KATHRYN KRAMER'S

A HANDBOOK FOR VISITORS
FROM OUTER SPACE

"A mad fairy tale that unexpectedly turns out to be true. Miss Kramer is such an engaging storyteller that we willingly submit, believing the impossible."
—THE NEW YORK TIMES BOOK REVIEW

"Romantic and surrealistic . . . muses over the end of the world with a gloom reminiscent of Doris Lessing and a wackiness befitting Tom Robbins."
—THE BOSTON GLOBE

"A delightful first novel with an uncommon amount of human wisdom and novelistic good sense. Kathryn Kramer is a natural."
—JOHN BARTH

"Nobody who loves novels should miss it."
—THE CHRISTIAN SCIENCE MONITOR

"The prose is transparent, its burden complex—a curious design, a fable-like shiver, a humor that casts a deep and subtle shadow."
—JOSEPH McELROY

A Handbook
for Visitors from
Outer Space

A Handbook
for Visitors from
Outer Space

A NOVEL BY

Kathryn Kramer

Vintage Contemporaries

VINTAGE BOOKS · A DIVISION OF RANDOM HOUSE · NEW YORK

First Vintage Books Edition, May 1985
Copyright © 1984 by Kathryn Kramer
All rights reserved under International and Pan-American
Copyright Conventions. Published in the United States
by Random House, Inc., New York, and simultaneously
in Canada by Random House of Canada Limited,
Toronto. Originally published by Alfred A. Knopf, Inc.,
in 1984.
The author wishes to thank The MacDowell Colony, Inc.,
and The Threshold Institute for assistance during the
writing of this book.
Portions of the poem "The April Wars," by Beth Joselow,
are reprinted by kind permission of S.O.S. Books,
Washington, D.C.
Library of Congress Cataloging in Publication Data
Kramer, Kathryn.
A handbook for visitors from outer space.
I. Title.
PS3561.R2515H3 1985   813'.54   84-25823
ISBN 0-394-72989-7 (pbk.)
Manufactured in the United States of America

It was meant to be a period of grace.
It was all of a long war
and no identification, no stamps,
no hungering after silk stockings,
no comrades on the assembly line
. . . .

no salutes no parades nobody
said nothing and it was nothing of you
and nothing on your back and nothing
in your pocket nothing on your lips
nothing in your eyes nothing to do
and nothing to do with it.

Beth Joselow, "The April Wars"

A Handbook
for Visitors from
Outer Space

Part One

Part One

The House at the World's End

(AFTERWORD AND PREFACE)

*A fine mist rises to the top story, mist created by the contact of the warm
earth with the cooler air of the atmosphere, and makes the house seem
even more desolate. The mist tapers into the attic, swallows the artifacts,
and advances down the stairs and along the hallways, scouring for signs
of life; through the bedrooms with their smooth beds; through the dining
room, the table's surface bare of china and silverware, the chairs' seats
convex; through the sitting room, whose doors onto the garden are ajar as
on a day when spring was coming. In the dim light (like that of dusk)
the folds of the drapes contain so many shadows that they appear to shift
even in the absence of a breeze, but no one is hiding behind, waiting to
jump forth and break the silence.*

*Scarcely any space is left now between the mist inside and the mist
outside, yet hope dies slowly. Life, the silence seems to suggest, might be
taken up again at any moment. The sun could pierce the clouds and the
mist evaporate to reveal a lawn sloping down to a swollen stream, where
children could launch paper boats, bearing messages for the world outside;
the mist could detach itself from the branches of an orchard on the other
side of the stream. And this orchard would be almost in bloom—one more
rain and one bright sun would burst the buds and cover the gnarled branches
with blossoms. Beyond the orchard, a road would lead through an avenue
of trees to a larger thoroughfare, thence on to villages, towns, and cities,*

where people would stop one another on the street to converse, feeling this to be an occupation of vital consequence.

But hope changes nothing; there seems to be no one left who can explain what has happened, why no one lives in this house anymore, who built it, with what in mind. And, if no one arrives, speaking welcoming words to dispel the house's mournful atmosphere, there will be no choice but to believe that the end was known from the beginning, this quiet was planned.

Before the war, death itself could seem imbued with a pastoral quality. We will die, people thought, but our grandchildren will bring flowers to our graves. Now for the first time they realized that there might not be any grandchildren; there might not be any flowers; there might not be any graves. When this last means of comfort—that picture of ivied slate with their names etched for future generations to ponder—came to seem delusory, it couldn't be ignored any longer: they weren't and never had been the center of the universe. The whole world and what they loved of it were parts of a tale spun in idle moments, its survival the happy ending they had supplied themselves on wintry afternoons when falling snow had made the indoors seem safe from invasion.

During the last days, people talked ceaselessly of the things they had seen, and each person tried to top his neighbor's story, believing his own information to be the most pertinent. A bumblebee was found intact in the root of a flower, a ship discovered berthed on rocks hundreds of miles from the nearest body of water, seaweed crusted on its hull. It was ascertained that people resembled trees, that trees copied branching water, that everything in the world was like everything. Is the world going to end today, do you think? people sometimes asked each other, but they asked it as if they were joking.

Now it is over. This world is empty; this house, like that so many once dreamed of owning, is deserted and easy of access. Flowers are arranged in vases in the bedrooms as if the owners were expecting guests. Everything looks especially neat and inviting, as if straightened up in preparation for a holiday. Suppose that someone were to happen upon this abandoned place. Would such a visitor remark, "How nicely laid out"? Or look for letters in desk drawers? Would anything of importance have been recorded?

Now a breeze starts up, presaging the disappearance of the mist. It comes from somewhere deep in the fog, or the fog is its visible, thick breath. Hearing the breeze, one can't help wondering if it is after all not dusk, as one supposed, but morning, the neighborhood simply quieter than usual, the birds fooled by the fog, everyone oversleeping. The silence contradicts nothing, and it seems possible that soon water will be heard running, or a voice calling a dog back in.

On All Fronts

The war had been going on for some time now, through sun and sleet, through lenient days when the buds bloomed according to the old seasons and the light breeze rattling windows and doors brought thoughts of white triangles scudding across a blue surface, through March thaws when the heavy, wet snow slid from the tanks like blankets from people asleep.

No one knew when the war had started, by whom or with what purpose. It had not been declared. Those who tried to join up could not discover where to present themselves. They knocked on doors of official-looking buildings, wrote letters to the government, but received no response. The government appeared to draft its forces according to some rationale not divulged to the public. Nor did it provide information about the progress of the war; ambiguous reports occasionally appeared in the newspapers but were printed in the back pages among advertisements for notepaper and knitting wool, so that one had to look hard to find them. Tradition, people complained, entitled them to more than vague uneasiness—someplace to volunteer their services for the wounded, a slogan or two, a battle hymn. But in this war there was nothing to do except wait around to see what would happen next.

Many even refused to believe there was a war on at all.

"Don't see anyone in uniform."

"No one I know has been killed."

The survivors of former wars, in particular, like the cranky generals playing cards on the lawn of the Old Generals' Home on the outskirts of Winston City, on the eastern seacoast of the United States of America, had a hard time taking this new war seriously.

"Who's the enemy?"

"How many of them are there?"

"Where are the troops stationed?"

"I don't get it."

"Battle is something you smell, but all I smell is lilacs."

A general sitting alone in a wooden swing objected. "You're so smug," he said. "This is a modern war. You're so out of date you couldn't smell it if it were thrust under your noses."

The others glared at him, then went back to their game, looking up from time to time to see if the Home was still there. The building had once been an orphanage for girls, and its somber rooms were haunted by their young ghosts, dropping hair ribbons on the faded uniforms folded over the backs of chairs. When they woke in the night, the old generals sometimes heard mischievous laughter.

"Marchons, garçons!" they yelled at some passersby, then cackled their old men's laughs.

A nurse came out of the building to see what the commotion was about.

"It's a long way to Tipperary," they began to sing when they saw her. "It's a long way to go . . ."

She sighed.

"Lose many today, Daisy?" one asked her.

"I'm not Daisy," she said. "I wish you'd stop calling me that."

The generals grinned.

"Rummy!" one of them proclaimed.

Sarah Simms, who lived a few blocks from this last barracks for men who had once commanded armies, was driving home with her groceries when it hit her: it was true. All the rumors and nervous talk she had pooh-poohed as so much warmongering by a peace-weary populace were not that; they were founded in fact. It was all suddenly so clear that she couldn't believe she hadn't seen it before. Now that she grasped it, she saw evidence everywhere: in the way people hurried along the street, competing for the quickest path of escape, in the way the street itself lay so passively between the rows of buildings. And the buildings waited like the condemned, the carvings and scrollwork on the old houses of government pitiful finery, worn for the firing squad. Yes, Sarah thought, the war must be real. There was an ominous quality to everything. Nobody could accuse you of being a worry-wart, a doomsayer, a pessimist when the world ran a constant danger of attack.

As if to confirm her impressions, there came suddenly, in the midst of traffic, a smell of cold mussel shells and seaweed, a feeling as if the air blew out of an unknown place, and Sarah shivered and wished the light would change. People everywhere hesitated. Even the cats, busy pulling loose threads out of clothing and furniture, looked up from their work and twitched their tails.

Then drivers honked their horns. The light had turned green. This is ridiculous! Sarah thought, hearing the words in her mother's voice. She simply needed to get home and unwind. There, she turned on the radio while she put away the groceries. She would make something special for dinner. Jason, her husband, would have a convivial homecoming. Over drinks they would joke about her wild imagination. Yet when Jason arrived Sarah could not explain to him what she'd been afraid of.

Cyrus Quince, the dissenting general's grandson (they had neither seen nor spoken to each other in five years), driving north from Winston to look up his old school friend Billy Daphne, had expected it would be a relief to be away from the tense atmosphere of the city, where everyone was so suspicious of everyone else that no one would meet your eye on the street, and if you so much as asked someone for the time the person acted as if you were asking him to give you some top-secret information. But even the gentle countryside of hills and fields, red barns and old white houses with green shutters, which Cyrus had remembered fondly from the year he spent there in boarding school, didn't seem peaceful. In a roadside diner where he stopped for coffee and a hamburger he heard local loggers and farmers speaking in the same foreboding tone so popular now in the cities.

He was so sick of all these dire hints. They reminded him of all the stories his grandfather had tried to get him to believe when he was little—some vast, mysterious conflict going on in everyday life. But it was a fairy tale, a yearning for days of yore when battle was glorious, noble steeds charging across rolling meadows, men fighting with swords, one on one.

It had been five years also since Cyrus had visited this part of New England, and, as he sped down the slope into Swanbury, past the turnoff to Fifield Academy, and then up the hill out of Swanbury, toward Amber, where Billy had lived, he felt sharply the loss of Billy's friendship (a loss for which he, Cyrus, was responsible), and abstract thoughts about the state of the world faded. What did it all have to do with him?

Symptoms of the war, nevertheless, did not abate. People found it increasingly difficult just to get through the day. They couldn't remember how they had ever found pleasure in their daily lives. They lost interest in working. They suffered from insomnia and lapses of memory. They became bored with their friends, tired of even their favorite foods. Everything seemed run-of-the-mill, insipid, stale. What had they ever seen, each privately wondered, in the one person they had once professed to love so earnestly? How had they ever fooled themselves into believing they were happy?

Thus the common mood was one of crossness, now and then superseded by a preternatural gaiety—a general ennui broken by brief riots of celebration. The newspapers, which gave such meager coverage to the front, were replete with reviews of the latest plays and films, debates about where the best meal in town could be eaten. As is usual in wartime, nightclubs thrived, not only because they offered diversion, but because their smoky, dimly lit rooms provided the palpable ambiance of the danger (anyone could have been a spy) people were beginning to crave. And it aroused passions they had never dreamed existed in peacetime. Perhaps such passions wouldn't last, but that in itself contributed to their force.

As an influential public personality (claiming to have been informed by "someone in the know" that when this war was over there wouldn't be any wounded, only all living or all dead) had suggested: why not have fun in the world's final minutes instead of whining while time ran out? The pursuit of pleasure had been declared a political act, a proof of esprit de corps among the new militia. In the Winston cafés, whose popularity increased daily as citizens abandoned their occupations and took up waiting for something to happen, endless libations were sipped in celebration of this new gnosticism.

"Life on the verge," Erik had gushed to the troupe (the regulars of Cyrus's acquaintance). "Everything tastes so much better when one is listening for boots on the stairs."

"What does *that* mean?" Cyrus had asked.

"He wants to know what it means! Isn't he archaic, ladies and gents? Wanting to know what something *means*!"

"He is a sap, isn't he?" Julian said mildly. "He pretends to be as free-thinking as we are, but his Little League, bake-sale, heart-of-the-country background sticks out all over him. Go ahead, put on your *High Noon* face and give us your Republican smile, Cyrus, you don't fool me."

"Yes," said Erik, "the poor soul. I'd feel sorry for him—if I knew how to feel sorry, that is. I think he secretly does believe in all the fables. The Bicycle Built for Two, Happiness in Slippers with Pipe . . . He may talk about war, but his ideas are straight out of Armageddon 101."

"You don't mean to say our knight in shining armor . . ."

"Knock it off, will you?" Cyrus protested.

". . . has a heart of gold."

"I'd tear my heart out of my body and sell it, if that's what mine were made of," drawled Julian, who was residing in Ante-Bellum Plantation Country at the moment.

"Oh, no! I would want to hang it around my neck!" sighed Erik, also in southern guise, but Julian scowled at him. When Julian said he was traveling alone, Julian meant it. Or did Erik think Julian was one of those people who didn't know his own mind? Like our noble cavalier . . .

Despite himself Cyrus laughed, and even though he told himself he was sick of them all—Erik, Julian, Miranda, Rudy, Suzanne, Karen, and even Gillian, who claimed to be in love with him—he found himself visiting them whenever he was in Winston. The Campers, they chose to call themselves, insisting that their ambition was never to live anywhere, only to camp. At present they were hiding out in an illicit residence on Ives Crescent, a semicircular street in an abandoned section of the city. At night they hung blackout curtains, purchased from army surplus stores, over the windows, and spoke in whispers.

They needed Cyrus, and he, though not always deliberately, let them think he played devil's advocate, that deep down he was no different from them—crusaders in search of true suffering.

Billy Daphne's mother came to the door of her trailer, and opened it a crack.

"Why, for pity's sake, it's you, Cyrus!" she exclaimed. "I almost didn't answer. These days, you never know."

"I don't need to come in, Mrs. Daphne."

"Of course you need to come in, Cyrus."

She held the tin door wide; nevertheless he had to pass sideways in order not to rub against her. She wore a purple-and-pink-plaid housecoat, buttoned with shiny pink buttons. Early on in their acquaintance Mrs. Daphne had confided to Cyrus that after her husband's death she had chosen never to wear any other colors. "Lavender is my special favorite," she said, "not that I'm glad he's dead, you understand." Cyrus, sixteen then, had assured her he understood, ignoring Billy making faces behind his mother's back.

Mrs. Daphne had seemed satisfied. "I'm sure you do, Cyrus," she said. "You're such a sensitive boy." "You're such a *sensitive* boy," Billy mimicked all the way back to Fifield on the bus, until Cyrus begged him to shut up.

"Sit down, you missing person," Mrs. Daphne commanded now, "and I'll give you something to eat. Like old times."

"That's all right, Mrs. Daphne. I stopped for something a little while ago. I just happened to be driving through the area and thought I'd see if by any chance Bill was around—it's been a long time since I've heard from him."

"Fancy that."

"What do you mean?"

Mrs. Daphne laughed—a dry, forced whinny. The effort caused her shoulders to heave forward; her face bent down as if she were trying to see a stain on her collar.

He glanced at the door.

"Mrs. Daphne, where is Bill? Is it true that he joined the army?"

She looked hurt for a moment, then wily. "I bet there's a lot of girls after you, aren't there, Cyrus? I could tell right off you were a heartbreaker."

"Jake Turner, our old headmaster, told me Billy joined up right out of Fifield."

"Didn't even come home to say goodbye," she spat out. "Called me up from a bus stop in Virginia. I tried to tell him he wouldn't like it. You think he would listen to me? Eighteen years old and he thought he was grown. Mark my words, Cyrus, Billy's going to get himself in big trouble, before the end."

But Cyrus laughed now at her sinister tone, relieved that nothing terrible had happened to Billy. "Didn't anyone ever tell you you're supposed to let children make their own mistakes?"

Mrs. Daphne, as if unable to help herself, reached out and touched his cheek. "You sounded just like a man right then," she sighed. "Who would have believed it?"

"I wouldn't know. Do you think I could have Billy's address, please? I take it he writes."

"Writes! Once a year, if I'm lucky. You call that writing?"

He grinned. "I call it writing once a year."

She looked at him, shaking her head, then turned to rummage through a pile of papers, from which she eventually drew forth an envelope. She tore off the return address and handed it to him.

"It's from the summer. Maybe it's no good. He might be out by now."

"Thanks very much, Mrs. Daphne." He opened the trailer door. As he turned to step outside, he heard her shuffling behind him.

"Goodbye," he said. "I'll tell Billy I saw you."

"Goodbye, Cyrus," she replied sadly. "I'll probably never see you again."

"What?" he exclaimed. "Why do you say that? That's ridiculous."

"I don't know. It's probably true."

The verifiable evidence of war being scant (troop movements kept top secret, the location of the field of battle unrevealed), no one knew at what moment ordinary life might come to an abrupt halt. The sense that their fate was hidden from them infiltrated every aspect of people's lives.

Even the past was not exempt from suspicion. Had things happened as they were written down, or had the records been falsified? Philosophers, inching belly-down along the spreading branches of maples in order to observe, unseen, the activity below, repeated smugly, "We knew it! We knew it! People should have listened to us before it was too late." The times might be shallow, as critics maintained, but shallowness, where by nature there should be depth, had to be false, like a trick-bottomed suitcase, or a bookcase that swung out to provide entrance to a passageway. Like the morbid poet who, hearing a live woman groaning behind a wall as she tried to free herself from a premature tomb, merely suspected his house of providing sound effects for his own melancholy fantasies, people perceived everywhere conspiracies intended to deceive them personally. They imagined messages, which they alone could not interpret, concealed between the lines of magazine and newspaper articles. The most commonplace phrases of speech seemed mysteriously encoded. They had the feeling their grasp of current events was incomplete. And the measures of relief from these anxieties were only too temporary: drunkenness, lying until scorched in the sun, exercise to the point of exhaustion. The malaise only deepened in proportion to the time spent pretending it did not exist.

Back in Winston, Cyrus stopped by Ives Crescent before heading to his grandmother's, where he was staying. The Campers, however, weren't home. They had gone "to pray," they had left a note saying, "for the dear boys on the line." Self-proclaimed atheists, they nonetheless had begun to frequent churches, although they claimed it was for the novelty, aesthetically pleasing, appealing to the ironic sense. They took communion, they said, to get away with it. They crossed themselves, but it was all in jest. Yet, when they thought no one was looking, they slipped into the curtained box and confessed to such a profound sense of guilt that the priest, although a veteran of many disbelievers' complaints, felt a genuine sadness.

"I am a traitor to my family, my friends, my country."

"Is that right?"

"You don't understand. I have betrayed everything I ever believed in."

"Such as?"

"Such as? How about love? I don't love anyone and no one loves me. And how can one live without love?"

"The taking of one's own life is a sin."

"I know that. That just makes me feel worse."

"You must pray for help."

"I don't know how to pray."

"You must try, my child. Is there anything else?"

"I beg your pardon, Father?"

"I said, 'Is there anything else?' "

"Well, no, not right now." Wasn't that enough?

"Very well. You may go."

"Yes, Father. Thank you, Father." No Latin? Not a phrase, no Hail Marias, nothing? A charlatan priest. "But I need to atone for my sins. Don't you take me seriously?"

"My child . . ."

"Without suffering there is no salvation! How can I be absolved without performing some penance?"

Perhaps fear nurtured this sense of guilt, perhaps the reverse. Whichever the case, people felt guilty and afraid. Although the enemy had not been identified, people feared betrayal and capture. They feared being mistaken for "one of them," whoever "they" were, whatever "they" represented. Terrified of compromising themselves, they attempted never to act with spontaneity or to speak their true feelings. Then they tried to relieve their own anxiety by frightening others. Jason Simms laughed and remarked, as he purchased a half-dozen cinnamon rolls in a bakery, that he no longer asked himself the "big" questions and unleashed terror in the heart of the saleswoman. She had remarked, "Mixing, baking, frosting, all that work and it gets eaten, and it never comes to an end. Seems you never get a rest until you die, doesn't it?"

She had thought she was being friendly. Apparently you couldn't discern even your own motives anymore.

"This wretched war . . ."

"This son of a bitch of a siege . . ."

"This infernal waiting . . ."

Gentlemanly epithets, as they crouched in their trench, these soldiers of contemporary conscience, their boots invisible under the previous era's sludge, bayonets rusting from the century's drizzle. They had nothing to do, no one to fight; they were stuck there, waiting for orders. While they waited, they thought about home, and, growing bored with their own love letters and photographs, exchanged these items up and down the line, until it no longer mattered into whose bright eyes they stared or whose phrases of endearment they read.

The colonel in charge of the regiment, conducting inspection of the troops with his next-in-command, the major, looked with distaste at the men crouched over their keepsakes.

"Can't they find something better to do with their time?"

"What would you suggest, sir? Praying for someone to take a shot at us?"

The colonel punctuated his stride with a sidelong stare. "That will do, Major. How often must I remind you that a shooting match is merely the smallest, most visible part of war? Waiting is what truly tests a soldier's mettle. You might even say that what makes a great warrior is not so much his might in battle as his constant readiness for it."

"Are you saying we might never see action, Colonel?"

"I'm saying this is action, Major."

"I see, sir." The major saluted and watched the colonel disappear down the line toward the tent. Yet increasingly he was uneasy. He thought of the Marne. He thought of Dunkirk. In those wars you knew what to do. And if you died, you died in glory, for your country . . . your country!

Sweet nation, one nation under God, God was simply the best general ever, that was all. Liberty and justice, babies even being stood up on bleachers by their parents when o-oh say can you see burst out of the p.a. system, the notes of the melody when you looked at them on paper going up and down like a cardiogram of the nation's heartbeat.

Oh, to be killed in action, to die a real soldier's death.

"Sometimes I wish I'd died then," a resident at the Old Generals' Home murmured. "If I'd known I would be put out to pasture . . ."

"We all have been. Every one of us."

The generals gazed down at their laps, at their once-muscled legs thin as dried wishbones in the regulation pale-blue paisley-patterned pajamas the Home issued to its residents, limbs across which had formerly stretched the patriotic green. What had it all been for?

Away from them, sitting on the lawn by himself, General Charles Street, Cyrus's grandfather, some fifteen years younger than the others, stopped his swing seat by pushing his cane against the ground and listened for what they would say next.

"You know what irks me the most?" asked General Eastlake.

"What does?"

"It's all this goddamn wishy-washiness. We spent our entire lives trying to make this country safe and sound, built its strength to such a point that it would be free from any threat, and listen to the way these college boys talk. This perpetual debate about the balance of power. . . . Hell, we've got the ammunition, why the devil don't we use it? The only correct balance of power is when we hold our side of the scale right down to the table!"

"It's only a matter of time before they try it on us."

"Saying we can't attempt anything because the other guy will get us back. . . . Good God, if everybody thought like that, we would never have fought any wars at all!"

"Maybe it's not too late," General Eastlake's roommate, General Martinson, suggested. "I mean to say, if we put our heads together . . ."

"Our last stand."

But this was too much for Charles. "What do you think we can do?" he shouted. "You quaint pearly-dentured blood-and-gore mushbrains. Are we going to march down to Washington in our bathrobes and flappy slippers? I can just see us, drooling on the steps of the Capitol. Ha!"

But they ignored him. Laying their cards on the table, they stood. It was time for bed, but, before they went in, they shared a complicitous look that Charles couldn't see.

In another part of Winston, café doors swung open to admit: Erik, Julian, Miranda, Gillian, Suzanne, Karen, Rudy, and others, hanging on each other's arms, laughing, pretending to be drunk on sacramental wine, tossing their hair, longing for an audience. They wished that they lived at the turn of the century, an era they felt more congenial to their sensibility than their own.

"The world will soon change beyond recognition, mark my words," warned Julian. "The Archduke will be shot and the shot will be heard around the world . . . or was that a different shot?"

But what did the details matter? It was transcendence they were after, as they scrambled for seats against the wall and began to talk—though not as if they wished to converse, but as if they were practicing speeches *sotto voce*.

"Erik and I," Suzanne boasted, "are thinking of joining up."

"We've been practicing our *maneuvers*."

"It was all the fault of those old radio broadcasts."

"They *were* sublime."

" 'It is 1940. France is falling. Soon all of Europe will grow dark . . . Duty! Honor! Fidelity!' they said, in these throaty voices. I felt so patriotic I would have given myself to the first man in uniform I saw!"

"Oh, Erik, I want to join up too!" Karen exclaimed.

"The more the merrier." Then Erik asked everyone, "Aren't we fabulous? Aren't we just too fearless for anything? Our country should be proud."

"Where is Cyrus, by the way, Gilly?" Miranda asked. "I thought you expected him tonight."

"Maybe he's at his grandmother's."

"Some alibi," Erik scoffed.

"I don't care."

"Still your hero, huh?"

"So deliciously ruthless . . ."

"But comrades! The tenderness concealed by his brusque manner . . ."

"The credibility with which good looks are endowed . . ." Erik yawned.

"Stop it, all of you!" Gillian cried.

"Unrequited love, how divinely hopeless."

Gillian burst into tears.

"You'd never make a spy, my dear," Erik said. "Let's not even *talk* about double agents."

"I wish there was a war—I mean it! I'd just go out in the street and wait for the bombs to fall. It would solve everything!"

"No, it wouldn't," Erik remarked, not unkindly. "Cyrus still wouldn't love you." He rose then from the table to put coins in the jukebox. The favorite tune of the moment was "Apocalypse." So popular was it that a parody already had been composed: "Apocalypso," a long, rambling, syncopated song; it too was played on jukeboxes across the nation. Orchestras embellished the melody with violins and cellos and played it outdoors on balmy evenings. "Dance with me," it finished. "Dance with me please. Dance a little longer for soon it will all be over, never any more to dance."

"I'm in love with that tune," Erik said, slowly describing a circle with his hips. "The composer ought to get a Purple Heart at least."

In the field, the soldiers went on waiting for the enemy to appear. Where were they? In another field somewhere, waiting for *them*? The joke was no longer funny.

The evening had turned chill, and a sloppy late snow began to settle on the colonel and major's tent, on the trench, on the tanks in their parking lot, on the stockpiles of ammunition, on the battleground the soldiers had been told they were defending. The snow made the soldiers recall a past they forgot had not been their own, a time in which respect for blood, love of the land, attachment to an ancestral home were paramount, a time when wars were fought (and on foreign soil).

With the snow had come a thick, damp air, and the soldiers shivered, yet they did not mind the snow because it safeguarded those memories they knew would dissolve when the snow itself ran off, leaving them with not even a dream to see them through their tour of duty. They hoped spring would never come.

"Careful! Somebody might be listening!"

In fact, everyone was listening. They listened to the neighbors on the left, the neighbors on the right, and everyone overheard everything. They even eavesdropped on themselves.

"Maybe it's a religious war," whispered Karen.

"What makes you think that?"

"I keep having these dreams . . ."

"Maybe it's a racial war," suggested Suzanne.

"No," Miranda said, "all wars are economic."

"They are?" They counted their change.

"Dear, dear," Erik mimicked. "We would gladly give it all away if this awful siege would stop. It is just so awful. Let the enemy attack, I say! Let them come down out of the sky, out of the trees, up from underground, from wherever they are going to come from, just let them be quick about it!"

They were brave then and ran out of the café. They were surprised to find that it was snowing. In the light of the streetlamp the huge flakes fell thick and fast. The streets were slushy. The Campers unlocked their bicycles and then brushed the snow from the seats. Hoisting their legs over the midbars, they saluted one another.

"Vive la résistance!"

"Keep the faith!"

"Long live the king!"

"Death to all traitors!"

"Give me liberty or give me death!"

"Down and dirty!"

"Let's go home, comrades."

They liked their sex neat, like whiskey. Who wanted to be left clinging to a memory of one spring dusk when her bobby socks gleamed white in the moonlight, when, his eyes being in shadow, she let herself assume the love in them? They had observed their parents, knew how the early years of marriage had degenerated into the later years, when the kids required all her attention, and she sewed name tags into coats and sweaters. They had seen how her hairdos had changed through the photographs—from long and luxurious to short, neat, manageable. They had seen how he had had to punch new notches to widen his belt and how he kept a bottle in the garage next to the oil for the lawnmower. And they had seen how their parents blamed one another for things not turning out as they had imagined they would way back on that moonlit night. Yet, even if Erik, Suzanne, Karen, Gillian, Miranda, Rudy, and Julian knew better than to believe the future could ever be what one had hoped, this did not keep other people from hawking such happiness on street corners, from advertising it on billboards, from even at times believing in their own ability to attain it with the faith that in the early part of the century had inspired someone to twist a waffle into an ice-cream cone when all the cups were gone.

Seeds of Conflict

It was an earlier decade, in Arborville, where Cyrus was born. In other places the world was changing fast, but here it continued to be an era of rest and relaxation, a still-innocent time of picnics and funny new dance steps, of cars as round and homey-looking as that pie made out of the fruit of Eve's fall, which everyone in the country ate with such gusto. It was a peaceful time, of sparkling days lapsing unmourned into velveteen nights, a landscape of the mind without electric wires. This might be the most volatile century in the history of the world, but in Arborville people were content just to enjoy life, make some money and have children, give their children the childhoods they themselves had missed. And in Arborville, in the heart of the country, childhood lasted longer than anywhere else.

Childhood is belief, and Cyrus believed in the world of his big white house, which stood in the middle of a big flat lawn surrounded by rosebushes and lilacs and forsythias. A cement walk ran from the sidewalk to the front steps, then around the side of the house to the backyard, where a swingset stood beside a sandbox (though he and Betsy no longer played in it). Here Cyrus had always lived with his mother and his father, his sister, Betsy, and his grandfather, Charles, who used to be a general. But he had resigned his commission and moved to Arborville when he heard that Cyrus was born because he wanted to make sure his grandson was brought up right. Cyrus's mother, Rose, mostly stayed in the house. Sometimes she was busy and put on a big apron and hummed and straightened things, but other times she lay in her room with the shades down and no one was allowed to make any noise. Cyrus hated it then—it felt like a rainy day.

In the morning Cyrus's father, Harold, went to work; at breakfast he went around the table tightening his tie, kissing Betsy and Cyrus goodbye. Back at his place, he stopped to drink the rest of his coffee, bending over his placemat so he wouldn't spill on his shirt; then he kissed their mother. Cyrus and Betsy watched; they reminded him if he forgot to. "You kids have all the luck," he said. The house was different once he left.

When he came home, the house changed back. The furniture seemed bigger, as though, if Cyrus wasn't careful, he might bump into it. Harold sat in the living room; Cyrus could go in but if he tried to tell his father something he had to talk quickly because his father was always listening for an end in the talk. If Cyrus didn't get there soon enough Harold would say, "Well, that's very interesting, Son," and pull the newspaper up in front of his face. When he came home, he liked his peace and quiet.

Cyrus's grandfather didn't go to work. His uniform hung in a closet upstairs. When Cyrus was bigger, he could try it on. His grandfather mainly told stories, and Cyrus loved to listen to them. His grandfather's voice was deep and soft like a lap, and when he began, "Once upon a time . . ." it made Cyrus feel as if he were about to eat something he had waited all day to eat. He felt cozy, yet also big, as if, should he go outside, he would find that his yard didn't stop at the sidewalk as it usually did, but instead rolled on, green and soft, covering the whole world.

Almost every day, between the time Cyrus came home from school and the time Harold came home from work, Cyrus and Charles would sit—in the kitchen if it was winter, on the front steps if it was summer—and Charles would tell Cyrus about the past. Charles had been a boy once too, but then he had grown up and gone to war and seen the world change. The world had been a happier place, where people did what they wanted without fretting about what other people might do to them if they turned their backs. But then all of this was ruined. People had to start worrying about things they'd never even thought about before and that made them cross.

"What's more, Corporal," Charles said to Cyrus, "people are getting crosser all the time, and why? Because they've come to realize that, no matter what they do or how hard they work, at any minute some imbecile can decide he's going to fight some other imbecile and pretty soon one of them will get mad enough and push a button and make the whole world pop like a balloon."

"What button, Granddad?"

"The one at the Imbecile Control Tower, Cyrus. It's a big black button and every time an imbecile walks by it big red letters flash and say, PUSH ME! PUSH ME!"

"They do?"

"Yes, and there's a kind of high screech at the same time, a very long shrill squeak that would make you or me shiver like fingernails down a blackboard do, but all the imbeciles love it. It makes them feel terrific. They dance around like a bunch of hooligans as if they're listening to the sweetest music."

Rose, sitting on the porch in a rocking chair, called out, "Mercy, Dad, what an optimist you are! To hear you talk, we might as well hide under the beds and wait for the sky to fall."

"If the sky falls you won't be any safer under your bed than out on the porch," Charles said. But he turned to smile at his daughter. He ought to keep his mouth shut. Why intone doom when she was happy? That happened too rarely these days.

Rose smiled back, and Charles saw her again as the child she had been before Sophie left them: like Cyrus, curious, alert, eager to right every wrong.

"Your mother's in a good mood today," Charles stage-whispered. "I like it when she's in a good mood, don't you?"

"Yes." But the subject made Cyrus uncomfortable and he said, "Tell me another story about the king, Granddad. Okay?"

"What king is that, Cyrus?" Rose asked sharply.

"The king," he said. He turned to look at her. "Once there was a king and he was a very contented man, he just sat around in his castle with his pipe and slippers and listened to the court jester's jokes, but all the imbeciles were always trying to get him to fight someone and finally this gave him such a big headache that he packed up his crown and snuck out of his castle in the middle of the night with the queen and the princes and princesses and came to America. Except he's hiding. It's up to us to find him and convince him to sit on the throne again."

"It is, is it?" Rose said. "I must say, Dad, you haven't wasted any time in indoctrinating the younger generation."

"Time is running out, Rosie." He winked at her, but she was no longer smiling.

"Let me ask you something, Cyrus," she said. "What makes you think there really is a king?"

"Mom . . ."

"Think about it. How do you know Granddad's not just making it up?"

"Are you making it up, Granddad?"

Charles laughed. "Ganging up on poor old Grandfather now, are you? For your information, Cyrus, the reason I know about the king is because I met him in the war."

Cyrus looked at his mother looking at his grandfather.

"Don't worry, I'm not going to reveal any state secrets." To Cyrus, Charles continued, "He was disguised as a common soldier. He thought that if everybody liked to fight wars so much, he ought to find out what they were all about. We got to be good friends, and he told me about his family, what life in hiding was like—he and his brothers and sisters, who lived with him, couldn't get to know anyone else for fear someone might discover they were of royal blood and turn them over to the imbeciles. It was awful always worrying about that. So he left his family and tried to be like everybody else."

"Dad . . ."

"It was the truth. And he tried. He didn't go back to his family and he met a very nice woman and they got married."

"What happened?"

Charles laid a hand on Cyrus's head. "I wish I could tell you, Corporal, that they lived happily ever after, but they didn't. You see, the king made a big mistake."

"What mistake?"

"He didn't tell his wife who he was. He wanted to forget about his past. Unfortunately, once you've got royal blood in your veins, you can't just pretend you don't. It's always there, boiling up and making you wish you were sitting on the throne, even if you really *hate* sitting on the throne. But I'll tell you something, Cyrus. People always know if you're keeping a secret. The king's wife kept asking him what the matter was but he wouldn't tell her. After a while she got fed up and ran away." Charles paused. "You see, Cyrus, secrets cause more trouble than they solve."

"Where did she go?"

"She went far away."

"Was the king sad?"

"He was very sad. In fact, I expect he never got over it."

"Where is he?"

"I'm afraid I don't know. I lost touch with him after the war."

"Then how do you know he got married?" Cyrus asked.

"You don't miss much, do you, Corporal?"

"No," Cyrus said, looking at his mother.

Charles looked over his shoulder to share his amusement at this reply with Rose, but she was not looking at either of them. She was sitting in the rocking chair, not rocking. Her face was lowered and she gripped each arm of the chair as if to keep herself from floating off. She was silent, but both Charles and Cyrus knew she was weeping.

Little by little, anxiety increased around the country, but the people of Arborville remained content. They thought all this talk of approaching war was so much hooey. They heard of people stocking food in their basements, building special shelters for protection during air raids, and they slapped their thighs and roared.

"They're out of their minds. Who would dream of attacking us?"

Arborville's nonchalance became so notorious that representatives from the government and the press arrived to determine why the Arborvilleans were so sure of themselves.

"Aren't you worried about another war?" they were asked. "Aren't you afraid of the effect it would have on your lives?"

"Hell, no, we're not worried about any war!"

"War! In Arborville?"

"We don't believe all that stuff on the news. We think the government's just trying to get everybody all stirred up for some reason."

"What reason?"

"How in tarnation should we know?"

Arborvilleans slouched in groups outside the hardware store around the questioner or peered at him down the Formica counter of the drugstore like planes waiting in line for an opportunity to take off. At first their self-assurance intimidated the pollster, but soon he became irritated and exclaimed, "But you're all asleep here! Can't you see what's happening in the world around you?"

"Now, now," the Arborvilleans soothed. "Don't get yourself worked up. It's just that we like things the way they are. We're not always looking for more in life than is there." They grinned at the interviewer. "You will report it as it really is here, won't you?"

But the interviewers suspected Arborville's complacence. They felt certain some arcane violence must lie dormant beneath the tidy lawns and trimmed bushes of the town, hidden antagonisms that, if left unexpressed, would have cruel repercussions in the later lives of the children who grew up there. They would move away and live in scantly-furnished apartments in gridded cities, their cupboards empty except for a bottle of gin and maybe a jar of olives, and they would slam doors and sing whenever they came home in order to avoid noticing the silence. . . . They would go to any lengths not to be left alone with the terrors that, now that they were far from Arborville, could no longer be kept repressed. The interviewers strove to induce the Arborvilleans to confess to feelings of enmity, distrust, and fear. "Don't you realize that at any moment we could all be killed?" they pleaded. But the Arborvilleans merely felt sorry for the interviewer.

"Cripes, you really think about that?" asked an Arborville farmer in ruddy-faced perplexity. "You poor dog. Better come out here and stay with us for a while. We'll straighten you out."

Then they would invite the pollster in for some pie—"lemon meringue, our favorite," unless, that is, it was peach, or blueberry, or butterscotch cream—and the pollsters succeeded only in getting fat in Arborville—Arborville! where everyone got up early and ate a hearty breakfast, where a day contained a day's work, where after work people sat on their porches and rested their eyes on the wheat gilded by the setting sun, or in town on the huge elms, miraculously free from disease. Arborville—where bronzed men on tractors enjoyed the atavistic companionship of their forefathers as they guided the plow in the furrow. Arborville—where nobody suffered from insomnia, where the air smelled of freshly baked bread and newly mown grass. . . .

Arborvilleans thought the outsiders were just envious. Arborville, they believed, was a wonderful place to live, a town anyone would be proud of, and, in the evening, when they sat out on their porches and chatted as dusk fell unnoticed about them, they told themselves how lucky they were to live in Arborville, when the outside world was such a mess.

"Couldn't be a better place in the universe to bring up kids," parents congratulated one another. "Let the Martians look down and drool. It's safe; the schools are good; the air is fresh, the morals untarnished."

"We used to go away for vacations," the people of Arborville told the visitors, when asked if they didn't "come on, admit it, just get the littlest bit bored?"

Well, they used to think they were obliged to get away. They'd pack the kids into the station wagon, drive out to measure the Redwoods, holler down into the Grand Canyon. Even went one year to Bermuda! But then it struck them as silly. Why should they leave the place they loved best on earth whenever they got a moment's spare time? The rest of the country could travel full-time if it wanted, but Arborvilleans no longer had any desire to go out and explore the world. Everyone else was welcome to come to them, if they wished, but they didn't like visiting other people. As far as they were concerned, Arborville was the center of the universe, and, one by one, the world's riches were sucked into Arborville's category of extraneous things. The pyramids of Egypt went tumbling, like dice, into the vortex of their self-satisfaction, the Taj Mahal, the jungles of Africa, the Eiffel Tower went end over end; the castles in Scotland, the white villas of Greece and Morocco—these in their turn were swallowed up, and then closer and closer to home: the Statue of Liberty, the Lincoln Memorial, the faces on Mt. Rushmore . . . until even the city fifty miles down the Interstate, where they had attended movies and fairs, was too much trouble to think about anymore. "Oh, it's just such a long way down, is the thing, and then you've got to come all the way back, and the kids are sleepy and cross. . . ." Hell, if they felt like going anywhere, why not go for a drive through Arborville itself, whose handsome founding houses still stood, capacious dwellings with enough clear space, front and back, to prevent any inimical party from reaching the porches unobserved, whose lilac and forsythia hedges kept the lines of demarcation cleanly drawn between neighbors? So they got into their station wagons, and, full of pride, ran the gantlets of huge elms that bent over the streets called Pleasant, Forest, Harvest, Oak, and so on out into the countryside, where lazy fields of corn and wheat stretched to the edge of the world.

"It doesn't make sense," the reporters said. "Someone will have to pay the piper." But, after all, they had their own careers to attend to. They had to go find out how the Vienna choirboys felt about their voices changing, get the scoop on the latest First Lady's plans for redecorating the White House. . . . They couldn't spend the rest of their lives in Arborville waiting for the townsfolk to confess they were just putting on a good show.

"So what's wrong with the Quinces?" Hugh Greenmantle, their next-door neighbor, asked his wife June impatiently. He was trying to read the sports section and he wished June would come to the point. "They've always seemed perfectly happy to me."

"I know, that's just it! How long can we keep pretending we don't hear the fighting going on next door?"

"Everyone has arguments from time to time, June."

"You know that mechanical bird Cyrus traded Huey for the aircraft carrier? The one that actually flew? Apparently Harold bought it for Cyrus on a business trip. Rose told me that when he found out Cyrus had gotten rid of it, he cried. He cried, Hugh!"

"June . . ."

"Well, Hugh, doesn't it make you think? If people like the Quinces, who we all thought had such a solid marriage, are having problems, how can we feel sure any of us are safe?"

Hugh frowned. "All I know is that if there are problems they must be Rose's fault. Hal Quince is an excellent fellow. I've known him since kindergarten. I'd trust him with my life!"

"What's going on with Hal lately?" Joe Williams remarked to his golfing partner, Tom Boxford. "He hasn't been himself in months."

"I know," replied Tom, choosing an iron for his drive. "He doesn't seem to want to discuss it though."

"Do you think something's wrong at home? Rose has always seemed kind of unstable to me. That way she looks at you like you might secretly be a maniac who carries a strangling stocking in your pocket. I remember once at a party she asked me if I had to drown or burn to death which I would choose."

Tom laughed. "Which did you?"

"I changed the subject, I think."

·   ·   ·

"Yes," said Susie Silton to Carrie Johnson over coffee, "I'm afraid there's definitely a snake in the garden. I finally got Rose alone after the bridge club and asked her if anything was wrong and she burst into tears. It seems the argument's over General Street. Harold thinks Cyrus and Betsy spend too much time with him; he complains General Street fills their heads with all kinds of unrealistic ideas. Rose thinks Harold's just jealous. But I don't know. I can see his point of view. It does seem odd, her dad living with them all these years."

"I agree," Carrie said. "It's not as if he's ill or can't afford to live anywhere else."

"Rose had a pretty rough childhood, I understand. She's never wanted to talk about it, but Harold told Bill once that her mother ran out on her dad when Rose was just a kid. Left her kind of fragile. Maybe her father feels she needs help with the children."

"She *is* pretty dreamy. Still, she's a grown woman. I'm sure she can manage on her own. I sometimes get the impression she thinks she's better than those of us who were born and raised here. Not that I like seeing her so unhappy."

"Yes, I know."

Carrie sighed. Susie refilled their coffee cups, and, thoughtfully, they sat sipping.

Meanwhile, in the Quince household (which the interviewers had not investigated), tensions increased. Harold, like the majority of fathers in Arborville who weren't farmers, worked at a job that made his existence away from the dining table, and apart from the weekends he spent working in the yard, impossible for his children to imagine. Yet he had never given this fact much thought until those jokers from out of town had started prying into everybody's private affairs. Their insinuating remarks had shaken Harold up more than he liked to admit. The things they said sounded so much like Charles. All this tomfoolery about the next war. Recently

Harold had told Cyrus that he didn't want that ratty old cat of Cyrus's sleeping in his room anymore—the thing had fleas—and Cyrus had replied that Jonzo had to be there in case there was a night attack so Cyrus could carry him down to the basement.

"Blast it, Cyrus!" Harold had shouted. "How many times have I told you there's not going to be a war? There's not going to be any attack!"

Cyrus raised an eyebrow—he'd learned that trick from Charles—and said, "I don't know, Dad. Granddad says you can never be too careful."

"Careful of what, young man? Would you mind explaining yourself?"

"Of the enemy, Dad," Cyrus said patiently. He sounded as if he felt sorry for Harold for being so dimwitted. "You should never volunteer information," he recited. "You should suspect everyone. Spies are everywhere."

"Spies!" Harold exploded. "All I know is that your grandfather is the one who'd better start being careful. One of these days he may find himself sitting up for a pretty little court-martial!"

Harold had tried to discuss his concern with Rose, but she was impatient with the subject. "Oh, Harold," she said, "it's just a game." A game! Couldn't she even see what was happening in her own house?

"What do you want me to do? Forbid my father to talk to his own grandchildren?"

He reminded Rose that they had agreed Cyrus would do something with other kids after school—take swimming lessons or join the Little League—but she always had some explanation for his failure to be involved in such activities. Either he didn't get along with the coach or the class was full or . . . He couldn't understand Rose's attitude. When pressed, she said, "There's a world outside Arborville, you know. And Dad encourages Cyrus's imagination." Imagination! Well, fine, but when a kid woke himself and the whole house up in the middle of the night screaming, "They're going to push the button! They're going to push the button!" it had gone too far.

For ages now, it seemed to Harold, he had been chanting: "*I'm his father, Rose. I'm his father,*" though he hadn't said it to her. He kept seeing Cyrus sitting with Charles on the steps, the two of them staring at him when he came home from work, as if he were a stranger.

Harold had always been proud to go to work. He was employed by one of the country's most venerable industries—it had grown to its tremendous size during the last war, but, unlike most of its counterpart war-boom firms, had been able to maintain its profit margin ever since by altering its capabilities to keep pace with the times. Harold had relished being a part of this industrial empire, but now he suffered because his children showed no interest in what he did. They preferred to be with Charles, acting out his military games.

Harold had tried to reassure himself that this was all right, that his was a life they would respect when they had grown up and moved away from Arborville and gone on to bigger and better things—progress his own efforts would have made possible. Then, he had thought, they would speak reverently of how he had instilled the basic values; they would think with tears in their eyes of his decades of uncomplaining support of his family and feel terrible that they had taken him for granted. Someday, Harold had believed, Cyrus and Betsy would come home to Arborville with their hearts in their mouths, their eyes glistening as old Hal, giving old Rose his hand to steady her, walked down the porch steps to greet them.

"This is what life's all about," sighed the major's wife. (This was in the good old days.) The major and his wife sat before a fire, she sewing, he reading and smoking his pipe. Their two children, a boy and a girl, were asleep in the nursery; the servants, though about, were unobtrusive.

She gazed at him fondly. Smiling to herself, she took a deep breath and it seemed to her the house itself pulsed through her blood. She breathed in at the front door and out through the dormers. She stretched and a board creaked. She could feel the kitchen dark and quiet now; upstairs, her bedroom waiting; beyond, the dormant life of the attic. The clock in the lamplit room where she sat gazing at her husband might have been ticking in her heart.

The major took his pipe from his lips and looked up. "Darling . . ." he began, then sighed.

"What is it?"

"I have decided to volunteer for active duty."

He heard her sharp intake of breath and saw her sewing drop from her hands. "But you said . . ."

"Neither I nor anyone else expected it to go on for so long. It's not right for me to sit comfortably at home while so many are dying on the battlefield."

"But it will be right for you to mingle your blood with everyone else's?"

"My country needs my services. It is my duty to go."

She looked at him, betrayed. He went on, "Let me remind you of how many women have bravely given their husbands and sons to the cause."

"Given . . ." she scoffed.

Scorn was not the weapon he had expected. Still, he wanted to fight a fair fight.

"Would you wish me to be a coward? To skulk at home while my countrymen fall?"

"A coward or a corpse," she said bitterly. "It is not much of a choice, is it?"

"What you should do, you see, is take notes."

"Notes, Granddad?"

Charles, Cyrus, and Betsy sat in the back yard, at the picnic table, having a "summit conference." They were drinking lemonade and eating chocolate-covered graham crackers. Harold and Rose, who were temporarily on better terms since Rose had discovered that she was pregnant, had gone away for the weekend to visit Harold's mother, who was ill in a nursing home in nearby Riverton. The instant the car was out of sight, a holiday had been declared at the Quince residence. Cyrus and Betsy had rigged a tarpaulin in the backyard—"on maneuvers," Charles said—and were going to sleep under it all weekend. They had persuaded Charles to go to the store for hot dogs and marshmallows—"not exactly battle rations," he complained, "but it will have to do." Now the coals glowed in the grill, and the outlines of things were growing blurred.

"Notes about what, Granddad?"

"What kind of notes?"

"Did you read in the paper recently where some people said they met some visitors from other planets, who came down to get acquainted?"

"Martians!"

"You have too conventional a notion of outer space, Grand-daughter. No—we spend so much time wondering what our next-door neighbors on Venus and Mars are up to that we forget there's a whole universe out there. We should be prepared for the visitors to be completely different from anything we've imagined, to have ways of doing things we've never dreamed of, ways of under-standing things . . ."

"Like what?" Cyrus asked.

"I was afraid you'd want to know. Well, maybe they can fly. Maybe they never need to sleep. Maybe they can find where they're going without maps, like Jonzo. Maybe they have ways of living many lives at once—say, if you wanted to be here and visiting your Grandma Quince at the same time."

"Ugh," Cyrus said.

"Yuck," said Betsy.

"Now, now. It's not her fault she's a crotchety old hag."

Cyrus and Betsy giggled.

"See, if she lived in outer space," Charles went on, talking to himself, "maybe she wouldn't be so unhappy. Maybe in outer space people don't misunderstand each other, don't leave each other like they do down here. Maybe in outer space they don't feel they have to keep secrets."

"What secrets?"

"That's what you have to find out, Corporal. Maybe in outer space they don't have wars. Anyhow, you two should be good at taking notes. Being officers, you already have sharper powers of observation than most people."

"Mine are sharp, Granddad. Betsy's the one who sleeps at her post."

"I do not!" Betsy, indignant, stomped off.

"You see, Corporal," Charles went on, "the world, at least as we have known it, might end in your lifetime." Charles scrutinized Cyrus, but he didn't flinch. Or was he getting sleepy?

"It may not, of course, but, if it does, it would be sad if no one had taken notes on what it had been like here in case anyone visited afterward. That's why I'm doing my best to teach you— train you to keep your eyes peeled."

"Keep my eyes peeled!"

Charles laughed. "You're a good soldier, Cyrus. I'm sure you'll make an excellent ambassador to other planets if you ever get a chance."

"I'll zap them right away with my space weapons!"

"Oh, no you won't. That's pure imbecile talk, Cyrus, imagining everyone in outer space is out to get us. Think how it must hurt their feelings. They want to come down and have a nice chat and ask us how things have been going on earth lately but, if they attempt to, imbeciles run out with guns and start shooting."

"But they might shoot us first. They might be on the wrong side."

"True, they might." Charles laughed. "The point is, Cyrus, one hopes that visitors won't be bound by the same distrust and suspicion that shackle us poor benighted human beings. In the meantime, pay attention to what goes on around you. Then at some point you can compile the information you've acquired. Make a sort of guidebook, a handbook—something to fit in the hand . . ."

"What if they don't have hands?"

"Insubordination! Something they can carry around with them, like a book you take on field trips to identify plants, or that tourists carry to inform them about architectural monuments and historical sites. Doctors have handbooks that help them diagnose ailments. . . . You listening, Corporal?"

"Yes, Granddad."

"You have to look at the world from their point of view. They might never have seen a house, for instance, or a yard, or a cat. If nobody's around to explain these things to them, well, they may not understand what anything is *for*. But if somebody had left behind some notes, they'd feel a lot more comfortable, don't you think?"

"Yes," Cyrus said. He yawned.

Charles smiled.

The moon edged up behind the roof, round and molten—the identical moon that through the ages had been responsible for the melancholy of princesses, for the madness of sailors, for the quickening of everyone's blood.

"It would be nice if we could go out there too," Charles said softly. "I'm all for intergalactic travel, aren't you?"

An airplane crossed the moon, like a bug. This airplane could have come from anywhere. It could have been going anywhere too: tracing a line from Arborville to a little house in the suburbs of Winston City or to an eccentric mansion in the New Jersey countryside. Maybe those who dwelled there would also look up and wonder about the plane. Charles sighed. Cyrus shivered suddenly and woke up.

"What?" he exclaimed, hearing the plane overhead. "Wait . . . four, five . . . six! Six airplanes today so far, Granddad."

"Good boy, Cyrus," Charles said. "If you only knew how happy you make me."

After Lark was born, there was whispering. This was worse than when Harold and Rose had yelled at each other. Now they scarcely spoke at all except during the long hours in which they shut themselves up in their bedroom. Cyrus, crouched at the keyhole, trying to hear what was going on, learned that it had something to do with the baby and whose fault it was he was the way he was. Over and over Harold asked Rose what about her past she was hiding from him, and over and over she said, "Nothing. Why would I hide anything?" Why would she? Cyrus wondered.

Sometimes Harold grabbed Betsy and squeezed her until she cried for him to let her go. Both Harold and Rose bestowed on the older children sudden, violent affections that frightened them.

Even Charles seemed affected. He wouldn't plan maneuvers and Cyrus was forced to resort to his friends, whose idea of battle was to hide in the bushes and jump out when he wasn't expecting it. But he soon tired of their crude concepts and instead spent his time patrolling the town with Jonzo, looking for things to record.

Then, mysteriously, the atmosphere would clear; Rose would sing about the house, and Harold renew his shouting at Jonzo. Cyrus and Betsy would play happily with their brother—Edgar Francis, Harold and Rose had named him; Lark he was called, because Rose said he was as happy as one. He was a baby who loved to be spoken to, and Cyrus and Betsy, who both adored him, could tell him anything and he'd grin and chortle, as long as they kept talking.

However, during his third year, when Cyrus was twelve and Betsy ten, Lark fell victim to obscure terrors. Discovering himself alone in a room, he would scream for "Granny."

"Lord knows where he got that from," Harold said. "My mother's been dead a year and yours he's never seen. Cyrus, Betsy," he called, "come in here a minute. You kids been telling Edgar stories?"

"Stories?"

"What kind of stories?"

"*Any* stories. You been making things up around him?"

"No, Dad."

"No, Daddy."

"Well, I don't want you starting either, do you hear me?"

"Okay."

"We won't."

But Lark was too small to understand that Granny was half invention. The only way to quiet him was to go on as they had begun; they first told him stories about Granny to entertain him anyway, just as they had once been entertained by Charles (who, though he had gone so far as to give Cyrus and Betsy each a photograph of their missing grandmother, with her address written on the back, had exacted from them their promise to keep this secret). So Betsy and Cyrus told Lark how nice Granny was, how she always had cookies in her pocket. "Cookies," Lark repeated, happy again.

"And she never gets mad," Cyrus went on, "although sometimes she gets a little sad."

"Don't tell him she gets sad, Cyrus."

"Well, she does."

"You don't know. You're just saying that because Granddad did."

"She doesn't have us," Cyrus retorted.

They argued, and Lark began to cry.

"Don't worry, Lark," Cyrus comforted him. "When you visit her she'll cheer up immediately."

"*I'll* tell you about the house Granny lives in," Betsy said. "It's a very small house, because she lives all by herself, but it's very pretty and there are lacy curtains at all the windows."

"Granny has lots of cats and dogs, Lark, and she talks to all of them."

"She sleeps upstairs in a big four-poster bed with pillows twice as long as the ones we have."

"*What?*"

"Because that's the kind people have who think in bed, stupid. And there's a tall clock downstairs and sometimes Granny wakes up in the middle of the night and hears it strike but always goes right back to sleep."

"Except sometimes . . ."

"Stop interrupting. Then, Lark, when Granny wakes up in the

morning, she always goes to the window and looks out over the town. . . ."

"Now who's saying what Granddad said?"

Betsy glared at Cyrus. "After she gets dressed she goes downstairs and has breakfast. And then you know what she does? She makes a cake."

"What cake?" Lark inquired.

"You're such an idiot, Betsy. Someday she'll make you one, Lark. We'll all go to visit her, with Granddad, and then we'll all live together for the rest of our lives."

It was a day so bright there seemed to be no shadows. Cyrus sat on the front steps of his house, a big white house on a street of big white houses, all freshly painted, with shutters that were never closed. Huey Greenmantle's father was waxing his car, rubbing it with a rag and then standing back and looking at his reflection in the newly polished surface. He saw Cyrus watching him and called, "What you up to, Cyrus?" but went back to rubbing his fender without waiting for an answer. Four doors down, across the street, Mr. Silton was clipping a hedge. Every few minutes he sang, "I wandered today to the hill, Maggie, to watch the scene below . . ." and then hummed the rest of the verse. Max, the Fosters' collie, ambled across the Fosters' yard to the sidewalk, stopping every few feet to sniff at something. When he reached Cyrus's lawn, Jonzo, sitting on the steps beside Cyrus, arched his back. "Just relax, Jonzo," Cyrus said. "It's only Max."

Then slowly he got up, went down into the basement, and removed his sneakers from the drier, where they lay like two dead birds, put them on, and set off, pursued by Jonzo, on his usual rounds. He strolled down to Main Street, still quiet for a Saturday, past the gas station: We Sell/Rain or Shine, into the hardware store, where he inspected the nail bins while he listened to the Saturday fathers greeting each other, "How goes the battle?" but his heart wasn't in it. So he left and walked back home again, rewinding the squares, each of which contained a smug-looking white house and a smug-looking green lawn, until he reached his own, which today looked no different from all the others. Charles was now sitting on the steps.

"Hey," he said, "aren't you going to salute?"

Cyrus flopped his arm to his forehead.

"At ease, soldier." Cyrus sat down a step below his grandfather. Jonzo turned in to the walk and meowed.

"Come on, Jonzo, knock it off!"

"How did inspection go? See anything out of the ordinary?"

"No."

"Hmm," Charles said. "Did you see anything?"

Cyrus shrugged.

At that moment, Harold came walking down the street, Lark on his shoulders, Lark's plump legs on either side of his neck, Lark's hands on his head: Lark was now three and a half years old. "Look out for the trees," Harold warned, whenever they passed under low-hanging branches, and Lark ducked. He was laughing, but with an undertone of fear, as if he thought his father had lowered the trees' branches on purpose.

"Stop, stop!" he panted, giggling harder as his father instead began to jog. "Daddy! Daddy!"

"Look out for the trees! Look out for the trees!" Harold shouted, and Lark shut his eyes as a fringe of maple feathered across his face, opened them just in time to close them again for the onslaught of fat, splayed oak leaves.

"Look out, buddy, look out for the trees!"

Slowing down, they turned in to the walk. Rose had been watching them anxiously from the porch.

"For goodness' sake, Harold!" she exclaimed, holding out her arms.

"For goodness' sake what, Rose?" He handed Lark up to her, over Cyrus's head.

"I . . ." she began, but then merely clutched Lark and hurried into the house.

With an effort Harold smiled at Cyrus and Charles. "Interrupting something? I wouldn't want to overhear anything top secret."

"Very funny," Cyrus said.

"Take it easy, Corporal," Charles said gently, but at this Harold lost control.

"Damn it all, Charles, I've asked you, over and over, to cut out the malarkey! What are you trying to do? Push me to the point where I have no choice but to ask you to leave the house?"

"Don't you dare ask him to leave the house! Don't you dare!"

"Hush, Cyrus," Charles said sharply. Cyrus, wounded, stared at him. Then Charles stood. He entered the house and climbed upstairs. Pausing at the door to Rose and Harold's bedroom, he saw Rose leaning out the window, trying to free a kite that had become entangled in the branches of a tree growing close to the house. "Rosie?" he said.

"I've meant to get this down for ever so long," she said brightly. "I keep forgetting to get around to it."

"Where's Lark?"

"In the kitchen with Betsy."

"Sweetheart . . ."

"I want to be alone, Dad."

He nodded, although she hadn't turned to look at him, and went from the room.

Cyrus had fled to the backyard and was scuffing the bare patch of ground under the swingset where he and Charles had often traced battle plans. Harold followed.

"Hey, champ," he pleaded.

Cyrus turned and swung. The punch landed on Harold's arm; Harold tried to grab Cyrus and hug him, but Cyrus wriggled loose and kept pummeling, though his swings were wild and landed without force.

"Hey, Cy," Harold said, ducking. "Hey, come on, now." He wanted to laugh but was afraid that if he did he would cry, so he stood still, accepting Cyrus's punches on his forearms, repeating, "Cy, come on now, come on."

Suddenly Rose screamed from the bedroom window. "Cyrus!" she cried, as if Harold were in some grave danger. "Stop it! Stop it this instant!"

Startled, Cyrus looked up. While he was off guard Harold made another grab for him, but he struggled free and then turned and ran out of the yard and down the street. Jonzo, who saw him take off, leapt yowling after.

"Stay home, Jonzo!" Cyrus yelled. "Why don't you just stay home?"

"Now look what you've done!" Rose cried.

Harold Quince lowered his head and accepted his wife's blame. But this did not change anything. Someone still had to make decisions, even if they were painful ones, like taking Lark away from home because under the circumstances it was the only thing that might save his life. And today was the day that, over two months ago, they had agreed Harold would take Lark to the Institute, which was located in New Jersey. Rose refused to look at the reality of the situation; he couldn't permit himself that luxury. Nevertheless, all during the plane trip east that afternoon, the only thing he could hear was her parting words to him, "You know what this will do to me, don't you, Harold?" "I'm not *doing* it to hurt you, Rose," he had reminded her, but he didn't even know if she heard him.

Harold recoiled as, at dusk, he and Lark drove down the wide, heavily-traveled highway on the hour's drive from the airport to the Institute. On either side of the road lay an area resembling a battlefield after it was all over: mountains of debris in the midst of which elephantine pipes rose into the sky, belching pale yellow smoke. A foul smell hung over everything. Lark, huddled in the far corner of the front seat, stared out the window. When Harold asked him if he was hungry, he jumped. Instead of replying he asked again, "Where are we going, Daddy?" He sounded so normal and healthy. Yet hidden in his genes were the agents of his destruction, already, if the doctors were to be believed, at work.

"To a school, Lark," Harold said gently. "I've already explained to you."

"I don't want to go, Daddy," Lark quavered. "I want to go home."

He jumped again when Harold yelled, "Damn it, Lark, that's enough whining!" But though his eyes filled Lark didn't cry but pressed himself even farther into his corner and mumbled, "Granny, Granny loves Lark."

"Granny!" Harold thundered. Then his vision blurred, and he pulled off the road. He sat hunched over the wheel, racked by sobs, while long trucks roared by and sleek limousines whished past, underlining his presence in the middle of nowhere, a place he would always be, alone with his inarticulate love.

He sat up at last; Lark was watching him, terrified.

"Daddy loves you too, Lark, do you understand that?" Harold asked, trying to smile. Lark didn't answer, and Harold reached over and gathered him into his arms.

"Don't cry, Daddy," Lark pleaded. "Don't cry anymore."

"No, Daddy won't cry anymore, Lark. I promise."

"They said he'll be fine, Rose," Harold said in a tired voice. (Charles had retired early, and Betsy and Cyrus had been sent to bed but were listening from the landing.) "They said he'll adjust in no time, so that by the time it . . . by the time he requires more help he'll feel at home there. They said that the younger they see these children, the better chance there is of helping them. And, with all the research being done, they said it's entirely possible that he may be able to lead a relatively normal life someday."

"He already was leading a 'relatively normal life,' Harold!" Rose cried. "What do they think they can do for him that I can't?"

"Now, darling . . ." Harold began.

"Don't talk to me as if I were a child," she said.

Harold closed his eyes. When he opened them, Rose was still there, a sentry guarding all sorrow, forbidding him to show any pain.

"I know you can care for him now," he went on, "but how would you cope later? The people at the Institute are trained to deal with children like Lark and we have to consider his welfare in the long run. We should also think of Betsy and Cyrus, whether it would be fair to them. . . ."

"Now, now, that's too much, Harold! If anything, Lark kept Cyrus and Betsy gentle and considerate."

"What I was going to say, Rose . . ."

"No, Harold, you're the only one who was uncomfortable having him around. He wasn't perfect enough for Arborville, was he? You were afraid the perfect Arborvilleans would shy away from us!"

Upstairs, Betsy began to cry, and Cyrus put his arms around her, whispering "Shh," but they had been heard, and Harold stormed up the stairs.

"You were eavesdropping!" he bellowed. "Get in your rooms!"

"You don't love Lark," Cyrus accused him. "If you loved him you wouldn't have sent him away."

Harold stared. Then he slapped Cyrus twice, hard. "Don't you ever, ever say that again. Do you hear me? Do you?"

Cyrus shrugged.

"You had better not." He grabbed Cyrus and pulled him down the hallway and into his room. He shouted at Betsy, who had taken refuge in the doorway to hers, to shut her goddamn door that instant and quit staring at him as if he were a freakshow. Then he followed Rose, who had come upstairs, into their bedroom.

"What the hell were you doing?" she demanded.

He stared at her. Then he pleaded, "You're my *wife*. Why aren't you on my side?"

Cyrus, lying face down on his bed, muffling his sobs in his pillow, vowed never to forgive his father.

Green Fields and
White Rooms

Even in summer the fog lay heavy on the mountains in the morning; in the evening it rose again from the valleys to swathe the house, making the world seem smaller than it was. The crickets told the sun to go down and it went and they told the moon to come up and it did, and the light went off in the kitchen and Billy's mother came out to sit with Billy and his father on the porch but no one said anything. They watched the fireflies, suddenly locating points in the dark, until Billy's father stretched and said, "How about it, Vinnie?" and then the three of them got up and went inside and upstairs and to sleep. As they slept, a breeze shifted the curtains and they turned in their beds, loosing their souls to go out into the night.

Billy knew his soul left him; that was why he had to say, "If I should die before I wake, I pray the Lord my soul to take," before bed, but he wished he knew where his soul went. He didn't see why, if it was his, it had any right to go off on its own.

Sometimes he woke up in the middle of the night and did not know who he was. He was in a dark room and felt his arms and legs but as if they were someone else's; he could see a body, lying in a bed; then he felt himself descending into the body until, suddenly, he was Billy again. His mother had told him this happened because when you woke up suddenly it sometimes took a minute for your soul to get back to your body, but this did not comfort him. It made him think that his soul could get lost and not come back at all and then he would never remember who he was.

He tried to be careful. He slept with his windows open, even in winter, so that his soul would come right in to him and not get mixed up and go into his parents' room as it might if it had to find its way through the dark house. And he kept his bedroom door shut so that his parents' souls, wandering, wouldn't try to get into his body. He hated it when guests stayed overnight; once when his mother forced him to share his room with his cousin Dwight Daphne, Billy stayed awake until Dwight was asleep and then tiptoed downstairs and slept in the den, the windows open and the doors shut. It was February and Mrs. Daphne's African violets froze and Billy caught the flu, but his parents didn't scold him because they thought his garbled explanation about not wanting to "get mixed up with Dwight" was his childish way of telling them that Dwight had molested him. "I always thought that boy was queer," Billy's father said. Dwight Senior, Betty, and Dwight Junior were not invited to spend the night again.

Billy saw his parents in the morning and the evening; usually nobody talked but sometimes for no reason they all started laughing and laughed so hard they could hardly stop. "Oh, my," Lavinia sighed, "listen to us." To Billy it seemed there was no one else in the world but them.

Billy feared his father, and as he got older he despised his mother for not standing up to his father, though he could remember that he had loved her when he was little and she had played games with him and had taken him on walks to find newts and caterpillars. But now she did not like to go outdoors. She said it was because her feet hurt—"I was born with delicate ankles," she would say—or because her back ached from mopping. Billy's father complained that a country woman should be up at dawn baking and gardening and feeding chickens (even though they had no chickens and he was too lazy to plow up ground for a garden). His mother left the house only to make her weekly trip to town, for which she prepared days in advance: sorting laundry, checking the pantry for supplies and writing the grocery list, which she organized in the order in which the products were stocked on the supermarket shelves. She told Billy that when she couldn't sleep, instead of sheep she recited groceries: meats, delicatessen, dairy products, canned fruits, canned juices, soft drinks, macaroni, flour, sugar, cereal, cake mixes, condiments . . . On shopping days, Billy had heard her telling his aunt Betty, she felt like her old self again. Her old self, Billy understood, was the self she had been before she married his father and had him.

One shopping eve, when his father was "out with the boys," Billy sat on the floor, leaning against his mother's chair; they were watching television. Lavinia was cheerful, as she always was before her day in town, and during the commercials she told Billy about her girlhood. "Oh, so many suitors I had," she said, speaking in the remote, prim way she used when speaking of her past, as if she actually had talked differently in those days, growing up in Amber, the daughter of a draper. She had been Lavinia Chalmers then, and had her mouth full of pins when Reginald "Gin" Daphne walked into the shop, looking for the veterans' office and full of resentment. "Sometimes I think about those days and I don't know how I got from there to here, Billy. It seems like two different people, and I don't know where the other one got to. Sometimes it seems like the best part of me got away."

The program came back on now, and Lavinia stroked her son's hair and sighed, not her usual groan, but a gentle exhalation, and Billy felt as if the girl imprisoned inside Lavinia's pale rolls of flesh had taken his mother's place. He was frightened. He was afraid that if he turned around he really would see her sitting there, laughing coyly, her lips pursed over the pins she said she had always kept between her lips to prevent the boys from stealing kisses. He jumped when her hand traveled down to his shoulder and pulled him against her. "Be careful, William," she warned, "you don't ever want to get mixed up with anyone."

"Yes, Ma," he said. "Ma, can I see what's on the other channel?"

Every morning at five, Reginald lurched into the hall, cursing if he missed the light switch. Billy, who was always awake, stiffened as he waited for his father to bang on his door and holler, "Rise and shine, William! Rise and shine!" But though it was hard to get out of bed, especially in winter, he didn't mind once he was out in the barn, blanketed by the smell of the cows and the muffled jangling of their bells. The rhythmic sucking of the milking machines soothed him, and he never tired of carrying the full buckets to the milkhouse, of pouring the warm frothy milk into the cool tank and watching it undulate over the vaning blade. If only his father hadn't been there, grumbling about every little thing, he would have been perfectly happy. But all his father thought about was how much milk each cow gave and whether he could get the inspector to certify his milkhouse one more time without having to install a new tank. If he hadn't had so much money he could never recover sunk into equipment, he would have just sold the damn place and bought some nice clean business, where the manufacturing machines didn't stink up the aisles. "And now your mother nagging me for a new TV, when already she's good for nothing but spending money. Jesus H. Christ, don't ever get married, Billy."

One night after a drunk, thinking to encourage his son to manhood, Reginald ripped a centerfold from one of the magazines he kept in his truck and taped it to the inside of the bulk-tank lid. In the morning he guffawed until he practically choked at the expression of horror on Billy's face when he lifted the lid and saw the picture. In fact, Reginald chuckled every time he thought about it until the afternoon, when he and Billy were out cutting softwood to take to the mill at Oakton, a tree fell the wrong way and killed him.

A month after Reginald's funeral, with the money she received from his insurance, Lavinia purchased a trailer and had it installed on the hill behind the house where the television antenna could draw better reception. Then she enrolled Billy in the private school in Swanbury ("Fifield is always delighted to discover promising scholars among the local population!" enthused the letter of acceptance); she wanted Billy, she said, to have a chance in life. Billy begged her not to make him leave Amber; he didn't see why he couldn't have a chance in life right there—he could do all the milking himself and still go to school—but Lavinia told him to stop fussing at her. By the time Billy left for school, she had sold off the herd and rented out the farmhouse to some city people who wanted to get back to the land. Encouraged by her sister-in-law, she altered her hairstyle and bought some flattering new house-dresses. She had "Short but Sweet" chiseled on Reginald's pink granite tombstone and she laid fresh flowers on his grave every Sunday, but other than that she couldn't see what else there was to do for him so she might as well not feel guilty about buying a color TV set, she'd wanted one for so long and, besides, it made everything much more realistic. She confided to the Dwight Daphnes that she had nothing against marrying again except she doubted she'd ever find a man as good as Reginald.

When Billy arrived at Fifield Academy, he was thirteen. Politely he explained to the headmaster that he could not sleep if anyone else was in the room, but Fifield's headmaster, Captain Turner (U.S. Army Disabled, shrapnel received—Received? Captain Turner had queried—in left eye, honorably discharged . . . Just in time, Captain Turner was fond of saying, since even before his wound he and the army hadn't exactly what you would call seen eye to eye), said he had heard that one before. It wasn't until Billy had spent several nights in a maintenance shed that Captain Turner had relented and assigned him the room he had since occupied alone in the attic of Bennet House.

During the first three years Billy was at Fifield, he made no friends. His classmates didn't dislike him; he wasn't the sort of misfit into whose bed other boys tucked snakes or who inspired them to locker-room scorn, like Kermit ("Slimey") Wilson or Liam ("the Skunk") O'Donnell. They simply never thought about him. Few of Billy's classmates would recall his face a year after graduation, although one or two might, in a middle-aged nostalgia, come across Billy between Daimler and Dodds in *Steeplechase*, the Fifield yearbook, and opine, "Now there was a dark horse if ever there was one."

Captain Turner prided himself on taking a personal interest in each and every one of his boys, but Billy somehow slipped his mind, until the day Cyrus Quince arrived at the last minute to spend his senior year and Captain Turner realized that Billy's room possessed the only remaining available bed on campus. To Captain Turner this coincidence seemed nothing less than fateful.

Thus, at the beginning of his fourth and final year, one afternoon when a leaf-detaching wind was opening and slamming doors along the hallways of Bennet House, Billy came upon Cyrus unpacking in his room.

At first Billy, who had spoken to no one since he had said goodbye to his mother that morning, stood stockstill in the doorway and waited for the stranger to explain. But Cyrus, after glancing up to see a thin, gangly boy of his own age, straight dun-colored hair traveling every which way, both scowling at him and squinting at the sun sliding down over the edge of the west-facing window, decided to say nothing. It was an advantage, Cyrus believed, to provoke the other into speaking first. Finally Billy roused himself to speech—with such hostility that Cyrus almost laughed.

"Who are you and what exactly are you doing here?" he asked.

"Setting up an Apollo space launch, what do you think?"

"This is my room. There must be some mistake."

"What kind of mistake?"

"Who told you to come up here? Don't take out any more clothes."

"Who told you?"

"Who what?"

Cyrus stopped unpacking and studied Billy. "Consider it from my point of view. I'm new here. I don't know you from Adam. Not that I know Adam. But how do I know your motives? Why should I take your word for it that you belong here instead of me?"

"What's that supposed to mean?"

"How do I know you're not a fugitive from justice hiding out in the attic?"

"Very funny."

"What I mean is, isn't there some sign you could give me so that I know you're one of us?"

"Cut the jokes, will you? I told you, this is my room."

" 'Cut the jokes'? 'Cut the jokes.' Nope, don't think that's it. Do you have anything else you might try? I'd like to cooperate, but you can't be too careful in this line of work."

"Just get out," Billy said.

Cyrus raised an eyebrow. " 'Get out'?" he repeated. "Let's see now. . . . Get out, out get, teg tou, toe tug . . ."

"Oh, go jump in the lake." There was a quaver in Billy's voice and Cyrus, hearing it, looked at him with interest. But at that moment Billy's attention was distracted by a photograph Cyrus had taken out of his suitcase and laid on his bed: an eight-by-ten glossy of the ugliest cat Billy had ever seen, glaring up at the camera with a half-gnawed mouse hanging from its jaws, its eyes slitted and its incisors bared.

"What *is that?*" he asked.

Cyrus glanced down, then picked up the photograph. "Here." He handed it to Billy. "This, I want you to know," he declaimed in circus tones, "is Jonzo! Jonzo the Great, Jonzo the Fearless, Jonzo the Mouse Slayer, Jonzo the Shadow . . ."

Billy made no reply; however, he sat down on the nearest bed. Cyrus gave a half smile; lips closed, he lifted his mouth to the left as if the right side of his face were paralyzed.

"I was thinking of bringing him out here, but I was afraid he wouldn't come up to Fifield's high standards. Besides, I don't think he would like marching in formation."

"Marching in formation?"

"You know, taps, reveille, ah-ten-SHUN!" Cyrus saluted. "Dear Harold thinks this is a military academy."

"He does?"

Cyrus sat down on his bed. "Because of 'Academy.' And because the headmaster's called 'Captain.' "

Billy smiled.

"Dear Harold thinks they can knock some sense into me here. Poor old Harold was just at the end of his rope."

"At the end of his rope?"

"Oh, yes. Dear Harold had really had it. He was at his wits' end. Another one of my wisecracks would have sent him right through the roof."

"Is he your father?"

"How'd you guess? Yep, Dear Harold and Dear Rose. How about you, who are your dear ones?"

"My mother's name is Lavinia. Vinnie for short. My father's dead."

There was a silence, and Billy looked out the window. "Three years ago," he apologized. "A tree fell on him."

He waited for the usual embarrassed remark of sympathy, but the new boy only said, "A tree? A *tree* fell on him?"

Billy didn't know what to say.

"You mean he was just standing there and a tree *fell* on him?"

Billy felt the new boy looking at him. Although they sat only a yard apart, the intensity of the other's scrutiny made Billy feel as if he were being looked at from a great distance; the look was of someone who can scan miles of empty prairie and discern in a speck of dust a band of horsemen approaching.

"We were cutting wood. My father did logging."

"You mean you were there?"

Billy nodded. The new boy's surprise made Billy remember how he hadn't felt surprised at all. He hadn't even gone to look at his father's body pinned under the tree, to see how badly his father was caught and whether he might rescue him by cutting the tree away with the chain saw. It had been as if what Billy had always known would happen had happened, and it had never occurred to him that Reginald might not yet be dead. He had picked up his jacket, dusted off the dead leaves and wood chips, and made his way home, where he had announced to his mother that she was a widow. He had never cried.

He looked back at the new boy. "What's your name, anyway?"

Cyrus, if surprised by this change of subject, didn't show it. Without shifting his long-distance squint from Billy's face, he reached down and turned up the tag on his suitcase.

Cyrus Quince, Billy read silently, 84 Summer Street, Arborville . . .

"I've never heard of Arborville."

"I'm not surprised. What about you, do you have some identification?"

"I'm Billy Daphne," Billy said, feeling stupid. "From Amber."

"I should have known."

"What do you mean?"

"Hey, don't play innocent with me. This is a dangerous line of work, you know. You have to watch yourself all the time. There's hardly anyone you can trust."

Billy shrugged. He felt hostile to Cyrus again, which made him feel disappointed at the same time. For a moment Cyrus had seemed different from the other Fifield students, but now Billy saw he was just as fake as everyone else.

Cyrus, used as he was to his flippancy's causing people to fall all over themselves trying to show they got his jokes, realized with some interest that this scarecrow-looking Billy Daphne person was actually annoyed with him.

"Well, listen, Billy, if you really don't want me to stay here, I can ask Captain Turner to assign me some other room. I mean, I don't want you to *catch* anything."

"Ha ha."

Cyrus sadly cupped his hand to his forehead. "You mean Captain Turner didn't tell you?"

"Tell me what?"

"I'm dying. Everybody in Arborville is dying. We've all got this terrible incurable disease—it's all hushed up so that the rest of the country won't panic."

"Sure."

Cyrus sighed. "I guess I can't blame you for wanting me to move." He stood up and began to put things back into his suitcase. "Oh, God, it's so hard, never being wanted, everyone running away screaming when they see you."

"What are you doing?"

"Leaving. What'd you think?"

"You mean you'd really go ask for another room?"

At this Cyrus paused and looked Billy in the eye. "I don't get a big thrill out of staying where I'm not wanted."

"Well, look, if you really want to stay . . . I mean, at least until you get settled around here and stuff."

"Forget it."

"Look, I'm *sorry*. You can stay."

Cyrus scrutinized him. At last he said, "Gee whiz, Billy, thanks so much. I really appreciate your kindness. The life of a dying person is so rough."

Billy grinned. Cyrus smiled his half smile back. Shyly, then, Billy watched as his new roommate unpacked the remainder of his luggage, made his bed, and propped his horrible cat's picture on his dresser.

Now the nuns marched in and Captain Turner, standing at the lectern, steepled his hands piously before him. Cyrus's arrival at Fifield coincided with the first year of the merger between Fifield Academy and St. Barbara's, a nearby religious girls' school, a move Captain Turner had fought and whose implementation he intended to make as difficult as possible.

"Holy Mary, Mother of Grace," he intoned in a barely audible voice, as the women in light seersucker suits and abbreviated headdresses filed past him to their seats. Mother Agnes, St. Barbara's pretty headmistress, shot him a contemptuous look. There was suppressed laughter in the assembly.

"Let us pray," Captain Turner exhorted, when the nuns were seated. He waited until all heads were bowed.

"Grant us, O great Commander-in-Chief on high," he boomed, "the power to resist temptation, or, when we can resist no longer, to give in with grace." He paused until the laughter had died down in the audience. He saw Mother Agnes staring at him and he winked. She blushed. Bless her dear habited heart, he thought. He grinned at her over the bent heads of the boys and girls until she bowed her head to escape his gaze.

"Let us pray, boys and girls, girls and boys, that this new experience for all of us will not prove altogether disagreeable. You boys, being in the presence of ladies, may have to watch yourselves, but I'm sure you'll rise to the occasion. And I'm sure that you girls, although attuned to the habits of the gentler sex when left to its own devices . . ." (he made certain Mother Agnes was listening) "will soon discover that beneath our rough and uncouth exteriors, we have hearts as soft as anyone's. Let us pray, Fifielders, St. Barbarettes, that the unaccustomed presence of the alien sex does not turn us from our righteous path. We pray that we may have the strength to work very very hard and to play very very hard, so that we can be tops! With Thy grace, Lord, we'll defeat Woodbine this year, cream St. Martin's, smash Willoughby-Wilcox, annihilate Trent . . ."

"Go, Fifield! Go, Fifield! Go, go, go!"

"Ah-MEN, brother!" Captain Turner acknowledged. He stepped down from the podium and bowed to Mother Agnes.

"How gallant." Mother Agnes, face fetchingly squared by her wimple, stood. "Now I'll pray. Do any of you know the *Lord's* prayer?"

"Yes, Ma'am!" cheered the boys.

"Yes, *Mother*," corrected the girls.

At this counterpoint, Captain Turner grinned. The sea against rocks, he thought—this one-eyed, self-proclaimed cynic who could yet not get through a day if he did not describe its events in exalted terms. Oh, my sweet congregation! he murmured. Yes, definitely, for once he was going to have some fun.

.   .   .

"You're really going to rub it in, aren't you, Captain?" Mother Agnes said after the assembly, as they sat sipping sherry in the sanctity of his office.

"Rub what in, my dear?" Captain Turner asked. "Here, let me pour you another."

"You may call me Mother Agnes just like anyone else, Captain."

"You my mother? Why, honey, if you were my mother, I'd still be small enough to fit in your lap!"

"Captain Turner, this wasn't my idea."

"Mine neither!" replied he. "Heck, I've always held that church and state shouldn't mix, though frankly I've never seen much difference between the two, Miss . . . couldn't I call you just plain Agnes? Or what was your name before you, er, hitched up with that feller on the . . ."

"I once bore the name Kelly Richmond, but I'm Mother Agnes now. If you can't bring yourself to address me as that, then don't call me anything. I'm trying to make this as painless as possible for us both, Captain Turner, and I'd be grateful if you'd be of some assistance."

"Now that's a pretty speech, Kelly Richmond. Where did you say you come from? I can't see . . ."

Mother Agnes stood.

"Aw shucks," Captain Turner went on in what he liked to think of as his "rebel" voice. "I'm not tryin' to get you riled up." He strode across the room and hovered over her until she sat. "Hell, y'all don't even wear your witches' costumes anymore—don't even wear your helmets except on special occasions like this morning. Anybody seeing you on the street would think you were just like any other young ladies, a mite conservative perhaps, but . . . So why did you do it? I mean, there's nothing different, except . . ."

"Except?"

"Well, hell, pardon my indiscretion, but you get that much fun out of celebrating the sacrament of marriage with some guy who's not even corporeal?"

"Well, Captain Turner," said Mother Agnes with a smile, "you'll never know until you try it, will you?"

"She's a wise one, that Mother Agnes," remarked Captain Turner to his table that evening at dinner. "There's a lot more to her than meets the eye."

The table included, besides his wife, Henrietta, and Assistant Headmaster Welch, who were always there, the new boy, Cyrus Quince.

"I think we're going to get along, but I still don't get it, why a good-looking young woman like that would relinquish the world. Must have broken her heart over some brute and decided to have done with the whole sex."

"Oh, for pity's sake, Jacob," said Henrietta Turner, refilling the water glasses. "Why don't you mind your own business for once?"

Assistant Headmaster Welch snickered.

"What for?" Turner grinned. "What could be more boring than minding my own business? I just can't believe a woman like that doesn't like men." He turned to Cyrus. "What's your opinion in the matter, Quince?"

"Maybe Mother Agnes just doesn't like you, Captain Turner."

Welch started to laugh, changed his mind and converted the laugh to a cough. Cyrus let his comment hang unqualified over the table and waited to see what form Turner's retribution would take. But, instead of seeming offended, Turner merely gazed at Cyrus thoughtfully.

"I think she likes me too much, if you want to know the truth. And is annoyed with herself for liking me." He grinned. "It's not often, after all, that a woman gets to enjoy the company of the opposite sex after swearing eternal fidelity to Mr. Self-Sacrifice Himself. A dead husband is not the most practical kind."

"Oh, really, Jacob!" Mrs. Turner exclaimed, like a train whistling. She spooned more food onto Cyrus's plate. "Can't you keep your imagination under control for once in your life?"

"My sensible Henrietta," Turner said, winking at Cyrus. "Where would I be without you?"

Cyrus started to laugh—stopped himself in time. Turner, however, had seen this.

"Aha!" he trumpeted, making everyone jump. Boys at other tables turned to stare. "So it's going to be the old silent treatment, eh? Well, I don't mind. A bit hackneyed, but I suppose as valid as any other opening."

"Turnip's really giving him the once-over, isn't he?" Cyrus overheard a boy behind him say. "Trying to find out his 'goals in life.' " They laughed.

Captain Turner waited. When Cyrus didn't speak, he crowed, "That's the trouble with the move, isn't it, Quince? It's all formula from then on in. You've relinquished that vital element of surprise!"

"Jacob, will you calm down?" Henrietta scolded. "How can these boys be expected to learn any manners with you setting an example?"

"Oh, relax. Everyone's used to me making a spectacle of myself." But in a quieter voice he said, "I want you to know that despite your antediluvian approach, Quince, you're an adversary of the caliber it's rarely my pleasure to do battle with."

Cyrus frowned. Turner pushed back his chair and retrieved himself from it. "Care for a nip, Welch?"

"Oh, why not, I always say." Welch stood also. "Be seeing you, Cyrus."

"Yeah." Cyrus nodded.

"Au revoir, mon ami," Captain Turner said, saluting. "I look forward to a continuation of our chat in the not too distant future."

What chat? Cyrus thought, but he said, "Sure. Okay."

"Christ, I sure do cotton to that boy," Captain Turner remarked to Ralph Welch when they were seated in his study. "Here, have another shot. Liked him from the first minute I saw him, more self-contained than any boy his age I've ever known, sitting in here with his parents, acting as if his being here was some kind of misunderstanding soon to be cleared up. They seemed a benighted pair."

"Oh?"

"Mother off in the ozone. Nervous as all hell. Lily, her name was—some goddamn flower. Father an ignoramus cut from the old pattern, that innocent, good-hearted type. They're the most dangerous kind. Hell, at least I know I'm a no-good son-of-a-bitch. Cigar, Welch?"

"No, thank you, Turner. I don't smoke."

This exchange was repeated every night.

"The father keeps saying, 'I've been with Amalgamated Something-or-Other for twenty-odd years now; we own our own home; we don't need a scholarship.'

" 'You like this kid?' I ask him. 'What do you mean, do I like him?' 'Do you like your boy?' I repeat. The boy's watching him. The mother's watching him. 'What kind of a question is that?' he says. 'He's my son!' "

Turner guffawed.

" 'Just wondering,' I say. 'Seems like half the folks who leave their boys here just want to get them out of the house. Make them uncomfortable or something. Sometimes I look around my dining hall and think what I've got is one big roomful of orphans.'

"The mother—what's her name, Daisy? Milkweed? Whatever. She's fiddling. Buttons and unbuttons her cuff. Swings her leg. A beautiful woman I might add. Aristocratic-looking—like Cyrus—the kind of lines that make it clear why we worship symmetry."

"Symmetry," repeated Ralph Welch.

"Would be more beautiful if she could calm down. The kind of woman I would risk . . . well, never mind, I know that's not your cup of tea, Ralphie. Anyway, the boy was looking so uncomfortable I took pity on him and suggested he take the dog for a walk. He didn't protest.

" 'I'm afraid we haven't been getting along,' Father Quince says as soon as his son closes the door. 'Cyrus had a younger brother—has, I mean—who was born . . . who has a genetic disease. He had to be sent to an institution. Cyrus has never forgiven me. And then this summer my father-in-law, who's lived with us since Cyrus was little, had to go into a retirement home. Cyrus was very attached to his grandfather and he holds that against me too. Mrs. Quince and I have both tried to discuss his attitude with him, but he refuses to listen. We thought it might be easier for him to be away from home right now.'

"He looks at me and waits for absolution. I let him wait awhile. Then I say, 'Seems to me you've sent a lot of people away in your time, Harold.' You know, omniscient-doctor tone, uninvited use of the Christian name—gets 'em every time.

"Sure enough, he looks abashed, but then the woman—Rose, that's what it is—begins to cry. Mr. Husband Quince looks over like he can't believe this is happening, then he gets up and goes to her wearily. . . . 'Oh, the trials we men have to endure!' I can see the thought broadcast across his mighty cranium, though he acts the comforting hubby. Puts his arm around her, speaks sweet nothings, strokes her hair."

Turner chuckled.

"The lady doesn't pay the slightest attention to him. She just sits there and cries like she does it for a living.

" 'It's been rough on all of us,' he apologizes to me. 'I'm sure you can appreciate that.'

" 'I can appreciate that,' I say. I excuse myself and go out to find the boy. I catch him engaging Gretchen in conversation, trying to induce her to chase a stick.

" 'She's a Seeing-Eye dog; she doesn't really know how to play,' I tell him, then explain that I train these dogs as a sideline. He's interested, and I suggest that anytime he feels like walking around with his eyes shut he can help me. He gives me that cynical-wistful smile as if it's something he'd like to do, but for some reason it's impossible.

" 'I get the impression you're not getting along too well with your parents,' I remark. 'They tell me you're angry at them because they were no longer able to take care of your grandfather at home.'

" 'That's a lie,' he says at once.

" 'What is?'

"But then he recalls he's talking to me, whom he's supposed to dislike. 'I don't really see what business it is of yours.' He strides off, calling Gretchen.

" 'I have a certain responsibility as headmaster of this school,' I begin—the usual recitation. He says, 'Just because you're the headmaster here doesn't give you the right to pry into people's lives.'

"You know me, Welch, I don't have a high tolerance for impertinence. But the kid had so much dignity he won my respect." Turner laughed. "Not that I intend to stop prying into people's lives."

Welch, who had drunk three shots of bourbon in a hurry, was scarcely listening, but Turner was used to this. He was accustomed to speaking monologues. "There's not a goddamn mind within a thousand leagues of here," he often said. Yet, because Welch rarely spoke, Turner could sometimes maintain the illusion that he was sympathetic company.

"So I go back in," Captain Turner went on, "and the mother's stopped crying. She's standing facing the bookshelf, running her fingers along the spines like a kid does along a fence. The father's back in his chair, memorizing the carpet. They turn the minute I come in, awaiting my verdict.

" 'Well,' I say. I make a big show of going behind my desk, looking through the kid's folder.

" 'If you're reluctant because of what I told you . . .' the father begins.

" 'We've got boys mad about all sorts of things here,' I say, 'Harold. He'll fit right in.' Old Harold stands, reaches for my hand, which I ignore. Took great pleasure in that. 'Thank you,' the mother says stiffly. 'I know we're very late.' Don't kill me with your gratitude, I felt like saying. I wasn't any too fond of her either, if you want to know the truth, though I felt sorry for her. Her sobbing was genuine enough."

"Noble sentiments indeed," said Welch. But he knew as soon as he had spoken that he had gone too far.

Turner, pacing, stopped and stared. "I can't see a whole hell of a lot what's got your goat, Welch. I never had the impression you cared too much for weeping women yourself."

"Got me there, Turner. She can cry her beautiful, aristocratic eyeballs out for all I care. What I fail to see is what you think so exceptional about the kid. Sure, he's clever enough, but standoff-ish, conceited . . ."

"Oh, hell, Ralph."

"I'm entitled to my opinion," Welch said primly.

Captain Turner heard this. "Handsome dog, though, you gotta admit."

Ralph Welch frowned.

Turner grinned. "What, spurned you already?"

Welch stood. "Turner, this is insulting and I refuse to discuss it further."

"Just let me explain one thing to you first, Ralphie. I know I hope for more from these boys than they'll ever achieve. I try to get them all revved up to do great things in life, but I know most will not last out the odds. The first hard fences and they'll choose to walk around. Come to think of the ambition to accomplish something in life as some adolescent dream. Something they be-lieved in high school. But it's worth all the energy I put into them if even one, just *one* of them . . . I trust my instincts about Quince, Ralph. He's thoroughbred as they come. Skittish, maybe, but strung taut as piano wire. You're a fool not to see it."

"Yes, well, that wouldn't be the first time you've called me that. Goodnight, Turner."

Turner sighed. "Sweet dreams, Ralph."

Once the major had left for the front, his wife could not bear to remain in the house. She therefore suggested to a number of her friends, whose husbands had also gone to war, that with their children they travel to a remote area where they would all be safer in the event that the war should come closer to home. Accordingly, they set out in caravan—gypsies, they styled themselves, but they jested, not intending to leave home forever.

The major's wife did not inform her husband, however, that she was going away. She excused this deceit by telling herself that it was better he should be able to think of his home—safe, unchanged, waiting—during his tenure in the field.

Thus the house and an entire way of life—an ideal against which future generations would continue to measure a world altogether different—were abandoned. One by one the rooms were shuttered and the twilight took over from the daylight as gently and unnoticeably as one parent relieves the other's watch over a sick child, and then the drapes were drawn, the doors shut. Sheets covered the chairs and tables, the beds and bureaus, and the piano. In the fireplace, in the kitchen stove, the coals were cold. The doors to the outside world were locked.

One early November day, when the air was as clear as it got anywhere on earth, Billy and Cyrus hitchhiked up to Amber, bought a sixpack in Raymond Lefevre's grocery—"What are you, Billy, twelve now?" Raymond winked—and went to break into Lavinia's trailer. Billy knew that his mother had gone to Winston for the weekend with his aunt Betty. Wafer-thin, he disappeared through the observation slit above the sink and in a moment stood in the open doorway, saying to Cyrus, "Listen, it's kind of a mess, maybe we should . . ." But Cyrus didn't wait for Billy to finish before entering.

"Holy shit!" he exclaimed. "She lives in here?"

"She's a pig. It's incredible."

Books—paperback mysteries and romances, detective novels and thrillers—listed everywhere in ready-to-topple stacks; mold had formed green craters in glasses lining the windowsills; spiderwebs were stretched like safety nets across the corners of the room. Cyrus made his way to a chair.

"Is it okay to move stuff?"

Billy kicked over several towers of books. "We ought to burn the place down."

"Billy . . ." Cyrus laughed. He picked up a book here and there and read their titles.

Billy tore loose two bottles of beer from the cardboard packet, rummaged in a drawer for an opener, and flipped the tops off. He handed a bottle to Cyrus, then opened the refrigerator to stow the others. Several jars and packages fell out.

"God, look at all that!"

"I told you, she's a pig. All she ever does is eat."

"She reads."

Billy kicked over another stack of books. "She's the most useless person who ever lived."

Cyrus nodded, accepting.

"Let's get out of here," Billy said. "I'm going to throw up if I stay in this joint."

"Yeah, okay."

Carrying their opened bottles, they left the trailer and headed up the field behind the house toward pine woods. Cyrus sauntered; Billy fell into his rhythm, though when alone he walked fast across this first field, going for the cover of the woods. Though in the habit of continuous banter, they didn't talk as they headed up the hill, Cyrus in front, Billy behind, wondering how Cyrus knew where to go. Soon they were in the woods, which were so thick and dark with unthinned spruce that they had to walk with their arms held out to fend off the boughs, but soon the spruce gave way to poplar and ash and some maple, their bark winter-gray; here and there a stand of birch shone whitely. An occasional poplar still held bright orange leaves, which quivered and rattled in the least breeze. It was three o'clock, but the days were short and the sun was already lowering. Its angled light made everything eerily brilliant and still.

They were still climbing when they came out of the woods. A grassy slope led up to a promontory of rock. They stood upon it, breathing a little shallowly, looking out at the mountains, which changed from brown to gray to bluish-gray and then to a clearer and clearer blue in the distance.

"I love this place," Billy said. "I've come up here my whole life."

"Yeah," Cyrus said, still looking out at the mountains. "It's beautiful."

"No one else ever came up here. My mother's scared to go in the woods and my father only went in to cut logs."

Cyrus nodded, then sat down, facing the view. He sat with his knees bent, his arms resting on top of his knees; in one hand he held his beer. Billy sat down a little way from him.

"I could live in a place like this," Cyrus said. "No one to bother you—except bears. Are there bears here?"

"You never see them."

"Just build some cabin and live in it. Nobody to tell you how to organize your life. Have you ever noticed how anxious everybody is to mind your business for you?"

"I guess."

"Like Turner. He drives me up the wall with all his questions. Why doesn't he bug *you*?"

"You're new." Billy knew it was more than that, however. Turner had never shown such interest in him.

Then Cyrus asked, "Have you thought what you're going to do, Billy? After this year, I mean?"

Billy shrugged. He was so skinny and loose-jointed that when he shrugged it always looked as if his arms were lifting out of their sockets. "Not especially. I don't think I want to go to college."

"When I was a kid I wanted to be a spy. I was thinking about that recently."

Billy smiled.

"Yeah. Pretty corny. I was dead serious about it, though. I used to practice all the time. Missions. I'd follow people around. Or try to get downtown without anyone I knew seeing me. You wouldn't believe some of the things I thought were disguises when I was little. It always shocked me when I'd be walking along in dark glasses and a big hat with my collar turned up and some grownup would say, 'Hi, Cyrus.'"

Billy laughed.

"It was my grandfather who got me doing it. He told me to always be on the alert. He said everyone in the world had hidden information they were trying to pass on and you had to be on the lookout for it. It could sound just like ordinary conversation, but it would contain a top-secret message. It drove me insane. I'd go to the store to buy a Fudgesicle and the store owner, Mr. Dubofsky, would talk to me about the good old days in Latvia or somewhere. I'd sit there waiting to hear the message. I used to have night-mares—for a long time I had nightmares about the bomb being dropped. Someone was about to push the button and I was the only one who could stop him, but I couldn't get there in time. Then it got confused with this other dream, a kind of torture session, and there was this inquisitor who had glowing cigarette ends for eyes and he was yelling things like, 'But what did Mr. Dubofsky *say*?' and I wouldn't know but he wouldn't believe me. I knew if I could tell him the secret message I could save the world from being blown up, but I couldn't, and he'd bend his face down toward me and then his eyes would kind of grow out of his head and just when he was about to burn me I'd wake up.

"It used to worry me a lot, whether I'd actually confess under torture. I tried to imagine tortures and whether I could stand them. Sometimes I yelled so loud in this dream I woke the whole house up. Dear Harold would have a fit. He thought it was all Granddad's fault."

"Why did he think that?"

"Granddad was a bad influence. Got me all excited with his wild stories. Dear *Harold* said. Anyway, I became so terrified of this nightmare—I started having it when I was about seven or eight, I guess—that I got afraid to go to sleep. I had insomnia for a long time. Sometimes I'd get up and go outside and walk all over town, staring at people's houses. Usually everybody was asleep but sometimes I saw a light on. I used to imagine we could have a club for people who couldn't sleep. We could have meetings in the middle of the night. Great idea, right? Jonzo practically always went with me. Sometimes Granddad would be waiting when I'd come back. He had insomnia, too. We'd make something to eat—we had to whisper. Mom caught us once—I guess insomnia runs on that side of our family—but I don't think Dad ever found out. He was a pretty solid sleeper usually, except when I yelled bloody murder."

"Your grandfather sounds pretty neat for a grandfather," Billy said enviously. "All my grandfathers ever talk about is boring stuff like how the prices of things are going up."

"Yeah. I never knew exactly what he wanted me to do, though. He'd give me an order, say, 'Take in Elm Street,' and I'd walk up Elm Street and back and when I got home he'd give me the third degree. Ask me if I saw anything suspicious. But I never knew what the hell to look for. I just counted things. Cats, dogs, how many people had their cars out of their garages, whether any mothers were hanging out laundry, stuff like that. Want to know how many houses on Summer Street have porches? How many fire hydrants there are in Arborville? How many people in Arborville have last names that begin with *Z*? At least, when I was eleven. Just ask Quince Information Service. It used to drive Dear Harold nuts." Cyrus laughed. "He'd come down to breakfast and I'd tell him he'd worn the same tie twice already that week and he'd throw a fit."

"What did he do?"

"Well, he didn't do anything. Just threatened to. 'God damn it, Cyrus, I've had it! If you don't start showing some respect, young man, you're going to be in serious trouble!' He's always saying junk like that. What an idiot."

Billy laughed. He admired the way Cyrus didn't take any shit from his father. "How did you remember all that stuff? Did you just get better at remembering, or what?"

"I don't know. It got so I couldn't help it. I kept records—index cards, filed in shoeboxes—but I didn't need to. I can still recite everything that's on them. That was Granddad's idea too—the files. I was supposed to be keeping records for people from other planets—people . . . well, whatever. I know, it's ridiculous, but I really took it seriously; I was convinced visitors from outer space were going to come down someday and I'd go out and welcome them and give them this guidebook that would explain the whole world to them, though Granddad's idea was to have the book as a kind of record of the way things were in case the world got blown up before the visitors from outer space got here. Don't ask me what was supposed to be *in* this handbook. Whenever I asked Granddad that question he'd say, 'Aha!' He was always saying 'Aha!' It drove me nuts. Tell me if this is boring."

"You really actually believed that visitors from outer space were going to come down to earth and you would show them around?"

"Shit, yeah! When I was lying in my room at night, trying not to go to sleep, I'd look out the window at the stars—my bed was right by the window—and I'd watch them all closely to see if they were really stars. Make sure they weren't spaceships instead. What I liked most was imagining how I'd be a welcoming committee for space visitors. While everybody else was hiding in their basements screaming, I'd just go out there and wait for the blinking lights to go off and the whiny whistling to stop and the door to open and then I'd walk right over and say hello."

"What if they didn't speak English? How were you going to communicate with them?"

"Don't ask me. I used to ask Granddad the same thing, but he just said that if they were clever enough to get down to earth in the first place they'd find some way of understanding us."

"Does your grandfather live with you?"

"He *did*. Since right after I was born."

"He doesn't anymore?"

Cyrus shook his head.

"Is he dead?" Billy asked cautiously.

"Dear Harold sent him away."

"How come? Didn't he like him?"

"Like him! For Christ's sake, Billy, he was such a terrible influence on me, don't you remember I told you? Always undermining Dear Harold's authority! 'Who's head of this household anyway, Rose? Me or him?' "

"It seems strange," Billy murmured.

"Everything blew up in August," Cyrus went on. "We had all just come back from visiting my . . . a relative, and Dear Rose was being her usual mysterious self. . . ."

"What do you mean 'mysterious'?"

"Oh . . . getting her feelings all hurt about something and

going off to her room. You could never tell when something would get her upset. And if you asked her what was the matter all she said was, 'You know perfectly well what the matter is.' If Dear Harold came home when she was upstairs, he'd yell at me and Betsy. 'Now what have you kids done? I've HAD it with these shenanigans!' Once I told him, 'Why don't you ask her yourself?' and he practically burned the house down he got so pissed. Anyhow, in August, they were having this huge fight, as usual, shut up in their bedroom, and I was in my room and had the door shut so I wouldn't hear them yelling, and then all of a sudden I hear Dear Harold storming out into the hall shouting, 'Okay, Rose, maybe I just will!' and next thing I know I look out the window and he's loading all of Granddad's stuff in the car and Granddad's come upstairs to say *goodbye* to me.

"He was *crying*, Billy. He was a general. Betsy wasn't even *home*."

Cyrus laughed shortly. "When Dad came back I told him I refused to go to school, to protest his idiotic behavior, and the next thing I know we're all stuffed in the car driving out here."

"Your grandfather was a general in the army?"

"He was kind of in charge of secret intelligence after the war, although no one knows about him. He's practically blind now."

"Why doesn't anyone know about him?"

"Well, because, if you want to know, my grandfather wasn't the most popular general in the whole world. In the end he had a big disagreement with intelligence about the way it ran things and resigned before he reached retirement. Actually," Cyrus added, "there are a lot more generals around than anyone thinks."

"Where is he now?"

"I don't know," Cyrus said curtly. He began kicking the ground with his heel. Billy watched his foot.

"Do you mean your father wouldn't tell you?"

Cyrus shrugged.

"Well, why doesn't your grandfather write to you?" Billy was still trying to absorb the information that all was not perfect in Cyrus's home. Cyrus had always joked about "Dear Harold" and

"Dear Rose," but Billy had thought of the Quinces as basically a happy family.

Cyrus squinted at Billy. "I would think that's obvious. He doesn't know I'm here. He might be trying to write to me in Arborville, but if he is Dear Harold would intercept the letters. They've probably got him all drugged up somewhere."

"If your grandfather was a general, wouldn't the army know where he is? Even if he didn't get along with them. Generals can't just disappear off the face of the earth. We could ask them."

"I never thought about that," Cyrus said guardedly. "But what makes you think the army would tell *us*?"

"Why would they want to keep it a secret?"

"I guess you aren't too familiar with the way the army works, Billy. They don't just give out information because you *ask* for it."

"But why would they want to keep you from seeing your grandfather?"

"I have no idea. I'm just saying you can't count on them telling you what you want to know."

"We wouldn't just go ask them, then. We could trick them into revealing where he is. We could even join the army ourselves and then start snooping around."

"Sure."

"Then if it seemed like they were covering something up, we could make a big stink and tell the newspapers and get the whole country up in arms about it!"

"I doubt it. I really don't think the country would get too excited about the fact that some person they never heard of lost touch with his grandfather, even if he was a general. And I don't particularly want to join the army. In fact, I wouldn't join it if you paid me."

"Even if it meant finding your grandfather?"

"Billy," Cyrus said, "you have to *kill* people. Or you could. Would you want to kill someone?"

"You only have to kill people if there's a war."

"There could be a war anytime."

"Then you'd have to fight anyway. They'll bring back the draft. It's better to join on your own. When you enlist, you can choose what you want to do."

"That's what they like you to *think*. They just tell you that to get you in. Then they tell you they're very sorry but you have to do something else instead."

"If you join with someone, don't they keep you together? I think it's called the buddy system."

"Look, nobody *likes* the army, Billy. They just pretend they do afterward. You know how fathers are always bragging about the good old days in the war and talking about their great long-lost army buddies? Well, one time I went into my parents' room, one morning when Dear Harold was sleeping late, and I had a tape recorder I'd gotten a kid in the school band to play 'Reveille' on, and I played it and then I yelled, 'Get a move on, soldier! What do you think this is, a honeymoon? Up and at 'em, soldier!' You know what happened? Dear Harold jumped out of bed practically before his eyes were open and saluted me! I almost died laughing. When I started to laugh, he gave me an incredibly confused look, but then suddenly he realized who I was and grabbed me and started shaking me. 'Don't you ever try that again as long as you live, do you understand me?' He yells a lot but this was different. Not louder or anything, just seriouser—more serious—whatever. I was pretty nervous. I thought he was going to punch me out."

"Wow."

"Yeah." Cyrus laughed.

He lit a cigarette, offered Billy one, and they sat watching the clouds on the horizon lose their color. It would be dark soon. Billy broke the silence first.

"Listen, Cyrus. Even if we didn't join the army, I could help you find your grandfather anyway."

"How?" He sounded suspicious, as if he didn't think Billy could be any help.

"I don't know *exactly*. We wouldn't just go out and look for him. We could have a plan, figure out the most likely places. There must be an address in your house somewhere."

Cyrus looked skeptical.

"We have to do something when we get out of that dump."

"That's true."

When Cyrus didn't say anything else, Billy asked, "Don't you want to?"

Cyrus, squinting at the horizon, didn't reply.

"I thought you were worried about him."

Cyrus tapped his cigarette on a rock to flick loose the ash, then inhaled deeply. He blew a long tunnel of smoke into the air. Billy watched it dissipate. Cyrus glanced at him, his eyes narrowed, deliberately, and Billy suddenly felt distrustful. It was the way he had felt the day they met, when Cyrus was being so cool, acting like he owned the place. Was Cyrus telling him the truth?

But then Cyrus shrugged. "Hell, why not? Let's look for the old dope." He flashed a smile, and Billy, after wavering a moment, was won back.

A fortnight later, Captain Turner received a telephone call from Rose Quince: she had bad news, she said, that she was afraid to tell Cyrus. His cat had disappeared. She knew how attached he was to it and she wondered if Captain Turner . . . Jonzo—that was the cat's name—had been despondent ever since Cyrus had left for Fifield, and then last weekend he had apparently just gone off somewhere.

"I feel terrible about it," she said.

"But why do you want me to tell him?"

"I thought it might be easier for him to be told by someone actually there."

About losing a cat? Turner wondered. Cyrus is tough, he felt like saying, I'm sure he can handle it. "Oh, what the hell."

As he hung up the phone, it dawned on him that Rose Quince was afraid to tell Cyrus the news. She must think he would hold her responsible.

Turner set off to Bennet House to offer his condolences. As he was climbing the last flight of stairs (Cyrus and Billy had the only room on the top floor; the rest was used for storage), he heard a cat complaining and Cyrus's voice scolding, "Come on, Jonzo, will you take it easy? If you don't cool it, I'll put you back in your box. You should be happy you're not still on the airplane." Billy was laughing. How the devil . . .? wondered Turner. Cyrus's sister—Cyrus had a sister, Turner thought he recalled—must have been his accomplice, but how had they gotten the cat from an airport without anyone finding out about it?

After listening a minute, he turned around and descended the stairs. He had a big grin on his face when he encountered Ralph Welch, who was on his way back across the quadrangle.

"What are you looking so pleased about?" Welch inquired irritably.

Turner winked. "For once I may have bet on the right horse. Ralphie, that's what."

Still grinning, he walked on, leaving Welch, who had forgotten their earlier conversation about Cyrus, fuming at Turner's smugness.

Although the major's wife wrote faithfully to the front, she remained careful to say nothing in her letters that might undermine her husband's illusion that she was still at home. She had ceased to think of this as deception; in fact, she had come to consider it a vital contribution to the war effort.

Things had changed since he left. She was working in a factory with other army wives, helping to keep up production while the men were away. For the first time she understood her husband's devotion to duty. The work was tiring, but she felt useful—she was laboring in the national interest. If her spirits lagged, she had the company of the other women to distract her. On the weekends they took their children to the beach or to the mountains.

In the meantime, with each communication he received from home, the major's uneasiness grew. No particular thing his wife wrote provoked it, rather, a strange sense that her letters weren't genuine. The passages in which she spoke of her affection and longing for him seemed too embellished to be natural. Then there were the passages in which she wrote about the house and its contents in minute detail, as if she were an agent handling its sale and he a potential client. When he received a letter containing a page-long account of the remodeling of their kitchen (we needed to modernize, she wrote), he requested a leave to visit his family.

The colonel said it was out of the question. "We need every man we've got if we're going to win this war," he said.

The major sighed. "I must ask you to reconsider, sir. I have reason to believe my family may be in danger."

"What reason? Didn't you receive a letter from home just today?"

"I don't believe my wife wrote it. It doesn't sound like her at all. I am not given to wild speculation, Colonel, but I believe that either someone is forging her letters or else ordering her what to write."

"Major, I seriously doubt . . ."

"How can we be sure of what's going on at home? Perhaps civilian letters are being censored in order not to cut down the army's morale."

"That's impossible, Major. If there were anything at home to be concerned about, I would have been informed."

"But innocence," proclaimed Captain Turner, "is to war what yeast is to bread. Innocence of people's true motives, I mean—including our own."

"Celibacy is necessary for concentration, that's all," Mother Agnes insisted.

They sat in Turner's study, Mother Agnes on the sofa, he across from her in an armchair. They had been sitting thus with increasing frequency over the past four months, describing these conversations as "conferences," in which they supposedly discussed the administration of Fifield–St. Barbara's merger. Yet they had discovered an ease in understanding one another, an intellectual congeniality, that soon had made pretense absurd, and they now freely discussed everything from their teaching difficulties to the state of the modern world. Nearly every day after her sixth-period history, Mother Agnes came by and chatted with Captain Turner until dinnertime. She looked so little like a nun it was positively sinful, he told her. In her snug navy-blue skirt, striped blouse, and short, neat haircut she looked more like a French schoolgirl than the head of a convent.

Mother Agnes, still as sure of herself as when she had been head of the debating team at Myers Junior High School, had always interpreted her vocation to suit herself. She had decided to become a nun one hot day when she was hitchhiking across Argentina following her graduation from college. "Hassles constantly," she had explained to Captain Turner. Then one day she had a brilliant idea, went to a market, bought six yards of black cotton, and sewed herself a habit. After that she was offered rides everywhere; people invited her to share their food; she prayed for their health and their children. . . . Mother Agnes had been a National Merit Scholar, a Phi Beta Kappa in college, and had been awarded a teaching fellowship at a prestigious graduate school, which she would have accepted had she not decided to try the convent instead. "Academia, government, business—what's the difference?" she joked. "I like my tyrants explicit."

"Shed your illusions long ago, is that it?"

"I hope so. I like to believe it's possible to face life head-on."

"What in hell for? We weren't given the capacity to delude ourselves for no reason." He grinned at her, and she grimaced.

But she had to admit she enjoyed his company. She believed Jake Turner was the only original human being she had met since a Bolivian revolutionary with whom she'd been in love for a weekend in 1965. Bandying words with this irreverent, melodramatic middle-aged melancholic kept her wits nimble. Despite their banter, they shared the attitude that one was put on earth to figure out how to get back into the Garden (not that Turner would have liked to hear his views so characterized) and she sympathized with the frustration he experienced in his efforts to persuade his students of this. And, although she felt she shouldn't, she also sympathized with his unhappiness with his wife. "I love her," he said, "but it's been twenty years since we had a real conversation. She accepts life, whereas I want to know why we got such a shoddy deal. She's hopeful, and I feel the world's going to hell in a handbasket. I believe man may have reached the end of his tenure on earth and Henrietta's still in a covered wagon heading west."

He spoke with such absence of spite that Mother Agnes could not help feeling for him.

For his part, Turner informed himself he was being greedy—the typically priapic, go-getting male—to want to know even more intimately this woman he liked talking to better than anyone he'd ever met in his life. Now, Jake, he lectured himself, what you and Agnes have is something higher, something the clayfeet couldn't even comprehend! You and she don't need *that*—you share *spiritual* goals. What's important is to support one another's ambitions. Yet, miserable fortune, he found her damned attractive, and no matter how hard he tried to transcend his baser yearnings, the subject was always circling around, sneaking back, dressed up in some new outfit, insinuating its purpose into the conversation.

"I like the convent because I can think clearly," Mother Agnes went on. "I could never think if I always had half my mind on a mate. One would be pondering some vital issue and in dear hubby would come, feeling grumpy, and one would have to placate him: 'Would you like a cup of tea, dear?' 'No.' 'What about a drink?' 'No!' 'But you should have *something*, dear.'"

Turner laughed. "It doesn't have to be like that." (Though who was he to talk?)

"Perhaps I exaggerate, but it's true. A woman who marries can never freely pursue the life of the mind."

"Couldn't you pursue it together?"

"The quest for truth and the desire to unite with another person are mutually exclusive impulses," she preached. "Believe me, I know."

"You sound pretty adamant about that. Do you mean to tell me the country's convents are full of mystics and geniuses?"

She sniffed. "Certainly not. Most of the sisters have as much intellectual rigor as marshmallows. And I suppose some do join to 'deny' their charms to the male sex. But I've gotten adept at detecting those novices who harbor the illusion that broken-hearted suitors will pine outside the nunnery wall, listening in frustrated agony to the otherworldly laughter of the permanently virginal. Today's convent is not a place of avoidance."

"I don't care, Agnes. I still say any woman taking final vows is thumbing her nose at the opposite sex. All that stuff about quest for truth . . . that's a sham. She's categorizing herself 4–F."

"Why not say she's a conscientious objector?"

". . . and in the process denying herself that most meaningful of life's dialogues."

"I assume you speak of the spiritual aspect of sexual union," retorted Mother Agnes. "There are other dialogues, though, that require solitude. That doesn't mean we don't love mankind."

" 'Love one man well and thou lovest mankind,' " he remarked. "I may be an ornery old coot, but I have done some thinking, even about the old Black Book, believe it or not, and it is my considered opinion that a vow of celibacy may actually be a kind of roundabout way of trying to get even with the Lord for kicking us out of the Garden." He chuckled. "Just think, every day He's got to look down and see the ones who are refusing to be fruitful and multiply."

"Well, Jake, if you want to play games with the Scripture . . ."

"No, listen—I'm serious. Hell, so old Eve listened to the snake. But if God hadn't wanted her to eat the apple He never should have planted the tree in the first place. Any mortal parent's got more sense. Once Eve did find out all the things He'd tried to hide, He couldn't take it, that's all.

"The Lord's just like any misguided father, not wanting his children to realize his imperfections, or the world's, because he's afraid they won't love him anymore if they find these things out. As if screwing up the relations between the sexes for all eternity isn't enough, He even makes His own boy pay. Hell, I'm all alone up here, Son, I'm not going to stand you any of that mortal happiness. . . ."

Jake shook his head ruefully, as if a student of his had disappointed him. "Except maybe the joke's kind of on Him in the end, because maybe all those gals of yours, claiming to hook up with sweet Jesus, and all those priests too, are escaping the intensest unhappiness He could ever think up to inflict, and that's the feeling of distance that can come between you and a person you love. Fancy, seems I may have argued myself around to your way of thinking."

He grinned at her and leaned back in his chair, stretching his feet across the ottoman.

"Are you quite finished?"

"For the moment."

"Let me say you have a unique way of looking at things. But I hardly construe the Bible as the charter of my organization."

Turner suddenly leaned forward. "Agnes, I just want to tell you that you're an extraordinary woman. I could argue with you while the sun went down and came up again and not once feel bored."

To his astonishment, she blushed.

"Heavens, am I breaching decorum?"

"Oh," she shrugged, "I think of having to defend my decision to take the veil as penance for my transgressions."

"Transgressions?" Captain Turner asked quickly. "What transgressions? I'd give my eye teeth to see you transgressing, Agnes."

"Who knows? Maybe you already have."

Turner stared. But before he had a chance to respond she stood and gathered up her books.

"Agnes . . ."

"I'll see you tomorrow, Jake."

"You just might do that," he stated.

As he tied Cyrus's blindfold, Captain Turner remarked, "When in the course of a human event, a man realizes he has made a mistake, he should just admit it, say he was wrong, and accept the consequences, don't you think?"

Cyrus groaned.

"Too tight?"

"No, but maybe you are."

"Beg pardon? Oh, ha ha, excuse my slowness. Okay, my man, here's the lady Ginger again. Let's walk down to the playing field and back. I'll proceed first with Maggie."

Turner and Cyrus, both blindfolded, set out across the quad with their dogs. To Turner's surprise, after Christmas vacation Cyrus had approached him and inquired if he would like some help with the German shepherds he trained as Seeing Eyes for the blind. An auspicious sign, Captain Turner had congratulated himself, though he had wondered what had occurred to soften Cyrus's attitude toward him. Cyrus, when questioned, would say only that he thought the experience might come in handy someday.

Turner continued to feel a keen interest in Cyrus, even though his efforts to become better acquainted with him had met with frustratingly little success. Not that he seemed to be alone in this failure. Although, from the first, students had made overtures to Cyrus—even Walt Daimler, captain of the soccer team and acknowledged commander-in-chief of Fifield's forces, wanted to forge an alliance with Cyrus—Cyrus, though polite, had kept his distance. If he had so far avoided being labeled a snob, it was only because he rebuffed all advances impartially. He appeared preoccupied, though by what Turner had been unable to discover. He spent time outside class only with Billy.

Turner tried to analyze the reasons for Cyrus's appeal. There were the obvious qualities: the good looks and extraordinary physical gracefulness. On the soccer field and the basketball court, he possessed such eloquent precision of movement that, in comparison, even Daimler could appear clumsy and pointlessly aggressive. Then there was that reserved cordiality of manner, in contrast to the jovial good nature of the usual Fifield favorites—though whence Cyrus could have inherited such gentility was a mystery. Yet there was more to Cyrus's attraction than could be explained by these essentially superficial characteristics, some component Turner could not isolate, but which he expressed to himself variously as depth, integrity, an almost physiological inability to be fooled by anything artificial or phony. If it wasn't too theatrical a thing to say in this day and age, the kid was good. Yet how he had become convinced of this, when Cyrus never confided anything in him, puzzled Turner. But Cyrus's reticence had merely confirmed his conviction that Cyrus's confidence was worth earning. Such was the perversity of human nature.

It was nearly April now; the first spring weather was seeping between the chillier layers, and, walking with their dogs, their own eyes covered, Turner felt he could speak directly into Cyrus's mind. The time was ripe, he believed, for more insistent probing.

"Sometimes in life you do things with the best motives in the world, but they turn out to be the wrong things. One morning you wake up and you can't pretend to yourself any longer."

The dogs had halted at a road.

"Ginger stop?"

"Yes."

"Good. You see, there's something in us in our youth that makes us not want to know ourselves. It's as if we'll never have to face up to our own mortality that way. As a result we tend to choose as friends . . ." He paused. ". . . even as wives . . . those people who will never force us to lay our cards on the table. We develop all kinds of artifices to conceal ourselves, and the amazing thing is, no one calls us on them. Does what I'm saying make any sense to you?"

"I never really thought about it." Inwardly Cyrus groaned. Here he goes again, he thought.

"I'm sure you've had the feeling that someone's a fake—that he or she's just not coming clean with you, haven't you?"

"I guess."

"Imagine then what it's like when you feel that way in regard to yourself, when you realize you've been living a lie so long you may not be able to be honest if you want to. It's no fun to wake up to that, I can tell you, but it's better than never waking up at all."

Cyrus didn't say anything.

"I don't think you'll have that problem, though. I have a lot of faith in you, Cyrus. I think you'll find your way around the pitfalls, though it may not always be easy. The world is made up of wishy-washy characters whose sole aim in life is to confuse others as much as they themselves are confused. Watch out for them. Above all, be honest with yourself. Have confidence in what you know. You may not be able to convince someone else of what you know to be right, but don't let that be a reason for doubting yourself. Well." He stopped. "That was quite a mouthful."

"I would say so."

Turner laughed. "Clearly I've said enough. But what about you, Cyrus? What's important to you? What *do* you want for yourself—in life, I mean."

"Me? Hell, I don't know." All these questions. A memory of his grandfather flickered before him—not as he'd been when Cyrus was small, but later, after Lark had gone away. Granddad had wanted everything to go on as before. He said you couldn't turn tail and stop fighting every time you suffered a loss. He was always nagging. Where's my officer? Where's the boy I trained? What he hadn't seemed to understand was that it wasn't right to go on fighting when Lark couldn't fight. Why did he deserve to live and Lark didn't?

Now here was *Turner* hounding him. *He* was special; *he* had a mission to accomplish.

"Come on, Cyrus. No dreams, no ambitions?"

"What? No, not especially. Not that I can think of."

"Well, I don't believe that. I think you just don't want to tell me about them. I'm sure you talk to your friends about the future."

"Not really."

"Not even to Daphne? You two spend a lot of time together. You must talk about something."

"No, we just sit and stare at each other."

"Is that right?" He paused. "Well, I won't press the point. But I do wonder why you distrust me. Have I done something to offend you?"

"What? That's ridiculous."

"Why are you so evasive, then?"

"What do you mean 'evasive'?"

"Why do you avoid answering my questions?"

"I'm not avoiding them. I just don't have anything to say. Besides, I don't see why you want to know all this stuff."

"Because, for crying out loud, I'm fond of you!" Turner exploded. "I even imagine that if you trusted me a little more I might be able to help you *get* what you want! Why on earth do you think?"

"I don't know," Cyrus said, embarrassed. "How should I know?"

"You *should* know," Turner said.

They didn't speak for a while, except to praise their dogs and give them directions. Then Turner abruptly asked, "Tell me, Quince, do you screw?"

There was another silence, then Cyrus snapped back, "Is your interest personal?"

Touché, Turner thought. "Sorry, just my dirty mind. I hope you'll forgive me."

"For what?"

Turner laughed. Then he forgot Cyrus for a time and lapsed into a private reverie, in which he thought—as he did ever more frequently—how intolerable his life with Henrietta had become. He didn't notice the diminishing sound of Cyrus's footsteps. When next he spoke and received no answer, he removed his blindfold to discover himself alone.

That night, in his bath, he still pondered Cyrus. He could not believe Cyrus to be as lackadaisical as he pretended—or as oblivious of others' opinion of him. He had been welcomed into Fifield society like a visiting dignitary, for Christ's sake. At the least, Cyrus must be aware of his attractiveness to the opposite sex, of the yearning with which St. Barbara's girls, lying on their stomachs on the hard ground, must watch his taut legs scissoring up and down the soccer field, maneuvering the leather ball around the backs and into the goal—they watched him with such intensity they seemed to be memorizing the experience. Turner thought of the way the girls always *leaned* against things, against tree trunks, walls, parked automobiles, supporting themselves in an attitude of exhaustion, making it seem an anomaly they weren't lying down.

What happened after the last whistle blew and Cyrus was hugged by his teammates for scoring the winning goal? What did the girls think about that? Turner wondered, exasperated. Did they envy that purely male passion? The nonchalance with which the boys treated their toned bodies? And how could the boys appear so unmoved by the girls' unetched faces, their lithe figures, their hair cut so that, when the wind gusted across the field, it assumed another but equally winsome arrangement, their laughter conspiratorial but rivalry checking their collusion when the players sauntered over in search of the captive water jug. They discussed the significance of their favorites' every gesture afterward in their bedrooms, Turner imagined—bedrooms bleached white, soft and without edges, like rooms in a dream. How could the boys appear always so unperturbed by the scent of the girls' sun-warmed skin, their coy glances? Could they not see how the girls flung themselves upon the altar of such insouciance?

What is your *problem*, Turner? he asked himself, as he submerged all but his head and his bony knees, which stuck out from the bathwater like red icebergs. He stared at them dolefully. You're a pitiful case, you know that?

He sat up, feeling a little hysterical, and the air above the bathwater struck him like a February wind and added to his misery. Maybe he had been there too long, he thought, stepping out of the tub and dripping soapy water onto the tiled floor. Maybe it was time he found another line of business. Was this the beginning of senility? Was he going to have this happen to him every goddamn year for the rest of his life? (Turner, now in his bedroom in his bathrobe, posed his questions petulantly to a portrait of his great-grandfather in old-fashioned military regalia.) Was he going to go on dwelling in this fool's eternity, imagining he could effect changes in the world because every year he was presented with a fresh batch of kids in whom to instill his fond hopes for a better future? Was he going to go on reiterating the same homilies each fall during convocation, go on producing temper tantrums when called for or playing Florence Nightingale when that was required, go on scolding boys for smoking in their rooms, for tunneling into the pantry, for sneaking off after curfew (pretending each time he had never before encountered so flagrant a violation of the rules)?

He was an actor who had played one part so long that everyone confused him with the character he portrayed. Wasn't there anyone who could tell he was acting, Captain Turner anguished, who would recognize *him* when he went backstage?

The devil with Quince, he thought, automatically sipping the cocoa Henrietta brought in for them to drink at bedtime. So Quince was outstanding, as sublime as they came, and maybe he really would do something fine someday, but on the other hand maybe he wouldn't, maybe he was a con artist, adept at seeming what others wished him to be. And, anyway, why was he, Jacob Turner, a grown man with a past and a future of his own, wasting his time being obsessed with a seventeen-year-old boy, turning him into some kind of arbiter in his mind?

Christ, can I be envious? Turner thought, and he sighed.

"Is something bothering you, Jacob?" Henrietta asked. "Why don't you come to bed?"

Captain Turner stared at his wife. Then he shouted, "Yes, something's bothering me, Henrietta! Can't you figure out by now what it is?"

Jason Simms hadn't yet tied the knot, but he and Sarah had been dating regularly through the last two years of college and then, this last year, after graduation, they had been living together and Jason had pretty much decided he'd pop the big question. He couldn't say the decision was inspired, exactly, but, after three years of intimate relationship, he knew Sarah by heart, and it comforted him to think of her always being around. She was familiar; Jason didn't miss the days of trying to figure out what was going on in some strange girl's mind. The only real problem they had was this recurrent complaint of hers that there wasn't enough passion in their life together. He thought her ideas were too romantic, but he felt that once they were married she would relax and be content.

Sarah, it was true, had been feeling that things were a little tepid. Life seemed flat and stale—a warning, she felt, of worse things to come. She had been out of a job for a while, and had been unable to find anything besides secretarial work, but that wasn't really it. It was something deeper, and she was becoming convinced that it stemmed from her relationship with Jason.

Sarah was glad, though, when he suggested they attend his high-school alumni weekend in April. They were living in Winston, and she was eager to get out of the city. It would be a five-year reunion for his class, and he sort of wanted to go back and see the old gang, now that he was a bona fide member of the C.C. world. "What world?" Sarah asked. "Cold, cruel . . . where have *you* been?" Jason said.

"Yes, high school," Sarah had sighed. High school had been so much more emotional than college. High school was when you first fell in love, when you talked to your best friend for hours on the telephone; there were so many intrigues, everything had that heightened, flushed significance. Sometimes she thought it was as if you saw color clearly only in childhood: it flared into brilliance during adolescence and ever after faded. She had read somewhere once that Americans were laughed at by other nationalities for clinging so nostalgically to an age everyone else tried to get through as quickly as possible; still she couldn't help it. She really hadn't felt very strongly about anything since.

On impulse she and Jason had taken out their yearbooks—Fifield's, which had been called *Divide and Conquer* in Jason's day, and that of Lindonville High, which was called *Agape*—a Greek word for "love," Sarah had explained, not meaning "open-mouthed." They had identified for each other the pictures of whom they had had crushes on, who had had crushes on them—the two, naturally, never coinciding. Sarah had felt close to Jason at that moment, a friendly kind of childlike closeness. He told her without self-consciousness what he had felt; for once his feelings weren't screened by sophisticated commentary and pseudo-sentiment. Sarah sometimes imagined that there were men who weren't afraid to show their feelings—maybe in the last century, or on farms, or possibly in foreign countries where it was sunnier and people were more content to live day to day. Jason just made fun of her for being sentimental. Was she? she wondered. How could she be sure?

She felt content for once, though, as Jason turned the car into the driveway that led through Fifield's grounds and parked in the lot marked VISITORS—under which some smart kid had added "From Outer Space." She was looking forward to seeing a part of Jason's past—maybe it would bring them closer. She wanted to meet Jason's old girlfriend Ellen, the first girl he had ever slept with, and she felt a pleasant mixture of jealousy and triumph at the prospect.

They left the car, crossed the newly-sheared grass of the quadrangle, and climbed the steps to the dining hall. At the door they were met by a middle-aged man with a diagonal scar running from his eyebrow to his hairline; the eye on that side obviously glass— he was handsome in a rough, pirate-like way.

When he saw them he called out, "Well, I'll be hogtied! If it isn't the venerable Jason Simms, dropped by to condescend for a bit!"

"Let me present the holy Turnip," Jason, grimacing, said to Sarah. "Captain Jake Turner, Headmaster-about-Campus."

"How do you do?" Sarah said. She hated it when Jason affected this self-conscious wit. She listened impatiently as he and Turner bantered. And what a pompous egotist that Turner was. Had Jason actually been fond of him? Finally Jason went off to get drinks, and Turner, excusing himself, turned to speak to a small, chic-looking woman, in a pretty, old-fashioned black dress with a round white collar, who had come to the doorway from within. Sarah was amazed at how his tone changed. She couldn't pick up all he said, for he spoke in a low voice, yet she could see from his expression that he spoke earnestly, with anxiety about the woman's response. Sarah, why do you always jump to conclusions? she scolded herself, altering her opinion of Jason's former headmaster. She realized he was one of those people who behaved superficially with everyone except the rare few whom he trusted and loved; with them he was gentle and sincere. She had to admire such reserve. God knows there was too much indiscriminate friendliness in the world, and she envied Turner's wife such devotion. The two of them entered the dining hall, and Sarah edged in after them.

"What's Mrs. Turner like?" she asked Jason when he returned.

"Mrs. Turner? Where?"

"Talking to Captain Turner."

"That's not Mrs. Turner. Mrs. Turner's over there behind the coffee urn, wearing the polka dots."

"Hmm," Sarah said.

"Hmm what?" asked Jason. Sarah's habit of implying some private knowledge exasperated him.

"I think Captain Turner's in love with that woman," she whispered. "They must be having an affair."

"An affair?" Jason looked dubious. "She looks like a librarian. Besides, I can't picture the old Turnip cheating on Henrietta. He's a lecherous old bastard, but I can't see him doing anything about it."

When Jason discovered that the woman was Mother Agnes, headmistress of St. Barbara's School for Girls, he was delighted.

"Your other woman's a nun!" he crowed. "Now do you believe me when I tell you you're always imagining that other people lead more exciting lives than you do? There couldn't be a more perfect example!"

"So what if she's a nun?" Sarah retorted.

A couple of Fifield students who had just come in caught her attention—juniors or seniors, Sarah judged—accompanied by a girl slightly younger. One boy and the girl were particularly attractive, similar-looking, in fact, dark-haired with skin tending toward pallor and the most astonishing deep-blue eyes. The boy was the more striking, though, and Sarah was immediately drawn to him. The girl was pretty, but more or less asleep in a typically dreamy adolescent way. Sarah wondered what it was about the boy that made him so noticeable. He wasn't doing anything, just standing in the doorway, checking things out, seeming very calm and controlled—probably that was it, he wasn't merely acting cool. His companions waited for him to make the first move.

At that moment he glanced over and noticed Sarah looking at him. Instead of looking away, however, he gazed back at her. Caught, she attempted a smile, to which he replied with a very engaging smirk. Sarah turned away then, feeling flustered; she could actually feel herself starting to blush. How absurd! She was at least five years older than he! But for the second time that evening she felt envious, this time of the girl with him. If not in fact his girlfriend, she at least was of an age to interest him.

As the three moved toward the hors d'oeuvre table, Captain Turner intercepted them and called, "Jason! Come over here a minute." Jason and Sarah approached. "Jase," Turner said, "here's a pair of my prize specimens for you to tell your real-life stories to. Cyrus Quince and Bill Daphne. And Cyrus's sister, Betsy, who's visiting."

His sister! That would explain why they looked alike! Then Sarah was embarrassed by the relief she felt.

"Cyrus, Bill, Betsy—this is Jason Simms, an alumnus, and his friend, Sarah . . . Danford, is it? Why don't you fellows chat with him for a while?" Turner winked at Jason. "I had fond hopes for him at one time. You can let me know if they were justified." He moved off.

"Old bastard still has a way with words, I see," Jason remarked, reaching over to run a proprietary hand down Sarah's back.

"Yeah, isn't he terrific?" the boy Cyrus Quince replied, though not as if desirous of pursuing the conversation. He mumbled something to his friend. His friend—Billy—laughed.

Sarah could tell Jason was irritated. So far the reunion was hardly proving to be the catchup, nicknaming, bullshitting-about-old-times Jason had led her to expect. Ellen hadn't come. In fact no one Jason knew well had shown up, and Sarah could tell he wished he hadn't.

When dinner was announced not long after, they were still standing near Cyrus and Billy and Betsy, and Turner motioned to them to sit at his table. A most peculiar dinner party it was. Turner engaged in some game of manipulating Jason and Cyrus into conversation, or, when they wouldn't cooperate, of baiting Cyrus, asking him if his dance card was full and other vaguely insinuating questions. Cyrus parried them in a half-annoyed, half-resigned way that made Sarah think he was accustomed to them. Jason was eventually captured by Betsy, and Sarah listened, amused, as Betsy explained her ambitions. She felt she was wasting her time in high school, but her parents wouldn't let her drop out and she couldn't join the Peace Corps until she was eighteen. She wished she had lived in the Middle Ages and been a monk, the kind who wandered among remote villages in a brown robe tied at the waist with a rope. . . . "You'd look cute with a rope around you," Jason remarked—it would have irked Sarah except for the fact that Betsy was so oblivious. From time to time Cyrus looked at his sister, and his expression—a mixture of affection, protectiveness, and amusement—touched Sarah. Since Captain Turner was monopolizing Cyrus (Sarah had hoped for a chance actually to talk to him), she tried to make conversation with Billy, who sat next to her, but he was so shy he made Sarah feel awkward herself.

Finally dinner was over. Jason, Sarah noticed, was fairly drunk and when, after the tables had been cleared and moved aside, a band began to play, he invited Betsy to dance. Ignoring her brother's disapproving look, she followed Jason off into the crowd. Cyrus, Billy, and Sarah stood together—Sarah felt a moment of panic. What should she say? Would Cyrus ask her to dance? Should she ask him? She felt about sixteen. Maybe she should ask Billy to dance, but then Cyrus would be compelled to find another partner.

"Hey, let's get out of here," Cyrus said, to no one in particular. "I'll get Betsy." He forced a path through the dancing couples but returned in a moment, unaccompanied. "She wants to stay," he shrugged. "I told her I'd come back in an hour or two."

As Billy and Cyrus turned to leave, Sarah abruptly asked, "Can I come with you? I . . ." She had in mind to say that she didn't much like dances and wondered if they might show her around the campus. Appear the grownup. But Cyrus broke in, "I kind of thought you were going to."

"Oh." So the attraction wasn't one-sided, then. She suddenly felt that her desires were transparent to everyone in the room, and she hurried out after Cyrus and Billy without further conversation. She wondered fleetingly if the St. Barbara's girls envied her—she a stranger and older—carrying off one of their blue-ribbon boys.

Outside, they all relaxed. They seemed a natural threesome. Sarah began to feel giddy. Cyrus and Billy, on their own, were delightful. Billy shed his awkwardness and Cyrus the slight superciliousness he had conveyed earlier (maybe because provoked by Captain Turner). They cracked jokes, were facetiously gallant to her. "Remember we have a lady with us, Bill," Cyrus said, cautioning Sarah not to ruin her high heels, though she wasn't wearing any, as they crawled under blackberry bushes and barbed-wire fences to reach the place Cyrus and Billy were going to show Sarah: their hideout. This turned out to be a clump of maples at the bottom of a cow pasture; once inside, Cyrus flopped down on the dead leaves. Sarah sat nearby, while Billy removed candles from a metal box secured in the crook of a tree and lit them. Then he too stretched out on the ground. Some black-and-white cows emerged from the darkness and formed a semicircle outside the maples and stared.

"Do you come here a lot?"

"To get away," Cyrus said, and Billy nodded.

Sarah laughed at the idea of their having anything to get away from. She warmed to their friendship, so fresh and undefensive. It was quiet and lovely, just the three of them and the curious cows. Maybe because of the soft night air, or the silence—such a change from Winston, where the exhaust fumes crept into the bedroom even as she and Jason slept—but she felt, too, as if she had escaped something. Leaning back against a tree trunk, letting herself forget everything except where she was, she listened as Cyrus and Billy began telling her some story, first about a cat, a heroic cat who had come on an airplane, surviving great hardship;

about dogs—blind dogs?—no, dogs for the blind—they trained them? to rescue someone? were they rescue dogs? . . . about themselves, their plans for the future: they were going to college, but for a reason of their own—some quest, some knight errantry, involving the dogs?

She wasn't actually listening, just smiling and watching them, accepting whatever they said, because she enjoyed the feeling between them, the fact that they would make plans together, the way they seemed to think themselves allies for life. Their intimacy was so spontaneous and playful, full of an affection, a tenderness, a particular kind of teasing she had never seen Jason express toward any of his male friends; he was always out to impress even them. She jumped when Billy yawned, stood up, and said, "Well, I guess I better be getting back. Have to finish my history paper."

"Oh!" Sarah started. "Do you have to?" She began to get up, then felt foolish. She looked at Cyrus. He didn't seem to be going anywhere.

"Okay, Bill, don't get ambushed. Check on Betsy, do you mind?"

"No. Nice to meet you, Sarah," Billy mumbled as he drifted off.

The cows, spooked, galloped away across the field, leaving Sarah and Cyrus alone with the dark and the sputtering candles and the sweet smell of the new grass.

"I hope . . ." Sarah began, but then stopped and settled back down beside Cyrus. Everything had happened so quickly; from the moment she had first laid eyes on him until she found herself alone with him out in a pasture not more than two hours had elapsed. Without saying a word to each other about it, it was as if they had been agreeing upon this moment all along.

She glanced at Cyrus lounging against his tree, sitting as motionless as some ancient king, and he was looking right at her, watching her, his eyes ready to smile—so relaxed! Sarah thought. How could anyone be so relaxed? and her heart beat faster.

Something, she felt, was about to happen—capital H, happen,

as she and her girlfriends had used to say. She felt the same fierce, blind desire now she had felt then, her body's insistence blocking every compunction, except it was even deeper and sweeter this time, because she had come to think she would never feel it again.

She looked quickly back at Cyrus; he hadn't moved or spoken since Billy had left, just kept watching her with that questioning, evaluating gaze, and Sarah wondered what he was thinking. But maybe she was reading into the situation. Improving on reality, as Jason claimed she tried to do. Or maybe she wasn't reading anything into it, exactly; that is, Cyrus probably was attracted to her too, but it wasn't some innocent passion, born of the spring night. Sarah remembered how she had imagined something similar the first time she had slept with Jason, and then it turned out he was drunk and was startled to discover her in his bed the next morning. Big deal, so a kid in some boarding school wanted to go to bed with her. He wasn't feeling anything special. Probably be describing to his whole dorm the next day how he scored with some alumnus's girlfriend. Or maybe he never had slept with anyone before and thought this a good opportunity to gain experience. Was he expecting her to act the older woman and seduce him? Was he waiting for her to make some move? What should she do? She felt uncomfortable, then resentful, as if her imagination's running away with her were Cyrus's fault. She looked at him crossly. He *had* to be aware of what was going on; she was sure he must be. Why didn't he reach over and kiss her? Didn't he want to? Was he mocking her?

Obviously she should just stand up, say, "Well, thanks for showing me your hideout," and he would be relieved and they'd walk back and life could go on.

Cyrus cleared his throat. "Sarah?"

"Yes?"

"What are you thinking about?"

"What?" She couldn't believe he'd asked that. "Oh . . ."

"Oh?"

"I don't know. Nothing."

"You seem pretty shy. Are you nervous?"

"About what?" He didn't answer. "Why should I be nervous? What do you mean?"

"What do you mean what do I mean? I was just asking. I don't have any ulterior motive."

"You don't?"

"Why, did you think I did?"

"I don't know."

"Well, I don't know either." He laughed. "Sarah . . ."

"What?"

"I was wondering . . ." She heard an awkwardness come into his voice. "I mean, I don't know you very well . . . very well! I don't know you at all! . . . but, ahem, what I'm *trying* to say," he said, sounding annoyed, "is, do you want to sleep with me?"

"Sleep with you?" Sarah echoed. She looked down at Cyrus's hands. He had sounded formal, polite. But maybe, she thought, really all he meant was did she want to, not would she; he was just curious.

"I don't know."

"Oh. I thought maybe you did."

He flexed his fingers and Sarah quickly shifted her gaze, as if she had been spying on him.

"Maybe I do."

He frowned slightly at this. Oh, for God's sake Sarah! "Not maybe, Cyrus," she said, sounding as awkward and formal now as he had. "I mean, I want to."

She was shy then, not wishing to look at him, but he was waiting, and at last she glanced up and then his eyes softened until he seemed to know something for certain, and he reached for her.

What she felt became a kind of race between what she wanted to happen and what was happening. Amazement at what she could feel strove with what she felt and radiated sensation to every surface of her skin where he was touching her. Where she had expected to find subterfuge there was no subterfuge at all; she could not believe she had met this person only hours ago—it felt so inevitable that she should be here with him like this. Cyrus already seemed more familiar than Jason did after three years; she knew what he was feeling when he said, "You're so soft," and, quietly, her name, "Sarah." The feeling of Cyrus—this *boy*, she kept saying to herself—against her, his body taut and smooth, joined with the sounds of their sighing and both mixed up inextricably forever with the touch of the cool yet warm air on her skin and the smell of the night.

Later—they didn't know what time it was, though the stars were all out by now—they started to walk back. Neither of them spoke, unless Cyrus said, "Here, look out for this root," or "There's a little stream up here, be careful," and she answered, "Okay," but he kept hold of her hand, and if they had to let go to crawl under a fence or make their way through brambles he reached right away to reclaim it.

"Oh, Cyrus, I wish we didn't have to go back," she said. He stopped walking and put his arms around her. (Jason, Sarah knew, with his firm belief in the necessity for keeping the demands of what he called reality in sight at all times, would have said, "Of course, Sarah, but we do.") Cyrus simply held her, and she held him tightly back. She felt so grateful to him it seemed all her blood still rushed toward him. Even if she never saw him again, she thought (though it was impossible to believe that in an hour she would no longer be with him—just as it was impossible to believe that four hours ago she had not known he existed), he had shown her that she could still feel something immediate and powerful. She simply would not allow herself to return to that horrible, empty feeling she had been living with for so long.

In the shadow of a building across from the dining hall they kissed goodbye.

"I don't want to leave," she said sadly.

He kissed her again.

"Can't we run away? Back into the woods. Bill could bring food. . . ."

He smiled. "Jason would come after us."

"I doubt it."

"You do?"

She kissed him.

"Do you want me to come with you? I mean, inside?"

"To protect me from his wrath, you mean?" She laughed. "No. I doubt if he even noticed I was gone."

Cyrus seemed taken aback at this, but he didn't say anything.

"Cyrus . . ."

"Yes?"

"I . . . Nothing, I guess. I'll see you."

He nodded. "Goodbye, Sarah."

"Goodbye."

He let go and she walked across the quadrangle. She didn't turn until she reached the dining-hall steps. He was standing where she had left him, watching her. He waved. She waved back once, then went in.

A second telephone call came from Rose to Captain Turner, with another request to convey bitter news. Lark had died, hit by a car like an ordinary child. It had happened a week ago—she was in bed; Harold was at work, and Betsy at school; they thought she had already told Cyrus—she had lied and said he would be on his way home for the funeral, which was tomorrow. Her voice broke.

"Dear God," Captain Turner said.

"Please," she said. "Please . . ."

"I'm so terribly sorry," he said, "but you have to tell him this yourself."

"But he will hate me," she said desperately. "He hates everybody else already. I don't want him to hate me too."

"He doesn't hate everybody! He's not grown!" Hearing what he had said, Turner felt ashamed.

"But I am not well," she said. "You can't understand. It's as if there's too much air around everything. Everything is standing by itself. I cannot bear glasses standing on the night table. Or books. Flat things are better but they are not flat every way you look at them. Sometimes when the blanket makes points on the bed I want to scream. I can't get up in the morning until the sunlight makes a path to the door. My son is dead and in order to go downstairs I have to hang blankets over the banisters."

She took a deep breath, but when he didn't speak she went on. "Betsy's been doing all the cooking. She makes casseroles. Harold took off from work but I couldn't stand to have him in the house, so he went back. He's driving Betsy to school now, although before she always took the bus."

He heard her breathe in again sharply.

"They burned Lark. I never even got to see him." Her voice faltered. "If I could just understand what's happening to me . . ."

"Mrs. Quince . . ."

"You see,"—her voice regained strength—"I know there wasn't always so much air. When the children were babies and I held them sleeping, then there wasn't. Cyrus was so serious even when he was asleep." She laughed softly. "He was always startled when he woke up. When I bent over his crib he looked at me suspiciously, as if I might be someone else. Betsy never seemed to notice when she waked up. Lark laughed when he saw me; he laughed at every-thing, until he became afraid. But Cyrus used to be able to comfort him, even when nobody else could."

"Yes," Turner murmured. "I can imagine that."

"He loved his little brother, Captain Turner. I never saw a child love another child so much."

Gently now Rose began to cry and Turner sat without moving in his study a thousand miles away. There was nothing to say; even the words he did speak into the black mouthpiece were de-formed by the distance. If he were there, he might take her in his arms and keep her head down against his shoulder and tell her there was a sense to life; when other people suffered, he was sure that there was. But he was where he was and this woman, nearing some edge, was somewhere else, and even if he said to her, "Hang on, I'll be there right away," ran out of Fifield and jumped on an airplane, she might have let go by the time he got to her and in any case his succor would be impeded by Harold, who would want to know what on earth he thought he was doing in Arborville.

Impotent, Captain Turner resented the telephone itself, with its illusion of contact, and he took the receiver from his ear and held it out in front of him; out of one end dribbled the ragged, faint sound of Cyrus's mother sobbing. I'm invisible, Captain Turner said to himself, and he felt inclined to perform some obscene act, to expose himself to this perverse black object that produced the sound of jagged crying as if the thing were something he had once purchased on purpose to hear the unhappy noise.

He laid the receiver on his desk and backed away, considering it. Suddenly he strode back, picked it up and shouted, "Will you listen to me for one second? What do you think I am, a suicide hotline? Tragedy isn't something you invented. Cyrus is *your* son, God damn it! Treat him like he belongs to you for once in your life!"

He slammed the receiver into its cradle. The telephone rang again at once; he was reaching for it when the ringing stopped.

"That poor Godforsaken woman," he said aloud. "May the Lord have mercy on all our souls!"

Captain Turner enjoyed the irony of calling on the Almighty when he felt it to be utterly no use. He started out to hunt for Cyrus. But, as soon as he was out of doors, out of the room that had become a part of the news of Cyrus's brother's death, he was overcome by a secret happiness, a sharp joy it shocked him to feel alongside the sorrow and compassion he felt for the boy he cared about so deeply. Standing still to examine it, he understood it to be the gratitude of the survivor. Someone was dead, but *he* was still alive, and with that thought he knew immediately what he had to do.

He would go at once to Agnes and ask her to leave the church and marry him.

The secretary came to summon Cyrus out of class. Everyone watched him leave. Outside, she requested him to go to his dorm and wait for a telephone call from his mother. Then his mother called. Apology and explanation surrounded like weeds the one thing she had to tell him: Lark was dead.

When at last his mother allowed him to hang up, he walked

very slowly back up the two flights of stairs to his room. As he climbed it was as if a film through which he had always seen things had dissolved. He noticed tiny nicks on the stair treads. The finish on the wainscoting was scuffed. The newel post at the third-floor landing was loose. Someone should be told—it wasn't safe.

In the room, Jonzo lay on the windowsill in a stripe of sun. Cyrus walked toward him, so slowly that the cat eyed him with suspicion. Jonzo shouldn't lie on the edge like that, Cyrus thought. He could so easily start in a dream and fall off.

"Lark's dead," Cyrus said to Jonzo, and stroked his back. Jonzo began to purr, stretching one front paw as far as it would go and curling his claws into the tattered surface of the sill. Flecks of white paint came loose and were carried outside by the breeze.

"Jonzo, why are you always tearing everything apart?" Cyrus asked. His voice sounded muffled and strange.

The cat stretched out his other paw and with his tail swatted the window casing twice, hard.

"You'd like to wreck everything, wouldn't you? You'd like to wreck everything in the whole world."

Jonzo meowed a parenthesis into his purring and Cyrus scratched his backbone. When Cyrus's hand reached his tail, Jonzo raised his flanks into the air. When Cyrus's hand moved back forward, Jonzo sat down again.

"He was such a little guy," Cyrus said to Jonzo, and broke. Standing by the window, he began to cry, occasionally lifting a fist to rub tears from his cheeks. Jonzo stopped purring and watched him.

Why didn't anyone tell me? he sobbed. Lark had died on Saturday—he had had to force his mother to tell him. Today was Friday. That meant that for a week everything he had done had been a lie.

On Monday they had played the final game of the season against Trent; at the last minute before the whistle blew and the game went into overtime he had broken the tie with a shot over the goalie's head, giving Fifield the league cup; he had rejoiced in the victory and Lark had already been dead for two days, lying in some strange room, his body broken, his life ground out. His eyes, clear and blue as Cyrus's own, had never lost their light; even the last couple of years, when it had become difficult for him to shape words, his eyes had shone. "Srus," he twisted out, but the pleasure in his eyes belied his tortuous speech. When it was time to leave, that last visit over Christmas, Lark had turned away, crying, and Cyrus had felt that by obeying Harold's command to get in the car he was destroying his brother. Twisting to look back again as they drove away, he had seen Lark rolling his wheelchair in pursuit and a nurse running behind and he had continued to look out the window a long while so that no one would see that he was crying too. He had sworn that as soon as he left Fifield he would get Lark out of that place.

But Lark was dead. His mind was playing tricks; it stole away into recollection, then rushed back, as if the ambushed fact would give way and not be true. Lark's death had happened at *one* particular moment, that was what Cyrus could not comprehend, and he kept cataloguing back through the week and at every point reexamining his own actions, his motives for them, as if he might discover some crack in the past through which he could slip into an alternate present, in which Lark would still be alive.

On Tuesday, he remembered, he and Billy had spent the afternoon down in the pasture—the first time he'd been down there since that night with Sarah. They were discussing their summer plans. Billy was going to come out to Arborville for a while or Cyrus was going to spend some time in Amber or maybe they were going to hitchhike out West. They were going to "rescue" his grandfather. (After Christmas vacation, Cyrus had told Billy he had discovered his grandfather's whereabouts: he was in a home for retired generals in Winston City. However, his eyesight had deteriorated to the point where he could neither read nor write. Therefore, Cyrus dared not risk communicating their plans for him by letter.) At Billy's urging, Cyrus had enlisted himself in Turner's service; at some point they could steal one of Turner's dogs for General Street. The three of them would set up housekeeping somewhere; Billy and Cyrus would get jobs, using false names; they would have to be careful.

Cyrus hadn't yet had the heart to tell Billy his grandfather didn't need to be rescued. The idea seemed to mean so much to him—you'd think it was *his* grandfather they were going to save. Cyrus had gone along with the plans, often forgetting Billy didn't know it was a fantasy. (It was certainly more pleasant than the way things actually were.) But the *fact* was he had lied to his best friend.

On Wednesday, after dinner, there had been a telephone call for him and it was Sarah. Jason would be out of town all weekend and she wondered if Cyrus might like to come down to Winston. She was trying to sound as if the idea had just occurred to her, but Cyrus could tell she was nervous. He had been nervous too when he first heard her voice—surprised. He hadn't expected to hear from her. When he said he would go—it wasn't so hard to sneak off; Billy would cover for him, and, even if he was found out, what were they going to do, expel him at the end of his senior year?—she had sounded so happy, and he was *glad* he would see her again.

While they were talking, Cyrus thought, Lark's body had already been burned. His ashes were in a box in a baggage room at some airport, waiting to be flown home. What a stupid idea it had been to see Sarah again; nothing could ever come of it. He was surprised she had even bothered to call.

The sun had left the windowsill and Jonzo vaulted down and twisted between Cyrus's ankles. Cyrus patted him perfunctorily. He took a box of dried cat food out of his closet and poured some into Jonzo's dish. Jonzo sniffed it, then walked away. Cyrus looked down at him, puzzled.

"Sorry, I forgot."

He took a can from the closet, opened it, and spooned the contents into the bowl on top of the other food. Jonzo began to eat at once.

Then, Cyrus took the suitcase from under his bed and began to pack. Three shirts, a pair of trousers, socks, underwear, a sweater.

Downstairs to the bathroom: toothbrush, soap, razor. The cat carrier out of the closet; Jonzo saw it and ran under Billy's bed. Cyrus pulled him out by a hind leg. Jonzo scratched and bit him. Ordinarily Cyrus would have provided Jonzo with a detailed explanation of the necessity for his imprisonment, but this time he shut him in the box, automatically careful not to catch his tail, without a word of excuse.

He looked at his watch: four-fifty. Billy would be out of class in ten minutes, back to the dorm in fifteen. If he went around back of the playing field, Billy wouldn't see him from the classroom building. If he walked quickly, he would be halfway to Swanbury by the time Billy got back to the room. A bus left for Winston at five-twenty-five. He knew of a place there where no one would ever think of looking for him.

Cyrus had never told Billy about Lark either. And, having not mentioned him the first day, when Billy asked if he had any brothers or sisters, he didn't know how to bring it up. Oh, by the way, I just happened to remember I have this brother. . . . He was afraid Billy might think he hadn't told him about Lark because he had been ashamed to. And now he couldn't allow a person who hadn't known of Lark to feel pity for him because he was dead. Nor could he face any sympathy for himself. He deserved no sympathy.

He considered leaving Billy a note, but he didn't know what he would say.

Apostasy
(Not to Mention Incest)

"Royalty in exile is a curse, like insanity or an inherited inclination to murder," the woman who had called herself the Crown Princess Theobalda said on her deathbed. "Find the cure!" she whispered hoarsely, and expired. (This was in New Jersey, in 1902.) But her son Langoustino (so named in tribute to one of the Crown Princess's gastronomical fondnesses, not by way of a clue to the Ludwickers' country of origin) was more impressed by the cleverness of his mother's epigram than by its entreaty and did little during his unofficial reign to advance the family cause. His only contribution was to produce, with the half-hearted assistance of a frivolous but apathetic local girl named Jeannine, four children to carry on the Ludwicker line. They were, in order of age: Dagobert, Xilipheupia, Constantina, and Sigismund, though they addressed one another as Tad; Xy, Xili or Pheups; and Sammy; Sigismund, inexplicably, becoming George. One of the few extant photographs from their youth showed them all together in front of the Ludwicker mansion, brandishing croquet mallets (croquet being the only outdoor game besides badminton of which the Crown Princess had approved), but this was a formal shot, and the children looked morose. Except Dagobert, that is, who was sneering.

Perhaps it was unfortunate that Theobalda had named her only son after an edible, because Langoustino (whom intimates called Gus) devoted his life to gluttony. "Frankly," he said, "I don't think there is a throne. I think Mother made it up. All I want to do is eat." Upon hearing her husband's words, Jeannine, who had married Langoustino because she thought he would take her away from New Jersey and all that it represented, slid into a decline and spent her brief remaining years at the Ludwicker mansion trying on the Crown Princess's jewels and weeping at her reflection in the mirror. The two younger children, especially, remembered her only from one sad portrait in which she stood by the mailbox in her dead mother-in-law's robes of state, waiting for a letter that never came.

Langoustino weighed 430 pounds the morning in 1921 when his body was discovered wedged in the ice chest, in which he apparently had become stuck while attempting to negotiate the release of a container of ice cream that had been trapped in an obscure region. He died of a heart attack, although, said the coroner, if things were called by their right names, it would have to be said he died of greed.

As the ropes lowered their father's coffin into its pit in the family graveyard, the Ludwicker children stared solemnly, but it was unclear if they grieved for their father *per se*—for Langoustino had not loved them or they him—or for the father they had never had. Such confusion between the actual and the longed-for, the concrete and the abstract, the individual and the general, was not unusual in the Ludwicker household. But whatever thoughts occupied the Ludwicker children's exiled minds brought tears to their eyes—except to those of Dagobert, that is, who was smirking. He was sixteen.

"I'm king now," he declared when the funeral was over. "Things are going to toughen up around here." (Hovering over him, his grandmother's spirit, not without malice, smiled.) "Now you have to do whatever I say."

He forced Sigismund and Constantina (eight and seven respectively) to prove their fealty by washing his feet, lighting his cigarettes, winding up his Victrola; he ordered them to catch frogs in the pond back of the house and to sacrifice them to the Ludwicker god. Dagobert's were not the most inspired tests of allegiance ever conceived, but perhaps this could be blamed on the area in which the Ludwickers lived, hardly a place to encourage belief in the efficacy of the search for such things as the Holy Grail or the missing half of a broken sword. "Still, we have to do something. Keep up tradition somehow, don't you agree, Pheupsy?"

Xilipheupia smiled. Tad was her king and liege lord and she never doubted that before long he would recover the throne and then he and she would reign, side by side. He never asked her to attest to her loyalty as he did Sammy and George; he demanded only her adoration and in return professed to treat her as his confidante and equal. They were only ten months apart in age, and, after all, they had been lovers for over a year.

For ten years, then, the young Ludwickers (whose surname was pronounced—and they knew what these words meant—"lewd vicars"), xenophobes and solipsists all, lived alone in the hideous elephantine edifice whose original section had been built by Timonius Ludwicker in 1768 and which had been added onto by every Ludwicker since. Dagobert had ironically dubbed the monstrosity "the Cottage." ("What a dreadful sight!" had exclaimed a late-nineteenth-century guidebook to New Jersey homes. "What a perfidy of design! What a mockery of everything reassuringly human in architecture—every style ever conceived by man seemingly represented therein: here clapboards, here stone caryatids, here brick and ironwork, as if a hundred blind architects had drawn up the blueprint. . . .") At the conclusion of this decade, Xilipheupia adored Dagobert even more than before; he had seen no reason to prevent her. Where else would he find someone who so perfectly fulfilled his requirements for lover, companion, audience? Loving her was like loving himself, and he told her this, saying that only in her presence did he feel certain of his existence. He described her spirit as an opiate, gently surrounding his, suffusing him with her essence; his core was solid, like a crystal, refracting hers. He could see all this happening, he said, as they talked.

Often long into the night they had lain, Tad's head on Xy's stomach, or Xy's head on Tad's stomach, stretched out like nave and transept on the dampening lawn, and wondered from whom they descended. From what royal root had sprung their exiled branch? What lapse of family was to blame for them? History's pages were rife with banished dukes, abducted princes, imprisoned queens . . . and *were* all those queens beheaded? How did one know for sure? A fact, Tad and Xy discovered, was only as substantial as one's belief in it. Though they did not know what to do with this discovery, they were quite proud of it and called vulgar those who accepted on faith the convictions of their fathers.

On one wall of the Cottage's ballroom, Tad and Xy had drawn the royal family trees of Europe. Sometimes they spent so long studying them that they felt their veins and arteries replicating that imperial tracery. They read avidly all the books of royal biography in the house, and compared their own features to those in the portraits. "I note a definite resemblance between your ears and those of Marie Antoinette," "Your chin is a dead giveaway for Edward VI's," they observed wistfully, searching always for the questionable reference, the dates that did not match up, the gap that would permit them entry into history.

Constantina and Sigismund, meanwhile, had no interest in such rarefied pastimes. Unlike their older siblings, they had not had the benefit of the desultory succession of tutors brought to the Cottage by Langoustino, or even of the facts dredged up by Jeannine Ludwicker (née Clark) from the fairy tale of her average girlhood.

Sigismund, it soon appeared, had inherited his father's voracity, and besides food only sports excited him—the glory of sportsmanship, to be precise. It was the contorted face of concentrated energy that he found appealing, the whole self directed toward one simple action, and his dearest wish was to be one of the figures frozen for eternity in the sports' photographs: the flap-hatted and jerseyed hitter's body caught just before it lunged at the fuzzy white sphere; the knee-socked and sleeveless figure suspended forever in space midway between court and basket, long arms outstretched, hands hooked as if the wrists rested on an invisible bar, the ball forever dropping toward the netted hoop. Best of all, he thought, would be to sustain injury in the throes of such an effort, and Sigismund wept to imagine his valor as, wounded, he yet played on, collapsing only after scoring the winning point, thence to be carried from the field on the shoulders of his jubilant teammates like the triumphant warrior that he was. Much of the time, he hobbled about the Cottage grounds on a crutch, wielded a slinged arm, or gazed balefully at the others, one eye covered by a patch. For his birthday, he purchased himself a neck brace.

Constantina, who at one time had hoped to find in Sigismund what Xilipheupia had in Dagobert, grew bored by her closest brother—by all of her siblings—and directed her passion toward an object from which reciprocity was unneeded: the family car. Initiating what was to be a lifelong infatuation with mechanical devices of all kinds, she taught herself not only how to operate the sleek machine, but how to repair it. As children they all had occasionally been taken on drives—to "survey the realm"—but Tad, Xy, and George were too preoccupied now by their own obsessions to care what might be occurring in the outside world and never made use of the car.

The long summer nights of her seventeenth year Sammy spent driving, exhilarated, despite the torrid air, because no matter what the ups and downs, the curves and turns, she was moving forward. Through the sweltering New Jersey dark, when the temperature never dropped, past the terraces lit by paper lanterns, where fox-trotting men and women strove feverishly to bring back their twenties—and the country's—the big elegant car oozed. Sometimes Sammy paused to stare at the dancers' febrile efforts, caressing the brake pedal with her bare toes as she watched, but she could not interpret their frantic motions. Before long, bored, she would lift her foot and glide away—on, on into the night.

But this was only a prelude. A prelude to what, Sammy was not sure, although, as she pressed the accelerator down to the floor, her heart pounding as the powerful creature lunged beneath her, she felt she could not bear the anticipation much longer. Then one predawn, when her forehead was clammy with sweat and her hair stuck to it in damp tendrils, she met Bib.

Bertram Block was his name (Bib to his friends) and when the car came screeching to a halt beside him he was standing at the edge of the half-constructed road, leaning on his shovel, waiting for some sign that he should get to work. He was helping to build a highway, he informed Sammy. "It'll be the greatest road in the country someday," he avowed. "It's only a dream right now, but someday it will be many lanes wide and will cut straight across the land! No one will be able to go anywhere without taking this road—no one!"

"Yes," Sammy breathed, "yes." His voice, she thought, was like the idling of a fine-tuned engine. She leaned against the front fender, her fingers caressing the chrome. She, who had never spoken to anyone in her life besides her immediate family, felt no fear or self-consciousness. This young man, in his worn overalls and squashed-looking cap, seemed to her the embodiment of her every inarticulate longing.

He, meanwhile, continued to speak about his job. It was his first one, but he hoped never to work anywhere else. How could there be anything more satisfying than to contribute to this magnificent construction? To watch as it grew from rockpiles and sand to a stretch of asphalt so long and smooth that even the good Lord himself would have been proud to win the bid to it?

Sammy listened, puzzled. She wasn't sure what this had to do with her. Impatiently she twined her arms around his neck and kissed him. "I love you," she said.

"Okay by me," replied Bib, astonished and a little shy. But he wasn't about to argue with anyone who drove such a magnificent auto and was feeling such enthusiasm for him, even if she was a little loony—dressed in that outlandish get-up (Sammy's favorite driving outfit of the time was a bathing costume that had belonged to Langoustino) and kind of forward. In fact—the sun rolling up over a sand dune, in its first rays the chrome trim on the cabriolet flashing and Sammy's hair blazing like gold—Bib was so moved that he grabbed her and held her tight. "You're pretty too," he said, "you know that? You're real pretty." But Sammy, who had not realized how late it was, thrust Bib away and jumped into the car.

"Hey, wait a minute. You just got here!"

"I've got to go home!" she called. "Tad hates me to be out after sunrise!"

"Who's Tad?" Bib yelled. "Are you coming back tomorrow?" But by then the car had disappeared into a cloud of dust, and whatever Bib Block may have felt about the fetching eccentric who had rolled out of the dawn in her big black limousine like every roadworker's dream dissipated with the truck exhaust of history because that day something happened that upset the Ludwicker household for a long while to come. By the time Sammy returned, the stretch of road had been completed and she did not know how to begin to look for Bib.

That morning when she slid the car into the garage, Dagobert was waiting, pacing, and he made her confess. Then he forbade her to continue her nighttime drives. Didn't she know it was dangerous? People could be after them—kidnapers and assassins! Did she wish to endanger all of their lives?

"But I love him!" she cried, startling her brother. "I'm going to marry him and live happily ever after!"

"Oh, you are, are you?" he teased her. "Does he have a title? You know I can't allow you to abandon your responsibilities to the crown."

"I don't care!" she wailed. "I'll abdicate!"

"You dope, you can't abdicate. You have to have something before you can give it up."

"That's what you think," Sammy said. She sat clutching the steering wheel. Dagobert slouched against an oil drum.

"That's what I know," he replied.

"It's easy for you to say. You have Xy," shouted Sammy. "You . . . pervert!"

"Pervert?" Dagobert blanched. "Didn't even know you knew the word."

"You think you're so smart."

"You're just jealous," he attempted, but she interrupted.

"I'm not jealous. You don't even know what love is."

"I don't, don't I?" Tad stepped toward her, but she rolled up the window and locked the door. She stared at him through the glass. Although she was unsure of the meaning of her own accusation, she saw that he wasn't.

In a low, serious tone she had never heard him use, he said, "Sam, please open the window. Just a crack so we can talk. I'm sorry I made fun of your friend. You can even marry him if you want. We'll make him a duke. Just open the window and tell me why you called me what you did. I need to know."

She remained silent.

"Please, Sam. I know I haven't always been very nice to you, but I'll make it up. I promise. Please talk to me."

But Sammy, enjoying this unexpected power, shook her head. She watched in amazement as tears came to Tad's eyes. Then he covered his face with one hand, like a parent pretending not to look while his child hides. Sammy turned in her seat to watch him walk, head bent, out of the garage. She felt worried and wanted to go after him, but her mistrust of him was of such long standing that even now she thought he might be acting to lure her out of the car. Eventually she lay down across the seat and went to sleep.

Dagobert walked a long time in the woods behind the Cottage. What was he going to do now? If Sammy was making friends in the outside world, it wouldn't be long before she would realize how unnatural was the life the four of them led at the Cottage. Sammy's "love"—unless Tad locked her in her room (and, tyrant though he might be, he was not, in his heart, cruel)—spelled the end of their peaceful family existence. How could he not have foreseen this? In truth, though, he alone was fully content with the life they led. He had seen signs of discontent in recent years. Xy longed to seize power—if they could only find out who had wrested it from them. George yearned to be a champion, beloved by the people. And Sam—she simply wished for a boyfriend, to drive around in her car with, like all the other girls her age in America. He alone was happy living in exile, with his own sister as his lover. (But, then, he alone of the four had any inkling of what the world beyond the Cottage was like. When Langoustino was still alive to rebel against, Tad had several times sneaked off to visit nearby towns, observed the inhabitants, and decided he did not like to be among people who did not know who he was.) He didn't *want* to go anywhere else, to dwell among commoners. Now he had no choice.

"Snapped?" Xy said, when at last he went in to her. "What do you mean 'snapped'? Do you mean snapped meaning broke, or snapped meaning fastened?"

He said angrily, "Can't you understand what I'm telling you? It's over between us!"

"Over?" Xy repeated, as if she had never heard the word. "What's over?"

He didn't answer, and to Xy it seemed that the crystal at Tad's heart had become opaque.

"What is it, Tad? Tell me! You matter more to me than my life!"

"Tell you what?" He shrugged, evading her eyes. "There's nothing to tell. I simply don't love you anymore."

"Not love me?"

"Will you leave me alone, Xy? Are you a parrot that you must repeat everything I say?"

"A parrot?" Her face was white and she trembled. "You're lying, Tad. I know you're lying. Something's happened. What is it?"

"I have to leave, Xili. Don't you understand? It's the only thing I can do. We have to say goodbye."

"Goodbye? But why? I don't understand. Where are you going?"

"I don't know. I don't know! To sea! To war! What difference does it make? Oh, Xili, don't you understand I've been a coward all of my life?"

"A coward? I never thought you were a coward. Don't leave me, Tad," she whispered. "Please don't leave me. I can't live without you. I will cease to exist." She felt her soul seeping out of her, even as she spoke. He possessed it and he would take it away and leave her empty. "Please, Tad . . ." she begged him, but by evening he was gone. He returned to New Jersey once, twenty years later, a visit Xilipheupia might have construed as a dream, and her resulting pregnancy as hysterical, had she not, nine months of self-doubt later, given birth to a daughter, whom she named Fritz Quadrata. But that was over two decades ago, and the Ludwickers were still no closer to escaping their exile than they had been at the time of Theobalda's plea. Xy believed Tad had been on the verge of discovering the truth about their heritage, perhaps had discovered it when he left, but although she continued the search on her own, chiefly by writing to heraldic associations to ask them to trace the Ludwicker family tree, she had learned nothing definite. They descended, came the various replies, from the noble line of Ludwigs of Bavaria; from Black Ludovico of Naples; from James, Lord Wicker, the Earl of Nightbrook; from the Ludovics, a family of bakers who had prospered in Paris in the 1500s. No record was ever located of the entrance of a Timonius Ludwicker into the American colonies, and it was likely that "Ludwicker" was an assumed name. Had this earliest known ancestor left no personal records?

Xy spent a period of some years ransacking the Cottage, hoping to come upon documents that would reveal the secret of the Ludwicker past, but from beneath the countless boards and stones she pried loose she acquired only a few lost rings and coins and many skeletons of mice.

Xy never doubted, though, that her grandmother's deathbed witticism demanded a literal interpretation. She believed that the legitimizing of the family throne, the recognition of their royal lineage, would cure her of her astigmatism: things would lose their double and regain their single sense. That is to say, she would know whether or not Tad had loved her. In order to survive his departure, she had told herself that he had been made to leave by forces beyond his control. Yet how, a different, less magnanimous voice demanded, could he have left her if he loved her?

Sammy never told Xy what she had said to Tad, but after he was gone their relationship gradually changed. No longer was Sammy the inconsequential sibling. She took over the running of the household and Xy came to depend on her in all practical matters, as if they had tacitly agreed that she would yield this sphere of control in payment for Sammy's not revealing her information about Tad's departure. This could have destroyed once and for all Xy's hope that he would someday return.

As Xy aged, however—she was now sixty-seven—her longing for Tad waned, as did her ambition to recover her ancestry. These desires now achieved fullness only on morose, drizzly afternoons when the yellow sulphurous smoke blew down from the oil refineries in the north and swirled about the Cottage, looking for a way to get in. Most of the time Xy—and George and Sammy— were content, diverted by their private interests: Sammy with her pursuit of the latest gadgets and her memorial drives up and down the New Jersey Turnpike; George with his "training"—jogging, weight lifting, calisthenics, batting practice—to keep in shape against the moment when he would be drafted by the major leagues; Xy with her books of history and biography, in which she ritually sought clues to her own existence—in other words, a life in some ways not at all untypical of the very rich.

They still recited their family tree, as had always been their custom before dinner, with the same feeling of cheerfulness and self-importance this invocation had always given them, and when the moon paused on its orbit above the Cottage they bowed, but they treated casually now the idea that they were born to rule, wore their cloaks like bathrobes, and padded across the red carpets to fetch their crowns from the cabinet as if to get a snack from the refrigerator. Nothing but some elementary catastrophe, it seemed, would catapult them out of resignation into strife.

Then there was Fritz (fair Fritz, ferocious Fritz, fretful Fritz . . . Cyrus would learn to torment her, discovering that she reacted to alliteration as most people did to buzzing mosquitoes), a pale, skinny child with the blood-red hair not seen in the family since the Crown Prince Febrilius. Xilipheupia was forty-five when Fritz was born, and from the first she adored her daughter—she sat by her crib, telling her all about Dagobert—but she was always a little afraid of her child, as if Tad had planted her as a spy in the household.

It was Sammy who actually cared for the tiny, despotic child: fed her, bathed her, changed her diapers, taught her to use silverware, tie her shoes, and, later, order things from catalogues and drive a car. Sammy fulfilled these duties with the same conscientiousness she had brought to the operation and repair of her automobile: she observed the creature's functioning, sent for owner's manuals, ordered accessories. It was to Sammy Fritz went if she hurt herself, if she felt ill, if she wanted attention. When she awoke from a nap she would stand up in her crib and wail, "Ammy!" not "Mama." Fritz didn't see another child until she was five, when Sammy, having read that this was the proper age, first took her to the dentist.

"Is that your Sammy?" Fritz asked another little girl and was shocked and saddened to learn that all children did not have Sammys, but mothers instead. While to Fritz, Sammy was a deeply loved and much-needed being, a mother was a remote, ambiguous personage who spent her time sitting very still, reading, inscribing things in a dark tome; who sometimes inquired suspiciously of Fritz if she was certain she hadn't seen her father that day. Fritz held tightly to Sammy's hand and felt deeply sorry for all the other children in the world.

If her aunt Sammy was Fritz's refuge, her Uncle George was her playmate. In his opinion, Fritz had been born in order to join in his games. When she was two days old he laid a tennis ball in her bassinet. "It's the early learners who become the greatest athletes," he explained when Sammy objected. He regarded Fritz's infancy as an unfortunate condition, a temporary sport's injury of sorts, and he waited impatiently for it to pass. Long before Fritz could talk she and Sigismund played contentedly for hours—games as intricate and never-ending as they were spontaneous. At ten she could shoot baskets from twenty feet and hit a fast hardball; the first time Cyrus played tennis with her, he never scored a point.

When Fritz was sick, Sigismund spread their Monopoly board across her bed, though neither of them understood money, and the goal of acquisition bored them; what they enjoyed was an obstacle course. Thus the Monopoly board was soon joined by the Chutes-and-Ladders board, the chess and Scrabble boards (they employed the letters not to make words—neither of them could even spell Ludwicker—but as part of a vast system of signs indicating routes and destinations, fates of capture, escape, and retribution too coded and elaborate for anyone else to understand). They were also in the habit (which drove Cyrus into a frenzy and made him refuse, after the first nerve-racking experience, ever to play with either of them again) of agreeing upon changes in the rules mid-game. ("It's immoral!" he raged. "Don't you understand that if you change the rules in the middle it can damage a position that was built according to the first rules? You think you're going to play one way and all of a sudden your strategy is meaningless— don't you see?" No, they didn't see at all; they could not understand his desire for fixed conditions. "It's boring to do the same thing all the time," they protested, mystified at his distress.)

Although each of the older Ludwickers sought to enlist Fritz into his or her particular ruling passion, she had other plans. Very early, she used her sense of hearing the way other children did those of touch and taste; she soon listened to the sounds things made when hit, kicked, and dropped with a look of expectation well-met. She banged spoons with evocative purpose, spending hours, once she could walk, traveling from room to room, composing as she went. Keeping track of Fritz's whereabouts, Sammy learned to recognize the timber of objects throughout the Cottage: the bed in Tad's old room, the clock in the upstairs hallway, the banisters, the refrigerator, George's golf clubs . . . When Fritz was three, Sammy bought her a violin, and the two became inseparable within a week. Fritz gave up the spoons (although she retained a vestige of this first musical habit all her life, tapping lightly with an index finger whatever she could reach as she strode through a room—giving her the appearance of an impossibly adept blind person), and fell so in love with her instrument that George, lonely without her companionship, became disgruntled and pouted.

Although Fritz could follow musical notation by the time she was four, the world remained her true score, and when she did play written notes, she used them as a base upon which to improvise. She rapidly lost patience with her tutors, who scolded, in one foreign accent after another, "But nein, non, Fräulein, Mam'selle, eet ees supposed to be played like zees!" "But I like eet like zees!" Fritz insisted, and they thought what a wretched child she was, to make fun of their poor English. In fact, Fritz believed her teachers spoke as they did because that was how one was supposed to speak when speaking about music, and she amused the first native-born instructor she had by assuming a unique medley of European accents during their lessons.

If Fritz was lonely, growing up in the dilapidated mansion situated on twenty-five acres of grounds off a little-traveled road a few miles from the town of Demetria, New Jersey, surrounded on all sides by white cedar hedges, with only Xy, Sammy, George, and her violin for company, she did not know it. She assumed all children lived that way. Nor did she think it unusual that her father should also be her uncle. (Xy had not sought to hide her parentage from her. Why should she, who had nothing to be ashamed of?) Fritz, however, believed not only that this double role was natural and proper, but that it was customary. That George was her uncle but not her father sometimes confused her; she often thought how much she would have preferred him to the mysterious Tad, whom she knew only from photographs and her mother's elegiac descriptions. (When she asked George why he wasn't her father, he replied, after considering a moment, that it was because fathers had to go away or die an untimely death.)

It wasn't until Fritz was thirteen and had her first period (an event that outraged and humiliated her) that anyone discovered her misapprehension. Sammy had finished explaining to Fritz the manner in which this bodily function was connected to the bearing of offspring (necessitating the further explanation of the manner in which offspring were conceived) when Fritz looked at her aunt and said, "But I can't have children, Sammy. I don't have any brothers."

"Silly. You don't have to have a brother."

Then Sammy's expression became rapt and wistful (so similar to Xy's when she spoke of Tad that Fritz grew nervous); she told Fritz about that morning thirty years ago when she had met Bib. It didn't matter that she had never seen him again; he had stolen her heart and she would remain faithful to him forever. "If once you give your heart," she said, "you can never get it back."

Sammy had meant to comfort her niece, yet Fritz was far more dismayed by this new information than she had been at the prospect of enforced spinsterhood. The idea that she could fall in love with, marry, even sleep in the same bed with someone she had not known since birth appalled her.

"I shall never marry!" she swore to her aunt.

"Don't worry," Sammy said, misconstruing this cry. "When the time comes you will have more suitors than you can count throwing themselves at your feet."

Fritz shuddered. So vividly did she imagine young men lunging at her ankles that she was no longer able to sit in a chair unless she curled her feet under her; at night she leapt into bed from a distance. She, who had always loved the dark, could not sleep without a light left on in her room, so sure was she that the moment she switched it off she would feel strong, strange fingers crawling their way up the mattress and under the covers.

The colonel's patience was wearing thin. For weeks now the major had sat slumped on his cot, eating little, sleeping less. He muttered under his breath; this wasn't like other wars, the terrain kept changing: first meadow and pine forest, now jungle; the scenery was a backdrop, shifted when one wasn't looking. The army were stool pigeons; if there really was a war going on, why didn't the colonel get on the phone to Headquarters and find out who the hell they were supposed to be fighting?

The colonel, however, knew these grumblings for what they were: the craving for certain comforts of home gone too long unsatisfied. War was life without women, men complained. . . . The colonel preferred quipping that war was life with them. He was what is known as a man's man. As much as he might enjoy the company of the gentler sex, it was the thought of men—wrangling cattle over the plains, clinging to the rigging of a ship plunging down mountainous walls of water, charging ahead with spears leveled and armor gleaming—that made his blood run high. (Not in any perverted fashion—he hoped that was clear.) It riled him to see first his men and now his fellow officer disgracing this time-honored brotherhood.

"Buck up now," he said. "Have a whiskey and forget about her."

"Forget about who?" the major asked, bewildered. "What are you talking about, Colonel?"

Same old story, thought the colonel. Goddamn female sex! he swore. Yet if he didn't let the major go, it would only get worse. First thing in the morning, he decided, he would send the major home to visit his wife. His house wasn't far from the front lines, after all: the airplane age had shrunk the distance between the two until it was negligible. Let him taste that famous domestic bliss for a week, the colonel assured himself, and he'd be begging to return to the front.

In the meantime, to appease him, the colonel told the major that they could anticipate an air attack tomorrow, many squadrons of bombers streaking across the sky. It was possible that none of the regiment would survive.

Cyrus and Betsy's grandmother, General Street's estranged wife, Sophie Street, was born Sophie Marie Laroux, the only daughter and youngest child of a once-large family that for centuries had owned vineyards in the Côte d'Or region of France. There had been a château, a park, a stable of horses, servants, an entailed fortune. . . . World War One put a stop to all this. It put a stop to Sophie's childhood as well. *The* war, it was called then. Sophie was eleven when Germany declared war on France and fifteen when the Kaiser abdicated. In the interim her four brothers had been killed and her father had died of a myocardial infarction, still referred to then as a broken heart. Sophie remained with her mother in the crumbling château, which had been requisitioned as an officers' headquarters during the war, until her mother's death of pneumonia in 1925, when she moved to Paris. There she made her living as a dressmaker. She did not visit the family estate again until 1951, when her great-uncle and last surviving relative died and she was free to do as she pleased with the property. She sold it. She had not returned to France since.

In 1933, Charles was a young lieutenant stationed in England. On his first furlough, he went to Paris. When Sophie saw him, he was standing in the Luxembourg Gardens, staring severely toward the Eiffel Tower, as if the city had just surrendered to him and he were debating what to do with it. When he noticed her observing him, he asked her if she were related to anyone in America. When she said no, he invited her to dinner. He spoke French impeccably—as Louis XIV might have spoken it. He was self-taught, he told her—one of the few things he did tell her about himself. A month later they were married. She was thirty and he was twenty-eight. Three years later, Rose was born. The marriage lasted seven more years.

The army was all mixed up in it. War had killed Sophie's brothers; indirectly it had killed her father, and she abhorred anything having to do with the military. Charles assured her he would leave the service as soon as his first tour of duty was over; like many young men, he said, he had joined up on a whim, not knowing what else to do with himself. But, when the time came, he elected to remain. He was engaged in valuable work in military intelligence, he argued; she ought to recognize that. She replied that he valued his work for another reason: it allowed him to feel that his own unwillingness to confide in people was justified in the interests of national security. He had never told her even where he came from! That, he answered, was a condition of their marriage to which she had agreed beforehand. "I was too much in love to believe you were serious!" retorted Sophie.

Charles had been a lieutenant when she married him; when he was made a general, she left him.

In February of 1951, eight years after leaving Charles, returning to France to arrange the sale of the château, Sophie spent a week in Paris with old friends. She knew they kept in touch with Charles. (In fact, they had given Charles her address, and, over the years, would keep him informed of her whereabouts.) A woman, Sophie thought, who could abandon her seven-year-old daughter because she could no longer bear the fact that her daughter's father would not supply her the facts of his biography did not have the right even to hope for forgiveness; yet memories of her early life with Charles, continuing on through their daughter's first years, when she was too happy to mind his secretiveness very much, accosted her so forcefully that she permitted herself to attempt a reconciliation and had asked her hosts for Charles's address. She wrote two letters: one to Charles and one to Rose. Then she returned to Winston.

At the time, Charles and Rose (then fifteen) were living in Washington, D.C., on Massachusetts Avenue, among the embassies. Rose, home from school before Charles was home from work, picked up from the entryway the letters the postman slipped through the brass slot in the door. The day she saw the two square envelopes with French stamps, she knew before she turned them over and read Sophie's name and return address (not in France but in Newbridge, near Winston City, where Sophie had settled for no better reason than that in 1946, when she had first come to America, her ship had docked there) that they were from her mother. It seemed to Rose that she had always been waiting for this moment. She was very calm as she carried the letters upstairs to her bedroom and set them on her desk. Then she began to pack a suitcase, keeping an eye on the letters all the while, as if she feared they might try to escape. Next she wrote a letter of her own. She addressed it to no one, but it said:

> *I am sorry to leave like this without warning, but certain matters necessitated my departure. I have discovered certain things, which need to be gone into. When I have gone into them, depending on what I find, I will come back. Or not.*
>
> *Don't try to find me. I have all the money, so don't worry, I won't starve or sleep in a gutter. I'm taking books with me; thus if I do come back, I won't have trouble catching up at school.*
>
> *Farewell,*
> *Rose*

She worried over the closure. How could she say "Love, Rose" when she was stealing her father's money and telling him she might never see him again? But "Farewell" sounded harsh, so she added a postscript.

> *P.S. Don't take this personally.*

Then she ran away from home.

Rose had always suspected the existence of some explanation for her adored mother's disappearance besides the one her father had always given her: that her mother didn't want him to be a general. Such reasoning made no sense to a seven-year-old, in whose mind all events revolved around her. Sometimes she hated her mother for leaving her; sometimes she hated her father for making her mother go, but she never stopped dreaming of the time when she would see her mother again.

Rose bought a train ticket to Winston. She intended to read the letters on the train, but, although she held them in her lap the entire trip, clutching them even while she slept, she didn't open them—and Rose was an intensely curious child.

It was five o'clock in the morning when the train arrived in Winston. Rose paid a taxi to drive her to Thornapple Lane in Newbridge. It was just beginning to grow light as she proceeded down the block. Reaching Number 53, she hesitated at the walk. The house was dark and silent. She imagined her mother, asleep, unaware of her presence. She imagined ringing the doorbell, her mother descending the stairs, sleepily opening the door: seeing her.

Then she walked back down the street. She didn't see her father again for five years. Then, living in Arborville, married for two years to Harold Quince, and having just given birth to her first child, Rose wrote to Charles. If he could forgive her for what she had done, she would like to see him. Would he consider visiting her and her husband in Arborville? They had a baby—his name was Cyrus Charles.

It took Rose's letter several months to reach her father, for he had resigned his commission not long after she disappeared, since then wandering alone about Europe, never staying in one place for long. But, when he did receive it, he set out at once for America.

That first night in Arborville, unable to sleep and hearing the baby cry and Rose getting up, Charles followed her downstairs. She was sitting in the shadowy living room, holding Cyrus in her arms. The light from the hallway was the only illumination. When she saw him standing in the doorway, she smiled. "He's not hungry," she said. "He just likes to know he can get me up in the middle of the night."

"A tyrant already." Charles entered the room. "May I hold him?"

The baby, pleased to have roused not one but two people, made soft sounds in Charles's arms.

"He likes you," Rose said.

"Not as much as I like him."

Rose laughed. She was very happy.

Then Charles said, "Rosie, I must tell you something. It's something I have never told anyone, not even your mother."

"Dad, you don't . . ."

She knew that more than anything in the world she did not want to hear what he was about to say. But he went on anyway, unburdening himself of his secret. She listened, appalled, to the story Charles told her, unable to believe it could be true, yet equally unable to think he would be inventing it. Simultaneously, she remembered Sophie's letters, still lying unopened in the back of her jewelry drawer upstairs. Their existence burned into her. It seemed to her she was implicated in her father's guilt; they were all of them guilty together. Now there would never be any escape from it.

"If you wish me to leave," Charles said softly, "I will do so at once. I can say nothing to defend myself."

Rose shook her head, weeping, and held out her arms for Cyrus. "I don't hate you, if that's what you think. And I don't want you to leave. But if we talk about it anymore right now I don't think I will be able to stand it."

Charles nodded, like one condemned, and left the room. As she held the baby close, Rose wondered if he knew what had passed between her and her father.

As for Sophie, when she received no answer to her letters, she accepted this verdict as final and never tried to contact Charles or Rose again.

She was sewing, that spring evening in 1973. She was sitting in her living room, and the front door was open; a vaguely salt breeze fluttered the petals of the daffodils she had arranged in a vase on a table in the entryway.

When Cyrus knocked, Sophie was not startled. Without hurrying she laid her sewing down beside the lamp, got to her feet, and walked calmly to the door. "Yes?" she said.

Except for the fact that her once-dark hair was now entirely white, Cyrus easily recognized her from the snapshot Charles had given him, which he still carried in his wallet.

"What is it?" she asked impatiently. She spoke with a slight, agreeable accent. She glanced at the cat carrier. "Are you selling something?"

At that moment Jonzo let out a wail.

"A cat?"

"Yes. I mean, no. I'm not selling anything."

"What is it you want, then?"

He made no answer, merely looked at her helplessly.

"I'm sorry," Sophie began, then stopped. She stared at him,

into his eyes—that same deep blue—and suddenly knew who he was. But still she asked, "Who are you?"

He tried to smile. "I'm your grandson, Cyrus Quince."

All that first night and the next, Sophie sat up with Cyrus, and they played cards until, exhausted, he fell asleep in his chair. Then, after first covering him with a quilt, she crept upstairs. Lying upon her bed, she at last let flow the tears she had been withholding—tears Cyrus would not allow himself. Yet she knew she wept for herself as well, for sorrows thirty years old. You old fool, she said, this changes nothing! Yet in her heart she felt something stirring into life, and when she fell asleep it was to spend, for the first time in years, a night free of reproachful dreams.

When Cyrus awoke, Sophie was in the kitchen, making breakfast. She was humming, and from afar he understood that she was happy. He didn't mind that she was happy, even though he himself was now indifferent, but it startled him to think that he might have had something to do with her happiness. He felt sorry for her that she was making such a mistake. Didn't she know he could not be trusted? That at a critical moment he would fail her, just as he had everyone else who loved him?

Sophie came into the living room. "You slept," she said, smiling.

She was so pretty, he thought wistfully, in her summery dress printed with tiny flowers. The skin of her arms was transparent; he could see the dark blue veins running up from her wrists.

He smiled back at her, so sadly and gently Sophie had to turn away to prevent him from noticing the tears rising to her eyes. "You can wash upstairs. I've laid a towel out in your room—the room to the right." While he was gone, she set the table: two plates, two cups and saucers, two sets of silverware. . . . How long it had been since she had done that! But Cyrus didn't return, and when she went to see what had become of him she found him sound asleep again in the guestroom.

For a long time, it seemed to Cyrus, things remained hazy, hazy and very still. He slept on for several days, getting out of bed only to drift outside and fall asleep again in the sun. Sophie had a tiny walled garden in back of her house; red, yellow, and pink roses draped the walls. He lay there in a wicker chaise and the heat kept him from thinking. Jonzo slept in his lap. He was twelve now and approved of this existence. Cyrus changed position infrequently so as not to disturb the cat. It took too much energy to move, anyway. He couldn't think. What was he doing, sitting there? He would sometimes reach out and close his hand over the thorny rose stems and then examine his palm, unable to believe that the blood speckling it was his. (He didn't know that Sophie sometimes watched him from within the house, and had to restrain herself from crying out to him to stop.) Once, for no apparent reason, he recalled a description he had read of a salamander being impaled on a fish hook; the writer described how, after it had been pierced, the salamander tried to hold on to the hook with its tiny feet. Cyrus kept thinking about this image until it no longer produced any emotion in him.

At the same time that everything was very strange, though, nothing was out of the ordinary. He couldn't really remember anything before the moment he rang Sophie's doorbell. He knew he had run away from school and that no one knew where he was, but it meant nothing to him. He didn't wonder what he would have done if Sophie hadn't lived in Newbridge anymore or if she had refused to let him stay with her. It was as if his blindness to all but his one compelling need to preserve the integrity of his grief had required her to exist, to let him in, making no complaint at having her past cracked open like that, to simply, with utmost graciousness, acknowledge him. His anguish for Lark required her to be there waiting, all her previous life nothing more than a preparation for the moment when he appeared on her doorstep. He had somehow known that, of all the people in the world, she was the only one he could bear to witness his suffering.

Although Cyrus had been with Sophie less than a week, they were already developing habits. After breakfast he went out to the garden, while she busied herself in the house. Once in a while she joined him outside and read or sewed. On these occasions, he grew uneasy when she left and soon followed her. On the third day after his arrival, she asked him to accompany her to the grocery store; they went out on each subsequent afternoon. It amused Sophie that Cyrus had become so solicitous he refused to allow her to carry home any of the groceries, or books when they went to the library. How did he think she had managed in the quarter century before he came? Yet she didn't mind pretending to be the frail grandmother he demanded.

Several times they encountered acquaintances of Sophie. She said, "I want you to meet my grandson, Cyrus Quince." The acquaintances were invariably astonished. "Heavens, Mrs. Street," they protested, "we didn't know you had one!" Sophie patted Cyrus's arm, and winked at him. "But I do—here he is."

One morning, when Cyrus was sleeping outside, Sophie searched among his things and found his address. Then she wrote the following letter:

Dear Rose,

Your son, Cyrus, is here with me. He arrived upon my doorstep a week ago, accompanied by his cat. I do not know how he found me but I assume that either you or your father must have told him I lived here.

He has not said, and I have not wished to ask, but I have received the impression that he has told no one where he is and so I have taken it upon myself to let you know he is safe.

Cyrus has told me of his younger brother's death. I am so terribly sorry. Cyrus must have loved him very much indeed for he is grieving deeply. Though of course I am not acquainted with any other persons of his age, it seems to me that he is too young to suffer in the particular way that he is suffering—to feel the powerlessness of love to save anyone from death.

I do not wish to add to your own pain at this time, and I am sure I have already done so by writing this. However, I must tell you that it is my belief that it would be best if you did not try to communicate with Cyrus but allowed him to communicate with you in his own time. He is very proud (as am I, as your father

*was—as I expect so are you), and will not accept sympathy.
Forgive me for suggesting this.*

*He may remain with me as long as he wishes. I am grateful
that he has sought me out. Perhaps in some small way I am to be
allowed to make amends for the hurt I have caused.*

Your mother,

Sophie

When Rose received the letter, Harold was at work. Unlike
the last time, she opened and read this letter from Sophie at once.
Standing in the hallway, she read it over and over, particularly the
signature: Your mother, Sophie. *Her* mother, Sophie.

How dared she? "It would be best if you did not try to communicate with Cyrus . . ." "He will not accept sympathy." How
dared she? Rose was furious—fury and despair were the only emotions that seemed to remain to her since Lark's death. Her mother
vanished, then reappeared when the fancy took her! In her rage,
it seemed to Rose she had also felt furious years ago when she
came upon her mother's letters lying on the hallway floor. Yes,
she had been right to do what she had done! Her mother had
deserved no reply. . . . Suddenly fear checked her. What might
her mother not tell Cyrus? Might they not, between them, piece
together her secret? At the least, Sophie would ask Cyrus why his
mother had never made any effort to see her, and he, having grown
up believing the reluctance to be on Sophie's side, would wonder.
He already despised his mother—of this Rose was convinced. How
much more he would despise her now.

Rose refolded the letter and put it back in its envelope. She
walked slowly into the kitchen; there she ignited one of the stove's
gas burners and touched a corner of the envelope to the flame.
When the fire crept close to her fingers, she threw the letter into
the sink and watched it burn out. She washed the black skinlike
fragments down the drain and scrubbed the basin. The kitchen
smelled of sulphur and ash—hell smelled like that. Quickly she
took eggs and milk and butter from the refrigerator, chocolate and
flour and sugar and baking powder and salt and cinnamon and

cloves from the cupboard; she made a cake: chocolate spice, Harold's favorite. When he and Betsy arrived home, its smell pervaded the house.

"What's the cake for?" Betsy demanded, as they surveyed the kitchen: the bowls, spoons, measuring cups everywhere, and Rose—in a flour-covered apron.

"Does a cake require an occasion?" Rose inquired cheerfully.

Harold and Betsy exchanged an uncertain glance as she returned to the counter, collected the utensils, and piled them in the sink.

"Cyrus called," she remarked.

She felt their stares but didn't turn around.

"He ran away but he's okay. He said he's okay. He apologized for worrying us. He's decided he wants to hitchhike out West with a friend." (In fact Cyrus had mentioned this plan in a letter they received just before he left Fifield.) Now she did turn. "I said I'd have to ask you but I thought probably it would be all right, if that's what he really wants."

She took powdered sugar and cocoa out of the cupboard and poured measured amounts into a saucepan.

It was Betsy who spoke first. "What friend? Captain Turner said Billy didn't know where he was."

"I don't know what friend, dear."

"Cyrus didn't have any other friends besides Billy."

"You exaggerate, Betsy. Cyrus has always had more friends than he knew what to do with."

Betsy, in reply, simply rolled her eyes.

"When did he call?" Harold now managed to ask.

"This afternoon, of course. You don't think I would have kept it from you?"

"No! But I'm not relieved at all by this news and I don't see how you can possibly be. I can't believe you actually told him it would be all right. What kind of parents will he think we are? God damn it, Rose, I want him on the next plane out here! Where the hell was he?"

"He wouldn't say," Rose faltered. "He . . ."

Harold now sat down heavily at the kitchen table. Betsy remained in the doorway, poised for flight.

Harold made an effort to remain calm. Rose was still in shock, the doctor had said. He shouldn't expect her reactions to things to be normal. Her lack of anxiety about the news of Cyrus's disappearance, for example. Even when the police came to question them—had they any idea where Cyrus might go? Did they think he might be suicidal—she hadn't seemed to realize the gravity of the situation. It was Harold who suggested the police visit General Street. But Cyrus had not contacted him.

"How did he sound? Did you ask if he had any money? Did he say when he'd call again?"

"He sounded all right. He didn't say anything about money, and he didn't say when he'd call again."

"My God, Rose!" Harold exploded. Betsy slipped silently away. "How can you sound so casual? Cyrus could be in shock. You know what Lark meant to him."

"What do you think Lark meant to me? How can you talk to me like this, Harold?" She sat down across from him, weeping. "How dare you talk to me like this?"

Contrary to what Rose believed, Cyrus and Sophie discussed neither Rose nor Charles. Cyrus was too dazed when he arrived to consider bringing up the subject of the long estrangement. And Sophie drifted with him in the peculiar timeless atmosphere of that first week. She was content to be entrusted with his care. She didn't want to say or do anything that might break the spell that seemed to have been cast upon them both.

When Cyrus began to feel more alert, he did think about his grandfather and his mother, but, believing Sophie preferred not to hear about them, he kept silent. Once, he knew, he would not have given in so easily. He would have insisted she tell him her side of the story. He would have wanted to acquire all possible facts, assemble them, and extract the truth of the matter. All through his childhood it had been his greatest ambition: to visit Sophie and convince her that she should give Charles another chance. Whatever he had done, she should forgive him, because he still loved her. But it had been a long time since he had felt that desire.

One night, however, Cyrus's ancient nightmare returned. The inquisitor with his familiar yet never clearly seen face leaned over him, his cigarette-tip eyes glowing, closer and closer to Cyrus's own, his scaly voice repeating, "Tell me who is to blame. Tell me who. You know that you know." Cyrus woke to Sophie shaking him. "Don't know what, Cyrus?" she asked. "You were yelling, 'I don't know! I don't know!' "

"I don't know?" He looked so confused—uncertain of who he was, of who she was, and of what they were both doing there—that Sophie gently reminded him,

"You were having a nightmare, Cyrus. You woke me with your shouting. Now, don't tell me you're going back to sleep. I have had too much experience of nightmares, my own and other people's, to believe you. If you wish to go downstairs and make some tea, I will come with you. If you prefer to sit in the garden and watch the stars, I will also. If you like, we will play cards all night. But if you intend to convince me that a nightmare is insignificant, you will not succeed."

"But, Grandmother . . ." Cyrus looked at her. She sat on the edge of his bed. The moonlight, sliced by the window shade, transformed his grandmother's long white braid into a gleaming rope down her back.

"Your grandfather . . ." she began, and stopped.

"What were you going to say?"

She sighed. "He often had nightmares too and shouted in his sleep. Most frequently he said, 'Forgive me.' I woke him and asked him what he wished to be forgiven for, but he always pretended not to remember what he had been dreaming."

Cyrus said nothing, but he nodded.

"In the ten years of our life together, Cyrus, he never told me a single thing about the years before he met me. Finally I could not bear it and I left him." She paused. "I was certain that his nightmares had something to do with his past. I used to look through his desk and bureau drawers when he was away from home for evidence of what he was hiding."

"You did!"

She smiled. "Yes, I did. I, Sophie Laroux Street, your grandmother, am guilty of espionage. I once searched through his desk in the middle of the night."

"Did you find anything?"

"I'm not sure." She looked at him, considering. Then she rose. "Wait here." In a moment she returned carrying a book, which she handed to him.

"This is the only thing I found that appeared remotely intriguing. Perhaps because it seemed worthless. Yet he kept it with him always." She laid it on the bed table. "Will you be able to sleep now?"

"Sure." In the moonlight they looked at each other.

"Good," she said and left him.

The next day Sophie left Cyrus alone while she attended an afternoon tea. She told him the other old ladies in the neighborhood would ride her out of town on a rail if she refused another invitation. Already they considered her devious and possibly dangerous because she so rarely attended their gatherings.

"You should wear dark glasses and take notes," Cyrus told her. "Then you'd really make them nervous."

"You think I'm joking," Sophie replied, "but I'm not."

Cyrus stood on the front steps watching until she turned the corner out of Thornapple Lane. Then he went indoors and called Arborville, collect. Harold answered.

"Cyrus!" he shouted.

"Hello, Dad."

"Cyrus . . ." Harold repeated.

"I just wanted to tell you I'm okay. I'm sorry if I worried you."

"You're all right then? Where are you?"

"Winston."

"Winston! What are you doing there? Your mother said you were heading west."

"West?" Cyrus repeated uncertainly.

"The West Coast. I've been extremely worried, Cyrus. I know you have a friend with you, but still, things happen. I don't like the idea at all."

"*What* idea? What are you talking about, Dad?" Cyrus was beginning to feel as if he had dialed somebody else's number and a strange man had mistaken him for his son. His father sounded as if he were calling from camp. His brother was *dead*. He had run away from school, and his father hadn't mentioned either thing.

"Hitchhiking. I wish I had been here when you called. Your mother . . ."

"When I called?"

"A few days ago."

"Dad, I didn't . . ." Cyrus could feel his stomach knotting. He gripped the receiver tightly and clenched his free hand as well.

"Listen, Cy," Harold said, and his voice was different now, uneasy, no longer hearty. "Son . . . Lark . . . I think you should know . . ."

Cyrus stared at the whitened knuckles of his fist.

"Know what? What?"

He heard his father breathe in deeply. "Cyrus, are you listening to me? Lark was killed instantly. It was an ambulance, going very fast, bringing another child in for emergency surgery. The brake on his wheelchair wasn't fastened securely and Lark was unable to wheel himself anymore, as you know. He wasn't even on a slope, but they think that he must have leaned forward and that was enough to jar the brake loose. Then when the brake released, the chair suddenly gained momentum. No one even saw he was moving until it was too late. The driver never had a chance to swerve. Lark was thrown out of his chair and landed on his head and his neck was broken. Do you understand what that means, Cyrus? He never felt any pain." He paused, but Cyrus didn't respond. "I thought it might help to know that. Maybe we can all be happy for Lark that in the end he never had to suffer. We all knew he didn't have much time left, and what could happen . . ."

As his father had been speaking, Cyrus had begun to tremble.

He shook so that he had to clench his teeth in order to keep them from chattering. He had been sitting on a straight chair beside the table on which the telephone stood; he slipped to the floor and sat with his back againt the table leg, his knees drawn up. He held on to the receiver as if it were being wrested from his grip.

Suddenly he interrupted violently: "That's not true! You know it isn't! You're just saying that now, but you're lying. You're lying!"

"Cyrus . . ."

"People always say that. *He never felt any pain.* They just say it to make the survivors feel better. Don't lie to me, Dad. It only makes everything worse." He was crying now. Harold could hear his stifled sobs.

"Cyrus, listen to me!" Harold shouted.

But Cyrus couldn't listen anymore. He wanted only to be alone again in his grandmother's house. This was what he had known would happen. They would try to comfort him. They would try to take away the pain, and it was all that he would ever have anymore of Lark.

Very gently, the way someone hangs up who has been secretly listening in on someone else's conversation, Cyrus replaced the receiver in its cradle.

When he heard the click, Harold repeated, "Cyrus?" Only empty space answered him. Absolutely frantic now, Harold slammed down the phone, jumped up, and began to pace. He had never felt so powerless in his entire life. How in hell had he allowed Rose to convince him that Cyrus was all right? First Turner, with his presumptuous remark that Cyrus would "heal himself in his own way," then Rose . . . What the hell was wrong with him?

Just then Rose walked in the door. "God damn it! Where have you been? Cyrus called again, Rose. He hung up on me when I tried to talk to him about Lark. I want this trip stopped, Rose. He said he was in Winston—I'm calling the Winston police."

"Harold, I don't think . . ."

"Rose, for Christ's sake! There's not *time*." He reached for the telephone.

Rose sat down. "There's no need to call anyone, Harold." She sounded very tired. "He's at my mother's."

When Sophie returned later that afternoon she found a note from Cyrus saying that he had gone into Winston for the afternoon. She was pleased. As she had hoped, by going off alone she had provoked him to make a private expedition of his own.

When he reappeared that evening, mysterious about how he had spent his time (setting a precedent for their future diplomacies), Sophie was not in the least disturbed. It was another sign, she thought, that he was young again.

From his childhood, the major remembered that the shutter on the pantry window had lost its latch. It had used to bang in a wind. "I feel it right here," his mother had said, pressing a hand against her head when she was so ill before she died (although the major was too young to understand that she was dying). "Clack, clack! I feel that I am going mad!"

"Don't go mad," he had pleaded. "I don't want you to go mad."

"There are things I have never told anyone. Things that I alone know. Now they have gnawed away my life."

"What things?" But he hadn't wanted to know. If they had made her so ill, they could make him ill too.

"There are no words anymore," she sighed, drawing him closer to her. "I have lived alone with these things too long. Now I can tell them to no one, even if I would. May you never know such solitude." She clutched him tightly. The little boy struggled, but his mother would not loosen her grip.

"You're hurting me! Let me go, Mama! You're squeezing so tightly!"

". . . so tightly . . ." the major murmured, as he levered the window open with a stick.

Cobwebs were strung thickly across inside. He cleared the

opening of them, then climbed through. The gray strands clung to him everywhere—to his face, hair, hands, and clothes—and would not let go. He stood inside the pantry, amazed.

Dust had fallen like snow on the shelves, coating the plates, settling in glasses like unfinished drinks after a party. He took a deep breath and blew; the dust rose in whorls, then drifted back down into a new pattern.

"Good God," he said softly. He stood listening. There wasn't a sound. No—there was a sound; he looked down and saw a mouse disappearing into a corner.

"Mouse?" he queried, as if inquiring after its health. The mouse didn't reappear, but he knew it was nearby in the dark, hunched over its paws, listening for him.

He advanced into the kitchen. The mice had been everywhere, places one would not have imagined they could climb to, as if they had carried little ladders with them and removed them afterward. Spider webs connected points on adjacent walls, but the webs were as empty as the house, as if only constructed to expedite an exodus that had long ago taken place. Where had everyone gone?

In the hallway, the major peered up the stairs. As a child, he had been terrified of these stairs, their shape, the sensations of mounting and descending, the strangeness of the fact that they were the only means by which one could move from one level of the house to another. He had forgotten this, but now, his family vanished without a trace, he felt his old terror returning to life.

"What we need is some light in here!" he exclaimed. He didn't wait to hear his voice resound in the stairwell but strode into the drawing room, tore open the drapes, unhooked and pushed the shutters into the outside air, rescued the caparisoned tables and chairs. Emboldened, he returned to the hall and started quickly up the stairs. He opened all the doors along the upstairs hallway; the rooms were tidy. No signs of a struggle. (Not that he really hoped to find them anymore.) At the end of the hall he opened another door and climbed a second flight of stairs. These led to the nursery, a large, unshuttered, airy room. The sun streamed in and the white-painted walls and rafters shone.

The major looked, mesmerized, at the small iron beds, the little table and chairs, the toy chest, from which he and then his son after him had taken their lead soldiers. Many a glorious battle had been waged on that nursery floor. Slowly, he approached the toy chest, lifted the lid, and looked in. The little soldiers were gone, and now the fear he had been keeping at bay swept over him. She had left him, and she had taken the children with her. He had been telling himself stories. The colonel had been justified in ridiculing his talk of infiltration and censorship—these were his own self-deceptions; he had invented a military invasion to account for the plainest tale in the world: lost love.

Sarah Danford and Jason Simms's apartment on Willow Street in Winston City was located on the second floor of a large late-nineteenth-century mansion, whose enormous size and ungainly character suggested that its architect had known when he designed it that its large founding family would disperse, its children move to distant states, their parents be removed to an old people's home, then the house itself sectioned off into rentable units. Sarah sometimes daydreamed about the place as it had once been: full of people of all ages—grandparents, aunts and uncles and cousins, mothers and fathers and sons and daughters, neighbors in and out—everyone shouting, laughing, bickering, happy; why couldn't life be like that anymore? Her loneliness seemed a punishment for some failure on her part—perhaps to understand what life was about. She had tried to convince herself that Jason was right, that she was romantic; but she refused to accept the fact that adulthood meant monotony. When she had met Cyrus, and found something in him she had given up believing possible, her dreams had flared violently into hope.

For a week after their meeting, until she decided to call, she spent most of her time gazing out the window, or lying on the bed, abandoning herself to a sensation she didn't remember experiencing since childhood—the sensation of being connected to everything else in the world by an invisible yet palpable ether; the shapes in the room had been soft shadows; the street noises, so raucous and distinct usually, were a homogeneous, companionable background. . . .

The morning of the Saturday Cyrus was due to visit, his friend Billy called. "Cyrus said to tell you he can't make it. He's got too much work to do." "Why didn't he call himself?" she asked. Billy seemed to hesitate. "I don't really know. He just asked me to." "I see," Sarah said. Then, "Are you sure he's all right?" "Fine," Billy replied. "He's just too busy to come down." Well, great, Sarah thought. If that was the kind of person he was, why bother about him? Several hours' acquaintance had hardly provided her with enough information to gauge his character accurately. He was just some bold eighteen-year-old out for a good time. She wasn't happy with Jason, and Cyrus happened along at an opportune moment; she pinned her hopes on him and he was perfectly willing to go along. Except what had all that *meant* then? That tenderness. That . . . what there were no words for. Had she imagined *that* as well?

Sarah was unprepared for the intensity of the loss she felt. She had to reach some understanding with Cyrus. She thought of calling back but decided against it. If he had been unwilling to telephone her before, even if she succeeded in reaching him the conversation would probably go nowhere. So she decided to write him. But one letter was too strident, berating him for his thoughtlessness; the next too plaintive; the one after that too flippant; another, written in a mood of defiance, seemed intent on impressing him with how invulnerable she was, yet, when she reread it in a subsequent mood of longing, its happy-go-lucky, devil-may-care tone sounded false.

She had been thinking about him ceaselessly, yet he was the last person she expected to see when she answered the doorbell that muggy Saturday afternoon in mid-June.

He stood there, wearing a pair of khaki trousers, a long-sleeved white shirt pin-striped with red, the sleeves rolled up to below his elbows, and penny loafers—if you didn't know better, you could easily mistake him for a typical high-school student: earnest, but not too earnest, president of his class maybe, all-round good guy, popular with girls, likable, cutting up sometimes, but not too much, a real sense of fun, and full of promise—a full-blooded American boy who would succeed in the prescribed fashion: a vice-presidency at some company or other; a two-car, two-child family—boy and girl of course, in that order. . . . Except this was Cyrus, just standing there, smiling in that wry, mischievous, yet somehow pained way out of one side of his mouth, his stance supremely relaxed in the way that looked like easy friendliness but was really a brand of reserve.

"Hello, Sarah," he said, and then she remembered his voice too—its uncommon masculine gentleness and distinguishing lilt—its charm.

"What are you doing here?" she asked.

He half laughed. "Are you going to let me in?"

"No," she said, turning, holding the door for him. He followed her up the stairs.

Sixteen steps to the landing, he counted, then the stair turned and there were eight more steps. A raggedy dark-green carpet was tacked to the middle of the treads. High ceilings. Twelve feet? Her apartment, number three, second-floor front, two windows in the living room, four rooms in all, on the small side . . . If he could keep counting, counting forever, then maybe it would not all slide, slide down into where everything was still happening: Lark's death; his abrupt departure from Fifield, not letting Billy know he was going; now his father's crazy questions; and, earlier, writing to his grandfather, lying to Billy about him—all these things happening at once, as if they were not separate temporal events at all but one event, and he couldn't make sense out of them, nor why he was standing here in Sarah's apartment, trying to think of an explanation for his presence. He could tell she was waiting for an explanation. But he knew that if he once began to speak of the things that had happened he would fall and go on falling. . . . He had half expected her to have heard about Lark and about his running away, but Billy must have kept his mouth shut.

Count things, he instructed himself; count the windows, the

panes in the windows, the books in the bookcase, the number of minutes spent counting. . . .

Sarah stood still while Cyrus strolled around the small living room: peering at pictures, tilting his head to read the titles of books, picking up small objects and examining them. Stalling for time.

"Cyrus?" He turned. "Do you have a search warrant?"

"No," he said. She was just waiting for him to make a move. He was reminded of the way Jonzo watched a mouse he knew could not escape. The hostility he felt toward her surprised him. After all, he was the one who had let her down.

Sarah merely stood now, letting him scrutinize her. She felt helpless to break the stalemate. What *did* she feel, she wondered?

At last, as if by a great effort, Cyrus approached her, his expression somehow appraising, and kissed her. (It was easy after that.) Sarah felt she ought to be indignant, but she wasn't. She responded, and after a while they went into the bedroom. (He felt a little uncomfortable with that guy's stuff around the room: a pair of tennis shoes sticking out from under the bureau, a shirt hung over the back of a chair. . . . Well, it had nothing to do with him.)

Cyrus was the same as before—it was she who was distant. (She didn't think he could tell, though.) It should have felt more licit this time, but instead it felt the opposite. He hadn't *said* anything. Just showed up, expected her to be there—what if Jason had been home? But once, when she cried out, he clasped her tightly, covering her body protectively with his own, even laying a hand upon her face, as if to shield her from some danger.

He touched the hollows below her hip bones, and the slope up to those ridges. Her skin was so soft—it felt like the silky material of the dresses his mother had worn when she was dressed to go out; she had always made sure his and Betsy's hands were clean before she would let them put their arms around her and kiss her goodnight. . . . What a strange thing to think about now. Sarah sighed, and it reminded him of the sound Jonzo made when he was asleep and someone stroked him and he didn't want to be waked up yet couldn't help liking it. She said "Cyrus" twice.

Afterward, he lay on his side, propped on an elbow, with his other hand pushing her hair off her face, touching her eyes, nose, temples, lips with his fingertips, a blind person establishing some-one's identity.

"What are you thinking about, Sarah?" he asked softly.

"I don't know—nothing."

She came back into focus. He was still observing her and laughed a little. "Where did you go? The moon?"

"Nearby."

They kissed. He could forget himself, like this. It was the only way he could forget himself.

He was sometimes afraid, as the summer wore on, that she was going to call a halt to things. He always half-expected her to say, Look, Cyrus, I can't see you anymore. She didn't, though. They saw each other nearly every day except on the weekend, unless Jason was out of town.

Fyodor Andrei Vladimir Sergei Petrovich Stoltzoff, a young Russian violinist recently emigrated (by way of Berlin and Paris, having departed the motherland at age three) to the United States, was responding to a newspaper advertisement for a violin teacher of the "highest caliber" to instruct a pupil at a private home in New Jersey. Fyodor had never been to New Jersey. It was August of 1973.

As he turned his car into the driveway, lined by the rocks, painted many colors, that Sammy had purchased from a mail-order catalogue, and observed the lawn—the sagging badminton net, the mildewed croquet set, the faded target from which several decrepit arrows drooped—and then the extraordinary building in the midst of all this, which looked as if a tornado had lifted portions of houses from all over the world and dropped them here, he wondered what kind of caricatures of human beings could live in such a place. It was so decadent! So capitalistic! Americans, he had found, did possess a certain warmth, but it was based on pride of ownership, and they lacked ideology and discipline. They were overwhelmed by nostalgia yet had no understanding of the past. They longed for Eden but, had they found it, would have wanted to redecorate.

The place distressed Fyodor so—he was of a sensitive, refined temperament that could not stand any sort of ugliness about him—that he was upon the point of backing out of the driveway to return to his apartment and its tasteful décor so restful to his anachronistic soul when a man, fifty to sixty years of age, chubby, balding, wearing a sports jersey and shorts, jogged around the corner of the house and up the macadam, dribbling a basketball.

Fyodor sighed and climbed out of his car (a sleek classical design that compensated him somewhat for the demise of the fiacre), then stood, staring at the man with an elegant distaste, which, however, seemed to make no impression.

"Who are you?" the man asked. "I've never seen you before in my life."

Just like a little boy! Fyodor thought. These Americans—they were all children! He had heard, from his acquaintances throughout Europe, about the American suburbs—a sort of no-man's-land between city and country—and the alienated people who lived there, but he had considered the stories exaggerated.

The man appeared frightened but held his ground, continuing to bounce the ball.

"I have just broken my record of shooting twelve baskets in a row," he said. "I shot thirteen. But Xy says thirteen is unlucky so I am attempting to decide if I should risk another shot to hit fourteen, but then if I miss it might be even worse luck, what do you think?"

Fyodor stared. A veritable naïf! he silently exclaimed, yet there was nonetheless something appealing about the man's ingenuousness, as with that of all children. A nation of innocents, Fyodor thought; they had never fought oppressors; their revolutionary spirit had died out several generations back. . . .

"I am Fyodor Stoltzoff," Fyodor said. "The violin teacher."

"Oh," the man said. He sounded disappointed. "Well, I'll take you to Xy."

"Who is Xy?" asked Fyodor, as he followed the man into the

house, where to his dismay he saw that the interior continued the dreadful disharmony of the exterior. A glance around the hallway showed Fyodor an appalling gallimaufry: suits of armor and iron maidens among duck decoys, rooster-shaped boot scrapers, old "Wanted" posters, glazed and framed; hundreds of pairs of shoes, everything from stiletto heels to thigh-high wading boots, were scattered around the floor; moose heads hung from the walls, their antlers draped with scarves, feather boas, and plastic leis—one of the moose wore sunglasses.

"Who are *you*, by the way?" inquired Fyodor.

"I'm Prince Sigismund," Sigismund said, surprised. "Who did you think I was?"

"I really don't know at all."

They passed through many more rooms, equally crowded, as if each generation had discarded nothing from the previous one—like Troy, one civilization built on top of the other, except that here all were visible at once. The effect, in the abstract one of pleasing continuity, was in actual instance perverse and horrible.

Now they arrived at a kind of sitting room, strewn with play-things: Fyodor noted a pinball machine, an Exercycle, a spinet piano; two parakeets squabbled in a cage, and in a large terrarium many small toads slept. The floor was strewn with mail-order catalogues from companies with such amalgamated and alliterative names as Econoknife, Gracious Greenery, Holiday Hobbies, Kitchen Korner, Picnicinc., Helpful Hair Hints, and so on.

Two women sat in this room. One was clothed in a long gray dress whose style had been popular at the turn of the century; her all-white hair was drawn back into a chignon. This woman, who seemed to be the elder of the two, sat reading. The other woman, shorter and plumper—Fyodor instantly deduced that she and the man who called himself Prince Sigismund were related—was dressed in modern yellow slacks and a frilly maroon blouse; her hair was dyed a metallic gray and she wore leopardskin slippers on her feet and an ostentatious ruby collar around her neck—fake, Fyodor thought with distaste. She was examining a catalogue. Neither of the two women looked up.

Sigismund walked into the center of the room, leapt into the air, and came down with a crash. At this the women lifted their heads; he rotated his arms, windmill-fashion, and they removed earplugs from their ears.

"Oh, she's stopped," the garishly dressed woman said.

"What is it, George?" asked the other. "Who's this? How did he get in?"

"It's another violin teacher."

Another? wondered Fyodor.

"He's called Fee-oh . . . Fee-oh . . . Who did you say you were again?"

"Fyodor Andrei Vladimir Sergei Petrovich Stoltzoff." Fyodor bowed (an old habit taught him by his White Russian great-aunts —he couldn't help it).

"How nice," the older woman said. "Are you related to the Romanovs?"

"A distant connection only," Fyodor replied, smiling suavely. "Fortunately for my safety."

"Yes, I quite understand. I don't suppose you know where they are?"

"Last I saw Anastasia, she was crawling under a barbed wire," he joked.

"Dear me, how very unpleasant," the woman said with feeling, and Fyodor continued to smile agreeably but was slightly discomfited, if the truth were ever to become known. She was being ironical, of course, and yet her irony was so subtle as to be mistaken for sincerity by any but the most discerning listener. It would not be the first time he had encountered this American fascination with royalty. For a so-called democratic country, its people were more in awe of royal blood than any European ever had been. Even the most sophisticated liberal-nihilists were not exempt. He thought sometimes they seemed to be a nation of illegitimates, these intrepid pioneers—their perpetual desire to make themselves agreeable betraying a deep nervousness, as if the true proprietors of their land might reappear and evict them.

The other woman said now, in a homey manner surprising

after the imperial dignity of the first, "Go right upstairs, Instructor Stoltzoff. I believe Fritz is in her room. It's the fourth door on the left."

Instructor Stoltzoff? Fyodor thought. "Fritz?" he inquired, but the women had returned to their respective reading matter and Sigismund had vanished. Thus dismissed, Fyodor bowed again (despite himself) and took his leave. After several false turns, he found his way upstairs and knocked on the appropriate door. Receiving no answer, he opened it and went in.

Fritz, who was standing at the window, looking out, violin and bow in hand, spun around and gazed with fright at Fyodor. With his ink-black eyes and the extravagant head of hair still believed, in certain circles, indispensable to a musician's success, Fyodor was not without a certain presence. Ordinarily he was well aware of the impression he made. But in this instance his attention was so riveted on the young woman that he did not observe that her reaction contained more fear than appreciation. The two stared at one another like two animals of different species meeting unexpectedly in the woods.

Never, Fyodor rhapsodized, had he beheld so striking a personage! That furious dark red hair! Those midnight blue eyes—he had never seen those colors together. Her features—nose, mouth, chin—were angular, but she made the conventional taste for softness and symmetry seem crass and vulgar. And she had the thinness and pallor he found so aesthetically appealing in women, emphasized by the simple black frock she wore tied loosely at the waist with a white scarf. She looked like a young girl in an orphanage, and very proud and self-possessed. Although she had done no more than turn around, he was also certain of her lynxlike gracefulness.

There was something so unusual about her that Fyodor, who prided himself on his recognition of the rare, the unique, the precious, felt a twinge in his acquisitive nerve.

"Allow me to introduce myself," he said, after the eternity he spent gazing at her was over and done with. "I was directed upstairs by your . . . by the people downstairs. I am Fyodor Stoltzoff, the violin teacher."

"You?" she replied scornfully.

"Why not me?" he inquired.

"Teachers are old," she stated.

Fyodor was not insulted. Her hauteur only increased her desirability. He required a challenge. He was tired of easy conquests, the hackneyed tactical maneuvers of the usual encounter. He suffered abominably from boredom. He was twenty-five but he felt that life was over.

"Perhaps you might play for me," he suggested, "and then I will show you that a teacher need not be old to instruct you."

"Play what?"

"Anything you like."

Fritz grimaced. Bored, she lifted her violin.

Fyodor watched her, amused. How artless she was! he thought, with a certain meted tenderness. Like a shy, wild animal . . . How *many* things there were in which he could instruct her!

Then Fritz began to play. After a minute, Fyodor was listening seriously. After several more, he was astonished. By the time Fritz lifted the bow from the last chord, he was weeping.

To Fyodor, who had heard many of the world's acknowledged virtuosos, it seemed that he was hearing music for the first time. Fritz's playing was cleaner, sharper, and purer than any he had ever heard. At one moment he ceased breathing, as she drew a note out so long he did not see how she could continue—if she had never lifted her bow she could have killed him. At the next, he felt certain he must expire anyway, as she expanded time, articulating crisply more notes at a presto tempo than he had ever believed possible.

Then there was the piece itself. Each new section sounded familiar; Fyodor kept thinking himself on the verge of identifying it. He recognized the trademarks of composers from all periods, from baroque to modern, so that if one were to hear only a portion of the composition one would think it derivative. But then the elements entered into dialogue with each other, contradicted and amplified each other, forcing the listener to wonder what synthesis could possibly be made of all this—not only that but to believe that the outcome mattered. Fyodor began to fear that Fritz had composed the music herself.

"My God!" he exclaimed, when at last he could speak. "Who *are* you? How is it that I have never heard of you? How is it that the world has never heard of you? Do you know you are doing what Plavitsky could never manage? What Gessini spent years attempting? No wonder you cannot find a teacher! I doubt very much that there is anyone who could teach you anything. It is incredible! But where have you performed? I don't understand how it is possible that I have never heard of you."

"I haven't performed," she said coldly. "I don't like people to listen to me play."

"You have never performed! But . . . you must overcome your stagefright and be heard! I take it as my personal duty to bring you to the attention of the world!"

Fritz had no interest in being brought to the attention of the world, but she said nothing. Unaccustomed to violent expression of emotion toward herself, she watched to see what Fyodor would do next. His praise had not flattered her, for she did not think of music as something for which she could take credit, and no one had ever extrapolated from a feeling for her playing to a feeling for herself. The discovery that this could occur introduced her to a possibility of power she had not known was hers to exercise. She wondered if this excitable young man, whose forehead glistened with sweat and whose long-fingered hands kept darting suddenly into the air like Sammy's birds trying to fly out of their cages, was falling in love with her. It happened, Sammy had told her, at first sight. Although Fritz had sometimes wondered what it felt like to fall in love, she was quite certain she was not going to do it with him.

Fyodor went on, and since he was unable to finish all that he had to say in his effort to convince her that she had no choice but to perform—it was her duty to the human race—he requested her permission to come again. Soon he was visiting every day.

They could change the world! he told her. To begin with she had—all on her own, if he was to believe her—broken through the impasse at which contemporary music had been stuck for some time now. She had simply transcended the seemingly interminable, dull, pointless debate between those who claimed music was felt by the heart and those who claimed it was apprehended by the brain. But naturally, as everyone knew, this debate was merely symbolic of the struggle going on all over the world between the forces of the emotions and the intellect, the self and the other, the individual and society, the masculine and feminine principles, good and evil, light and darkness, yin and yang, father and son, mother and daughter, father and mother, mother and son, father and daughter, friend and enemy, thesis and antithesis, law and order. ("Stuff and nonsense!" called out Sigismund. He came dribbling his basketball through the ballroom, whose acoustics, Fyodor insisted, were the best in the house. "Sorry I can't play longer, but I'm trying to break my record of getting all through the Cottage in an hour." "Don't get lost again!" Fritz shouted after him.) Could she not see the revolutionary significance of her art? he pleaded. The universe cried out for synthesis, harmony (not counterpoint), singing in unison even!

Before he met her, he went on, deciding to illustrate his point in more personal terms, he had despaired of finding a woman who was his equal. (You're not *my* equal, Fritz thought, but continued to listen in silence.) He had encountered no one with his capacity for passion; he had felt all alone in a world of wall-to-wall carpeting. "We live in a country all our own, you and I," he avowed, though it was not, he privately felt, without similarity to the country of Tolstoy, or perhaps even to the terrain explored by the great Dostoevsky (whose Christian name, after all, was his own). And her family as well, he continued, he considered exceptional. For a first mistaken moment, it was true, he had thought them merely callow to an incredible degree—too fearful of the world around them to seek a more fulfilling existence. But the obsessive nature of their interests (not to mention Fritz's own genius) had so impressed him that he had quickly changed his mind. If anything, he thought, they were like the divine idiots who had charted the far reaches of the soul and thence returned. Never had he met any group of people so transcendent to their daily lives. (Fritz's symbolic account of her incestuous parentage was a perfect case in point.) He envied them their possession of such spiritual tranquillity. He, a restless, homeless soul, had sought it all his life.

One evening, when Fyodor had come to the end of his soliloquy, and Fritz could think of nothing to reply to him, out of curiosity, out of a sort of spite, she allowed Fyodor to make love to her, although she would not let him touch her until she herself had removed the white scarf about her waist, her black dress, and her white underclothing and had folded them on a chair beside her bed.

"Ah, my Fritz," Fyodor said, "you break my heart."

The pallor of her skin was so extreme, the skin so tautly stretched over her bones, that he was almost frightened. He had known many women (though never loved any of them until now, he prided himself) and knew they considered him a skillful companion at love, but now, to his horror, he felt his excitement subsiding. Fritz's stance was so unsuggestive—she neither approached him nor seemed shy but stood without clothes as unmoved by his presence as when playing her violin—and he felt shaken by her coolness. If only she would walk toward him, or smile, but she merely stood, waiting, watching him. For a fleeting moment it crossed Fyodor's mind that she did not know what was about to happen, but the absurdity of this was too great for him to consider it seriously. However, the idea of it was not unexciting, and by keeping it in mind Fyodor succeeded in forgetting her, and when later, feeling he had possessed her, he said, "Ah, my Fritz, you are so enigmatic—I wonder if you feel anything for me at all," he was merely, he believed, employing lover's rhetoric.

He arrived the next afternoon bearing roses, but, as it turned out, did not deliver them. Sigismund, as on the first day, met him in the driveway.

"Fritz doesn't want to talk to you," he announced. "She won't come out of her room until you leave."

"I'm afraid I don't understand," Fyodor said, feeling himself turn pale. "Is she ill?"

"No," Sigismund said, "she isn't. You disgust her and she despises you. A person like you has no right to love a person like her. You are a pervert and a maniac. If you ever try to see her again, she will kill you."

Finished with his message, Sigismund stared at the young man, who seemed on the verge of doing something sudden and perhaps unusual. Sigismund did not understand what was going on at all. He watched Fyodor as he watched Fritz when they played basketball, trying to guess which way he might next dodge or feint. This was some kind of new game and he felt he might like to join in, but he was not sure he understood the rules.

This morning when he had gone upstairs to see if Fritz would come outside, she was standing in the middle of her room, her arms at her sides, looking at her violin, which was impaled over a post of her bed. He began to cry when he saw it, but she shouted furiously at him to stop. Then she told him to say those things to Fyodor and not to come back until he could promise Fyodor was gone forever.

Fyodor had no idea how long he stood in the driveway, dazed, wondering what to do. Finally he slipped into his car and drove away. Eventually the concentration required by driving restored him to at least a modicum of his usual *amour-propre*.

Mad! he exclaimed. She's mad!

Totally unprepared for life, he said to himself—as he crossed over the George Washington Bridge. The New World of perpetual childhood, inability to accept the reality of others—only in America, he said.

Investiture

At Chive University's Foreign Studies School in the nation's capital, Cyrus sat with his feet on the desks of its most renowned professors. "Call me Jack," they said, or "Smoke?" Among themselves they agreed, "He's the stuff." "He plays them close to the chest." "He'll do the distance." The clichés saved for special occasions. These were men who had played key roles in shaping the nation's intelligence, who had had (in many cases still had) access to the highest levels of classified information, men who were interrupted in the middle of lectures and taken by political limousines to *somewhere secret* to be asked their expert opinions about delicate national and international situations.

These men were short-haired and clean-shaven; their firm jaws and flawless teeth bespoke countless glasses of milk drunk by them as youngsters; their elegantly tailored suits were as similar as uniforms. To glimpse one of these men through his half-open office door—sitting at his desk, jacket hung over a chair, shirtsleeves rolled up, tie loosened—was to partake of a forbidden intimacy.

"The enigmatic Charlie Street's grandson," Cyrus's professors noted, eyebrows lifted. "A chip off the old block?"

They had not known General Street personally, but knew him by reputation, knew how, owing to his brilliance at deciphering codes and predicting enemy movements, he had leapfrogged the ranks to become one of the youngest generals ever, going on, after the war, to help organize peacetime intelligence. A hard-to-dispel mystique still surrounded General Street. No record of his existence was to be found in any of the country's archives before the moment in 1931 when he walked into an army recruitment center to enlist. (The details he supplied the officer on duty at the time did not bear up under subsequent investigation. An historian, researching a book entitled *Unknown Generals from All the Wars*, was unable to verify any of them.) Furthermore, early in 1951, Street quit the service abruptly, leaving behind him a legacy of dangling sentences. "If I had understood what the war was really about . . ." "If I had known what it was I fought for . . ."

Perhaps as a result, the faculty at Chive tried to investigate Cyrus's own background thoroughly, and they had their methods, effective if not always orthodox, of obtaining the information they wanted. They questioned those who knew Cyrus best (except for General and Mrs. Street, both of whom refused to answer any questions whatsoever). From these various points of orbit the central personality would be circumscribed.

They learned that Cyrus left Fifield Academy, the boarding school he attended, in the spring of his senior year without telling anyone where he was going and that he spent the following summer with his maternal grandmother, Sophie Street, née Laroux, estranged wife of General Street. She had not been in contact with her husband or her daughter for three decades. ("I'm only telling you this," Rose Quince said, "because it seems in Cyrus's best interest that everything be out in the open now." What did she mean by "everything"? And by "now"?)

General Street, who had lived with his daughter throughout much of Cyrus's childhood, was now a resident at the Old Generals' Home in Winston City (along with old battleaxes Eastlake, Martinson, Finch, and others). Cyrus had not been in contact with his grandfather since Street left Arborville at the end of the previous summer. Mrs. Quince said Cyrus "simply walked out of the room" whenever the subject of General Street was mentioned. "He was very angry at us about that," his father said (Mr. Quince was reached subsequently at his office). "He refused to recognize that his grandfather was becoming a burden on the household, in particular on my wife—though quite possibly the Old Generals' Home is not a good place for him; he's surrounded by other old men pursuing similar dreams of grandeur." *Dreams* of grandeur? "But there comes a point when you accept the fact that you can't take care of everyone in the universe."

Cyrus's headmaster, Jacob Turner (who continued, in civilian life, to refer to himself as "Captain," although he had hardly been a career officer), expressed astonishment at the revelation of Cyrus's kinship to General Street. "That scoundrel!" Turner exclaimed. It appeared Turner had served under Street in the last war. The general, he proclaimed—it seemed in typical exaggeration—"made the goddamn army bearable."

The faculty at Chive, though not indifferent to the high esteem in which Turner held Cyrus, were more impressed by Cyrus's evident knack for arousing devotion while revealing little about himself. (This was a talent that could prove a tremendous asset in an intelligence career.) That of his high-school roommate, for instance: William Daphne (nicknamed Billy), whom Cyrus had given as his "personal reference" on his application to Chive. (Daphne also applied to Chive but was not admitted; shortly following his high-school graduation he enlisted in the armed forces.) Billy "worshiped" Cyrus (Turner's word), and his discovery that Cyrus had, one, never told him of his younger brother (news of whose sudden death precipitated Cyrus's flight from Fifield), and, two, lied about his relationship with his grandfather, maintaining that his parents refused to divulge Street's whereabouts, left Billy "deeply embittered."

Cyrus's father, when told of his son's deception, claimed not to be surprised. Cyrus had always refused to look reality in the face. When confronted by a fact emotionally unacceptable to him, his intelligence, ordinarily highly organized, lucid, and rational, gave over to an almost somnambulistic state in which he would indulge in the most irrational behavior. Not only that, but he seemed later to feel duty-bound to stand behind whatever absurd position he had taken. "Not that I think I always handled it correctly," Mr. Quince said. "Cyrus is so bright that whenever he behaved immaturely you just wanted to shake him. It was hard to remember he was still a child. And then, Mrs. Quince and I devoted so much worry to Lark that we often forgot to worry about Betsy and Cyrus. I blame myself for not taking stronger measures. Insisting General Street live elsewhere a long time ago, or sending Cyrus away to school earlier." Mr. Quince accused General Street of fostering in Cyrus "impossibly idealistic expectations of himself and the whole world." Moreover, since Cyrus was small, Mr. Quince complained, Street had attempted to instill in his grandson a "practically Messianic sense of responsibility for the human condition—that is, encouraged him to think he could do something about the mess the world was in." What mess was that?

The faculty at Chive found this all quite intriguing. However, they did not think Cyrus's father gave him enough credit. Though they admitted it was unusual to find someone of Cyrus's young age so concerned with what, in their profession, was tantamount to "cover," they believed his obfuscations were strategic, not inadvertent. Clearly he knew that the information he concealed must eventually surface. (A parallel might be drawn to the anomalous situation of a fact registered in both highly classified and unclassified documents, as was discussed at length by C. G. Niles in his well-known *What IS a Secret? The Hows, Whys, and Wherefores of Governmental Classification*—i.e., that a secret was not a secret was not a secret.) What end such strategy might serve was not a question that occurred to them. They believed Cyrus knew what he was doing.

The faculty regarded in the same light the evasiveness with which Cyrus replied to *their* questions, particularly to those about his future. He was just playing hard-to-get—this endeared him to them. Those students who were always down on their knees before them in their eagerness to be accepted into the intelligence community did not interest the faculty. One didn't apply for induction into their classified brotherhood; one was chosen. Cyrus was a natural; he already played their sophisticated game of hide-and-seek. He had felt the call. And, quite aside from all this devotion-to-duty business, how else, in this day and age, but by gauging the limits of one's control over others was a man to find adventure? One could not, after all, run away to sea—simply roll one's belongings into a bandana and loiter about docks awaiting a likely-looking skipper. As for exploration, the world's mountains had been scaled and flags planted atop them, the jungles penetrated, the sources of the mighty rivers located. There *was* nowhere new to travel except deeper into the intricacies of the human mind. (Outer space, it was true, remained unexplored, but to date individual interplanetary adventure could be counted largely an imaginary exercise.) And it was in the country's most secret service, the faculty at Chive fondly believed, that this territory was best explored. If in fact Cyrus did harbor "scruples" about their activities, they did not doubt that these would be overcome.

They fed him tidbits of classified information to develop his appetite. "Now, Cyrus, this is what the *public* knows, but here's the story behind the story. . . ." The revered Professor H. himself took a special shine to Cyrus and invited him to register for his for-upper-classmen-only *Principles and Practice of Intelligence Gathering*. On occasion he took Cyrus with him when he went down to the tenth floor below ground of the Intelligence Archives, where the top-secret documents were stored. (The theory was: let him browse at will among forbidden facts, and he would become addicted to them and crave the companionship of other initiates.) H. casually depressed the five-digit code that had to be punched on the elevator's keyboard to direct the elevator to Negative Ten. He let Cyrus know he knew Cyrus had seen. He invited Cyrus to play tennis and to meet his wife and daughter, whom Cyrus dutifully dated. And once, when by mistake Cyrus walked into a private conference in H.'s office and, startled to see in the flesh a prominent member of government he had heretofore seen only in black-and-white, did not immediately back out, H. said, "No, stay, Cyrus. Shut the door and join us. I'd like you to hear this—you don't mind, do you?" The other opened his palms in acquiescence.

"What did you expect?" Miranda asked him.

They were sitting in the coffeeshop after H.'s class. H. had assigned them their term project: to follow an unwitting person and discover whatever they could about him or her. Cyrus had said the whole idea gave him the creeps.

"Did you think covert activity was *nice*?"

"No, but I didn't expect to be engaged in it."

"How can you be so naïve? Everyone and his twin brother knows that the Foreign Studies School is basic training for spies and diplomats."

Cyrus shrugged.

"Why did you come here, then?"

"I don't know, really. The idea was originally a joke."

"A joke!"

"Well, a dare, kind of. I used to talk to my roommate in high school about war and spying and how war now *is* just spying, and he never really believed me. He thought spying was necessary to prevent war. He said I couldn't *prove* it wasn't. Sure I could, I said. Don't ask me what I meant. How? he asked. Infiltrate, I told him. *Pretend* to be a spy but not really be one—be a kind of double agent but not for any side, just to find out what is really going on. . . .

"I basically applied here for the hell of it. I didn't actually expect to get in."

"Come on, with your connections?"

"Just because my grandfather was a general doesn't *automatically* qualify me to be here."

"It doesn't hurt."

"I don't even know about that. He didn't leave on good terms. They might just as well have decided I was 'unsuitable material.' "

"But they didn't. And I'd like to know what your secret is, if it's not your grandfather's influence."

"Influence! He's in a retirement home, totally blind, hasn't had anything to do with the army, the government, or anything connected with intelligence for over twenty years!"

"Okay, not influence, but they still know you're General Street's grandson. You've been here two months and the big H. is salivating all over you. You're saying it's just force of personality?"

"I'm not saying anything. H. is an idiot."

"He's not an *idiot*, Cyrus. You're an idiot for saying something like that. His outlook may be totally warped but that's something else. If he wasn't so intelligent, then his smooth voice and his perfectly perfect haircut wouldn't make me feel so sick to my stomach."

"I'd watch out, if I were you. You're being seduced, and pretty effectively, it seems to me."

"That's ridiculous."

Miranda looked impatient. "H. seeks you out. He admits you to this class—that *never* happens. He invites you over for dinner every other week, doesn't he?"

"It would be folly to deny it."

"He fixes you up with his daughter, Miss Finishing School herself. What's her name?"

"Tiffany."

"Tiffany, Jesus. What do you *talk* about?"

"Not much."

Miranda smirked. "What about H.? What do you talk about with him?"

"Who knows? Strategy. Freedom. The American way. My future career. For some reason people always want to organize my life."

"Why is that, Cyrus?"

"Why, because I'm so exceptional! I'm a rare specimen among young folk these days. Most of us are pleasure seekers, always after the latest thrill. I, on the other hand, know what's really at stake . . . according to him."

"At stake?"

"You know, Miranda, the survival of the free world."

"Oh, that. But what do you talk about specifically? What about when you go down to Negative Ten? What do you *see*?"

"Nothing worth writing home about."

"You won't tell me, you mean."

"There's nothing to tell."

The truth was that, despite himself, he was beginning to feel uncomfortable telling Miranda what he had heard and seen. Not that there had been anything so overwhelmingly exciting. So far he hadn't even been able to understand why the documents he had seen *were* top-secret. Or what was so confidential about the discussions he had overheard H. conducting with members of government. It was just the idea that he knew pieces of information that might be of value to someone who knew how to fit them into the big puzzle. Even though he could never go down to Negative Ten and look up whatever he wanted just because he knew the elevator code, somebody else might be able to. An enemy, to be exact. He felt as if H. had infected him—was transforming him into a leper who would have to live only among other lepers. Yet, if he was totally honest, he had to admit that sometimes he got a thrill out of knowing secrets. He actually caught himself looking at some ordinary person on the street and thinking, I'm Cyrus Quince, and I know something you don't know . . . and feeling superior. Was that sick, or what? But if he *was* that depraved, wouldn't it be more honest to admit it? Already it was tiring him out—always resisting.

What you want to do, you see, Corporal, is to let everyone else tell you who you are. Let them create a false identity for you; that's the way the best spies work. You don't have to make up a thing; everyone else will take care of that. After a while, even if you slip up and reveal your true identity, no one will believe you. That's when you know you're safe.

"You say you want to find out the truth," Miranda scoffed, "but you don't want to let anyone else in on it."

"I'm beginning to wonder if that's possible—I mean, to find it. How do you sort out all the information?"

"You sound like them," she taunted. "You're getting that same patronizing tone. 'I'm afraid, my dear, that the situation is simply much too complex for you to judge.' "

"Cut it out, will you? You know I'm on your side."

But was he?

Cyrus had met Miranda in H.'s class and immediately admired her spunk. She was the only student who dared to disagree with H. His supercilious remarks tidily vanquished most students, but Miranda would not back down if she believed she was right.

She was a sophomore and, she insisted, the Foreign Studies Schools's only radical. She had been in Paris in '68. That she was fourteen at the time was irrelevant. Her fellow students were persuaded, though the faculty weren't. Her father, a career officer in the foreign service, had pushed Miranda to apply to Chive, and they thought her rebellion was directed against him and would be outgrown.

Although Cyrus had wanted to get to know her right away, she, having observed the red-carpet treatment he received from H. and some other faculty members, rebuffed his approaches. When she discovered—via the grapevine (it was against his principles to trade on his grandfather's reputation)—that he was the grandson of General Street, who had the cachet of black sheep, she seemed to decide it might be useful to become acquainted with him after all.

They began to be friends. Miranda had two constant companions. Erik, her nominal boyfriend, who had dropped out of Chive after his first year to pursue his love of theater, and—to Miranda's dismay—of his own sex; Julian, another sophomore, who intended one day to study international law, and who had no interest in Miranda's politics but listened to her lectures because he had fallen in love with her (then Erik fell in love with him).

Cyrus was relieved that Miranda had no romantic interest in him; he still felt very confused about Sarah, whom he missed—terribly, at first, sometimes saying her name aloud as he lay in the uncomfortable regulation bed in his narrow dormitory room, especially after he had waked himself up in the middle of the night with his own shouting, and lay, sweating, his body burning wherever the inquisitor had put out his cigarette. He would switch on the light beside his bed and lie motionless, staring at the ceiling. At these times he imagined Sarah so vividly he almost could feel her lying beside him, and he would decide to leave Chive—just walk away as he had from Fifield, take a train to Winston, and tell her he couldn't stand it. He wanted to *be* with her, that was all. But they had agreed it couldn't work out after the summer. He was only eighteen, Sarah had said; he was just beginning college; he didn't want to be tied down to one person at this point. How did *she* know what he wanted? He didn't argue with her, though, because he thought she herself wanted to be free of the relationship and gave these reasons as excuses.

They had also agreed to write, but Cyrus had not written. He found it too painful, and anyway she didn't write him. Probably better that way. It wasn't that he stopped missing her, but after a while he just got used to her absence. (He had had a lot of practice.)

One day, while attempting to straighten up the incredible disorder into which his room had fallen, he came across the book Sophie had given him. For the first time he took a good look at it. It was an architectural guidebook to New Jersey homes, published around the turn of the century. When he had examined it in Newbridge, he could not imagine what importance it could have held for his grandfather. He had kept it in order not to hurt Sophie's feelings. But now—probably just owing to the atmosphere of secrecy at the Foreign School—he was less inclined to dismiss it. He visited filling stations in the vicinity of Chive until he found one that had a road map of New Jersey. That evening at dinner, he asked Miranda if he could borrow her car for the weekend.

"Where do you want to go?" she demanded.

"I'm afraid I can't tell you. It's a secret mission."

"I'll bet."

He laid his hand across his heart. "It's highly classified. Even my family isn't allowed to know. But trust me. I have our best interests at heart."

"Our?"

Cyrus assumed H.'s most dismissive tone. "That's rhetoric, my dear Miranda, in case you didn't know."

"Oh," she said, "I *should* know by now."

Cyrus never did tell Miranda precisely where he went that weekend. Of the first three houses pictured in the guidebook, the first was no longer standing; the second was a private insane asylum; the third was standing, but barely, and signs reading "DANGER—KEEP OUT" were tacked to its boarded-up windows. The fourth house—an enormous, incredibly strange-looking place, but which for some reason Cyrus liked the looks of—was not only standing but appeared to be occupied. Upon presenting the guidebook to the tall, elegantly attired elderly lady who answered the door, Cyrus was admitted into the house.

"That book was Tad's," she said. She didn't seem curious as to how Cyrus had come into possession of it. "Who's Tad?" Cyrus asked. Yet even before the lady—Xy Ludwicker—identified him as Dagobert Ludwicker, an older brother who had disappeared forty years ago, and presented Cyrus with a picture, Cyrus had a pretty good idea who Tad was. The photograph, Xy said, had been taken shortly before he disappeared. It was a photograph of the two of them, and Xy sat on her brother's lap in a starlet's pose: her arms were around his neck and she was gazing longingly up into his face. He, however, looked directly at the camera, or, as then, at the viewer, and as Cyrus stared back into young Tad Ludwicker's eyes, he felt as if he were going deaf. His ears filled with the sound of a wave rolling in to shore, building and building with the expectation of release, until he thought he was going to explode, but the wave did not break. The sly grin, the mischievous glance, the slightly asymmetrical features . . . none of these had changed with age and Cyrus immediately recognized Charles.

Xy was watching his face. "What is it? Do you know him? Where is he? Is he . . . alive?"

"Alive?" Cyrus repeated. "I . . . I have no idea. I've never seen this person before." It was the first thing that came to mind to say. He had spoken from instinct. *Cover yourself, stall for time, put the burden of proof on whoever suspects you.* Later, of course, he explained his reaction to himself in various ways. Until he could figure out why his grandfather had kept his original family secret, what point was there in telling anyone else what he had discovered? Particularly Xy Ludwicker or Sophie. They were both old; such information could upset them for no good reason. Maybe Tad wasn't even Charles after all; there could be some other explanation for the similarity. A twin brother given up for adoption in infancy. Some other bizarre coincidence. It was too crazy, and the longer he looked at the picture the less marked seemed the resemblance. Furthermore, at that moment Fritz appeared, and it didn't take long for Cyrus to realize that, since he had not spoken immediately, to suggest some clandestine connection between Charles and Dagobert would only make Fritz, whom he understood to be a kind of adopted daughter, or ward, of the three elderly Ludwickers, more suspicious of him than she was already. She was the kind of person who would be furious if she thought anyone was keeping a secret from her, even for a minute. And he didn't want her to be furious; he wanted her to fall in love with him—as precipitately as he had done with her, despite the fact that through the whole of that first afternoon she sat stiffly on a sofa, glaring, never addressing a single word to him.

Cyrus returned the next weekend and then the next (hitchhiking from the railroad station in Demetria)—driving Miranda and Erik and Julian wild with curiosity—and suddenly he was happy. He had forgotten what it felt like: to be happy. It wasn't the same as with Sarah. For one thing, Fritz wasn't involved with someone else, from whom their relationship had to be concealed. (Even though he drew out the mystery for the benefit of his friends at Chive, Cyrus fully intended to bring Fritz back to Washington one day with him for a visit.) But, besides that, Fritz was different from Sarah. She didn't hide her reactions; he always knew right away whatever she was feeling, and her straightforwardness was a tremendous relief to him. He began to trust her and was able, for the first time, to talk about Lark. (Fritz cried when he told her.) He also told her about Charles—not who he was (though he meant to tell her that soon; together they would figure out what to do about it), but how much he had cared about his grandfather when he was little and then, as he got older, how his grandfather seemed less and less admirable; all he did was complain about the world. "If the country would listen to me, I'd have things straightened out in half an hour!" he shouted, stupid things like that, but taking himself seriously, whereas he used to be joking. Cyrus grew embarrassed to invite friends over; his grandfather would always butt in and begin ranting and raving.

In general, Cyrus grew less reserved; he took Chive, H., and their claims upon him less seriously. He even thought about inviting Miranda and Erik and Julian up to the Cottage with him one weekend—he'd love to observe their reactions when they saw the place and met the Ludwickers. Around this time Sarah wrote to him, confessing that she was in love with him and expressing her desire to see him, but, not knowing what to do about this, he wound up not doing anything.

One evening when he and Fritz were lying in bed, snuggling together, chatting about this and that, she said, "Cyrus, there's something I have to tell you. I haven't been telling you the truth."

"About what?"

She spoke in her usual matter-of-fact tone, and he expected that she was setting him up for something—a joke, an endearment.

"I'm not really adopted," she said.

Startled, he drew back to see her face. "What do you mean, you're not really adopted?"

"I'm not adopted." She avoided his gaze. "Xy really is my mother; Sammy really is my aunt and George my uncle. I don't just *call* them that."

"But . . ." He tried to picture the family tree. If Xy was her mother and Tad was Xy's brother and he was Tad's grandson— if he *was* Tad's grandson—they were some kind of cousins, weren't they? Second cousins? Cousins-once-removed? "Why didn't you tell me in the beginning?" he asked, puzzled. (He didn't suppose it was a tragedy, though.)

"Because Xy and Tad . . . Because Tad is my father." Her voice was so low he could barely hear her.

"*What* did you say?" he shouted.

"Tad's my father. You heard me."

"Then you mean he's not really your mother's brother? Why does she pretend he is?" Yet, even as he said this, Cyrus had the sensation that it was no longer he who spoke. Merely his voice, reciting someone else's lines. Lose a cousin, gain an aunt, he thought, with sudden, hysterical levity. His *aunt*? What did that *mean*? Was this incest then? Could it be incest if you didn't know the person first? Was it against the law? This possibility seemed so ludicrous that he nearly laughed aloud. His hand lay on Fritz's arm; he stroked her bare arm, moved his hand back up and touched her breast. I'm touching my aunt's breast, he thought. Fritz inadvertently sighed, but drew away from him.

"You don't understand what I'm saying, Cyrus. He *is* her brother."

"Who's whose brother?"

She sighed again, this time from exasperation. "Tad is Xy's brother. Xy is Tad's sister. Xy is my mother. Tad is my father. Now do you understand? And why I didn't tell you?"

She raised herself to look at him. This time he wished he could avoid *her* eyes. He nodded dumbly, trying to pull her back into his arms, but she resisted.

"I never thought anything was wrong with it. I thought it was normal. For a long time, when I was little, I thought you could have children only with your brother. I was resigned to never having any. I understood that that wasn't so after a while, but I still didn't know there was anything wrong with a brother and sister . . ." She paused. Her voice, when she continued, sounded bitter. "Fyodor told me. He told me the name of it: incest. It's against the law to marry people you're close to. It's one of the most shameful things there is. They can put you in jail for it." Tears stood in her eyes. "Do you hate me, Cyrus? Do you think I'm evil too?"

Mutely, he shook his head. She looked at him searchingly. "Yes, you do! You do hate me! You're just like Fyodor!"

"Fritz, I'm not like Fyodor." He closed his eyes.

"Why won't you look at me, then? If you're not ashamed?"

Why wouldn't he look at her then? How could he look at her? What could he say? He couldn't tell her now who *he* was.

"You don't love me anymore," she said coldly.

"No, Fritz . . ." He forced himself to open his eyes. Looking straight into hers, even smiling, he said, "That's not it at all. I just feel bad for you. But I don't think you're evil—why would I think *you're* evil? If anyone is evil . . ."

Finally believing him, she slipped back into his arms; as they made love again, Cyrus commenced the process of burying all thought of what he now knew. There was never any doubt in his mind that if he told her who he was—who *she* was—he would lose her. And it wasn't so bad, after a while. This new untold knowledge simply dissolved into everything else he had not told people. He had not told Billy about Lark or his grandfather. He had not told Sarah about Lark, about his grandparents' long estrangement, or about the fact that his grandfather happened to live only a few blocks from her apartment. He had not told Sophie that Charles was in Winston or that the book she had given him had led him anywhere, let alone where it had led him. He had told Miranda and Erik and Julian next to nothing about Fritz, wanting to surprise them with the Cottage. Now he certainly wouldn't tell them anything.

After a brief vacation from subterfuge, Cyrus went back underground. This time he stayed there.

The news from the field grew worse and worse. His Excellency the Special-Ambassador-at-Large-in-Times-of-Crisis had been called in to Acting Headquarters by his superiors.

"Now's the time," they said. "Go out there and knock 'em dead."

"Knock who dead?" he inquired.

They smiled, acknowledging his sense of humor. "Ambassador, you know the situation. The troops are in the trenches, ready for battle. But where's the battle?

"There have been a few desertions—not many, but enough to concern us. An officer belonging to a regiment in the 29th Division has gone AWOL. As we said, enough. Indications of more problems ahead."

"But what do you want me to do? My job is to negotiate with an enemy, not manufacture one."

"This is a special situation, Ambassador. If it's helpful, you might consider the troops' suspicion of us as the enemy. Their concept of war is very old-fashioned. Look at them! In trenches, in biplanes, in phantom jets . . . It's enough to make you cry, their childlike faith in these things. Yet if we don't keep them occupied . . ."

"I see."

"Excellent," they said. "We knew you would."

Throughout his long diplomatic career, the ambassador had learned that the best way to get two opposed parties to agree upon a point was to convince each that he wanted what the other wanted. It was a long, delicate process, he informed people who asked how he went about it: interminable questions to be posed, opinions sounded, positions stated and restated. But what happened was nothing logical. Time after time the ambassador had seen how, although at first the party of the first part said he would accept only such-and-such a solution and the party of the second part said he would accept only a solution opposite in every particular, over the course of time, the party of the first part and the party of the second part grew so familiar to each other that each began to confuse the other's position with his own. With the ambassador's gentle coaxing and rephrasing, it eventually appeared to them that they had been in agreement all along. They shook hands, the best of friends.

The ambassador had then often been asked, Of what use was he in the process? Was not the course of time the true resolver of differences?

No, it was not, he had always replied, and for this reason: although his role *during* negotiations was insignificant—a tape recorder could produce the same effect—it was at their conclusion that his presence was vital. For then the two leaders had to be able to explain to their respective constituencies how it was that they now agreed when previously they had not agreed at all. The ambassador saved them from the embarrassment of having to admit they had misunderstood one another. They could blame it all on him. "It was *his* fault!" they could say. "*He* misrepresented everything!"

"How fascinating, Your Excellency!" people said to him. What he was saying, in effect, was that he was a sort of sponge, soaking up the miasma of distrust between antagonistic persons, unencumbering them, enabling them to trust one another? Though wouldn't one fear letting the wrong thing slip? Indeed, after a time he *himself* must hardly trust anyone at all! No? Well, a noble calling, to be sure.

Yes, how noble I am! he would think, feeling proud and honored. His life was being spent in a good cause, and how many people were able to say that?

"Just one thing," the ambassador said, as he turned to leave the room.

"Yes, what is it?"

"This is the last time I do this."

It was November 26, Cyrus's twenty-third birthday. Four years had passed since his first visit to the Cottage, and by now he was an accepted member of the Ludwicker household. While at Chive, he spent many weekends and most vacations with them, driving back and forth between Washington and New Jersey in the car given to him at the beginning of his sophomore year by Sammy (she donned overalls and repaired it when it broke down). He visited Sophie occasionally, his parents never. He had last seen them at his graduation from Chive the previous June.

Betsy had gone to college in California; she visited him several times at Chive. The last time they argued violently, at first about politics—he said she was naïve; she said he was cynical. (Secretly he envied her belief in the value of the work she did; "lettuce strikers" her kind were called at Chive—those who bothered to involve themselves in ephemeral, "local" issues.) The argument went on to involve more personal things. She accused him of cruelty for never visiting or writing to Granddad or going to Arborville; he suggested she mind her own business. He had no feelings for others, she said; just because Granddad got on his nerves, he had no right to blot him out of his life. He told her to bug off—she didn't know what she was talking about. Enraged, Betsy said she was disowning him as her brother, he was turning into such a lousy human being. Please yourself, he said. They hadn't written after that.

At the end of Cyrus's junior year, Miranda and Julian had graduated from Chive and with Erik departed for Winston, where they metamorphosed into the Campers and took up vagrancy as a way of life. They recruited Karen, Suzanne, Rudy, and Gillian, with whom, offhandedly, the spring of his senior year, Cyrus began an affair.

All of the Campers, Gillian included, knew of Fritz but had never met her. They knew she lived in New Jersey (he had met her through relatives, he said), played the violin excellently, had dark red hair, and didn't like to go anywhere. (She was too busy, Cyrus explained vaguely.) She always beat him at tennis, was several years older than he (this contributed to their exotic picture of her), couldn't cook—she lived with her mother, an aunt, and an uncle, and her aunt did all the cooking. They gathered that she was rich and that she gave Cyrus whatever he wanted. Supported him, in fact. Never once had he worked at a summer job. H. and other faculty members offered him various internships but he turned up his nose at them. Now that the Campers had to scramble for money, they resented the easiness of Cyrus's life.

He had remained more candid with Miranda than with the others, but even to her, when she hectored him at least to tell her what was so wonderful about Fritz to keep him devoted for so long (if not her money), he would say merely, "We just get along, that's all." "She makes no demands on you, you mean," Miranda retorted. "I bet if she knew how you manage to entertain yourself when you're not with her she wouldn't be so easygoing." "It has nothing to do with her." "Harmless fun, right?" "Well, more or less."

Without having had to work very hard, Cyrus had maintained

a high academic standing at Chive, graduating near the top of his class, and had had several job offers—though none as splendid as the Campers (or he himself, though he wouldn't admit this to anyone) had expected. H.'s ardor had cooled during Cyrus's senior year. He had tired, finally, of having to cajole Cyrus. He had gone to great lengths to encourage him and met only coyness. To hell with him, he thought. Cyrus was too old to have to be sweet-talked like a virgin into bed—he knew where his bread was buttered. Let him *ask* for something for a change. Since his graduation, Cyrus had divided his time between Winston City and the Cottage. When Miranda inquired if he wasn't growing bored, living the good life, he replied that he was waiting for inspiration to strike.

Cyrus had driven down from Winston that afternoon for his birthday, and tonight the Ludwickers were giving him a party. Dressed up, Xilipheupia in velvet and diamonds, Sigismund in a black turtleneck with the number sixty-four sewn on it in many-colored sequins (his present to himself on his last birthday), Constantina in a gold pantsuit, her hair dyed a new shade, entered the sitting room. They greeted one another with the effusive formality of people who had not seen each other in years.

Cyrus and Fritz, on the couch, Cyrus sitting, Fritz reclining, her legs angled over Cyrus's knees, exchanged a look, what Xilipheupia called the "Dagobert smirk."

"Happy birthday," Fritz said, drawing him down to give him a kiss. When he sat up, she curled her feet beneath her, snuggled against him, and laid her head on his shoulder.

"Yes, hasn't the weather been glorious lately?" Sammy said. "Do have some of this." She squirted cheese out of a can onto a cracker. "You bend the nozzle, you see, like this, George." He, juggling three tennis balls, did not answer. Sammy poked the cracker into his mouth.

"Thanks," Cyrus said to Fritz. "Actually, Sam, it's been pouring all day and it's as cold as Alaska."

"Alaska," Sammy said thoughtfully. "Where they live in snow houses and eat blubber. I never believed that, did you?"

"Sure, I believe it. But then I'd believe anything—I'm very gullible."

"Gullible," Sammy repeated. "I see—gullible."

"Now that you are twenty-three," Fritz whispered, "does this mean you have attained full maturity?"

"Mmm," Cyrus replied, his mouth full. "Wait and see."

"Only if I have to."

"You have to," he said, pulling a lock of her hair. "There are others at this party besides ourselves."

"Happy birthday, Cyrus," Xilipheupia addressed him solemnly. "I do hope there may be very many more."

"Thank you very much, Xy. I hope there will be too."

Fritz sat back and regarded him indulgently. "Will you look at him, Mother?" she demanded. "He is so smug. He looks like he swallowed a cat."

"What cat?" Sigismund asked, ceasing to juggle. "What cat, and, moreover, what is the subject under discussion?"

"Sometimes I think he's only after the throne," Fritz teased. "Sometimes I don't think he cares about us at all."

"She's being provocative," Cyrus remarked to Xy. "Don't be provoked."

At this exchange, Xy looked anxious. Sometimes she felt the implications of Fritz and Cyrus's talk flitting about her mind like hummingbirds, never setting down.

"When you curl your lip like that, darling," she said to Fritz, "I see Tad all over again. It's not only in your expressions, it's in how you walk, in certain tones of voice. . . . It must be true that blood is thicker than water—royal blood, at least." She sighed. "I wish I might see him, just once, before I die."

"Maybe you will," Cyrus remarked.

"Why do you say that?" Fritz asked, startled.

"No particular reason."

"You've never said it before."

"Come on, Fritz . . . Why don't you sit down, Xy?"

Xy sat, so did George, and Sammy came over from the bar with a tray of drinks.

"This punch is something new," she said. "I got the recipe from *Elegant Eating*. See if you can guess what's in it."

"I don't see that I said anything wrong, Cyrus," Fritz said, miffed. She scuttled away from him and picked up her metronome from the coffee table. She placed it on her lap as if it were a pet and set it ticking.

He sighed. Xy regarded them uneasily. Armies were creeping up to the borders, but as yet she did not know their strength or where they came from.

"Have you been enjoying yourself out in the world, Cyrus?" Sammy asked. "You've been gone a long time."

"I have," he said. "Unfortunately it looks like I'm going to have to go back tomorrow."

"Tomorrow!" Fritz exclaimed.

"I didn't get a chance to tell you . . ."

She simply stared at him, hurt. The others did as well.

"Something came up."

"What came up?" Sammy inquired.

"Something I have to do."

Fritz now watched him silently.

"Why can't you do it here?" Sammy asked, bewildered. "If there are things you need, they can always be ordered."

"Sam, have mercy . . ."

"I received some wonderful new catalogues while you were gone," she continued eagerly. She searched through stacks on a table.

"Don't bother, Sammy," Fritz said icily. "He just wants to be back with his *real* friends in Winston."

"I wish I had some real friends. I could use some."

"Perhaps I could use some as well."

"Perhaps I could too," said George.

Fritz, after staring at Cyrus another moment, suddenly pushed the metronome off her lap and ran from the room. Soon antagonistic wails began to slither into the room from above and roil about the ceiling like vapors.

Cyrus sighed again. "I'm sorry. I didn't mean to spoil the festivities."

"I think she's upset because you're going away so soon," George said.

"I think so."

"The last time you left she cried for days. She didn't think you were ever coming back."

"She plays everything in the top octaves when you're not here," said Sammy. "We have to wear our earplugs all the time."

"She wouldn't play at *all* with me. Not even basketball, and that's her favorite."

Xy, remembering that day years ago when Tad had also been taken by an incomprehensible, inexplicable urge to depart, asked, "Are you going to war, Cyrus? That's what Tad did. He said there was always a war going on somewhere. You could just find one and go to it."

"Fancy that."

"In war you wear a uniform," George remarked, "like sports. But you don't have a big number on it."

"George . . ." Xy protested.

"What?" he asked. "Just what?"

"War is not the same as sports. Don't you know anything?"

"Ten points, Xili." Cyrus laughed.

Xy looked mystified yet not displeased.

"What did she do that she gets ten points?" George asked furiously. "It isn't fair. I don't even know what we're playing!"

"All's fair in love and war," Sammy said. She had returned to the sofa with her arms full of catalogues, and sat down beside Cyrus. "I learned that in *Quimby's Quotable Quotes*."

"Cyrus has never liked to play by *our* rules," George said gloomily. "He always makes Fritz and me play *his* way."

"Come on, George. Will you stop giving me a hard time?"

"He always tells Fritz and me we're crazy, to play the way we do." There were tears in George's eyes.

"Crybaby!" Sammy said. She opened a catalogue. "Let me just

show you a few things." She riffled the pages. "Here, look at this! Windshield wipers for your eyeglasses—there's a little battery you wear behind your ear, now isn't that a good idea? And here—a circulating vase, like a fishtank; it keeps the water running through a filter and flowers last up to twenty-four hours longer! And here's a reminder diary that lists all the things the average person needs to do in a day, everything from getting out of bed to eating lunch to brushing your teeth—it's all here. Now what do you have to say, Cyrus?"

"Pretty nifty stuff, Sam. You going to send for it?" He closed his eyes, letting his head fall back against the sofa. If he could just stay like that . . . He stood up.

"I'm going to go see what Fritz is up to. I don't hear her playing anymore."

He found her in her room, lying face down on her bed, a pillow held over her head. He could hear her stifled sobs as he shut the door. For a moment he stood watching her; he felt bad, yet he also felt remote. What good would it do to comfort her, apologize, promise to return very soon? They had been reenacting this same scene for months. She cried that he no longer loved her; he insisted that that wasn't the problem. She wouldn't leave the Cottage; he refused to spend all his time there—what hope was there for them?

Meanwhile Fritz was crying, lying on her bed crying. It broke through to him temporarily and he went to sit beside her. Laying a hand on her back, he said, "I'm sorry. I shouldn't have sprung the news on you like that."

"Please leave me alone," she mumbled.

"Don't, Fritz. I said I was sorry."

She turned onto her side; her face was tear-stained. "It's not that you're going again, Cyrus, that's not it. It's you. You're not the same. Ever since you finished going to Chive . . . Can't you go back there?"

"I graduated!"

"But you said they wanted you to stay. If you stayed, then we would be happy again."

"Fritz . . ."

"Do you love someone else?" she asked in a small voice.

"No." That at least *was* true.

"Then what's wrong with you? Why are you so unhappy?"

Suddenly Cyrus remembered something. He was sitting on the front steps in Arborville—it was before Lark was born. He had gone outside to be alone. He had done something wrong—he couldn't now remember what—but had gotten in trouble because he had lied about it. Charles followed him outside. He had heard from Rose what had happened and was very angry. It was the only time Cyrus remembered his grandfather *being* angry with him, in fact. "Promise me you'll never lie anymore, Cyrus," he said. "The most important thing in the world is always to tell the truth to the people you love. If you lose that, you lose everything. Will you promise me never to do it again?" Cyrus had promised.

The funny thing was, he vividly remembered how he had silently added a contingency clause to that contract: *I'll never lie to you.*

"Fritz, listen," he said eagerly, "why don't you come with me? Just this once. Then if you don't like it, for whatever reason, I promise not to ask you anymore."

She shook her head.

"But, Fritz, I'd be with you! I wouldn't leave you for a minute! Why won't you even go once? It's not fair."

"I can't, Cyrus!"

"But Fritz, no one *knows*."

Fritz morbidly fancied that people would fathom her dark secret at one glance. She refused to believe Cyrus's reassurances to the contrary. He was tempted to tell her he sometimes doubted if most people would even be all that shocked. They'd probably be fascinated. They thought incest was something that happened in movies from France. Sometimes he couldn't take it seriously himself. Incest—what was that besides a word? He'd once looked it up in the dictionary:

The crime of sexual intercourse or cohabitation between persons related within the degrees within which marriage is prohibited by law. *Spiritual* (in R. C. Ch.): Marriage or sexual connection between persons related by spiritual affinity . . .

But what did that mean, really? Wasn't the incest taboo invented by royal families to keep themselves from dying out because of hemophilia? They needed fresh blood.

"Sometimes I think that's just your excuse. You say you love me, but you're not even willing to go out in the world with me. If you won't even try, I guess then I *don't* see how we can stay together. I can't stay here the rest of my life."

"Like us, you mean."

Cyrus didn't answer this.

"All right, then," Fritz said abruptly, "I'll go."

"What?"

"I'll go! That's what you want. I'll go with you tomorrow. But I can tell you now no good will come of it."

When it hit him that she had actually said yes, he had the horrible feeling she was right.

She didn't accompany him in the morning, however; he said it would be better to wait until the next time; this visit would be too rushed. She seemed relieved—he knew he was.

Stopping for gas halfway to Winston, he reread the letter he had received the day before on his way out of town. It had been forwarded to his Winston post office box from Arborville.

My dear Cyrus:

I am only too aware that you may think my writing to you an old fogey's sentimentality, and if you do and choose not to reply, I will accept your decision. I know it is not considered smart, or cool, or whatever you past-disregarding, tradition-trampling young folk say these days (not that I'd necessarily group you with the multitude) to attempt to retrieve lost connections; it's the fashion now to forge ahead, to "profit from" relationships and do better in the future. (An alarming trend, though I'll spare you my socio-

political analysis of the phenomenon. Do I hear you saying, "Thank God"?) To me, though, people aren't ciphers, one replaceable with another. Often, over the past years, I've found myself thinking about you, wondering how you were getting on, and now, calculating that you've finished at Chive and are at last embarking upon "real life," it seems an opportune moment to find out what you're up to.

As for what I'm up to . . . The year you were at Fifield was one of turmoil for me. What everyone in the whole school, I expect, knew before I admitted it was that I had fallen in love with Agnes Richmond—Mother Agnes, as she was then. (She chose to retain Agnes instead of reverting to Kelly, a decision I heartily applauded.) The ensuing complications, I daresay, are obvious. To abbreviate an interminable tale: it ended happily. We have been married for three years and for the past two have been living in an apartment in Winston City. Agnes decided to go for her doctorate at Winston State, and she's now in the final throes of writing her thesis.

I, on the other hand, have been occupied more ignominiously, though at present I am managing a bookstore, the least distasteful of the numerous employments I've attempted since resigning my post at Fifield. I continue to work with my dogs on the weekends at a kennel owned by friends, and my fondest dream is of moving back to the country to pursue that work full-time.

But the best news of all: last September I became a father. We had a girl, Lilith Richmond-Turner, who is truly the joy of our lives.

So these are the highlights, as the newscasters say. What about you, my friend? Are you about to launch upon a brilliant career in the Diplomatic Corps? Will we read your name in the papers before long? I'd love to know.

I have lost touch with nearly everyone from my "former" life, but I can't tell you how much pleasure it would give me to hear from you again.

Yours in friendship,
Jacob Turner

At the foot of the page, he had written his address and telephone number.

Cyrus stood in the bare, frozen garden behind 9 Ives Crescent and yanked the cord that hung down through the ivy. Above he heard the muted tinkling of the bell. Julian stuck his head out a third-story window. "Ahoy, there!" he called. A rope ladder tumbled down. So ridiculous, Cyrus thought. The stairs within were intact, but the rope ladder made the Campers feel more like fugitives.

"Long time no see," Julian said, as Cyrus climbed in over the windowsill.

"Right."

"Cyrus?" queried Miranda. She came into the large, unfurnished room they kept empty for exercising. "What gives? You have a fight with your true love?"

"No, just some unfinished business to attend to."

"More secret missions." Miranda rolled her eyes.

"Nothing so exciting."

"Well, come in. Stop standing on ceremony."

They migrated into the next room, where Karen, Suzanne, Rudy, and Gillian sat on the floor in a semicircle around a kerosene heater. They were playing poker. "Cyrus!" they chorused.

"At ease, at ease." He dismissed them with a salute.

To Gillian, who rose to embrace him, he gave a tangential kiss.

"I thought you were going to be gone several weeks!"

"So did I," he said, laughing. He ignored her questioning look.

Erik, having heard the commotion, arrived from downstairs, wearing a sheepskin-lined aviator's helmet, a baggy tweed overcoat, and gloves. He was deep in the midst of writing a play.

"How the hell can you type?" Cyrus asked.

"I'm not typing. I'm talking into a tape recorder. What are you doing here?"

"I'm beginning to wonder. You pay a friendly visit, and everybody thinks you have ulterior motives."

"We don't have to think; we know you have them. I sometimes think they're the only kind you do have."

"Very amusing."

" 'Very amusing,' " Erik minced. "Doesn't he sound peeved?"

"Give me a break. I just got here." Not that this ever made much difference to the Campers. They weren't big on preliminaries.

"What's the trouble, Erik?" Julian asked. "Creative juices not flowing?"

"Not even oozing, dear heart. Wretched characters."

"How are they misbehaving?"

"Turning into you and Miranda, that's what."

Erik removed his gloves and coat and tossed them into a corner, then wedged his way close to the heater.

"I thought that was your intention," Cyrus said.

"Us in the abstract, not us in ourselves," Miranda said. "It's supposed to expound Camper philosophy."

"Whatever that may be."

"Oh, Cyrus, you know perfectly well."

"I know what you *say*. You've been talking about it since you moved to Winston. As far as I can see, though, your 'philosophy' is just a rationale for not getting jobs."

"Look who's talking."

"But I don't have a rationale. I'm just not doing anything, pure and simple."

"And that makes you superior to us?"

"I didn't say that."

"It makes him pure and simple," Erik said.

All laughed, including Cyrus.

"Why don't you play the section you wrote yesterday, Erik?" Miranda asked. "Erik wrote a wonderful speech—if it doesn't convince you our intentions are serious, nothing will. Please, Erik?"

Erik groaned, but he went downstairs to fetch his tape recorder. Cyrus lounged against a windowsill; Gillian curled on a mattress beside him. (Mattresses supplied the only furniture in the room.)

"Okay, all you theater buffs," Erik said. "Assume a properly awestruck pose." He set the recorder in the center of the room and depressed the "Play" button. While he, feigning boredom, went to look out a window, his voice began, almost chanting.

> *Yes, everywhere we will establish residence in abandoned areas, in the bombed-out sectors of contemporary consciousness, in the ghost towns of the nuclear soul. In secrecy and stealth we will multiply our number. We will swell to a world-wide, continually relocating population, all personal and international boundaries dissolved. Anywhere at all will be home because everyone will camp and Campers will recognize each other at first glance; we will achieve the kind of solidarity experienced by persecuted religious sects in former times. . . .*

"Ah, persecuted, yes, one must be persecuted," Erik interrupted his voice, but he was shushed.

> *. . . And then one day our number will be so great that, if we all take a deep breath and blow, the old society will float away from us like a dried-up dandelion. . . .*

Erik strode across the room and switched off the recorder. The Campers applauded.

"That's so beautiful, Erik," said Miranda proudly.

"A lot of pompous blither, in my opinion," he answered.

Cyrus remained silent. He still wondered what it all meant, but he was surprised to hear Erik sounding so sincere, and felt uncomfortable saying anything. But Miranda was looking at him expectantly.

He shrugged. "It sounds good. I still don't see how you're going to make this dream come true. I mean, just for once, I'd like to hear a specific plan of action."

"Oh, you're so goddamn smug!" she exclaimed angrily. "It's easy enough to sit on your high horse and look down on the folly of any effort to change the status quo. We may be hopeless idealists, but at least we put ourselves on the line."

"I'm not trying to be smug. I just want to know what you're

going to *do*. You have all these grand ideas, but I have yet to hear how you're going to put them to work."

"A belief isn't invalid simply because you can't put it into practice," Julian remarked.

"In my opinion, it is," said Cyrus. "It's empty words, otherwise. Just something to make yourself feel better. If everyone who has so much to say about the great crisis the world is in actually had done something about it instead of sitting around discussing it, something might have been accomplished."

"But, Cyrus," Miranda protested, "you have to change people's consciousness before you can change the world."

"Okay, how are you going to do that?"

"*Talk* to them, first. Explain to them what you believe and why. If that doesn't work . . ." She shrugged. "Then use more violent means. Anything in order to convince people that the old way of thinking about things, the every-man-for-himself and all that, is what's responsible for the mess the world is in today."

"I don't believe people could ever stop thinking about themselves first. I think it's naïve to think they could."

"Look, Cyrus, the reason people think about themselves first is because they're scared not to. They're afraid if they don't look out for themselves someone else will get the better of them. But that's just because they believe the great Dream is still attainable. Can't you see how tyrannical this ideal—this Home Sweet Home with the perfectly happy family in it—has become? What a sense of failure people feel when they don't achieve it? But, instead of realizing that it's the system itself that's responsible for their failure, they blame themselves for it."

"Maybe they should."

"I can't believe you're saying that, Cyrus!" Miranda exclaimed. "I guess I knew you'd been getting more conservative, but I didn't realize you were already ossifying! And you're the same person who used to sit around at Chive talking so anti-establishment, but you were really just playing one side off against the other, weren't you? Agreeing with me and meanwhile getting more involved with the Department. I guess I'm glad that at least you're finally showing your true colors!"

"All I'm really saying, Miranda, is that the more you find out about things, the harder it is to have clear-cut ideas about them."

"That's just evading the issue."

"It isn't, it *is* the issue. You make it sound as if some group of Machiavellian government officials sat around one day and plotted everything."

"Plots don't have to be talked about or written up on some drawing board to exist, Cyrus. There are always these forces at work. We have to fight them, that's all. We have to convince people that it's our distrust of one another that's at the root of what's wrong."

"Maybe it's well-founded," Cyrus remarked.

"No—that's the plot."

The plot, he thought. Like supermarket tabloids, always uncovering hidden connections, seamy secrets. *Hitler didn't die in Berlin after all but escaped and is building a new army. Queen Elizabeth the First did have children who will soon rise up to reclaim the British throne. Man in Peoria, Illinois, claims to be King Arthur reincarnated . . .* As if these things would really mean anything if they were true. The irony was that not only Miranda but the entire intelligence community thought this way, with its billions of top-secret documents—always trying to discover the *big secret that would explain everything.* At Chive you were taught to believe that the apparent reasons things happened were never the true reasons. Nothing was what it seemed; appearances were deceiving; the only thing to fear was fear itself; there was no enemy like the enemy within . . . . well, not that they were all the same thing. But there was no escaping it. Either you imagined that some secret knowledge (which, if you could once discover it, would enable you to rule the world— or, at least, fix everything that was wrong with it) was held by a foreign government or by subversive elements within your own population, and *they* were the enemy; or it was withheld by your own government and *it* was the enemy. If you couldn't find this secret seat of power, you blamed yourself for not conducting an effective investigation.

Yet he hadn't needed either Miranda or intelligence to teach him to think like that. Someone else had taken care of that a long time ago.

A handbook for visitors from outer space, Charles had ordered him to write. It would EXPLAIN THE ENTIRE WORLD! He remembered thinking how it would suddenly appear everywhere, like Gideons Bibles; visitors from outer space, consulting it, would understand what had happened in the world to make it come to an end. But if you grew up expecting the world to end—even though it might be next to impossible to actually imagine this happening: the whole world just *stopping*, the war to end all wars (once the First World War had been *that*) maybe even being started by one crazed person in a vindictive moment—it warped your thinking; you looked at everything with a jaundiced eye; and you could never relax your vigilance. If you did, and everything blew up while you weren't looking, it would be your fault.

"I think you like to think there's some plan on the part of the government because it makes you feel you can do something about things, whereas I don't really believe it's possible. It's too late now. It's only a matter of time until someone—or not someone, a short-circuiting computer—pushes the button."

You could get yourself all worked up, waiting—you felt hopeless and it made you crave something real to fight about, so much that you actually got to the disgusting point where you *envied* people who lived in totalitarian societies the curtailment of their liberty, envied the guerrillas you watched running for cover on television, the people who could be put in jail if they expressed the wrong political opinion. Gee, if only *we* had some outright oppression! It seemed despicable to him, like the Campers playing at being social outcasts, claiming they knew what it really felt like to be alienated. (But what was he saying? Was he saying that he did?) So they lived illegally in a condemned building in a derelict section of Winston. Big deal. They were as much a part of society as anyone; they just liked to pretend they weren't.

He had watched them so many times, working themselves into frenzies while they chewed beef Stroganoff and drank wine some poor peasant had probably worked for next to nothing to pick the grapes for. First they got all fired up about the inflated arms budget, then cruelty to laboratory animals, the population explosion, water pollution, air pollution, deforestation—you name it. (Betsy was the only person he knew who ever actually did anything.) Talk *was* cheap.

"Exactly the attitude that will be to blame if we do blow ourselves up," Miranda said. "You've given up before you started. It's the way you are about everything. You don't do anything because you're scared you might fail."

"Now, wait a minute . . ."

"Cyrus, you can't separate your political beliefs from your personal ones, even if you think you can. For instance, I think it's silly to believe love can last a lifetime. That's just another of those myths, those impossible ideals of perfection that end up making us all miserable. The pair is out-of-date. You probably would feel much better if you exorcised those moldy old ideas once and for all."

"What are you talking about?"

"Look, I know you pretend not to feel guilty about your two girlfriends. . . ."

"Miranda . . ." Julian objected.

"What?" She looked at him, then at Gillian. "I thought one of our rules was to speak frankly about these things. In my opinion, Cyrus does one thing but believes another. The immorality of infidelity is outmoded; all the old taboos are falling. And why shouldn't they? Be honest, Cyrus. Can you tell me one good reason?"

He gave her a hard look, then said indifferently, "Not I."

"To me a couple is a nauseating entity, insular, smug, bourgeois. . . ."

"Whereas *we* are so happy!" Julian remarked. "I want Miranda, she wants Erik, Erik claims he wants me. We are all loved—so what if by the wrong person?"

"Builds character, having a craving to resist," Erik said. "I should know." He blew a kiss to Julian, who, grimacing, pantomimed a catch and threw the kiss on to Miranda; smiling at both of them, she grabbed it out of the air and put it in her pocket.

Cyrus, studying Julian, absently laid his hand on Gillian's head, rested against his knee.

"I thought you were all supposed to live happily ever after."

Julian looked at him frankly, "So did I."

Two days thence, Cyrus went to Jake Turner's apartment for dinner. He felt uncomfortable at first, not so much with Jake (as Turner insisted upon being called)—he seemed exactly like his former self, although more easygoing; it was Mother Agnes (just Agnes, Cyrus kept reminding himself) he had to get used to. There she was, wearing blue jeans and a T-shirt, her hair long; being affectionate with Jake and their little girl, acting like any normal wife and mother. He was not a Catholic—he didn't even know if there was a Catholic church in Arborville—yet, somehow, he couldn't forget that she had been a nun; she had made an eternal vow of chastity, and she had not kept it. Even if there was no God to smite her down, didn't her own conscience trouble her? Wasn't there some part of her that, remembering her convent self, looked askance at her married life?

Well, maybe not. Maybe other people didn't feel the strength of allegiance to past selves that he did.

At the moment Agnes was at the counter that separated the kitchen and living-room sections of their big loftlike apartment, rolling out piecrust. Part of the kitchen area was out of sight behind a partition. Jake now stuck his head from around the corner and called,

"What do you drink, Cyrus? Bourbon, scotch, martini, Bloody Mary? My very favorite queen—no dithering there. Didn't agree with you? Whack! Off with your head!"

"I guess I'll have a bourbon on the rocks."

"Sounds good to me too."

When her father proceeded into the living room with the drinks, little Lilith Richmond-Turner ventured forth from the safety of the kitchen and stood beside her father's chair, smiling slyly at Cyrus. He said hello to her, and she hid her face against Jake's arm.

"Don't let this coy behavior fool you, Cyrus. Once she knows you a little better you'll long for the shy stage to come back." Jake smiled at him. "Now, in ten words or less, what's happened to you in the last four years?"

"Well, I went to Chive, graduated, and now I'm not doing anything. How many is that?"

"Same old Cyrus. Man alive, I used to want to throttle you sometimes!"

Cyrus smiled vaguely.

"*Speaking* of which . . . It sure threw me for a loop to find out you were old Charlie Street's grandson! Why didn't you *say* something?"

"What do you mean?" Cyrus said, startled. "He isn't that well known. It didn't occur to me."

Jake looked astonished. "But surely he told you I served under him! I was more or less his aide-de-camp through the war. We got to know each other pretty well."

"You what!" Granddad *knew* Turner?

"What a bizarre coincidence, then. I simply assumed, when I learned from that ruffian at Chive who called up to get the low-down on you that you were Street's grandson, that he had recommended you come to Fifield. Shows what an egotist I am, I guess."

Cyrus was trying to think back: whose idea *had* it been that he go to Fifield? But those days preceding his abrupt departure from Arborville (and preceding *Charles's* abrupt departure from Arborville) were such a blur. But Granddad knew Turner. What did Turner know about him?

"Where is he now?" Jake asked.

"He died right after I got out of Fifield."

The instant the words were out of his mouth, Cyrus couldn't believe he had said them. He fully expected Jake to say, "Why, you liar!"

Instead Jake said, "What a damn shame. I would have loved to see that man again. You know, he was responsible for getting me involved in training dogs. They ran messages behind enemy lines." He looked sad. "Funny I never saw anything in the papers—not that I read them religiously."

"There wasn't a lot of coverage," Cyrus said, feeling sick. Why had he *lied*? Well—he knew *why*. If Jake found out that he was living in the same city as his former commander, he would be sure to visit him and would discover that Cyrus hadn't been to see him since before Fifield and would want to know the reason. That was why. But knowing why absolved him of nothing. Now he had one more fake story to remember, more fake details to devise to back it up.

"I suppose not. It's a sad day, though, when the country forgets the likes of him. I heard via the grapevine that he departed the service in less than its good graces—maybe that had something to do with it. Did he ever tell you the story?"

"Not specifically. He didn't like what was happening in intelligence. He thought it should be dismantled except for a skeleton organization, not built up the way it was."

"I'm with him there, but I don't quite see . . ."

"Jake," Agnes called. "Sorry to interrupt, but I need a hand getting the roast out of the pan."

"Excuse me a minute, Cyrus."

When her father left, Lilith tottered over toward Cyrus, a fierce look in her eye.

"Grrr!" she growled.

"Grrr?" he repeated, laughing. Then he got down on his hands and knees and growled back. Lilith shrieked. She turned, tried to run, then reverted to a crawl and went as fast as she could toward the kitchen. Arrived within a zone of safety, she turned around and bared her teeth at Cyrus—he crawled away; she returned in pursuit. He let out cries of terror as he made for safety behind the sofa.

"Grrr!" growled Lilith. "I monster!"

"Oh, no, help, help, she's captured me!" he cried, as she clambered onto his back and caught his neck in a stranglehold. "Mercy! Mercy!"

"Give him no quarter, Lil!" called Jake. "That's my girl."

Cyrus freed himself and sat back on the couch with Lilith on his lap.

"You like children, don't you, Cyrus?" Agnes remarked, smiling.

"Other people's," he answered with a laugh.

"Looks mutual to me," said Jake, returning. Lilith now had her arms around Cyrus's neck. He was feeding her bites of cheese and crackers.

"As I said," Jake went on, "I regret not having seen your grandfather again. At some point I'd be interested in talking to you at length about him. I'd like to know more about his background, for one thing. He was generally evasive about questions he considered personal—a quality I respect, although I thought he carried it to extremes." Jake grinned. "A tendency—if I may be so bold—it seems to me his grandson inherited. But, for now, I'd like to hear more about you." Jake went on to ask all about Chive. Luckily Cyrus didn't mind answering these questions. Then, during dinner, Agnes took up most of the conversation, talking about her Ph.D. thesis. Cyrus became almost relaxed. It caught him completely off guard when, as they were sitting in the living room again after dinner (Lilith had been put to bed), Jake said,

"Do you ever hear from your old buddy Billy Daphne, by the way?"

"Bill Daphne?" Agnes chimed in. "That nice shy boy from Amber?"

It sounded almost as if they had rehearsed their questions.

Jake nodded. "He was seduced by Uncle Sam's beckoning finger, you know."

At this Cyrus forgot himself. "What?" he exclaimed. "What did you say?"

Jake regarded him curiously. "Joined up right out of Fifield. Surely you knew that."

Cyrus shook his head.

"You can't be serious." Jake waited. "Well, I *am* astonished. I was certain you would get in touch with him. It never occurred to me . . ." He shook his head. "He was a wreck when you disappeared like that. I was almost more worried about him than I was about you."

Cyrus avoided his eyes.

"What happened? The two of you were so close."

"My brother died," Cyrus said sharply. "That's what happened."

Jake didn't flinch. "Yes, I know, but why did that mean you had to drop all contact with Billy? Understand me, I'm not saying it wasn't a tragic event. You were in shock and reacted to the news by getting the hell away from everything and everyone—which I, for one, have never criticized you for. In fact, I had such confidence in your own ability to know what you needed that I said so to your parents. A damned irresponsible thing to do, when I think back on it—not to mention insensitive. But I still don't understand why you didn't contact Billy later!"

Cyrus shrugged. "We didn't stay in touch, that's all. He didn't write me either."

"He wouldn't, though. You were the one who left. You know, Cyrus, he never had a single friend until you came along. I was afraid he had gone permanently down some rabbit hole or other. Before you arrived, he lived off in a world of his own. It was more than just being shy or dreamy. He seemed out of contact. A difficult home life, to start out with. Father dies violently, afterward mother can't stand having the kid around. . . . Some question of whether Billy did all he could to save his father. Think of the guilt he must have harbored."

"What the hell are you talking about?"

"Didn't he ever speak about it to you?"

"I knew he was there when his father died, if that's what you mean."

"His father was killed when a tree he was cutting fell on him, as you know. But Billy apparently didn't even go to see if there was anything he could do to help him. He ran right back to the house to tell his mother his father was dead."

"He *was* dead."

"But Billy didn't *know* that. His mother asked him later if he had tried to save his father and he said he never thought his father might still be alive. It was plain to the men who went to bring him out of the woods that even if he hadn't been killed instantaneously nothing Billy could have done would have saved him—he was literally crushed. But there was still that unpleasantness associated with it. I'm sure afterward Billy must have blamed himself for not trying to do anything. I know his mother certainly did. I don't know how much time you ever spent with her, but in my opinion she was a very intelligent woman, although very ignorant. She came down to talk to me once Billy's first year at Fifield—I was concerned about Billy and had asked her to come. She told me Billy and his father hadn't gotten along and that she got upset every time she looked at Billy after his father's death."

"That's just wonderful."

"But she had the sense to know how unhealthy it would be for Billy to be around her. And I think that in her own roundabout way she had even figured out that the reason she felt so antagonistic toward him was because she herself wasn't all that unhappy to be rid of her husband. 'It's not like he's any more gone now than he ever was.' I remember she said that."

Jake now smiled at Cyrus. To Cyrus his smile was grotesque.

"I don't know if I ever heard Billy laugh until you came along. An unlikely pair if ever there was one: a boy from a cultured family, the grandson of the most intelligent man I ever met in my life—not that I knew that at the time—and a boy from the backwoods. But suddenly Billy seemed like a normal kid. Still shy, but not lost to the world anymore." He shrugged. "But maybe I'm wrong. Maybe you didn't realize . . ."

"Realize *what*?"

"How much you mattered to him, Cyrus." Jake exchanged a rapid glance with his wife.

"Do you think he didn't matter to me?"

"If he did, why didn't you write to him?"

"I never told him about my brother," Cyrus said quietly.

"Yes, I know," Jake said impatiently, "he mentioned that, but . . ."

"I think I can understand," Agnes said. Cyrus looked at her, startled. He had practically forgotten she was there. "You felt you had lied to him, so . . ."

"I did lie to him." He looked at Agnes. He was beginning to feel very nervous. Suddenly to be talking about all this . . . And Jake's sickening hints about Billy murdering his father . . . Suddenly his uneasiness turned to rage. What gave Jake the *right* to talk about people like that? Summing them up as if they were dead and buried! Who did he think he was—God?

"Perhaps you're being a little too hard on yourself, Cyrus," Agnes suggested. "Maybe you didn't tell him about your brother originally because it hurt too much to talk about. He was already dying, wasn't he? Then, when he did die, suddenly like that . . ."

Cyrus interrupted her coldly. "It was a lie. Everything else is irrelevant."

Jake and Agnes stared at him—Jake looking exasperated, Agnes looking concerned. I can't stand this, he thought, I just can't stand it.

"Excuse me, I don't mean to be rude, but can we please drop the subject? I know you mean well, but . . ."

"I had no idea it was such a sore subject with you," Jake said. "It certainly doesn't seem to me like a simple case of not staying in touch."

"Let it go, Jake," Agnes interrupted.

Jake shrugged, annoyed. Then he sighed and grinned. "I guess you can see who's boss in this house."

Cyrus forced a smile in return. He took his leave shortly thereafter, however—and he would have been quite happy never to go back. He supposed he had gone in the first place out of curiosity; he wanted to *see* Jake and Mother Agnes as husband and wife. Although he had tried at Fifield to convince a skeptical Billy that there was something going on between Turner and St. Barbara's headmistress, he had not imagined they would ever *act* upon their attraction.

But now he needed Jake and Agnes; he had to have a place for Fritz to stay when she came to Winston. For obvious reasons, she could stay with neither Sophie nor the Campers. Therefore, he had no choice but to swallow his pride and accept Jake and Agnes's subsequent invitations—they seemed eager enough to have him back. (Just wanted to get him all figured out, he thought.) He did enjoy seeing Lilith; he began to babysit for her occasionally.

Fritz's actual visit turned out to be somewhat of an anticlimax. Cyrus was more nervous than she was, wondering what Jake and Agnes would make of her. But evidently, though they liked her, they didn't take her stories about her upbringing literally; they thought she was being witty. It wasn't until her third or fourth sojourn in Winston that anything unusual enough occurred to make them think she was other than a little eccentric.

Jake had suggested they attend a concert at Winston's Symphony Hall. It was the first concert Fritz had ever been to, and Cyrus had difficulty in making her understand that one was supposed to maintain silence. She was astonished at the audience's passivity. "Do you mean they *have* to listen to you?" she whispered to him incredulously. "Well, more or less," he replied, equally incredulous.

After the performance, Fritz announced that she was going backstage to talk to the violinist.

"What's going on?" Jake demanded, as he, Agnes, and Cyrus tried to keep up with Fritz, who was proceeding rapidly.

Cyrus rolled his eyes. "She's planning to tell the violinist what he did wrong."

"You're not serious! Tell the greatest living maestro of his instrument how to play it?"

"Something like that."

"Oh, Cyrus," Agnes pleaded, "you've got to stop her. She'll be embarrassed to death afterward. I didn't realize she was this naïve."

"You prevent her, Agnes. When Fritz has made up her mind . . ."

Indeed, by the time they elbowed their way through the crowd surrounding the performer, it was already too late. The showdown was in progress.

The violinist—a man in his early seventies, balding, tufts of fading pale hair surrounding his skull like seats in an amphitheater, looking very elegant and perspiring in tuxedo—was listening coldly to Fritz. The crowd about them was gradually falling silent.

"The concerto was capable," she said rapidly, "but flat, especially in the middle. The sonata was not too bad. But the ending was sour and you cannot find C-flat at all."

The maestro surveyed Fritz. She, oblivious of her effect, tapped her foot impatiently. Arrogant minx, he thought. But, despite himself, he was unsettled, and he did not like to be unsettled.

"So you did not approve of the ending," he said sweetly. He turned to the onlookers. "Did the rest of you not like the ending?" No one spoke. "Well, then." He reached for his violin case, took out his Stradivarius, and offered it to Fritz. "Perhaps my young critic will be so kind as to show me how it is to be played."

Fritz, seeing the violin, felt soothed. She was not afraid of the maestro, but the number of people hemming her in made her nervous. Her fingers quivered with eagerness to touch the instrument. In fact, she was gazing at it with such longing that the maestro felt a twinge of jealousy. No one had ever dared to look at *his* violin like that before!

But she didn't take it. "I can't play in here," she stated, at which several people snickered, construing this as an attempt to evade her predicament. The maestro knew better.

"Let us go where you can, then," he said. "Nothing could be simpler."

Seizing Fritz by the wrist, he walked her briskly back out onto the stage. The last of the departing audience, seeing him return, began to clap confusedly and to shuffle back to their seats.

"No, no!" he shouted. "Out, out! Ushers, clear the hall!"

When the hall at last was emptied, he again offered Fritz his violin. This time she accepted it at once.

Those who had followed on stage whispered. That the heavens did not open and a lightning bolt spear the young woman for her impudence was simply evidence that God was overworked. The maestro motioned to them to hush.

Then Fritz played. She ignored the score the maestro held out to her. She did not repeat the pieces in their entirety, merely those sections about which she had spoken.

"Do you see?"

The maestro received his violin from her hands without a word. The silence deepened in the hall until it would have been possible to hear an angel falling off the head of a pin. He, who had thought no one in the whole wide world besides himself could overcome certain quirks in his violin, felt like a cuckolded lover.

It was not until he had replaced the instrument in its case that he broke the silence. His face bore the faint trace of a smile. "Come with me, Nemesis."

Fritz looked for Cyrus. He gestured for her to go on. Even he, who did not consider himself to know anything about music, had had no difficulty recognizing that Fritz's rendition was superior to the famous violinist's—purer somehow, truer to what the composer must have intended.

"You could knock me over with a feather," Jake announced. "You said she was good—you didn't tell us she was that good!"

"I guess I didn't really know myself."

Meanwhile, Fritz had vanished into the wings with the maestro. When they emerged over an hour later, he greeted those spectators who remained.

"Would you like to know how I feel?" he asked them. "I feel like a child who has been told he may go out to play. Do you realize how long it has been since anyone dared to criticize me? This young woman's name," he took Fritz by the arm, "is Fritz Quadrata. I guarantee to you that before long it will become a household word."

Among the onlookers who had witnessed both the original encounter and now the maestro's concession of victory, skulking in a corner so as not to be observed, was Fyodor Stoltzoff.

·   ·   ·

As the jeep that had brought him to the front lines sped away, the ambassador looked about him uneasily. He stood all alone on a plain, like a lone tree guaranteed to draw lightning, while, as far as he could see in every direction, trenches sliced the earth. From the air it must have looked as if a giant spiderweb were laid out on the ground. Rusting matériel of all descriptions—tanks, cannons, fighter jets—was parked in the angles of the web. In its center, not far from him, stood the tent of the colonel in charge of the regiment. A real old-time soldier, his superiors had told the ambassador; a real diehard.

It was a sunny day, balmy and breezy, early spring. Some of the men had removed their shirts. They were chatting, telling jokes, telling stories, smoking, throwing darts, playing cards, playing chess and checkers, eating and drinking, singing, humming, whistling, shaving, writing letters, bathing, napping, sunbathing, doing pushups, doing deep kneebends, sketching, reading, winding their wristwatches . . . They appeared relaxed, even cheerful, which surprised the ambassador, who had come prepared to find men on the verge of despair. Instead he found men who clearly had made a life for themselves in the trenches. The ambassador was confused. Of what exactly was he supposed to persuade the soldiers?

He decided to speak informally with them first to sound out the situation. He walked to the nearest trench and squatted at its edge.

"Hello there, men," he greeted them, in the hearty manner he had been practicing.

Only a few glanced up.

"You another reporter?" one asked.

"A reporter? Why . . . why, yes, as a matter of fact, I am."

"Thought so. You know, we've had it up to here with you guys and your dumb questions. Don't you ever get tired of hanging around, looking for a war story for the *Hometown Express*?"

"The people at home are always glad of news," the ambassador ventured.

"You call this news?"

"I suppose it must grow monotonous after a while."

The soldier shrugged.

"Don't think about it much anymore. It's just the way things are."

"But don't you have a family? Don't you miss them?"

"Of course I do. What kind of a question is that?"

"Did you ever think about the fact that they must miss you?"

"Look, Pops," the soldier said irritably, "what are you driving at? I'm just like everyone else, doing my duty."

"And never once questioned that it was the right thing to do." The ambassador sighed and stood, gazing down the trench. He had come prepared to quell a mutiny but there wasn't one. He should simply return to Acting Headquarters and inform his superiors that the situation was under control. They would be pleased. It was not inconceivable that they would award him another medal.

Instead he sat down on the edge of the trench. "Would you like a cigarette?" he asked.

The soldier shrugged. "Never say no to that."

They both lit up.

"What's your name?"

"Robert Jones. Bob. What's yours?"

"Andrew Martin." (It sounded strange in his ears, plain like that.)

The soldier held out a hand. The ambassador shook it warmly. What a direct, unaffected young man, he thought. Had *he* ever once been like that?

As he contemplated what he was about to say, the ambassador felt a momentary compunction. Bob Jones and his fellows had made their separate peace. Was it kind—was it *right*—to suggest to them that it was not their destiny to which they had acquiesced but a state of suspended animation?

But he no more than hesitated. "Listen, Bob, I'm not a reporter, I'm an ambassador, and there's something I have to tell you. . . ."

It was now several months after Fritz's triumph at the maestro's concert. She had been traveling regularly to Winston with Cyrus—

to prepare, with the maestro's assistance, for her concert debut in May. Her attitude about the world had altered dramatically; not only was she no longer afraid, she was already blasé. She was interested solely in the world of music and spoke incessantly about "Pierre"—the name the maestro was called by his intimates. Pierre this, Pierre that. It was all getting on Cyrus's nerves. He began to regret ever encouraging her to leave the Cottage. Why *had* he? he wondered. She was basically happy there, as long as he visited frequently, and he realized now that he had taken for granted being able to do so whenever he felt like it. Now she was often busy with her own plans when he felt like going to New Jersey. Furthermore, although the course of their love had not run smooth since his graduation, as long as Fritz refused to leave the Cottage, whatever difficulties they were having could be blamed on that. Now they couldn't be. He now had no choice but to face the fact that he had hidden his identity from her for four years—thus hidden *hers* from her as well. She still showed no particular curiosity about his life, did not wonder why he introduced her to none of his friends besides Jake and Agnes, or to his grandmother, who he had told her lived in Winston. Nevertheless he felt that it was only a matter of time until the web of secrecy he had woven around himself began to unravel. The Campers—Miranda and Julian especially—pressed to be introduced to Fritz. Jake was becoming curious about the Campers. Sophie, though so far she hadn't asked him anything, he knew had sensed a change in him the last few months. He often felt her looking at him with concern, and he dreaded the moment when she would say, "Is something bothering you, Cyrus?" For he found the prospect of lying to her abhorrent. He never had specifically *lied* to Sophie; he simply had neglected to mention certain things. He had been able to count on her reluctance to ask "prying questions." And now Fritz was going to play for an audience. Maybe she'd become famous, and then . . . ACCLAIMED VIOLINIST DAUGHTER OF GENERAL AND GENERAL'S SISTER! FRITZ QUADRATA IS A UNIQUE YOUNG WOMAN—IN MORE WAYS THAN ONE! MYSTERY GENERAL'S SECRET FINALLY REVEALED! He could see the headlines now.

He knew he had to do something, and he knew he had to do it soon. What, though? He couldn't pull one thread without unspinning the whole cloth. Anyway, where would he start? Whom would he talk to first? Fritz? *Guess what, Aunt . . .* Sophie? *Hey, you know that book you gave me the night I had the nightmare? Well, you'll never imagine what I found out. . . .* His grandfather? Just show up at the Old Generals' Home one day . . .

Hi, Granddad, it's Cyrus, remember me?

Cyrus? The boy I used to sit with on the steps in Arborville? The one who had nightmares all the time? Yes, I believe I recall you.

What about the stories you used to tell me, when we sat out on the steps? Do you recall them? About the missing king and how finding him and getting him to sit on his throne again would set the world to rights?

He could see him nodding, amused. *You always were a gullible child.*

Well, guess what? I found him.

Cyrus the sleuth.

I found his family too. Xy, Sammy, George. Your sisters and brother. And you're him.

I knew I could depend on you, Corporal.

Except you have more of a family than you think. You have a daughter. You and Xy. Her name is Fritz.

You don't say.

Or did you know that all along too? Was this part of your master plan? That we'd meet and fall in love? So I could suffer as you did?

But this he couldn't conceive of his grandfather answering, because it was on this that everything hinged, wasn't it? Whether or not Charles knew about Fritz? That was why he couldn't visit him now; it was bad enough what his grandfather had done, but if he had *known* what he was doing . . .

In the end it was a simple coincidence of events that jarred him loose, knocked him out of the orbit he was describing around life and set him on a collision course with it.

On this afternoon, he was babysitting for Lilith and had taken her to the park. It was late March, a bright, blustery, but not very cold day, and he hadn't felt like staying inside. He was in a particularly lousy mood because Gillian had insisted upon accompanying him. He tried to dissuade her—for one thing, Lilith didn't like her—but knew it was a lost cause. Ever since Fritz began coming to Winston, Gillian had become very possessive. Whenever Fritz wasn't around, she demanded Cyrus spend every minute with her. Nothing he said had any effect. He kept getting the feeling she was trying to force him to take some firm position, make some cut-and-dried decision that would resolve *her* uncertainty.

She asked him if he thought they should go on being involved, now that Fritz was around so often. Do you want to stop? he asked her. It wasn't that, she said. What was it then? He had never led her on. He told her at the beginning he had a girlfriend whom he loved. Sometimes he felt Gillian was hoping he and Fritz were on the verge of breaking up (not that far off the mark, actually), but even if Fritz was out of the picture, he couldn't see wanting to be more attached to Gillian. But he didn't know how to say this to her. And, unless he stopped visiting 9 Ives altogether, he couldn't figure out exactly what "breaking up" with Gillian would consist in, since they weren't officially a couple in the first place. That, and she made herself so available. Once he said to her, "Why don't you just tell me to get lost? If it causes you so much pain . . ." She just looked like she didn't know what he was talking about.

At the moment Gillian was sitting on a bench in the sun, and he and Lilith had just turned onto the brick walk that led down to the duck pond when he heard a woman's voice remark, "Such a pretty little girl."

"Thank you," Gillian replied.

Kneeling down on the pretext of tying his shoe, Cyrus listened.

"And your husband seems devoted to her."

"Yes," Gillian said in a pleased voice. "He's a wonderful father."

What? Cyrus exclaimed. Furious, he started back up the walk. Lilith's wail stopped him. He turned. She stood, looking after him woefully, and he hurried back and picked her up.

"I'm sorry, Lilith, I didn't mean to scare you. I wouldn't leave you." She wrapped her arms around his neck. "Don't cry, Lil. Do you want to ride piggyback?"

She nodded tearfully, and he hoisted her onto his shoulders.

"I'm a horse, Lilith. Can you say 'horse'?"

" 'Orse," she said.

"Good. Now say, 'Giddy-up, horse, giddy-up.' "

"Gee-up, 'orse," Lilith said. "Gee-up, bad 'orse."

"Bad horse!" Cyrus exclaimed. Laughing, he began to jog. "What do you mean, bad horse?"

Suddenly he stopped. What had immobilized him was a memory—although it was not exactly the memory itself that arrested him but the way he was remembering it. It was in Arborville, a bright, shadowless day nearly ten years ago. He was sitting on the front steps with Charles, and coming toward them down Summer Street was Harold, with Lark on his shoulders; it was the day Lark was leaving for good—his father was taking him away. But now it was as if he wasn't only watching his father; he also was his father. He wasn't only Cyrus, trotting down a brick walk in Winston City with Jake Turner's eighteen-month-old daughter on his shoulders; he was Harold, hurrying down Summer Street with Lark. He was intensely conscious of his hands holding Lilith's plump legs, her tiny hands clasped around his forehead. It was as if some message were being transmitted from her flesh to his, and suddenly it dawned on him. She trusted him! My God, he thought, how could she possibly trust him?

Cyrus had never felt sorry for his father before in his life and the feeling stopped him dead in his tracks. The next day, as if on a whim, he drove up to Amber and visited Mrs. Daphne.

Part Two

Part Two

Unconfirmed
Troop Movement

A vector of sun traveling straight down through the universe and into the window of the bedroom at the Old Generals' Home in Winston City that General Eastlake shared with General Martinson struck General Eastlake full in the face. "Berthe," he murmured, "Berthe . . ." and flung an arm over the edge of his bed. But he did not awake and soon had plunged into a deeper dream, in which General Martinson's snores figured as the rhythmic rattle of machine-gun fire in the distance.

General Eastlake was in heaven. Heaven was full of generals. They were having a feast and everyone was eating a lot: roast suckling pig, jaws propped wide with apples; pheasant under bells of glass; and General Eastlake's particular favorite, roast beef with Yorkshire pudding. They washed everything down with hearty German beer and dainty French champagne.

"There's your antipathy right there, Otto," General Eastlake joked to Bismarck.

"I couldn't agree more," replied Bismarck, and they clinked glasses and said, "To your health." "To yours."

Caesar ambled over, wearing his short battle dress.

"God, man, your knees are tan!" General Eastlake exclaimed.

"In the name of Mars, how could you fight with cloth clinging to your thighs?" Caesar retorted.

"It's true, your legs must have scared whole armies away," General Eastlake told Caesar.

"A standing army is a great mischief," proclaimed Ethan Allen, who had been leaning on his musket, listening. He was growing deaf. "I thought so before Madison did."

"Who is he?" Caesar whispered to General Eastlake. "I keep forgetting."

"Ethan Allen. He fought the British in our revolution—thinks he won it all by himself. Got this damnfool idea that only small bands of militia, fighting on their home territory, can win a war."

"Harrumph," Caesar remarked. "Peasant."

"Eastlake!" shouted Napoleon from the field where he was choosing a team for baseball.

"Julius!" responded Alexander the Great.

"Charlemagne!"

"Attila the Hun!"

Soon General Eastlake was at bat; he had swung and sent the ball spinning up into the nimbus clouds that floated about heaven in the shapes of cannons and tanks and fighter jets, but he never made it to first base because the breakfast bell jangled loudly in the corridor outside his room, and, waking suddenly, he stared at his drab, uncelestial surroundings and at General Martinson, sitting on his bed in his bathrobe, putting on his slippers.

Martinson chuckled. "What did you dream this time, Ted?"

Eastlake sighed. Slowly he hoisted himself to a sitting position. "My mind is going, Jack," he said gloomily. "It's the end. I may as well face it."

"It was a dream. We all have dreams."

"Not like mine you don't."

"Look, Ted," Martinson said, "your mind's as clear as a bell."

"Don't try to comfort me, Jack. You sound like a goddamn nurse. I'm eighty-eight years old. I'm a feeble old man, conjuring up visions of glory."

"I still believe we could have a role to play. Our final battle may yet await us."

"Don't kid yourself. No one cares what we think. They sucked the juice out of us and threw us away. Who wants to learn anything from history? People prefer to think the world started when they were born."

Charles, making his way to breakfast, paused outside their door and caught the latter part of their conversation. More of the same, he groaned.

Then he grinned. Bending to the keyhole, he puckered his lips and softly began to whistle. "When Johnny comes marching home again, hurrah, hurrah, When Johnny comes marching home again, hurrah, hurrah . . ." The plaintive tune carried faintly into the room.

"Jack," Eastlake said morosely, "I hear music."

"Don't worry, I hear it too. Whistling, it sounds like."

". . . the men will cheer and the boys will shout, The ladies they will all turn out. . . ."

Hearing footsteps approaching the door, Charles straightened and walked briskly down the hall to his own room. He was in it with the door shut before Eastlake got his door open. Though blind, Charles was spryer than Eastlake, his elder by fifteen years.

"God damn it, Street, I know it's you!" Eastlake shouted down the corridor. "Nobody else possesses such a warped sense of humor! If you weren't blind as a bat and I weren't lame as a duck we'd settle our differences in a more direct way, I hope you realize that!"

"If I knit one more sock," Peg Jones remarked, "I'm going to go stark, raving mad."

Peg, the soldier Bob Jones's wife, sat at her kitchen table with her best friend and next-door neighbor, Nan Thurston. They had been sitting there for years.

"I'm serious, Nan. I can't stand it anymore. I simply can't stand it."

"But, Peg . . ."

"Aren't *you* fed up? We're supposed to believe there's a war on but where's the evidence? I haven't seen any flag-draped coffins, have you?"

"No, but . . ."

"Soldiers on stretchers? One single limping hero?"

Peg shrugged.

"Have you heard of anyone receiving a telegram informing that so-and-so is missing in action?"

"No, I haven't, Peg, but . . ."

"But *what*?"

"Well, there may be military reasons for not announcing what's going on."

"No doubt. That's just the point. The military is supposed to work for us, not the other way round."

"But what can we do?" Nan asked impatiently. "What power do we have?"

"I don't know, but I swear before the day's over I'm going to think of something. And for starters . . ." Peg threw her half-gusseted sock, needles and all, into the trash can. "I feel like getting smashed," she announced. "I feel like getting smashed and not sobering up for a week."

Nan stared. Then suddenly she laughed. "Well, the kids won't be home until four-thirty . . ."

Peg glanced at the clock and then at her friend and grinned. She rose, fetched the rum from the dining room and the Coca-Cola from the refrigerator, and mixed two drinks. Then she and Nan went outside to sit in the sun.

Harold got out of the house around nine. He had been counting on getting an early start—he had a big day ahead of him: mend the back steps, scrape and paint the bulkhead, clean out the garage, and take a load to the dump; get to work on the yard . . .

He had asked Rose to wake him when she got up at seven, but at ten past eight he awoke on his own to the smell of bacon frying.

"God blast it," he exclaimed, marching into the kitchen. "I asked you to wake me up, Rose!"

"I'm sorry, dear. You just looked so contented, lying there. I couldn't bear to disturb you."

"Contented! I'll look contented when I'm dead too!"

"Now don't be silly, sweetheart. Sit down and let me pour you a cup of coffee."

. . . And serve him scrambled eggs and bacon, insist he have another pecan-caramel twist . . . Jesus God, in two years he would be fifty and everyone knew what life expectancy was for men these days.

At least he was out now, though, and he waved to the other fathers who had also escaped from their houses: Hugh Greenmantle and Pete Foster and Bill Silton, Bill singing "When You and I Were Young, Maggie" just as he had done every Saturday morning for the past twenty years.

"Hal!" called Hugh, and Harold strolled over to the edge of his yard and Hugh strolled to the edge of his and they stood talking over the fence; Hugh held a rake in one hand like a staff. "Never get all the leaves before the snow catches me," he said, and Harold answered, "I know what you mean."

"How about you? What have you got on the agenda?"

"Got to mend the back steps and paint the bulkhead."

"Again?"

"Every damn spring. It's the gutters. But it's easier to repaint the bulkhead than replace them."

They contemplated this together. Then Hugh asked, "Any news from Betsy and Cyrus?"

"Betsy's still lost in the jungle," Harold said, and they both laughed. "Teaching things to the natives they'll never need to know. She's eaten alligator."

"Good lord. Won't be seeing her for a while, I guess."

"Doesn't look like it."

"What about Cy? Still looking for his niche in life?"

"Not sure what he's up to exactly. Never been much of a letter writer."

"None of them are."

"I suppose not." Except that while Cyrus had not come home once since leaving Arborville, Huey, Jr., and Harold's other friends' sons reappeared every Christmas and summer; some had even returned to Arborville for good.

"Huey still liking law school?" Harold asked.

"Loves it. Simply loves it."

"Think he'd ever want to practice here?"

"Don't know," Hugh shrugged. "Not much excitement, in a legal sense, in a town like Arborville."

"Well," Harold said, "they're not ours to keep."

Once, they might have gone on to discuss their jobs at Amalgamated, but that subject had become taboo since Harold's trouble had started. Everyone knew that Harold had been taken off a number of the big accounts, and it was rumored that Burney, the president, had said to him, "Maybe you need to take some time off, Hal."

"Guess I better get this show on the road," Harold sighed, and Hugh said, "We're not getting any younger," and they separated.

Did June get upset if Hugh didn't eat her coffee cake? Had June, like Rose, begun to cook new and exotic foods? Whenever he asked Rose if they could just have plain old pork chops and applesauce for once, she said, "Oh, Harold! Where's your sense of adventure?"

And now she was at work on the house. New curtains in the kitchen. New slipcover for the couch. He couldn't walk into a room and sit down—he first had to look for the chairs. Last week he had arrived home from work to find she had ripped out the wallpaper in the dining room. He was apprehensive now each time he came in the front door.

In their offices at work, the men displayed photographs of their families. On Harold's desk were four: one of Rose, taken on their honeymoon, riding a carousel pony—she was stretching a hand toward him, her hair was blown back, and she was laughing; and there was one of each of the children. Lark at his third birthday party, wearing a pointed party hat and looking excited. Betsy on the swing in the backyard, grinning. And Cyrus, about ten, sitting on the front steps with Jonzo.

The general work area on the third floor of the building where Harold's office was located held seventy-five employees when filled to capacity. Down its center ran two adjacent rows of chest-high partitioned cubicles occupied by the junior executives; on either side of these rows sat the secretaries in two columns; around the room's circumference were glassed-in offices belonging to the senior executives. Each of the room's four corners was walled opaquely from the central area, and these were the vice-presidents' offices. It was to one of these that Harold had not long ago been promoted.

Before that, Harold, like all the other men, had formed the habit of wandering around the general work area. Rarely, it seemed, was any man between the rank of junior executive and that of vice-president to be found in his own office.

A vice-president, however, was expected to stay put, and it was when Harold could no longer leave his office that his difficulty began. For he realized why, all those years, he had not wanted to sit at his desk. He was trying to escape from his family, whose smiling faces reproached him for not having kept their lives free of pain.

Harold now also had nothing to do. The two junior executives assigned to work exclusively for him between them took care of all his responsibilities. He sat in his office with the door closed. It occurred to him that he had worked all his life in order to earn walls on all four sides of him. From now on the room would grow smaller and smaller, until one day it fit him perfectly.

In order not to go mad, Harold began to read, something he hadn't done in years. To avoid discovery, he read small paperbacks whose pages he could rip out a few at a time and transport to work in his inner jacket pocket. At his desk, he concealed them between sheets of inventory reports. By now he had torn up the majority of Cyrus's and Betsy's libraries. He embarked upon each book—from *Heidi* to *The Plague*—with the same polite attention, restraining his interest until he had decided whether or not the author might ever have experienced anything similar to his, Harold's, situation. If the author passed this crucial test, Harold then read on with uncritical abandon, hoping to acquire some understanding of his own misery.

In his eagerness, he grew careless. One day when he went to lunch he left several pages from *Hamlet* on his desk. The pages were heavily underlined and marginated with such comments as "Come off it," and "Just go stab him, will ya?," which P. D. Burney, whose habit it was to enter his vice-presidents' offices when they were not in them, did not notice were not in Harold's handwriting. He said nothing to Harold, but he began to keep a special eye on him.

By this time, though, Harold was too preoccupied by his own thoughts to care what anyone might be thinking of him. It seemed to him that for years an insidious struggle had been going on in his marriage. It had started when Charles came to Arborville. Before, he and Rose were perfectly happy. But something happened then. Harold had understood that her father was simply coming for a visit, but a few days after his arrival Rose announced that he was going to stay with them. She accused Harold of heartlessness when he objected. She had never been altogether his after that.

When he took Lark to the Institute, that was another point scored against him. When Lark died, Rose behaved as if he had no right to grieve. She was the one permitted to collapse; he was required to comfort, to stand firm while she faltered. He was only the father.

Rose, Harold now saw, had never believed he loved his own children. She did not *want* to believe it. He did not understand why this was, yet he was convinced it was true. For as long as he could be made to appear the villain, she would remain innocent.

One day Harold, sitting at his desk, simply began to cry. A normal, happy family—that was all he had ever wanted. That was what Arborville had once considered them. What a joke! Already they had been losing Lark. Then they lost Cyrus. And Betsy—she was dutiful, but she didn't enjoy her visits home.

It wasn't that other families didn't suffer tragedies—Harold had never thought of himself as singled out by misfortune. But other husbands and wives survived the hardships that life saw fit to bestow upon them. They remained allies—friends. But he and Rose—after the first brief happy years of their marriage—had become enemies. When the children were gone, they had achieved a truce, but it had left them strangers.

"What's the matter, Sarah?" Harvey said, smiling, "Cat got your tongue?"

"What?" she asked, startled.

Jason laid a hand on her shoulder. "It will take a while for the movie to wear off. She's probably just wishing someone loved her as much as Jules and Jim loved Catherine." He laughed, but he looked at his wife a little wistfully.

Ursula grinned. "Who doesn't?"

Sitting in a café, drinking cappuccino and eating cheesecake, they discussed the film: whether Catherine's killing herself and Jim by driving them both into the canal signified that she loved Jim the best; whether Jim had "known" it was going to happen; whether Jules was in fact "happy" as he walked away through the cemetery at the end after having watched his wife's and his rival's coffins being slid into the crematorium. . . .

Sarah listened to them analyzing the triangular love affair in their world-weary, "cultivated" voices. In fact she hadn't been wishing someone loved her as Jules and Jim loved Catherine. She had been thinking that Jules hadn't loved his wife much at all to have allowed her to become so confused, to have not insisted she break off her affair with Jim. That wasn't unselfishness, it was passivity. It left Catherine no way of demonstrating to Jules—and to Jim—how their "love" had destroyed her except by destroying herself and them.

Suddenly Sarah mumbled "Excuse me," and pushed back her chair. It tipped over, causing everyone in the restaurant to stare, but she didn't stop to pick it up. She grabbed her purse and rushed into the street, nearly knocking over a passerby, who then shouted at her furiously—so angry! Why was everyone so angry? At the least opportunity their anger leapt out.

She hurried on, turning around once, but naturally Jason wouldn't have followed. He would have considered that to be "giving in to hysteria." He considered such scenes "unbecoming." "If you want my attention," he said, "all you have to do is ask for it." You didn't *ask* for attention! What did he expect her to do? Make an appointment, bring a list of what was bothering her? Didn't he understand anything?

She walked on; ludicrously, it was a beautiful night: April. The night air was mild. She could smell spring. It had been on a night just like this, five years ago, that she had met Cyrus Quince. Cyrus . . . She had thought she would never get over him. She had never felt for anyone what she had felt for him, yet how clumsily she had handled the relationship. First she had been overly reticent, then, when he had probably forgotten all about her, she had written him such a passionate letter it still embarrassed her to think about it. He must have been scared to death. If she hadn't written it, if she had written it earlier, if she had told him from the beginning how she felt about him instead of waiting for him to tell her first . . . it still distressed her to think about it. In many ways, although she had resigned herself to the fact that she would never see or hear from him again, had finally stopped *expecting* to, her feelings for him remained unresolved. Then—less than a week ago, late on a Saturday afternoon, she had seen him.

She was standing at the living-room window, gazing aimlessly down into the street. In the bedroom Jason was watching a basketball game on television, shouting his encouragement or denunciation, when she saw Cyrus approaching. She recognized him instantly—no mistaking that walk, the way he always had of settling back on his heels after each step, like a much older, or heavier, man. As he neared her building, he glanced up at her window; she waved eagerly. Cyrus! she thought joyfully. Coming to see her! After all this time . . .

Without even thinking she ran out of the apartment and down the stairs. But he had not stopped. By the time she was out of the building, he was half a block farther down the street.

Her heart sank—he had not been coming to see her after all. Still, it was *Cyrus*, and though she had no shoes on, in her stocking feet she followed him, dodging behind the elms and maples that grew at twenty-foot intervals in the grassy strip between the sidewalk and the street. No willows on Willow Street—he had been the one to point that out to her. That was one of the things that had endeared him to her the most, the funny little things he noticed. . . .

She pursued him for several blocks—out of Willow Street into Gloucester, then into Elm. Suddenly he halted and stood staring across the street. He was directly opposite the Old Generals' Home. There was only one old general out on the lawn, sitting on a swing seat, rocking himself back and forth with his cane. Sarah had often noticed him there. He sat out in all weather, always alone. Even when the other generals were outside, he kept to himself. She had smiled at him on occasion but he never responded.

Now Cyrus stared at him, as if trying to make up his mind about something. For an instant she thought he must be trying to decide whether or not to visit her, and she was on the verge of calling out to him, when he crossed the street. She moved to the other side of the car behind which she had been crouching, thankful that no one else was on the street to observe her. (Though someone was.)

Cyrus halted again, only ten feet or so from the general, but he continued to swing slowly back and forth, oblivious. Then Sarah realized—he was blind. That explained why he never acknowledged her greetings.

But why did Cyrus stand and stare? What could interest him so?

Suddenly the general stopped the swing and turned his head. "Is someone there?" he called out.

Cyrus made no answer.

Again the general asked, "Is anyone there?"

This time Cyrus turned. Hearing the footsteps, the old general rose. He took several steps. Sarah froze.

"Who *is* it? Why don't you speak?"

Cyrus, halfway back across the street, hesitated, but then came on.

Terrified that he would see her, Sarah moved stealthily around the car. What on earth was the meaning of his strange behavior? (Fyodor Stoltzoff, concealed behind a tree a little farther down the street, was asking himself the same question.) When Cyrus passed, Sarah could not resist gaining a closer glimpse. Cautiously she craned her neck and gazed at him over the bumper. He was hurrying now, his head bent, seemingly oblivious of his surroundings. Then Sarah saw why: he was crying.

She was standing now on a bridge—a long, low bridge supported upon arches like a Roman viaduct—spanning a dark river. She had stopped to peer down over the railing. Cars sped past behind her. "Don't jump, lady!" someone shouted out a car window. I wasn't thinking of it, she retorted silently, though it was true the impulse was inevitably suggested by the water itself, its inviting darkness, its oblivion-promising depths. But what would that solve?

She was thinking now of the fact that she had never confessed to Jason that the summer before their marriage she had carried on, on an almost daily basis, a love affair. She recalled that she had not agreed to marry Jason until after it seemed certain Cyrus was not going to answer her letter. (She had called his dorm once, just to make certain he was still at Chive—that nothing had happened to him. Whoever answered the phone said he was away for the weekend. To her that fact provided incontrovertible evidence that he did not miss her.)

But it was the same thing now. She said to herself she still cared for him, but at the least sign that this was not reciprocal she backed off. So he hadn't been coming to see her—so what? She could have called to him! What was the worst that could have happened? That he would refuse to speak to her? That he would be indifferent? Well, better to find out than to treasure an illusion the rest of her life. Then, later, he was crying, and she let him walk on uncomforted, telling herself she would be intruding, but really not wanting him to discover she had followed him. Always thinking first of herself, as if she were too precious to reveal her feelings to anyone. She was sickened to think that once again her diffidence had cost her Cyrus.

Sarah hurried home in order to pretend to be asleep when Jason arrived. The next morning she waited to get up until after he had left for work. (He didn't seem very eager to confront her, either—tiptoeing about, making the minimum of noise.)

At ten o'clock, she left the house and walked the few blocks to the Old Generals' Home, breathing a sigh of relief when she saw that the blind general sat in his usual spot. She crossed the lawn and halted before him.

"Excuse me . . . ."

"Yes, what is it? Is that you, Dora?"

"No, it's . . . You don't know me." (Should she call him "General"? "Sir"?) "My name is Sarah Simms. I live not far from you in the neighborhood, and I often go by here. In fact, I've said hello to you but . . . well, I didn't realize until recently that you couldn't see me."

"I see. You thought I was a cantankerous old codger and came to confess your mistake."

"No, not exactly. I mean, I did kind of think that, but that's not why I came to see you. The real reason is . . ."

"There are no real reasons. If I've learned nothing else in my lifetime, I've learned that. And I've certainly learned to suspect those eager to lay claim to knowing them."

Sarah murmured, "I only wanted to ask you . . ."

"Well, what is it?" he asked impatiently.

Taken aback by his gruffness, Sarah did not at first reply. Indeed, if she had known he was so crotchety she would have thought twice about approaching him. Remembering why she had done so, however, she made herself go on.

"It's kind of a long story, but a few days ago I happened to notice an old friend of mine, someone I hadn't seen in a long time, doing something peculiar." She hesitated. "Well, that's not exactly true. I'm afraid this is all going to sound crazy to you," she added apologetically.

"You flatter yourself," he said. But then, as if hearing dismay in her silence, he tapped the seat beside him. "Sit down, Miss Simms."

She obeyed, feeling more uncomfortable than ever.

"Well," he demanded, when she did not continue, "are you going to go on?" He laughed sarcastically. "I haven't got all day."

"It will only . . ." But then she understood. He was *lonely*— that was why he was so belligerent. Poor old fellow. This realization restored her composure.

"Are you . . . What is your name?"

"I go by the name of General Charles Street."

He really was a general, then. She hadn't been sure. It had always seemed strange to her that so many of the nation's former commanders should have nowhere to live but in the Old Generals' Home. When she passed by the place, she thought of all the military secrets they still must know that very well might go with them to their graves. She had harbored a fantasy of getting to know them—maybe even working at the Home as an aide—and of their confiding in her what they knew. She would be admitted into their deep, masculine mysteries. . . .

"As I said, General Street, I live not far from here, and on this day last week I was looking out my window when I saw this person coming down my street. I was certain he was coming to see me, so I ran downstairs to meet him, but . . . well," she shrugged, "he wasn't. I was embarrassed. So," she sighed, disgusted, "I followed him."

"How did you prevent 'this person' from seeing you?"

"I hid behind trees and cars."

"I see." He sounded vaguely amused. "What shameful behavior did you indulge in next?"

She laughed. "Nothing else. I just followed him. I wanted to see where he was going."

"And where was that?"

"He came here."

"Here?" General Street was startled. "What do you mean?"

"He came as far as the Home. I watched from across the street. I'm sure he never saw me. He came over here—you were out by yourself—and looked at you. He . . ."

General Street's expression had grown uncertain, but he still sounded self-possessed. "Yes, I recall now. I heard someone and asked who was there but, receiving no answer, naturally assumed it was an idly curious person desiring a closer look at a feeble old military man."

"I don't think so, General Street. He's not the idly curious type. That's why it was so strange, and that's why I came to see you. I feel worried about him."

"Worried?"

She went on unwillingly. "When he came back across the street he was crying. Because I was so . . . well, I didn't speak to him because I felt ashamed to have been spying on him. I'd been invading his privacy, really, and . . ."

"You say he was crying?" General Street interrupted harshly. "What was your friend's name, Miss Simms? You didn't mention it."

"Oh—Cyrus. Cyrus Quince. He . . ." But at the look on General Street's face, she stopped. "What is it?" she exclaimed. "What's wrong?"

He shook his head.

"What?" she repeated, alarmed. "What's the matter? Is Cyrus . . . ?"

"No, no," he said. He was smiling strangely. "It's nothing like that. But, you see, you gave me a shock." When he next spoke he sounded inordinately pleased. "You see, that young man you so shamelessly trailed is my beloved grandson."

Fyodor Stoltzoff was in a quagmire of indecision. A few months ago, Fritz Quadrata had reentered his life. At the time he had spied her at the concert, he could not have been more miserable. His career had come to a standstill. He was penniless. He had been unable to attract a woman to his bed in months, and moreover was not confident that if he had he could have—as it were—taken advantage of her presence. Finally, he recently had been diagnosed as having a severe ulcer and had been told his recovery depended upon the eating of cottage cheese. Cottage cheese! He! Who possessed the world's most discriminating palate! Then, in the midst of his misery, Fritz had reappeared, a forgotten strain of music suddenly heard anew. Fritz, the only woman to whom he had vowed eternal love! And who had spurned him! Yet he had been certain she would suffer for it. Who else would ever visit that demented household? But there she was: out in the world, among friends, with a lover (rather too boyish, good looks in the Phrygian mode, Fyodor thought disdainfully, yet this disparagement provided no solace). Fritz's evident fondness for her companion pierced Fyodor's heart like an icicle. That he might, by cruel fate, be prevented from having her he could bear; it was tragic, and how few lives these days attained the heights of tragedy? But that someone else might possess her was not to be borne. Her triumph over the maestro twisted the knife.

Fyodor begrudged Fritz no amount of musical success. Always he had adored her talent—what was he saying?—her genius! But *he* had discovered it! *He* should have been the one to bring it to the attention of the world. He would have been her mentor, her fondest adviser, upon whom she would depend—for everything! Now she was to achieve acclaim without him!

It was no happenstance, Fyodor was convinced, that, this past weekend, had thrown Fritz's companion in his path. He was driving through an outlying district of Winston when he noticed his rival (for this was what Fyodor considered him) crossing a street. Instantly, Fyodor pulled his car over to the curb, leapt out, and took off in pursuit. He worried that he might have been observed, but the idiot appeared too preoccupied to notice anything. He didn't notice when a young woman (pretty, Fyodor noted, if not particularly distinctive-looking) ran out of an apartment building and chased him in her socks! Fyodor himself barely escaped being run smack into by her; however, she too seemed oblivious of everything but her own quarry. (He kept looking over his shoulder to make sure that *he* was the last in line.)

Fyodor, too, observed Cyrus's tears, and his curiosity mounted. He continued to follow Cyrus until, after several blocks, he climbed into a car and drove away. Fyodor decided to give up the chase, returning instead to the Old Generals' Home. Posing as a journalist interested in writing a feature about retired commanders, he induced an attendant to show him about the place. (He found her most obliging—also agreeable to look at—not stupendous, like Fritz, but gentle, and very pleasant to converse with.) The generals were napping, she apologized, except for General Street, out on the lawn. If he wished . . . No, no. For the present he preferred to speak with her. Would he perhaps care to come into the office, then? Indeed he would. There she gestured at a wall on which hung photographs of all the generals in their prime. "There's General Street," she said. "He was very handsome, wasn't he?" Fyodor glanced at the photograph and was about to turn away, when something compelled him to take a closer look. He had seen that face before—but where? Then suddenly, like a Cossack galloping over a steppe, the answer came to him. In the Ludwicker family album! General Charles Street was none other than Dagobert Ludwicker, the brother of Xilipheupia Ludwicker! Fyodor was overcome by excitement. He had made a dramatic discovery! If only he could comprehend its significance!

"Do the generals' families visit them often?" he inquired, trying to imagine what a journalist might ask.

"No, not very often," the attendant replied.

"What about General Street?"

"No. But his daughter lives in Arborville; it's a long way. His grandchildren never come—no, that's not true, his granddaughter did come occasionally. To hear him talk about them, though, you'd think they came once a week. Cyrus and Betsy. You've never heard a more doting grandfather. It makes me so angry sometimes. If people realized what even an occasional visit means to an old person . . ."

"You have a heart," Fyodor said. "That is clear to see."

They began to speak of other things besides generals. Her name was Dora. He told her his. He let her wrest from him the fact that he suffered from an ulcer. Eventually he confessed that he was a violinist undergoing reverses of fortune—the only reason he stooped to something so disreputable as journalism. Of course, he went on, an exile could not be choosy. He ought to be grateful to the country that had given him asylum after politicians in his own country, his beloved Motherland, had become so literal-minded that his family had been compelled to flee, to lead thereafter an ignoble, furtive existence among the ranks of the homesick.

"How very dreadful!" Dora exclaimed.

"No, it's simply my fate," he said.

She would make him a milkshake, she announced. It could not do him any harm and would perhaps cheer him up. She was too kind, he protested.

By the time he returned home that evening, Fyodor felt better than he had in quite a while. It was almost with indifference that he dialed the Ludwickers' telephone number.

Fritz herself answered, and Fyodor attempted to sound unlike himself.

"I'm calling for Cyrus."

"He's not here. He's in Winston." Then she grew suspicious. "Who is this?"

"A friend," Fyodor could not resist saying, before he hung up. (It was an unfortunate indulgence, for in speaking those two additional words he had allowed Fritz to recognize his voice.)

Fyodor, meanwhile, could scarce contain his excitement. Dagobert Ludwicker—if Fritz was to be believed, her father—was her lover's grandfather! (Fyodor had long ago decided he had been mistaken not to take literally Fritz's claim. Sometimes he even thought everything might have turned out differently between them had he believed her at once.)

Sitting at the center of this essential secret, Fyodor felt very powerful. He felt that he held many people's lives in his hands. Surely, he thought, in this knowledge lay the seeds of his revenge. And perhaps that might have been the case, had Fyodor informed Fritz of his discovery at the time he made it. Instead, he delayed. He wanted first to learn for how long Cyrus had been aware that Fritz's father and his grandfather were the identical person. For, if he could prove to Fritz that her lover had lied to her, might she not, even now, turn for solace to him? But how he was to find out what he needed to know Fyodor had no idea.

It is a commonly held belief, in this day and age, that a person's hidden desires can impede the realization of his conscious ones. Though Fyodor was familiar with this theory, he had always held himself aloof from it, believing that unconscious motivations were characteristic of plebeian temperaments. Yet he began to fear something was at work to hinder the accomplishment of his revenge. He, with his brilliant mind, could form no suitable plan of action. Was it possible, he wondered, that he had underestimated the strength of his desire to hear Fritz play again? Not only to hear her play, but to hear her applauded, to hear her talent recognized? For he knew of her approaching debut. And if he dealt his blow before she performed . . .

A person's hidden desires are principally understood to be malevolent, but, when the goal pursued is revenge, the reverse could be the case. Alas, Fyodor began to fear that his best motives, scheming underground to outwit his worst intentions (even contriving to disguise themselves as these worst intentions!) were going to get the better of him after all.

Mutiny

In a back corner of the gardens behind the Cottage, past the rose trellis, the grape arbor, the boxwood maze, the fountain out of whose unicorns' horns water trickled slowly into a stone basin, greenish with algae, and not far from the Ludwicker family graveyard, a small stretch of lawn had been kept open between the pacing grounds of exile and the pedestrian woods, where Constantina had set up a picnic table, a set of covered swing seats, and a charcoal grill. She was very fond of cookouts.

At the moment she was in the kitchen, mixing sour cream into a package of desiccated onion-and-beef flavoring subtly complemented by the addition of various herbs and spices. She stretched to remove a platter from a cabinet above the refrigerator.

"See how it's divided into triangles for different kinds of chips and crackers with a circle in the center for the dip bowl to sit in?" she asked.

Cyrus, extracting cubes from an ice tray, nodded.

"I know you think I'm not aware of what goes on, Cyrus, but I know raw vegetables are quite popular; potato chips went out of style but now are back—they have them flavored with chives or barbecue. I still prefer them plain when they go with a dip, though, don't you?"

"Indubitably."

"Bacon is bad, eggs were bad for a while but they're regaining respect. In South America there are chickens that lay blue ones with no cholesterol in them. Ask me anything, Cyrus, I bet you can't ask me anything I don't know."

"I believe you, Sammy. When have I ever doubted you were up to date?"

"Up to date," she repeated, pleased. "Like the news. Up to the minute they keep you informed. The news is one of my favorite programs."

"Entertaining, huh?"

He sliced lime and squeezed it into his glass. Fritz wandered in from outside, wearing a white bathing suit.

"Want one?"

"No."

Sigismund, dribbling his basketball, entered on Fritz's heels. He observed Constantina arranging paper cups and plates on a tray.

"What's all this for, I'd like to know?"

"A picnic, nincompoop. Can't you tell the signs of a picnic at your age?"

"A picnic? Good show, after the game, a picnic!" Sigismund "George" Ludwicker faked a throw at a basket, swiveled rapidly, and protected the rebound from an invisible opponent.

"Billy Daphne's coming," Cyrus remarked. "An old friend of mine from high school, with his girlfriend."

"They are? When?"

"Tonight."

"What did you think the picnic was for, halfwit?"

"How would I uncover your sneaky motives, hemophiliac? Do they like to play croquet?"

"I don't know, George. You could always teach them."

"That's true," he said. "I could be the coach."

Fritz now asked, "Why are they coming? Why did you tell us only yesterday?"

"Billy called yesterday! They had already left Magnolia Junction."

"You could have told him not to come."

"I invited him, Fritz."

"You never asked my permission."

"I didn't know I had to. In case you forgot, you told me I could invite people here whenever I wanted." Cyrus spoke impatiently, but he was startled. Fritz had never pulled rank on him before.

"But not him," she said.

"How can you say that? You don't even know him."

"I don't want to."

"He's looking forward to meeting you."

"Why?" Fritz asked apprehensively. "What did you tell him about me?"

"Nothing!" Cyrus exclaimed. "I *told* you—I wrote him and asked if he wanted to get together at some point. I haven't seen him in five years. I mentioned you. What's so strange about that?"

"Why are you suddenly seeing him now?"

"I don't know. I felt like it."

"Something is about to occur I don't know about," Fritz stated.

"Such as?"

"Ever since Fyodor called . . ."

"Fyodor Stoltzoff! You didn't tell me he called!"

"Well, I'm telling you now."

"When was that?"

"A few weeks ago."

"What the hell did *he* want?"

"He . . ." Then she stopped. "I don't know. I hung up on him before he could speak."

Then Fritz looked at Cyrus in astonishment, feeling both horror and incredulity, as if she had looked into a mirror and seen not her reflection but the face of a stranger. For, except in the very beginning, when she had concealed the truth about her parents, she had never lied to him. And that time she had lied only because she was ashamed, with no cognizance that by lying she had gained control over the situation. That she could now do so by keeping from Cyrus the essential fact (that Fyodor had asked for him) was what she had—all in this moment—understood. It was a revelation such as she had not experienced since the day she first played for Fyodor and observed the power her music gave her over him.

In the wake of that first sensation came a second: she knew, extrapolating from what she herself was at that instant feeling, what a certain expression in Cyrus's eyes, which she had never before been able to decipher, signified. He had been lying to her—about something—for a long time now.

Suddenly (for the first time ever), Fritz felt a great curiosity to discover what was hidden. Although she had no inkling about the *nature* of Cyrus's lie, she saw that he must have lied in *order* to provoke in her the desire to find out his secret. It was because he envied her general Ludwicker lack of curiosity—had often been angry at her because she showed so little desire to know the world outside the Cottage. ("I just don't understand why you don't at least want to see what the world's like before you decide you're not interested in it!" he had raged.) Fritz in her turn had marveled at his need to investigate, just as now she marveled to learn that audiences demanded a program. She could not, Pierre insisted, simply improvise on stage! Some strategy—however subtle and unusual—must be adhered to! She must give people something to take home with them! "But I don't want them to take what I play home with them!" she replied, scandalized. It was enough that they were to be allowed to listen at all! Pierre had practically spluttered, trying to convince her. "Yes, it is all very well, you are nervous, you have never been away from home in your life, but it makes no difference! None of these things are adequate excuses for what you propose to do. Call me old-fashioned if you like . . ." (it had never occurred to Fritz to do so), "but my deepest belief is that to produce a tension and not to resolve it, in full conscious-ness of what you are doing, is morally reprehensible and must be prevented! What difference, my dear, does it make how magnificently you play, if there is no *order* in your music!"

Fritz had not understood him in the least—not, that is, until this moment. She now *did* see. If she could find out Cyrus's hidden knowledge, it, like the introductory chord in a musical composition that contained the organizing principle of the whole, would render intelligible the battle that had been at play between them in recent months, maybe always.

"When did you see Fyodor?" she abruptly asked.

"What!" exclaimed Cyrus. "Have you gone crazy? Why on earth would I see him?"

She looked unsatisfied.

"Fritz, I don't even know where he lives, let alone what he looks like!"

"I just don't know," she remarked. "I think you're in a plot with him. Maybe you're in a plot to overthrow the succession."

At this, Sammy and George stared at Fritz. These were accusations of treason! They were highly relieved when Cyrus replied in his ordinary way.

"For crying out loud," he said in disgust. "He's just an idiot, Fritz. It's not even worth worrying about him. Come on, why don't you have a drink with me and relax?"

"I don't want to relax," she said.

"Have it your own way, then."

"Are you having another fight?" George ventured.

"No, we're not having a fight," Cyrus answered. "At least I'm not. I'm going to lie in the late-afternoon sun and drink a toast in honor of my high-school reunion. Anyone who wants is welcome to join me."

"Thank you, but I have to make the dessert first," Sammy said. "I'm creating frozen ambrosia; you purée canned apricots and incorporate miniature marshmallows into the fruit pulp and then freeze the mixture in ice trays. You may want to serve it with whipped cream; it's optional. It's especially handy for busy people who want an elegant dessert but prefer not to take up their precious leisure time with food preparation."

"Sounds great."

"How long are they going to stay?" Fritz asked. "Maybe I'll go away while they're here."

When Cyrus merely rolled his eyes in reply, she left the room.

"Now she's in high dudgeon," Sigismund said.

"I wish I knew *why*."

"Any friend of yours is a friend of mine, Cyrus," Sammy said. She had heard this line on a TV western but until now had never found an opportunity to use it.

Cyrus frowned. "It would be nice if Fritz felt the same way."

Later, Japanese lanterns were lit and placed on poles around the clearing, and the redwood stain of the picnic table was hidden by a yellow tablecloth on top of which were arranged dishes in various pastel colors containing chopped onions, tomato slices, pickles, sauerkraut, and lettuce; jars of relish, ketchup, and mustard; larger bowls containing potato salad, cole slaw, macaroni salad, and baked beans; a tray of hot-dog and hamburger buns beside a sheaf of paper napkins printed with butterflies; a pile of plastic knives and forks and one of paper plates; a jug containing lemonade, whose tap was positioned over the table's edge above a cup on the ground; a stack of paper cups with foldout handles; several large metal spoons and two unopened bags of marshmallows. Xilipheupia, Sigismund, Cyrus, and Fritz, sitting in folding lawn chairs in a loose semicircle, were watching Constantina lift a platter of hot dogs and hamburgers from a TV tray beside the grill when the gong at the front door was struck.

Constantina looked absorbed. She had been trying to decide whether the hamburgers or hot dogs would take longer to cook so that she would know which to put first on the grill. Sigismund, who had taped his knee and was sporting a crutch in honor of the guests' arrival, had been attempting to look noble but instead looked anxious, for he was uncertain if there would be enough hamburgers for him to have more than two. Xilipheupia looked benevolent, even regal. Her faraway look told the watchful Fritz that she was thinking about Tad. When little, Fritz had had the feeling her mother was keeping her father's whereabouts secret on purpose, and it had seemed sneaky of her to ask if *she*, Fritz, was hiding him. Having so recently understood the power conferred upon a person who conceals information, she wondered what advantage her mother could have gained by pretending not to know where Tad was if in fact she did.

Cyrus was observing Fritz. She looked baffled and sad, and he had been about to say something to her—he didn't know what, just something to bring her back—when the gong sounded. He jumped up, then, giving her a last look, sprinted back to the house. Before the gong's hollow reverberation had ceased, he had reached a small white gate from which a walk led around to the front of the Cottage.

"Around this way!" he shouted, as he opened the gate. "We're all out back."

Then Billy came into sight around the corner of the building, and Cyrus's face broke into a grin.

"Billy!" he shouted. "I can't believe it! How *are* you? How was your trip?"

"Hello, Cyrus," Billy said quietly, the broad smile with which he had at first, spontaneously, responded to Cyrus's enthusiastic greeting narrowing, his expression growing polite, reserved.

Then, noticing Cyrus's smile change also to a more formal one, Billy turned. "This is Arabel Gillespie," he said. "Arabel, Cyrus Quince."

"Nice to meet you," Cyrus said.

"How do you do."

Suddenly Cyrus laughed. "God, Billy, you're not even skinny anymore! Did he ever tell you how skinny he used to be, Arabel?"

She smiled, but said nothing.

"Well, take it from me. I was an eyewitness."

I was an eyewitness too, it strangely occurred to Billy to retort. Meanwhile Cyrus was leading them back through the garden. In the dusk, Billy glimpsed statuary and pathways, disappearing into undergrowth.

"You're sure this is your girlfriend's house?" he demanded.

"I've always been under that impression," Cyrus said, grinning at Billy over his shoulder. (Billy remembered that particular grin now—Cyrus had something up his sleeve.)

As they neared the clearing, Cyrus remarked, "Maybe I forgot to mention—she's a member of an exiled royal family. They've lived here for generations. This is their ancestral estate."

Before Billy had a chance to respond, they had come upon the Ludwickers themselves.

"Well, here they are, everybody," Cyrus announced. "Billy Daphne and Arabel Gillespie. Billy, Arabel, allow me to present the Ludwickers: the Crown Princess Xilipheupia, the Princess Constantina, and, on her left, Hungry Prince George, future sports chancellor of Ludwickerland."

Sigismund beamed. "Bill Daphne! Well, well, Bill Daphne . . ."

Who was this joker? Billy thought.

Then Sigismund turned to Arabel. "And you, um . . .you'll excuse me for not getting up, um . . ."

"Arabel," Cyrus reminded him.

"Yes, Arabel. I was injured in a game this afternoon and am in a very great deal of pain."

"You are?"

Cyrus was observing, amused, then glanced at Billy, trying to catch his eye. He would have given a lot to know what Billy was thinking right then. He couldn't wait to talk to him alone. God— the stories he could finally share!

"Basketball," Sigismund said. "The most important game of the season, too."

"I'm sorry to hear that. I hope you're better soon."

Suddenly Fritz stood, glaring at Cyrus. "I knew you hardly noticed me anymore," she exclaimed, "but I didn't know I had become invisible!"

He looked at her, astonished. "Fritz! I didn't forget you! Don't be ridiculous." He went to her and put his arm around her shoulders, giving her an imploring look.

"Hello, Fritz," Billy said.

Arabel moved closer to him, taken aback by Fritz's outburst. Billy took no notice of her. Fleetingly, Cyrus wondered how long they had been together. She seemed several years younger than Billy and pretty shy.

Fritz pulled away from Cyrus and stepped toward Billy.

"I don't like you," she stated. "I never wanted you to come." To Arabel she added, "I don't like you either. I command you both to go away immediately!"

"Fritz!" Cyrus exclaimed.

"This is *not* Cyrus's house. It's mine, and I forbid you to stay another minute!"

"Fritz, stop it!" he said furiously. "They're our guests!" But George and Sammy—and Xy—were wondering if he was going to be a match for her this time.

Fritz, looking at him coldly, answered, "So are you." Then she strode past Billy and Arabel and made her way back to the house.

Cyrus stared after her angrily. Then he shrugged. "As I guess you can see, she's not used to strangers. Don't take it personally, though. She acted the same way the first time I came." He appealed to the others. "Right?"

"Yes," Xy replied. "But we have to be very careful." She looked seriously at Billy and Arabel. "I'm sure you under-stand. One can never tell when someone might be an enemy of the throne."

"Thanks a lot, Xy. That's very reassuring." He winked at Billy, but Billy was regarding him impassively. "Never mind. Come on, have a seat. Let me get you something to drink. And don't worry about Fritz. She'll be fine as soon as she gets a little more used to you. Really."

He smiled apologetically at Arabel. He was grateful when she smiled back. It was more than Billy was doing, and Cyrus was beginning to wonder if it had been wise to invite Billy to the Cottage. The visit certainly wasn't off to a very promising start. Had he let himself get carried away by the past after his visit to Amber? Though it wasn't until he had made his unsuccessful attempt to visit his grandfather that he had actually written to Billy—he had been desperate and in his desperation had let himself imagine that, of everyone in the world, Billy was the one person in whom he could confide. For once tell someone the whole truth. His desire to do this had grown so urgent that he had conveniently forgotten Billy might have changed. He had been inviting the Billy he remembered, not this new, bitter-seeming person who acted as if he had already made up his mind not to believe a word Cyrus said. Billy's sole interest seemed to be to make sarcastic comments about anything and everything—and to drink. Cyrus didn't approve of the way Billy treated his girlfriend either.

Underneath his reluctant understanding that Billy's visit was not going to rescue him from his difficulties, Cyrus began to feel bitterly sad. Where was his old friend? Jake Turner's words returned to haunt him. Had Billy been this messed up even at Fifield and he had been oblivious of it? Did he remember a person who had never existed? Or had something destroyed that person?

But he refused to think it might have been he. He did not have that kind of power over other people's lives—he resented Turner for his insinuation that he did. That was exactly what his grandfather's problem had been, too, and Cyrus hated them when he thought about it. Because they had failed to accomplish what they wanted in their lives, they pinned all their hopes on him, and then, when he didn't live up to their expectations, they were angry at him! What was it about him that encouraged people to *do* that? It was the same with H. at Chive.

But in fact he knew—or thought he was coming to see. It was what Miranda had said on occasion. Because he kept too much to himself, he let people go on believing what they wanted. The trouble was that here he was trying to remedy this situation and Billy wouldn't *let* him. That's what killed him. People said they wanted to hear the truth but, like the Campers, if you actually told them what you thought they didn't want to listen.

Over the next ten days, Cyrus's first impression of Billy was borne out. The time passed in miserable stalemate. Billy didn't want to believe Cyrus wasn't responsible for every misery that had befallen him since Fifield, for everything from joining the army to the failure of his relationship with Arabel. (What did he expect? Inviting a girl he had barely met to accompany him to a strange place—and you couldn't get much stranger than the Cottage.) And Cyrus refused—he absolutely and categorically refused—to accept responsibility for all this. He had wanted to talk to Billy as a friend—he had wanted *Billy's* forgiveness. But he felt that in order for Billy to agree to do this, he would have to subjugate himself entirely to Billy's view of what had happened. He saw how he could do this. He saw as if a real, physical distance were involved, how he could make a kind of leap and be what Billy wanted. (Be what everyone wanted. Accept the blame for everyone's unhappiness.) He saw how he could do this, but he would not. It would be like drowning, like giving himself up to some religion, though it wasn't God asking him to sacrifice himself; it was other people (although, even if it had been God, he hoped he would have had the courage to refuse).

As the days passed, it seemed to Cyrus that he ought to have foreseen all this. He blamed himself for not having considered the consequences of inviting Billy to the Cottage—the effect on his relationship with Fritz, among other things. What he could not have foreseen, however, was the added complication in the person of Arabel. From the very first night, when Billy almost totally ignored her—practically from the very first smile she gave him, he had known (he didn't know *how* he knew, but he knew) that if at some point sides ended up being drawn, Arabel was going to take his.

To begin with, Billy blamed his want of caution on the climate. On the vegetation that had urged his feelings to take forms unnatural to them. He now recalled with revulsion the frowzy willows and cypresses, the wisteria rushing up over the houses. It seemed to him that if he had been in Amber when Cyrus's letter came, able to look out at the clean lines of still winter-stripped maple and elm, he would never have taken the bait. In Magnolia

Junction, deep in the South, where Billy had spent his last two years of military service, the wanton sun had lured him off his guard, had blinded him so that he thought Cyrus was sincere in his desire to see him.

There were too many leaves down there. Creepers and vines and tendrils. Everywhere he looked something grew. Houses didn't burn there; the vines pulled them down. The vines insinuated themselves even into stone, widening cracks until entire walls and pillars toppled. Decrepit mansions careened sideways like ships. Chimneys stood alone in fields, the houses that had clothed them gone to earth long ago.

Even the flowers were part of the conspiracy. Fat and gaudy: vermilion, fuchsia, tangerine, magenta . . . When Billy closed his eyes, their garish afterimages swam before him, jeering at him for having let himself be fooled.

The air in Magnolia Junction was thick and wet, never silent. Mosquitoes and gnats incessantly hummed. It rained sometimes, but it was a devious rain. You couldn't sense it coming. Without warning everything was dripping, as if the rain hadn't come from the sky at all but instead had been sweated by the huge leaves, had oozed from under the houses' eaves. The rain never cooled the atmosphere, so thick and hot that the cats and dogs had to sleep on their backs, their paws in the air.

You could never be alone. You couldn't walk in the woods because the branches were netted together in impenetrable barriers, and the vines grew so thick and fast that even if you once entered the woods the vines would grow over the opening while your back was turned and you wouldn't be able to get out. Billy had never felt able to think clearly unless he was all alone.

Then there was the town itself, everyone sitting behind the wisteria hanging over their verandas, keeping an eye on you, making sure they knew your business. And they acted like you knew theirs, too, calling their parents "Momma" and "Poppa" to your face, instead of "my mother," "my father," as if they were *your* parents too, as if everybody in the world was one big happy family.

They loved to sit, wallowing in the scent of the magnolias, on their porches and discuss their ailments, their every little ache and pain. Death is a part of life, they said, maintaining they were not afraid to die, though if Death had come before they were ready, they would only have pretended to welcome him. They would have invited him in, with that unrelenting hospitality for which they were so famous, and have set Death down in the best armchair, stuffed him full of rum cake and chess pie and sweet pickle until he was so full he fell asleep, right there in company, and snored. Then they would have tiptoed over to the fireplace and taken down from above the mantel the gun their grandfather used in the war—they always kept it loaded just in case. Then they would cock the trigger and shoot Death full of sulphur and lead. Billy knew they would have done this to Death without batting an eyelash, if they had had the chance.

Magnolians talked all the time, and at first Billy thought they were just being friendly, but now he saw how their talk had conspired like the undergrowth in the woods to disguise the separateness between all things, and he recalled with loathing their chatter, their accent that splayed out words like rose petals blowzed open by too much heat.

There was a bar in Magnolia Junction called the Calypso where the soldiers stationed in the town spent their off-duty hours—bragged and swaggered and swigged liquor. They addressed each other by such names as Slim and Drake and Hog and Scotty, punctuating their sentences with winks, saying, We're rough and tough, mean and nasty, aren't you aching to find out for yourselves? to the damsels of Magnolia, who sat perched on bar stools and smiled at the soldiers and maintained that they were.

Billy had been a regular too, nicknamed Daffy by the others, though he had learned not to display the absent-mindedness that had earned him that *nom de guerre*. With practice he had acquired a personality superficially indistinguishable from those deployed by Slim and Drake and the others. Easygoing, devil-may-care, nominally resentful at the restrictions placed on them by army life, despite the fact that many stayed on in Magnolia Junction after receiving their discharge, loath to abandon their requisitioned identity. Billy had been among those who remained, seemingly content with the life of card games, drinking, casual sexual encounters— in the enjoyment of these pastimes, running through his savings. Sometimes he thought of applying for a VA loan, returning to Amber, and putting the farm back into operation, sometimes of going to a brand-new part of the country, starting out fresh—he didn't know at what. He had been trained as a mechanic in the army, but he didn't want to spend the rest of his life figuring out why some engine was malfunctioning.

Into this limbo dropped Cyrus's letter. Billy now, ten days after his arrival at the Cottage, remembered as clearly as if they were still occurring the events of the evening when he had decided to take Cyrus up on his invitation to visit.

In other parts of the country it might still have been winter, but in the South spring had arrived and that night the Magnolia maidens were dressed in gauzy garments in colors as flamboyant as the area's flowers. They spoke some language—it wasn't narrative speech—that was a kind of lush declension of sighs and coos guaranteed to arouse the soldiers' coxcombry. Like slow-moving willow boughs the girls oscillated from soldier to soldier, and even when pausing never altogether sat, but leaned, perched, or hovered, practicing this same choreography every night. The soldiers all called them Honey and they called the soldiers Sugar and, since they were all each other's understudies, no one was ever without a part.

That evening Billy was sitting in a booth with some of his buddies, sipping a beer, and observing the action, though his thoughts were occupied with Cyrus's letter, which rested, folded double, in his shirt pocket. Cyrus Quince, arch-traitor, popping up in his life again, wanting to get together—"for old times' sake." Cyrus Quince, the greatest liar the world had ever known.

Billy was watching the couples dancing—he didn't often dance himself, but that night he suddenly had an urge to. Sliding out of the booth, he approached a girl sitting at the bar. The tune commencing on the jukebox was an old sweet song, and when the girl—her name was Arabel Gillespie, which was all Billy then knew about her—slipped off the bar stool and into his arms as compliantly as if she had been waiting for him to ask her, Billy felt that things were about to go his way for a change.

Later they went to bed and a week after that he asked her if she felt like going North with him for a visit, and she said she did.

Billy now, stretched out on his bed at the Cottage (after the first few days, Arabel had moved out of his room), took Cyrus's letter out of its envelope and reread it, examining every line for evidence of intent to betray he might have overlooked.

Dear Billy,

Just happened by the old stomping grounds the other day and thought I'd drop by your place and see if you were around. (You weren't, by the way.) Your mother gave me your address. I really hope this reaches you.

Believe it or not, Billy, I didn't know you had joined the army until last week, when Jake Turner (remember him?) hit me over the head with the news. (He hasn't changed too much.) I've been seeing him and Agnes, ex-Mother Agnes, sometimes when I'm in Winston. Did you know they got married? (You owe me ten bucks—remember our bet?) Anyway, I was pretty surprised, I have to admit. I never thought you were really serious about enlisting. (On the other hand, I wasn't serious about Chive, and I ended up going there for four years. I graduated last May. Don't know what I'm going to do now.) What are you doing? Your mother said she thought you were out of the army by now. Are you? Or are you going to stay in and be a general? (General William Daphne—I can just see you.) Speaking of generals . . .

I don't know exactly how to put this, Billy, but I'm really sorry about everything. Not telling you about my grandfather, or about my brother, Lark. There's no excuse. It was a pure and simple lousy thing to do. Sort of a lot has happened in my life since then that's made me realize I was probably pretty messed-up when I was at Fifield. (Naturally I'm perfect now.) I guess what I'm saying is that I'd like the chance to try to explain. I was thinking, if you're out of the army, maybe you'd feel like coming to visit. I spend a lot of time at my girlfriend's place in New Jersey. (We've been together four years.) Her family has an enormous house, and you could stay as long as you want. (In fact, you could stay here the rest of your life and they probably wouldn't even notice.) Anyway, they love visitors. (They're nuts, but friendly.)

Otherwise, I could drive down to Magnolia Junction to see you, or wherever you are if you're not there (assuming you're in the continental U.S.). I really don't care how far away you are (actually, Outer Mongolia sounds pretty good right now). Just let me know—that is, assuming you feel like writing back. I'll understand if you don't.

Well, Billy, I hope you're healthy, wealthy, and wise, and having a wonderful time, wherever you are. (Also hope your hair's grown out by now.)

Yours truly,

Cyrus

No, there was no particular clue. Cyrus was too clever for that. Billy saw that circumstances had conspired to set him up—the southern climate, the people in Magnolia Junction, Arabel's sweet smile—then Cyrus could work his will. Billy remembered how, over the week before he decided to go to New Jersey, whenever he reread the letter his eyes kept returning to three words only: "I'm really sorry," in that familiar script, the letters elaborate and joined, but angular, not looped. . . . Billy had always thought Cyrus had the most distinguished handwriting.

Left to her own devices, Arabel Gillespie explored the Cottage. Sometimes she danced as she traveled along the corridors; she shivered in this huge dank house, and it warmed her to dance, set the Magnolian blood coursing through her veins—Magnolian and what else? Would she ever know?

(You're lucky, Polly Farquhar had said, most people spend their lives in search of anonymity but you don't have to worry about that. They don't want to recognize that blood means those things about themselves that can't be changed. They think if they disguise themselves then destiny can't take them by surprise, but a person so busy hiding from himself not uncommonly mistakes somebody else's destiny for his own. That's not freedom at all. Someday you'll know what I mean.)

Arabel didn't know who her father was. Twenty years ago her mother, Annie Gillespie, had preceded her on the Calypso's bar stools, and one night, as the Magnolians put it, her luck ran out. She never would say who the father was—if she knew. She mooned about in the most disgraceful way, as if motherhood were an evil fate devised for her personally, and, following her baby's birth, lapsed into soliloquy and drink, neglecting the child shamefully. It was true that in Magnolia Junction everybody minded everybody else's business, but if this hadn't been the case, Arabel would not have survived. She grew up thinking of all houses as home, though; after she first ventured to Aphrodite, the old Farquhar estate, when she was five years old, she had spent more time there than anywhere else.

It was a tumbledown place, since the end of World War Two the refuge of Palomina Farquhar (Polly), a once-talented ballerina who had been crippled when an inexperienced partner failed to catch her at the end of a flying leap. Since then she had spent her days on a chaise longue, wrapped in shawls, kept company by an old black man named Gabriel—her servant, supposedly, but many Magnolians believed lover. When they walked by Aphrodite on warm evenings they heard her and Gabriel cackling like hyenas. Nobody in Magnolia officially approved of Polly and Gabriel, but they accepted them because they couldn't remember a time when they hadn't been around, and when, shortly after Arabel's tenth birthday, Annie Gillespie was found drowned in a swamp outside of town, all Magnolians looked with favor on Polly's request to adopt Annie's child. This was done.

Polly did her best to get her new daughter educated. She sent her to school, but it didn't stick. She tried also to teach her to dance, but, though Arabel was gifted, she exercised no more discipline in this pursuit than in any other. Worried about Arabel's future, Polly scolded her. "What are you going to do when I'm gone? I won't live forever, you know." "I don't know," Arabel answered, unperturbed. "I'll get work." When she came home one day and announced that she was traveling North with a young man named Billy Daphne, one of the Calypso's soldiers, Polly didn't know what to think. She feared that Arabel, used to Magnolian friendliness, was ill-prepared for the hostilities she would encounter elsewhere. On the other hand, Polly hoped for more for Arabel than to remain in Magnolia her whole life—end up like her mother, probably. Already she was spending more time than she would confess at the bar in town. How often would such an opportunity for escape present itself?

Polly had another reason for preferring that Arabel depart at this time, too: she was dying. (A few months, a few weeks now, the doctor had said. The cancer was progressing quickly. But it's the liver, Polly, he said—an easy death—if you can call death easy. You can call death what you want, she retorted. I just call it death.) She could not abide the thought of her beloved child, so much like life, standing by while she sank into her grave, witnessing her pleas for mercy from a deity she did not believe in.

So Arabel, unburdened by the knowledge that Polly was preparing to abandon her, resided still in the assurance of Polly's and Gabriel's eternal affection, the unending sultry afternoons when she had curled up on Aphrodite's listing veranda beside Polly's chaise with her head against Polly's knee, Polly stroking her hair and in her scratchy old voice telling stories, while Gabriel, sitting on the nearby steps and puffing his pipe, chuckled at nearly everything Polly said. Arabel missed them, but she was not homesick. She was too preoccupied with the task she had recently set herself: winning Cyrus away from Fritz. It was to distract herself from her impatience with the progress she was making on this front that she began to explore the Cottage. There was a lot to explore.

There were eighty-five rooms altogether, not including attics and cellars and bathrooms (to Arabel's if not Billy's amazement, Cyrus had enumerated all this for them the night of their arrival);

thirty-three of these were bedrooms. There were thirty-nine rooms on the first floor, thirty-eight on the second, eight in the tower; there were two hundred and twenty-seven doors, including those of closets; two hundred and forty-five windows; fourteen staircases (Theobalda had been so fond of staircases that eight had been added during her reign alone); fifty-five beds, twenty-two of them with canopies; three hundred and seventeen chairs; fifteen sofas; forty-five fireplaces; twenty-seven chimneys; eighteen chandeliers; two hundred and twelve tables of all sizes and descriptions; two hundred and seventeen electric lamps; one hundred and twenty oil lamps; seventy portraits of Ludwicker relatives in the portrait gallery. . . . It was between the portraits of Constantin Ludwicker, Theobalda's father, and Manuel, Theobalda's husband, known to posterity only as Manuel the Gardener, that Arabel was standing when Cyrus kissed her. A mistake, he realized at once. He could tell by the way she kept her arms around his neck afterward that she thought it signified more than it did.

At the time they had been playing hide-and-seek, Cyrus and Billy and Arabel and George, and Arabel was It. Cyrus had concealed himself behind the drapes in the portrait gallery but had changed his mind—too obvious—but at the moment he stepped from behind them on his way to a more secure hiding place she marched into the gallery. "Shh!" he whispered. Basically it was to prevent her from calling out, "I found you!" that he pinned her against the wall between the two portraits and kissed her. It was just a spur-of-the-moment kiss. It didn't *mean* anything.

When Cyrus, five years earlier, had investigated the Cottage, its seemingly innumerable chambers, shadowy corridors, hidden staircases, and secret passageways had aroused in him a feeling of dread, as if with each door he opened he feared to come upon new evidence of ancestral treachery. But no one had taught Arabel there was any such thing as trespassing, and once Cyrus, rounding a corner and seeing her dancing, was amazed at the fearless way she sped down the corridor into the gloom, unperturbed by all those closed doors. He had never imagined that anyone could move like that: leaping, twisting, bending, springing, as if rocketed, into thin air. She flung herself with such abandon into empty space that even after she moved on it still seemed animated. It was as if he could see the afterimages of the poses she had for an instant maintained stretching away from him down the corridor like a line of girls, all of whom looked exactly like her, their outflung hands just meeting at the fingertips. And each girl grew progressively less ethereal as she gained distance from him, until, at the end, there was Arabel herself.

He wouldn't have minded continuing to watch her—it was soothing, as if she were choreographing a yearning of his own to escape immobility that he hadn't the skill to satisfy—but when she reached the end of the corridor and was about to turn, he slipped quickly out of sight, feeling a strange shyness. (This occurred prior to the fatal game of hide-and-seek.)

The colonel stood before his tent, watching as the lieutenant shouted orders at the soldiers climbing out of the trenches. They moved, it occurred to the colonel, with the same reptilian slowness that must have characterized the first slogging onto *terra firma* of man's evolutionary ancestor. Then he woke up to what was happening. "What the hell!" he bellowed, striding down the line, ignoring the troops, who booed and hissed and mockingly blew kisses.

"Would you mind informing me, Lieutenant," he asked, "that is, if it's not too much trouble, what the devil is going on here?"

"Not at all," the lieutenant replied affably, looking him in the eye. "Mutiny. That's what it's called, Colonel. Mutiny."

"Mutiny, my ass. Come off it, Lieutenant. Did you feel the need for some exercise? Tired of running in place? Or were the boys anxious for a better view? Come on, what gives?"

"I really don't have time for a bedside chat, Colonel. Let me just put it plainly. The men have decided they've had enough and I'm with the men. They asked me to take over for the march home and I agreed to. They no longer recognize your authority."

The colonel stared in disbelief at the lieutenant. Then abruptly he turned and headed back to his tent.

When the colonel had concluded that the major was not going to return, he had promoted this lieutenant, who before then had never been out of the trench, to serve as his second-in-command. He saw now that it had been a grave mistake. The lieutenant was suffering from the dizziness of high altitude. But mutiny? How could they *mutiny*?

In his tent, the colonel took from beneath his cot a locked metal box and unlocked it. Inside sat the camp telephone. He removed it, set it on his desk, and sat down. He had long ago committed to memory the secret number of the emergency line to Head-quarters, and he now dialed it. He had never done so before. *Only in case of dire emergency* . . . the condition echoed in his memory. He felt a thrill finally to be in a position to dial this number—a sensation he regarded as unseemly, but which he could not suppress nonetheless.

It took a moment for the recording he was hearing to make sense to him. "We're sorry, the number you have dialed is not in service at this time . . ." Then he heard space funneling out at the other end of the line.

For a moment the colonel sat and stared at the telephone. Then, slowly, he stood and moved to the entrance of the tent. The soldiers were falling into formation now. They were presenting arms, about-facing, high-stepping, saluting. . . . And then the lieutenant yelled, "Forward, march!" and off they went, off into the spring day. Left, right; left, right . . . Off the battlefield, into the countryside. Left, right; left, right . . . beating their retreat into private life.

One afternoon, Cyrus, Fritz, Billy, and Arabel went for a drive in Sammy's Model-K Lincoln: Cyrus at the wheel, Fritz beside him, Arabel and Billy in back. Nobody spoke. Cyrus drove slowly along the road that traveled west from the Cottage through farm-land, its meadows less steeply sloping than those around Amber and Swanbury, though its aspect was similar. The windows were rolled down and warm air, smelling of new grass, blew in, riffling their hair and their clothing. Cyrus, glancing in the rear-view mirror, saw that Arabel had closed her eyes and turned her face to the wind. Billy, gazing out his window, looked bored. He might as well be driving a hearse around, Cyrus thought.

Approximately three miles west of the Cottage, the road entered the town of Demetria, where, Cyrus noticed, the Red Cross was holding a blood drive in the local armory. They wanted to leech the spring fever out of the afternoon.

Suddenly he braked, turned the car to the right, and slid to a stop at the curb. "Thought they might need some new blood in there," he said. They were all looking at him as if he were out of his mind. "Anyone else want to come? It's a patriotic obligation, you know."

"Right," Billy said.

"You're joking, I hope," Fritz stated. "They take your blood and give it to someone else—you never know to whom. You could be walking down a street and pass a stranger who had your blood in him."

Cyrus looked at her incredulously, then laughed. He got out and slammed the door. Leaning back in through the window, he said, "Don't bother waiting, I'll walk home. See you traitors later."

He had progressed about a block, congratulating himself on his escape, when he heard someone running after him. He turned to see Arabel. Reluctantly, he waited for her to catch up. "Decided to do your duty after all?"

"No. I just wanted to talk to you."

"Oh," he said.

"Why are you always avoiding me, Cyrus? Have I offended you?"

"Why would you have offended me?"

"Because, ever since that time . . ." her face flushed, "we kissed, you've avoided me."

"I think you're exaggerating."

"What do you think I'll *do*?"

He glanced at her. "It's not what I think *you'll* do." But before she could react to this (anymore than she already had, that is; she was smiling to herself, and he wondered what brilliant thing he was going to say next), he said, "Arabel, I thought I explained. I'm not free. I know it may be hard to understand. I realize to you it may seem as if Fritz and I are not getting along, but . . ." he frowned. "I love her."

"Then why . . .?"

"I don't know why! Does every kiss have to have a reason?"

"Don't you like me?" she asked.

He stared at her. Her indignation reminded him of Betsy. (She even looked somewhat like her—like him too, he guessed.)

"I thought I just explained. Come on." He pushed against her lightly. "Don't look so sad. Please." They had now reached the steps of the armory. "Things will work out with Billy—he'll get over . . . whatever it is he's upset about."

"I'm not interested in things working out with Billy."

"Well, I can't do anything about that."

Just inside the door, in the vestibule, a man sat at a table handing out forms to be completed by prospective donors. The forms requested such information as individual and family history of disease, last time blood donated, adverse reactions—if any—to having blood drawn. . . . A moment after they had begun to write, Arabel tapped his arm.

"What?"

"This part where it asks about hereditary illness—what should I do?"

"What do you mean?"

"I mean I don't *know*," she whispered angrily.

"Well, just put that—put you don't know." He looked at her curiously.

When they had completed the forms, they joined a second line to await the actual blood giving. She was noticeably quiet.

"Are you nervous?"

"No, are you?"

"Is something else wrong? Arabel . . ." He looked at her more closely. Then he had an inkling. "Is it because of your parents?"

She nodded.

"Arabel, I'm sorry, I didn't mean . . . I'm sorry if I upset you. Do you want to go?"

"No."

Funny it hadn't occurred to him at once. Billy had briefed him on her family history, but she seemed so light-hearted he hadn't considered it might obsess her, just as Fritz's did her—as his did him. He felt admiration for her suddenly. She didn't stop to wonder whether she might make a fool of herself, did she? He would never have admitted not knowing who his father was the way she just had. Or, earlier—simply asking him bluntly if he liked her.

"We're next. Are you sure you want to do this? It's still not too late to change your mind."

"I'm not going to change my mind," she said.

"Well, don't faint, okay? I don't want to have a fainting woman on my hands."

Soon they lay, not on adjacent cots, but at opposite ends of the room, as their blood was collected in transparent pint containers. Cyrus, trying to raise himself to get a glimpse of Arabel, was ordered by a nurse to lie still. This same nurse had complimented him, as she had inserted the needle into his arm, on having "nice, accessible veins." "I've been working on it," he answered.

At last he was allowed off the cot. He crossed the room to where Arabel lay, glancing with a certain nausea at the jar filling with blood.

"How are you doing?"

She opened her eyes and smiled at him wanly. "All right."

"I'll wait for you outside."

Feeling slightly dazed, he sat down on the grassy embankment between the armory building and the sidewalk. In a short while he heard footsteps crossing the grass and she sat down beside him.

"How do you feel?" he asked.

"Okay, I guess."

They looked at each other. They were both wearing the same queasy expression. He began to laugh—so did she.

"Last time I do that for a while," he said.

"I thought you were so brave."

"Who said so?" Then he added, "We're all alone, you know. We've been abandoned."

"You told them to leave."

"I didn't think they *would*, though. Billy, at least, ought to know you can be weak after you have blood drawn."

"Do you feel weak?"

"Well, less so than I did inside."

"Then let's walk back."

"You feel up to it?"

"I feel fine now."

"You'd probably say that if you were dying," he remarked.

"What?"

"Nothing. Come on, then. Let's hit the road."

When they left the outskirts of Demetria, they walked along single file, Cyrus in front, for about half a mile. Then he stopped and turned.

"We can cut across country here. These fields will bring us to the woods behind the Cottage. It's a lot shorter—and nicer. Want to give it a try?"

She agreed, and they climbed over the rail fence and started out. Cyrus bent to pick a dandelion. "Matches your dress," he said, attempting to affix it in her hair. Impatient, he propped it behind her ear. He wished she would stop looking at him so lovingly.

"Don't!" Sigismund shouted.

"Don't what?" Billy asked.

It was the next morning, and they stood in the gardens behind the Cottage, Billy pointing a pistol at Sigismund.

"Don't shoot."

"You just shot me."

"That was different."

"But that's the game." Billy laughed. "It's only a blank."

"I don't want you to shoot me anyway. I don't like this game anymore. Let's play croquet instead."

"What are you scared of?"

"I'm not scared," Sigismund said, backing away.

Billy kept the pistol aimed at him.

The screen door slammed. Cyrus came down the back steps, carrying a cup of coffee. "What do you think you're doing?"

"Shooting George, what does it look like?"

"I'd prefer he wouldn't shoot me, Cyrus." Sigismund moved toward Cyrus, his eyes on Billy. Billy swiveled, squinting, his arm out.

"I'd prefer he wouldn't too. Come on, Bill, will you cut it out? You're making him nervous."

"Not you, though?" Billy pointed the gun at Cyrus.

"Yes, now me too. Are you happy?"

Billy shrugged. He walked to the unicorn fountain and laid the pistol on the stone rim of the basin and sat down beside it. "George asked me what games we played in the army, that's all. We used to play a kind of Russian roulette, although it wasn't the real thing because we didn't use a real bullet, and we didn't aim at ourselves. We used blanks, and whoever drew the blank had to buy the next round of drinks. It's no big deal, Cyrus."

"People can die of shock from having blanks fired at them, you know. They never find out it was only a joke."

Sigismund, glancing from Billy to Cyrus, said, "I'm busy now, I think I remembered. I hope very much that you will excuse me. I would very much like to stay, but . . ."

Cyrus moved aside to let Sigismund pass. When the door shut behind him, Cyrus sat down on the steps and took a sip of his coffee.

"He *asked* me to show him," Billy said. "I didn't force him to play. Besides, you act like his father. Don't you think he can take care of himself?"

"He asked you to stop and you wouldn't."

"He shouldn't be such a sissy."

"It's none of your business what he is. Just leave him alone, all right?"

"You think you can run everybody's life, don't you?"

"I don't think I run everybody's life." Cyrus looked at him. "Why do you think that?"

"For obvious reasons."

"What obvious reasons?" When Billy refused to answer, Cyrus said, "Why don't you just *say* it, Billy! You're so obviously pissed off at me—you have been since the moment you arrived, but you won't say anything."

"I just think you treat the Ludwickers like babies. Like the way you just helped George out! And they're always making ridiculous comments—what they say about the army, for instance—and you just let them go on thinking these crazy ideas."

"*You* try to tell them. Then you'll realize why I stopped bothering."

"Why don't you ever take them anywhere? I can't believe they've lived here their whole lives and never left. They even get their groceries delivered. I still can't believe they're for real."

"Get used to it. They are."

"You ought to charge admission. All that royal family stuff. And that show they go through every night at dinner, saying all their ancestors like grace."

"Tell me about it." Then Cyrus asked repentantly, "You want a cigarette?" He tossed the pack to Billy, who lit one and tossed the pack back. Seeing Cyrus feeling for a match, he threw a matchbook too.

"The Calypso? What's that?"

"A bar in Magnolia Junction. Where I met Arabel."

"Oh, yeah, she said . . ." He laughed.

"I don't see the joke."

"It's hard to picture her in a bar, somehow."

"What's so hard about it?" Billy's tone was sarcastic. "She slept with every Tom, Dick, and Harry that came into the place." He laughed in a private way—a bitter, mirthless snicker that reminded Cyrus of the way Billy's mother laughed. It gave him the creeps.

"Surprises you, huh? Take my word for it, though. She's a real slut. She may not look like it, but it's true."

"That's a pretty lousy thing to say about your own girlfriend, don't you think?"

"My girlfriend . . . She latched on to me when she found out I was leaving town. Wanted a ticket out of Magnolia Junction, that's all."

"I find that hard to believe. I think she really likes you."

"Right. That's why she's been throwing herself at you."

"That's not true."

"Fritz noticed. You're the only one who pretends it's not happening."

"I'm not pretending because it's not the case." It wasn't, either. Anything she might now be doing he was responsible for. He couldn't tell that to Billy, though. So here he was, once again keeping something from him. If you paid more attention to her, he felt like saying, she would lose all interest in me.

"You wouldn't mind getting her in the sack, though, would you? Why don't you just admit it?"

Cyrus stared at him, then exclaimed, "What's *with* you? You act like you want me to go after her! Are you just trying to pick a fight or what? I'd really like to know."

Billy responded coldly. "I'd like you to be honest for once."

"I'm being honest! I've told you I like Arabel." He frowned. "I even admit I think she's pretty—attractive—whatever you want me to say. She also happens to be relaxing to be around, probably because she's younger. Mainly it's probably relaxing because I know she's your girlfriend."

"Don't make me laugh."

"I wasn't attempting to."

They regarded each other with hostility.

"You're as deceitful as ever," Billy said. "I can't believe I thought you could have changed."

"Why did you bother to come then? If that's how you felt."

"You invited me."

"I wanted to see you," Cyrus said simply.

Billy looked dubious.

"No one's forcing you to stay, you know."

"Thanks for telling me."

"Billy!" Cyrus said. "I *told* you in my letter I was sorry—about all the stuff that happened at Fifield, and I meant it. I don't know what else I can say."

"I don't believe you because I still don't see why you had to lie, except that you didn't trust me to keep my mouth shut." Billy spoke bitterly. "I would have told you about something like that. I thought we were friends, but you were just making a fool of me."

"I wasn't! You were the only person I liked at Fifield, for God's sake. I didn't tell you because I couldn't!"

Billy shrugged indifferently.

"I loved him!" Cyrus exploded. "Can't you understand anything? I couldn't tell you because I loved him!" He went on in a quieter voice, "He was going to die and I couldn't stand it. *I* couldn't stand it, did you hear that? *He* never complained once. He knew too, although everybody said he didn't. Everybody pretended he wasn't dying. The doctors, the nurses, my parents. They said it was 'better that way.' It would 'keep his spirits up.' Can you believe the idiocy of that? He was *dying* and they were worried about keeping his spirits up! He was nine years old and he was incredibly smart.

"He couldn't talk much after he was about six. What he had was some kind of deterioration of the nervous system. It's a congenital disease, and it's very rare—only a few thousand people in the country have the particular defective chromosome that causes it and your husband or wife has to have it too or something that complements it, I forget exactly, but even so it's rare—Betsy and I didn't get it. Anyway, Lark could always understand everything perfectly well, but for some reason people are so stupid they think that if you can't talk you don't understand what's said to you. Except I'm really to blame because I *knew* he could understand and I never talked to him either. I imagined conversations. I wanted to ask him if he was scared to die. I wanted to tell him that if he had to die I would stay with him the whole time. And I wanted him to know that I would never forget him. No matter what else ever happened in my life, it would never be the same after he died." Cyrus's voice broke, briefly. "I never said any of those things. Every time we visited, I told myself I'd wait until the next time. I'd tell myself there was no point in upsetting him for no reason. The truth was that I couldn't accept the fact that he really *was* going to die. Then he had the accident."

His eyes shining with tears, Cyrus looked at Billy. He laughed, embarrassed. "It was like the plot we had to rescue my grandfather. It could never have happened, and I knew it perfectly well, but sometimes I almost believed it would. But it was the same thing as with Lark: I was selfish. I didn't want to see my grandfather because it would upset me. I kept remembering how much I loved him when I was little—I thought he knew everything in the whole world, and I *believed* everything he told me—and then compared that to how I'd grown to resent him. . . . I didn't want to talk to Lark about death because I couldn't bear to. I pretended I loved them both, but I didn't. You don't treat people like that when you love them."

Billy felt confused. As Cyrus had spoken, he could recall his former love for him—for the Cyrus for whom he *had* been the only likable person at Fifield. Cyrus had often preceded his statements with the avowal, "I never told anyone this before." And Billy had believed him. When Cyrus had accepted his offer to help locate his missing grandfather, Billy felt for the first time in his life that his help was worth anything. When Cyrus left, he felt mocked. He had, in the five years since, lived with the belief that Cyrus had known of something in him—some hideous fault or undependability—to merit such treatment. Now here was Cyrus, not simply offering a full pardon, but denying he had judged him in the first place. Where would that leave him?

"Is your grandfather still alive?" he asked uncertainly.

"Yes. I still haven't been to see him." He half laughed. "I tried. I got about ten feet from him and then I left."

"Ten feet?"

"He's fully blind now. He couldn't see me."

"You didn't say anything to him?"

Cyrus shook his head. "Bill . . ." He gazed at Billy, feeling extremely nervous. Here goes nothing, he thought. "There's something else about my grandfather I haven't told you."

"What?"

Cyrus noticed that the sneer had disappeared from Billy's voice. In his relief, Cyrus grinned.

"*What*?" Billy demanded.

Standing, Cyrus asked, "You feel like going for a drive? I don't particularly want to talk here."

"I guess. Sure." Billy stood also, leaving the gun lying on the fountain. Cyrus tossed the cold dregs of his coffee on the grass.

When the two of them had disappeared around the side of the house, Fritz, who had been watching from her bedroom window, ran downstairs and claimed the gun.

No sooner was Cyrus's car out of sight around a curve in the road than Fritz was in hers and driving away herself—to Winston.

Fyodor Stoltzoff's address and telephone number were listed in the Winston telephone directory, and eventually Fritz succeeded in finding his apartment building. It was a decrepit structure, and the front door was unlocked. As she made her way up the sagging stairs and along the dark hallways in search of Fyodor's apartment number, she felt in her handbag for the gun.

Fyodor was slow to open the door. "Yes?" he said. Then he saw who it was. "Fritz . . ." he murmured. "It is you! But you must not come in here! I would not wish you to see the sad circumstances upon which I have fallen. . ." He looked wildly over his shoulder at Dora, lying among the rumpled bedclothes. "Let me fetch my shoes, and . . ."

"I don't want to come in," she said. "I came only to ask you a question. Why did you call Cyrus?"

"I . . . Fritz, my dearest, we cannot talk here. Please."

"Answer my question."

"The answer is too complicated."

"I demand to know it now." She brought out the pistol and aimed it at his chest.

"You cannot be serious!"

"Tell me!"

"No, I will not." She wanted to know! She was not supposed to want to know!

"Very well, then."

Fritz was not a woman to stall for time—she pulled the trigger. It merely clicked impotently. She fired a second time; this time there was a stupendous noise, and Fyodor staggered backward before he realized that he had not been hurt.

"Your gun is broken," he sneered.

"It's Billy Daphne's stupid gun!" she cried, flinging it down the hallway. "No wonder it doesn't work!"

She then ran from the building. Fyodor, infuriated, hurried to the window of his apartment that faced the street and leaned out.

"Ask your beloved Cyrus who his grandfather is!" he shouted. "Then you will think twice about scorning me!"

"You do not know his grandfather's name?" asked the maestro, perplexed. He had not doubted Fritz's story, not for one minute (for which she, who liked him already, liked him still further), though he was most alarmed to hear she had threatened the violinist Fyodor Stoltzoff, who had the reputation of being a madman, with a gun—not only that, but had left the evidence behind her.

"You are lucky," he said, "that it was Stoltzoff you threatened. He is too vain to consult the authorities. But you must promise me never to do such a thing again."

"How can I?" she replied. "I threw away Billy's gun."

The maestro groaned. "Do let us be sensible, Fritz. Now, who else do you know who is acquainted with Cyrus and who might know his grandfather?"

. . .

It was early evening by the time Fritz rang the doorbell of Jake and Agnes's apartment. Jake professed himself astonished, though of course delighted, to see her. Agnes and Lilith were out shopping. Fritz cut him short, announcing she had come only to ask him a question. It was with difficulty that he prevailed upon her to sit down.

"Shoot," he said.

"What do you know about Cyrus's grandfather?"

"Do you speak of General Street?"

"Yes. He really is a general then?"

"Was," Jake replied.

"He isn't anymore?"

"He's dead!"

"That's not what Cyrus told me. He told me he lived in a retirement home in Winston."

"Maybe he did live there. He's dead now. He died around the time Cyrus got out of Fifield."

"He was still alive when Cyrus went to Chive."

"Well, that . . ."

"I think I would have known if his grandfather had died since I knew him," Fritz said.

"I should think you would," Jake said, but he sounded annoyed. "Evidently our friend has some difficulty in keeping the facts straight where Charlie Street is concerned. But I'm afraid you're going to have to have it out with Cyrus. I don't see how I can help you."

Fritz was tapping her foot impatiently. "Is Cyrus wicked?" she asked.

"What did you say?" Jake gasped.

"I said, 'Is Cyrus wicked?'"

Jake shook his head. "Forgive my incredulity, but how can you ask such a thing? *Why* are you asking such a thing?"

"Is he a liar?"

"Fritz . . ." Jake looked distressed. "That's a harsh accusation. Cyrus has always kept his own counsel. Yet I would have thought that with you . . ."

"Did you know his grandfather?"

"You mean Cyrus didn't tell you . . .? I must say there certainly seems to be a gap somewhere in your communications. I served under General Street in the war, Fritz."

"What war?"

"The World War," Jake answered in amazement. "The Second." At a loss, he asked, "Would you like to see a photograph of Cyrus's grandfather? I have one I know even Cyrus hasn't seen, since I took it myself. I keep meaning to show it to him."

"I don't want to see it," Fritz said, alarmed. "I don't like to look at photographs of people I don't know."

"Come on," Jake chided her gently. "It's Cyrus's mystery grandfather. I'm just trying to reestablish a little sense of reality here."

Jake went into the bedroom and Fritz sat stiffly, listening to the ticking of the clock on the mantel. Its inexorable one-two, one-two, usually merely dull to her, was jeering. Jake returned, bearing a battered cigar box, and sat down beside her.

"I'll spare you my old girlfriends and all the ones of myself at various stages of my career," he said, shuffling through the photographs. "My high-school graduation, my first wedding . . . my parents' wedding! Good God, didn't know I had that! Ah, here it is!" he exclaimed triumphantly, drawing forth a curled and yellowy snapshot. "I took this on a furlough we had in Rome. At the Colosseum. He didn't know I was taking it. He would have ducked— one of those people who hates to have his picture taken. Here— have a look."

Reluctantly, Fritz accepted the photograph. It showed Charles, still wearing Tad's mustache, sitting on a crumbling stone wall, elbow on knee, chin in palm, looking pensive. Fritz had often seen Cyrus assume this same posture.

"So that's him," Jake said cheerfully. "The missing grandfather. Good-looking chap, isn't he? Doesn't look . . ." Happening to glance at Fritz, he broke off in mid-sentence. Fritz was trembling. Her face, pale ordinarily, was drained entirely of color.

"What on earth's the matter?" he exclaimed. "You look like you're going to pass out!"

"I'm not," Fritz said. Her voice was eerily calm. Jake suddenly wondered if she was quite right in the head.

"What's wrong, Fritz?" He laid a hand on her arm. "It's only a photograph."

Fritz attempted to stand, but she was trembling so violently she had to sit down again. Jake regarded her with concern.

"He can't be dead," she said. "He can't be."

"Fritz, I . . ." Something must have happened, something that had knocked her off the beam. A fight with Cyrus? "Can you tell me what the matter is?"

"Nothing is the matter." She handed back the photograph. Then she tried to stand again and this time succeeded. "I have to go, that's all. I have to find him."

"But, Fritz, General Street is dead."

"No," she said, "he isn't." She now sounded exultant. "General Street is my father."

The maestro took this news in stride. At his suggestion, she telephoned all the Streets whose telephone numbers were listed in the Winston directory; thus she came upon Sophie. Without identifying herself, Fritz demanded to know the whereabouts of General Street. Sophie replied haughtily that the General did not keep her informed. "Is he alive?" Fritz asked. "Who is this?" Sophie demanded. "I can't tell you," Fritz answered. (The maestro had coached her not to give away this information.) "Then I'm afraid I cannot help you," Sophie responded, hanging up.

"Never mind," Pierre comforted her. "We'll find him. And we'll find out where your family comes from, too. We'll study all the family trees in the world, if necessary."

Next Fritz telephoned the Cottage and ordered Cyrus not to attend her concert. They had planned that he would persuade Xy and George and Sammy to attend as well. But now she maintained that it would make her too nervous to have her family in the audience.

"Why have you decided that now?" he demanded. "And why did you leave without saying goodbye? Did you take Billy's gun?"

"Yes. I had to shoot Fyodor."

"You WHAT?"

"I don't wish to speak about it."

"Fritz, I'm coming up there."

"No, you are not."

This tug of war continued until Pierre grabbed the receiver from Fritz's hand and said icily, "You try my patience. Do you not respect Fritz's wishes? Or are you of limited intelligence? She requests you to stay home!"

By the end of the first day of their mutinous march, the regiment had broken up into companies. Bob Jones marched with the men from his hometown, his friends and neighbors: Howie Thurston, Mick Savely, Dave Chubb, and others. The lieutenant, whose name was Bernie Wilson, was among them. They had all known each other since they were knee high to grasshoppers.

It was dusk on the third day when they came upon the major's house. They were tired, but in high spirits, and had been singing and joking and laughing, groaning as they reminded one another of the simple pleasures of home. A hot shower and then a cold beer in the backyard—the angels could *keep* heaven! But, when they rounded a bend in the road and saw the great house standing in the dusk, steeped in silence, mist rising from the fields all around, they grew quiet. They had been straggling, but as they crossed the expanse of ground between the road and the house they instinctively drew into formation. They gazed uneasily at the upper windows, expecting gunfire to burst forth. When they reached the front steps, Bernie whispered, "Halt, you guys. I'll do this." After the first day, he had given orders only in jest, but now they did as he said, and he climbed the steps and dropped the brass knocker.

But nothing happened. No one answered.

"Nobody home," Bernie announced in a singsong voice, but none of them laughed.

"This place is spooked," Mick Savely whispered. "All this fog everywhere . . ."

"It's like being in an old black-and-white movie."

"I feel as if I've been here before," Bob mused.

"I get that feeling too—in a dream or something."

"Hey," Bernie said, "you guys are giving me the willies. Knock it off, will ya? I'm going to go in and have a look around. Put on a few lights, it will seem like home sweet home. We'll build a fire—I'll bet you there are fantastic fireplaces in this joint—pitch our tents in the ballroom . . ." He caught Mick in his arms. "Want to dance?" Then he turned the doorknob. It was locked. "We'll find a way in. We're requisitioning this place!"

They circled the house, brave again, but it was Bob who found the open window into the pantry. He almost shouted to the others, but he didn't. Instead he climbed in and shut the window softly behind him. He wanted to be alone inside. Why did he feel he had been there before? How did he know where to go?

The house was full of shadows, yet enough light remained to enable Bob to make out doorways and windows, to avoid the looming furniture, as he traveled through the first floor and made his way to the second. As he started up the narrow steps to the top story, he felt very strange. A fetid smell, faint when he began climbing, overwhelmed him as he opened the door. Reluctantly, he struck a match, in order to see more clearly what he had already seen.

The other men were still circling the house when they saw a light flare in an upper window and simultaneously heard a yell.

"Break the door down!" Bernie commanded

By the time they found Bob, he was sitting on one of the child-sized beds, staring dully before him. From a rafter, above a tiny overturned chair painted with bright-colored birds and flowers, the major's body hung.

They cut the major down and buried him by moonlight beneath a towering oak. When they had shoveled the earth back into the grave, they broke branches from the tree, stripped them of bark, and fashioned a cross from them. On it they carved the major's name and the date. Not knowing what else to do, they fired a military salute. Then they headed back to the mansion.

"Come on, Bob," Bernie said. "Come on in with us."

Bob stared silently at the major's grave.

"He's dead, Bob. We gave him a decent burial. We fired a salute for him. There's nothing else we can do."

"I know. I'd just like to be alone for a minute."

"All right. But don't be long." He clapped him on the back. "And that's an order."

Bob smiled absently. "Sure, Bernie."

He waited until Bernie was out of sight. Then, taking out his pocketknife, he knelt in the fresh earth and carved on the cross: KILLED IN ACTION.

Sliding the bow, which she did not forget was made from the hair of horses, across the strings, which she did not forget were made from the insides of cats, Fritz studied the audience's faces. She waited until they were comfortable, swaying and smiling, believing she would give them what the first strains had led them to expect; then she broke their hearts.

When they began to drift away on some tender adagio, she stepped up the tempo, shifted key, raced from assonance to dissonance. After the first shock, they would become determined not to be seduced again and would concentrate in order to maintain their perception of the more melodic sections as part of a cacophonous whole, as merely a lull before the inexorable victory of pandemonium. Yet such was Fritz's skill that each time she persuaded her audience anew that the disharmony had been the aberration, not the other way round. Once again they permitted themselves to believe that in the end the beloved familiar would triumph over the dread unknown.

Fritz did not play from a score, nor did she direct her gaze into the middle distance; throughout the concert she looked directly into the eyes of her audience—caught each alone and stared him down. The audience grew hypnotized; they began to feel about her as certain falsely accused prisoners, when time passed and they were not freed, did about their captors, since their captors knew when they would be released. Just as, over time, such prisoners grew to wonder if they were guilty after all, so did Fritz's audience begin to worry that they might bear some responsibility for the confused state of the psyche her music portrayed—she stared at them so accusingly, as if she played what she saw in their eyes.

On occasion, the wrongly accused were taken from their cells and tortured, and it was learned that under torture people could be made to confess to sins they had never committed, thereafter would even believe they deserved punishment, might beg for more of it, submit themselves to it body and soul, hoping thus to assuage their sense of guilt (even though, being unmerited, it could never be dispelled). What was just beginning to be discovered, however, was that a torturer studied his victims for clues to his own feelings, and the question was raised as to what might happen were the victim, so seemingly helpless, to say, Do not worry; you are *capable* of love. It is because you doubt this capacity in yourself that you torture *me*. Yes—it even came to be thought that the tortured were to blame for the torturing, that the torturer should be absolved. . . .

The maestro, listening in the wings (he had not wanted to sit in the audience for fear they would look to him for direction on how to react to his protégé's performance), began to realize that, despite Fritz's assurance to him before the concert that she had now conceived of a suitable conclusion to the piece, she had said so merely to appease him. In fact she had lost herself in the argument and was powerless to resolve it. He saw that to her piece there was no foreseeable ending; there was no possible conclusion, and there was no extrication from this impasse.

Yet he did not want to believe this was so. Can you not take a stand anyway? he beseeched her. Do you truly believe it is impossible to discover who is doing what to whom?

He feared that, when the audience recovered from being

dumbfounded, they would jeer, and he began nervously to tap his feet—Fritz's own habit—wishing now simply that she would stop, even on a questioning note.

The next day it was raining; at the Cottage fat, slow drops runneled down the window glass, built on the tips of pine needles until, attaining a critical weight, they fell. It was a gloomy, persistent rain, and to Cyrus, awaiting Fritz's return, it seemed there had never been any other weather. There was even fog, loitering about the lawn like pieces of fallen cloud.

He had begun expecting her about two o'clock (pacing up and down, though never straying far from the front windows), but it wasn't until nearly six that he heard her car drive in. He hurried into the entrance hall and was waiting there when she dashed in out of the rain.

He merely stood, waiting for her to speak; fleetingly he thought he had never seen her look so lovely: the run from the garage had left her pale cheeks lashed with color, and her skin seemed practically to shimmer. Her hair was pinned up but the humidity had curled loose strands around her face, softening it, and he wanted to go to her and embrace her, wet raincoat and all, but he did not dare.

He waited, instead, but when at last her eyes collided with his, she did not have to say a word. One look was all it took.

Cyrus thrashed out of sleep. He came up like a diver out of oxygen and lunged into consciousness. His heart pounded, and it seemed to him that someone was in the room. Had the door just closed? He sat up, breathing shallowly.

A trickly light, the moon's, was scattered about the room, the moonbeams broken by the pine tree outside his window. Often he had fallen asleep to its branches' low soughing, trying not to notice his breathing evening out. Fritz said that when he slept he breathed in four-four time. Even in sleep her hearing was so acute that if the rhythm of his breathing changed she woke instantly. Whenever he had cried out in a nightmare, she woke up and then woke him. Then they had talked, or gone for a walk, checking first to see if Sammy and George and Xy were about. Somnambulists all, the Ludwickers continued in sleep their daytime activities; it was not unusual to find George shooting baskets under the stars, Xy, her eyes closed, sitting in an armchair turning the pages of a book, or Sammy baking a cake in the unlit kitchen.

He switched on the light beside his bed and looked at his watch. Three o'clock in the morning—the hour, Charles had once told him, when the shift changed in heaven, the hour most people died. The angels' attention strayed. *That's why you wake up, Corporal. Someone has to keep an eye on things.*

Cyrus leaned back against the headboard, propping himself up. His head was splitting, his mouth was dry, and he was still wearing his clothes. How had he gotten where he was? Who had helped him to bed? Who had laid a blanket over him and turned out the light? He didn't remember doing any of these things himself.

He did remember Fritz's arrival, meeting her in the front hall, realizing what he had suspected after her phone call—that she knew, she had found out about Tad; he remembered leaving the room and going into the dining room and taking a bottle from the sideboard and deliberately setting out to get drunk. After that, his memory yielded little.

He got up now, went out into the hallway and into the bathroom, took two aspirins and brushed his teeth. Then he advanced down the long carpet toward the stairs; the Mickey Mouse night light punctured the windowless dark of the hall; everyone, it seemed, slept.

Downstairs, he stood and listened. Not a sound. Even Xy, Sammy, and George, he thought sadly, were asleep in their beds.

Quietly, like a custodian, he made his way around the Cottage, opening doors one by one, entering rooms, making sure that everything was as he remembered. After all the rain it was a cloudless night, and a large aqueous moon had windowstriped the rooms. All the shiny objects throughout the Cottage glinted: candlesticks, doorknobs, suits of armor, brass lamps, andirons, silver pitchers. . . .Everywhere the fey, intermittent light tried to trick him into believing the shadows held some company. The loneliness he never permitted himself to feel in the daytime he could never defend himself against in the small night. During those stray hours, when one day had ended but the next had not yet begun, his defenses were stripped away, and it was always then that he missed Charles the most. It was then that he would remember how, in Arborville, it was always Charles who heard him leave the house if, unable to sleep, he sneaked out for a nighttime ramble. Charles would be downstairs waiting when he came home. They would sit in the kitchen, putting on only the small light over the sink, and whisper. Charles always winked at him the next morning at breakfast. Cyrus wondered if Charles, when he was Tad, had wandered through the Cottage in the moonlight. Had he too sat and watched Xy and George and Sammy doing things in their sleep and wished for them to wake up? Was that why he had been so sympathetic to a little boy's insomnia? Those nights in Arborville—had he been thinking of another house a thousand miles away? Had his grandfather been homesick all his life?

Cyrus heard again his grandfather's deep, soft voice, telling a story so Cyrus could go back to sleep, Charles interrupting himself with his wry, gentle laugh; he saw his grandfather's veined, knotty hands, resting on his knees; and he saw the faraway look in his eyes. And, as always, on the other side of his mind he saw young Tad Ludwicker, with his flamboyant mustache and mocking smile, the two of them standing before him as if for judgment.

Until now he had found them guilty. He had beheld them without pity until sadly they turned away from him and disappeared.

But tonight, when he looked at them, they looked back at him unashamed, saying, *You understand now, don't you? You know now what it means to love what you must lose, and you will learn what it is to live in exile, how what you have lost will not let you alone, will deny you happiness in what you have, until all you have left are the tales you told yourself.*

Charles seemed to smile wistfully at this wisdom but Tad shrugged impatiently, as if tired of so much fine sentiment and desiring to be permitted simply to enjoy life, the way he had before he developed a conscience to trouble him.

Instead of vanishing, though, as they always had before, Charles and Tad turned away from Cyrus and regarded one another: the gentle, resigned old man who lived alone in his world of dreams, and the restless young one, wanting to go out into the world and wrest it into the shape of his mind. Oblivious of Cyrus now, of any lingering desire of his to prevent them, they moved toward each other and were conjoined.

He had returned to the stairway and now climbed back up and walked down the corridor past Xy's, Sammy's, and George's rooms, stopped outside Fritz's door and carefully turned the knob. It was unlocked. He went inside, shutting the door gently behind him.

In the moonlight he could see her clearly, sleeping on her side. As he watched, she murmured and turned onto her back, tossed an arm over the edge of the bed. He smiled. When sleeping alone she was a violent and passionate sleeper, but when he slept beside her she could sleep an entire night without moving, as long as he didn't move.

He stood a moment longer watching her, then sat down on the bed. She didn't wake. Stretching out, he lay beside her and pressed against her; still asleep she turned toward him. He put his arms around her and kissed her hair, and she sighed, nestling closer, sleepily stretching an arm across his chest. He tightened his embrace. Suddenly she was wide awake.

"Cyrus . . ."

"I love you," he whispered.

"I love you too. I wish I didn't but I do. I wish I hated you. You don't know how much I wish I hated you."

"You know, don't you?"

"Yes."

They whispered between kisses, caresses, exchanged hurriedly, before the memorized gestures seemed strange to them, before their new knowledge of one another filtered into their blood.

"How did you find out?"

"Jake Richmond-Turner."

"Jake!"

"He had a picture of Tad. He was with him in the war."

"How did you know that?"

"I didn't. I visited Jake to ask him about your grandfather."

"But what made you visit him?"

"No one thing. Fyodor calling—he asked for you, you know."

"For me!"

"I don't know what he wanted."

"Did you tell Jake about Tad?"

"I told him the man in the photograph was my father."

"You did! What did he say?"

"I think he thought I was crazy. I never felt less crazy in all my life. So much made sense suddenly." She laid her hand on his face. "Did you keep it secret because you thought I would forbid you to come here anymore if I knew?"

"You would have!"

"Maybe. But I feel so sorry for you."

"You feel sorry for *me*?"

"Because that's not the real reason you didn't tell me."

"What do you mean?"

She merely repeated, "It would be so much easier if I could hate you, but now I am in pain thinking about your pain. I never hurt for anyone else before, and I don't like it. I can't think. I thought I could finish my composition—I never even cared to finish anything before, until I knew you were lying and I saw that photograph. All the way driving back from Winston I could see the way to the end and I thought that when I saw you and made you know what I had found out I would be able to play the rest, but then you looked so bewildered and hurt."

"But I love you, Fritz. I don't want to lose you, don't you understand? No one else knows me. No one else in the entire world!"

"No one knows me either. No one ever will—except you. That is our fate. We're doomed. That's what it means to be a Ludwicker.

Now I know how Tad felt when he left. Now I'll be like Xy, missing you all my life."

Except you'll have Tad, he thought.

"Don't say that. I'm here, Fritz. I'm not leaving you."

"Please just hold me." They were silent awhile. Then Fritz asked abruptly, "Did he know about me, Cyrus?"

"Granddad?"

"Tad. Mother said he did, and I always believed her, but Sammy said he only came back one night. He came into her room also and kissed her and she thought it was a dream until she got up in the morning and saw how happy Mother was. Did he know about me, Cyrus? I want to know the truth."

"No, I don't think so, Fritz. But I don't know."

"Jake said he's dead. Is he dead?" Then she added fearfully, "Did he die since you've known me?"

"He's not dead, Fritz."

"He's not dead! Oh, Cyrus . . .I knew it! Where is he?"

"Where I told you. In Winston City at a home for retired generals."

"You mean you *see* him?"

"I don't see him. I haven't seen him since before I went to Fifield. I could never have gone to see him and not told him about you. He's the one person I could never lie to. It seems strange, after all the lying he did. But I promised him I wouldn't. And I guess I've never really stopped loving him, even after I found out what he did. I think that's partly why I couldn't tell you—I thought I would have to hate him."

"No," she said, "you were afraid he would love me better than you. I am more closely related."

"What?" he exclaimed.

"I love him, too, Cyrus."

"But how can you? He's my grandfather."

"He's my father."

This was where they stopped. They grew sleepy. Cyrus was almost asleep and thought Fritz was when she said, "Would you mind going back to your room, Cyrus? I would like to be alone now."

"All right," he agreed.

She was gone when he got up in the morning.

Billy and Arabel were eating breakfast together. Billy had been somewhat friendlier to her since he and Cyrus had gone for their drive.

"How's your head?" Billy asked.

"My head?"

Billy laughed. "I've never had so much trouble getting a drunk to bed in my life."

"That was you?" Cyrus smiled wanly and sat down. About noon, he wrote down his grandmother's telephone number in Winston for Billy and Arabel. He told them to stay at the Cottage as long as they wanted—he wasn't sure when he'd be back, and took off for Winston in pursuit of Fritz.

That evening, Arabel received a telephone call from Magnolia Junction informing her that Polly was dead. Billy drove her to the nearest airport and paid for her plane ticket home.

"Are you going to come back?" he asked.

"I don't know," she answered. "I can't think about anything now." She didn't ask for his address in Amber, and he didn't offer it to her.

As he walked to the parking lot, it occurred to Billy that once again death had come into life, like a wedge driven into a log, and split the living apart.

The Lines Are Drawn

Most old women boarded the trolley after rush hour. That way they avoided the stampede of the nine-to-five anonymous, too proud of having evolved beyond sentimentality to let the old women who rode early sit down. The cars were crowded with these efficient and ferocious commuters, who shifted their briefcases and furled umbrellas from hand to hand and thought their competent thoughts, trying to ignore the old women who had the audacity to want to go on living, even though anyone could see they had nothing and no one left to live for.

The commuters did not like to be reminded that life ended in pettiness, that one could spend one's last days counting: pennies and pills, hours of sleep and bowel movements, friends remaining; that one was doomed to undergo the body's slow degeneration. First the back would become less supple; then cataracts would creep over the eyes; the hair would thin and whiten; the internal organs would begin to fray. All the grand emotions would be reduced to discrete nuggets: *Yes, that was when I knew love. That was when I was happy.* Scenes from the past that once had blossomed in the heart into eternity would dangle in the memory like charms from a bracelet. (Although Sophie could have told them it was not like that.)

No old men rode the trolley. *They* didn't live in little houses in the suburbs, counting every cent; you never saw *them* on their way into town in the morning, grasping tight to life. The old men were all downtown, slumped on park benches or in the doorways of derelict buildings, wearing mismatched socks and five-day beards, hands clutching the necks of bottles even while they slept. And what did this say about the sexes, that the old men came loose at the seams, lost buttons and stopped shaving, while the old women put more locks on their doors, hoarded toast they had not finished, washed themselves as frequently as cats? Poor old men—the old women had thrown them out! Gotten what they wanted from them (children, maybe; houses, possibly) and then chucked them into the street. Into the grave.

Who went to war? demanded the young men—youthful up-and-coming doctors, lawyers, bankers, stockbrokers, business-men. . . . Who risked their lives in defense of the country? In defense of the country! In defense of old ladies riding the train! And look how men were rewarded! They were evicted from their homes! (If they lived . . .)

But the young women too were frightened by the old women, for they did not want to become like them. They did not want to be left alone, afraid to go out after dark, having only each other for company. The statistics were plain: men died first. Men got shot down at the height of their glory; women were left to do the remembering. But the young women did not want to believe this. They did not want to believe there was nothing they could do to prevent widowhood. That was why they had to get out of the house.

Sophie Street, who resembled every other old lady (wore the same flannel culottes beneath her dresses, maneuvered her arthritic arms through the same chemise straps, carried the same black tetrahedon-shaped handbag, and, in summer, one of navy-blue straw) was certain that she was different from the others. She refused to believe that life had finished with her; she could not respect her neighbors—the way they gave in to fate. Their relentless discussion of the details of bodily decay disgusted her. Had they no pride? Did they not know that if one abdicated one's pride one had lost everything?

"You always were standoffish," Charles had said to her recently, when she had told him she had no friends. "You always kept your distance. Did you think you were so special?"

Wasn't she? She wasn't going to think she was like everyone else at this late date. So even though she stood like so many others waiting for the trolley to round the corner to carry her downtown, and once aboard sat as daintily as a spoon angled in a silverware drawer, all the while her heart beat in anticipation.

She would not die without getting what she wanted. That made no sense. Why would she always have been waiting for something if there were nothing to wait for? Anyone with half a brain could reason that out. And Sophie believed in justice. She had banked everything on there being a moment of reckoning, when she would ask Charles why he had allowed her to leave him.

Sophie scarcely slept anymore; she merely lay in the dark and listened for the refrigerator to start up with its sound like someone clearing his throat. What sleep she had felt like a waking dream: she did not lose consciousness of the room; instead things began to happen in it. Jugglers slid out of the walls and danced, leering at her with black-and-white faces. Her four dead brothers, her father, her mother, sat down at table, conversing happily, but there was no place set for her. Sometimes her former maid Ermentrude, whom she had engaged when Charles had to entertain, appeared in her black uniform and white apron and they disputed over the evening's menu. And always there was Charles, reciting his litany of accusations.

"Hello, Charles," Sophie would say. "Has anything changed?"

"No, my dear heart," he would reply, twirling his mustache.

"If only you would break yourself of that habit, dear, you would look so dashing."

He would refrain for a moment, but then, at an uncomfortable juncture in the conversation, he would absent-mindedly reach for his mustache again and begin twirling it. Nevertheless, he was a fine-looking man, his hair dark and wavy, his bearing militarily erect; he hadn't aged as Sophie had.

For a while they would chat about little things (just as they once had done in their tiny apartment overlooking the rooftops of Paris, an entire lifetime together stretching before them, so Sophie had thought)—what they were reading, what they would have for dinner that night—but eventually they would arrive at a pause and then Charles would ask, "Do you want to hear how the war is going, dear?"

"No," she would say, "I don't wish to hear about it."

She would turn onto her side and look at the wall. Charles would have to flatten himself up against the wallpaper to get her to look at him again.

"I know it is a painful subject to you, but if I can't discuss it with you, whom can I talk to?"

"Talk to someone who believes in it."

"But why don't you believe in it?"

"Because no one has ever explained it to me so that I can see the sense of it."

There would be another pause. She always knew what his next question would be. "Why did you leave me?"

"You know why I left you. You would not tell me about your past."

"What had my past to do with us?"

"It had everything to do with us."

But when she reminded him that she had repented, and asked him why he refused to forgive her, he would fade into the wall and her mind would go blank until dawn.

The nights, however, ever since she had received the phone call from that young woman asking for Charles, something different had occurred. Charles appeared but kept his back to her. Though she entreated him, he refused to speak. In the dream she thought he had died, and she accused him, "What have I now to live for?" Yet she woke each morning full of hope, knowing that the only death had been of her dreams. If she saw Charles again now, she knew that she would see him old and frail as she was, and she would know all that he was or wasn't at last.

Now the trolley descended underground; in the tunnels the windows became mirrors, and Sophie gazed at her reflection: a prim old lady in a dark-blue suit, holding her pocketbook on her lap. Who in the world, observing her, would believe she still suffered from passion? But then the car slowed to a stop, and, as she disembarked, her thoughts became fully occupied by the prospect of choosing material for a new dress, although it seemed absurd to do so when she possessed dozens already, when the prices were so high these days—when she was so old.

When they heard the tramping of feet, they were afraid and hastened through their houses, shutting windows and latching doors. To the children, however, the excitement was the same as when their mothers yelled, "Quick, the windows!" when it was about to rain.

In fact it was a sunny day, and Bobby and Emmy Jones had been playing, as they often did, on the bluff at the edge of the town where they lived with their mother and their friends and their friends' mothers, now that all the fathers were at war.

Emmy and Bobby often played war. They played with Laurie Thurston and Patty Savely, who lived on either side of them, and Rudy and Davy Chubb, who lived across the street. If none of their friends could play, Emmy and Bobby played with each other. Emmy was nine and Bobby was six-and-a-half.

Fifteen minutes ago, they had raced into town and bolted up the main street toward home, yelling like town criers, "Soldiers are coming! Soldiers are coming! We saw them from the ridge!"

Peg had intercepted them as they zoomed into the yard. By that time they were pursued by a throng of other children and mothers.

"How many soldiers? What color were their uniforms?"

"Millions of them!"

"Army-colored . . ."

Now Peg and Nan were on the phone. The windows above their kitchen sinks faced, and Peg and Nan amplified by gesticulation what they said over the instrument.

"I phoned Meg and Louise. They said they would spread the alarm up past Franklin Street."

"What about Fairground Road? They're the closest."

"They already know. Mary Jean called me."

"Did we bring this on ourselves, Nan?"

"Oh, the kids were exaggerating their number—it's probably our boys after all."

"Why don't you and Laurie come over and wait with us? It seems pointless, all of us barricaded in our separate houses."

Upstairs, Bobby and Emmy were arguing about the best place to hide. Under the bed, Emmy suggested. No, Bobby said. They would look under the beds right away. He thought in the clothes hamper, with clothes on top of you. Emmy said forget it; she saw a movie once where a soldier stabbed a laundry basket to see if anybody was in it.

"If it's Daddy," Emmy said, "I bet he'll be wearing lots of medals."

"For being brave."

"For being wounded. For getting shot."

"Daddy wouldn't get shot. He'd be too quick."

"It doesn't matter how quick you are, you still get shot. After wars, lots of men have limps."

"Daddy won't."

"He might. He might be missing a whole leg. He might have to be in a wheelchair forever."

"I'm going to tell Mom what you said."

Bobby, pursued by Emmy, ran down the stairs.

"Emmy said Daddy might have his leg shot off and be in a wheelchair! But he won't, will he?"

"Emmy!"

"I'm only telling the truth." She glared at her mother. Bobby, looking from one to the other, chose Emmy and moved next to her. Under ordinary circumstances Emmy would have repulsed him but now she took his hand. At this, Peg's eyes filled. Turning, she heard Emmy whisper to Bobby, "I'll protect you, don't worry. I'm not scared of any stupid enemy."

"But we don't have any guns."

"We can spray them with Windex. I saw a lady on TV spray it at a burglar. It has ammonia in it and it blinded him and she got away. See, if they try to come in the house, you be standing on the hall table and spray it at them. I'll be hiding behind the door with a rolling pin. Then when they're stumbling around trying to see I'll jump out and bash them over the head."

"Okay," Bobby agreed.

Kneeling, Peg hugged them. "You sweethearts. Nobody's going to attack us. It's just Daddy coming home. We're being extra-careful, that's all."

Nan and Laurie came racing across the yard.

"Laurie insisted we run," Nan said, grimacing, "for cover."

Peg laughed. While she and Nan stood at the window, the children huddled at the table. Emmy and Bobby explained their plan of defense to Laurie, who nodded thoughtfully.

She said, "What I'll do after Emmy hits them with the rolling pin, when they're all knocked out, is take their guns away from them. Then we'll be armed."

"Can you believe them?" Peg whispered.

Nan rolled her eyes. "They're thrilled! They're ready for battle! How did they *get* like this?"

Cyrus had been staying with Sophie nearly a week. Upon his arrival in Winston, he had telephoned the maestro's house; an unfamiliar voice informed him that Miss Quadrata not an hour ago had left with Pierre to visit friends of his who owned a house somewhere on a lake. They were expected back in two or three days. Cyrus left his telephone number. When, after three days, she had not returned his call, he called back. This time he was told that Fritz had been given his message but had departed that morning with Pierre for a concert tour around the country that could last as long as two months!

At once Cyrus called the Cottage, with the intention of persuading Billy to join him in Winston, but Billy and Arabel were gone. Sammy told him what had happened. Next Cyrus called Billy's mother; she was curt. No, she had not seen or heard from Billy. Did Cyrus think she kept an answering service for her son?

Even the Campers weren't around—they had left several weeks ago for a trip across the country. They hoped to recruit new members along the way. They had pressed Cyrus to accompany them— he was beginning to wish he had. Anything would have been better than the restlessness from which he was suffering. He couldn't keep his mind on anything. He couldn't sit still long enough to read a book. He wouldn't have minded a good roughhouse with Lilith, but he wasn't about to visit Jake and Agnes. He spent an entire futile afternoon trying to telephone Betsy in South America. When late one night he arrived home (having, in the course of the afternoon and evening, watched four movies) to find a note from Sophie ("A Sarah Simms called—she said you might remember her as Sarah Danford. She'd like you to call her back"), he didn't stop to check the time before he dialed her number.

He woke both Sarah and her husband up. He did his best to sound apologetic, but he didn't suppose it was very convincing. Sarah spoke in monosyllables. More cloak-and-dagger stuff. Can you not talk because of Jason? That's right. Say yes or no, then. Yes, she said. Do you want me to call back in the morning. Please. Actually, are you working? I don't have to. Shall I come over? About ten? Again yes.

It was exactly ten o'clock when Cyrus rang Sarah's doorbell, and he felt somewhat nervous. He had been so overjoyed to have something to do with himself when he came in and saw his grandmother's note that he hadn't even considered what it might be like, seeing Sarah again. Or why she was suddenly calling after all this time.

But it wasn't like that—there was scarcely any uncomfortableness at all. It could have been five years ago—it was even the same month—when he came to see her after running away from Fifield. (The only difference was that this time everyone had run away from him.) She looked the same, acted the same—maybe was slightly more outgoing. They talked about different subjects: she asked about Chive; he asked about her jobs. She wasn't happy with her present one—didn't know what else she wanted to do, really. He allowed as how he was in a similar state, though (he laughed) he couldn't even say he'd been working. Been freeloading. At the moment he was thinking of returning to Arborville for a while. His father had said at his graduation that if ever he needed a job . . . At least he'd be earning some money while he tried to decide what else to do. He didn't want to go into any kind of government work. The only work he had ever come close to liking was working with Seeing-Eye dogs. It still got to him, whenever he saw a Seeing-Eye dog—the confidence those dogs had in themselves. There they were, responsible for leading people around, across streets, into buildings, up and down stairs, through doorways, and around corners; for preventing them from bumping into other people and tripping over obstacles; yet it didn't even occur to them to question their trustworthiness. They didn't wonder if they were capable of the job entrusted to them, let alone worthy of such trust.

Sarah wondered what had become of her intention of convincing Cyrus he should visit his grandfather. That short-tempered old general of whom she had grown so fond . . . Of obtaining from him an explanation of his failure to do so. Before he came, this had seemed pressing, but now that he was here, actually in her living room, sitting on the couch, drinking coffee—she sat at the opposite end—it seemed immaterial, the only pressing issue her acknowledgment of the fact that nothing had changed at all; he had not sat in this room for five years but it might have been yesterday.

"So how's married life?" Cyrus asked.

In an almost offhand way, Sarah told him that she was planning to leave Jason. The only reason she hadn't yet told him was that he was right in the middle of a big project at work and if she burdened him with the news it would be difficult for him to finish.

Cyrus mentioned Fritz briefly then. They were temporarily split up, he supposed one would say; she was gone for a couple of months. Just as well, actually—they had had no time apart in over four years.

They didn't speak of their own past—but, then, why would they? It was in the room with them; they had hardly been anywhere else together; and when, during a silence, Cyrus stood and strolled to the window to look out (the same window at which she had been standing when she saw him walk by), Sarah didn't have to muster very much courage at all to go and stand beside him. When he turned, she simply went into his arms.

And it was actually all right, more all right than he would have expected. It didn't even feel like a betrayal, and with anyone else right then, he thought, it would have. But somehow, because Sarah had preceded Fritz, it seemed not inappropriate that the first woman he slept with after making love to Fritz for very possibly the last time should be Sarah. Mostly, he guessed, it was just friendly—even though they wound up spending more of the day in bed (until dangerously close to the time for Jason to come home from work, in fact), and then spent there more of the rest of the week, than could very well be attributed solely to altruism, comforting each other in time of distress, etc. He decided that for right now he might as well enjoy it while it lasted. He was going to Arborville at the end of the week.

Sarah, determined not to say anything that would close any doors prematurely, decided in the end to say nothing about having become acquainted with his grandfather. She felt dishonest, but she didn't want to press her luck. Cyrus was so genial, so expansive—she was afraid to do anything that might make the No Trespassing signs go up.

Before he left, she tried to take his picture, but he adamantly refused. He launched into a harangue about how he despised photographs, the very idea of them; when you looked at photographs it was as if the people were dead; besides, you never knew when someone might try to blackmail you with one. At first she thought he was kidding.

Sarah wondered about him, when she could sufficiently withdraw from the mesmerizing effect his personality exercised on her. She had seen him weeping because—for whatever reason—he was unable to bring himself to visit his grandfather, yet something in him must have been stronger than his sorrow. At times he seemed to feel so much and yet in speaking of his feelings to negate them: which was the real Cyrus? When they said goodbye, too . . . They promised this time to stay in touch, but, feeling out of countenance with herself, Sarah said, "I love you, you know, Cyrus." He said, "I love you too, Sarah." After the anguish she had suffered for not having said those words before, they seemed said too casually, as if there had never been any doubt of it, but as if loving someone made no difference to the way things would turn out.

Cyrus felt Sarah's sadness when they said goodbye, and he would have liked to say something to comfort her, but what could he say? His days of making promises were over. Still, it made him feel cast adrift, to leave her like that. He knew she thought he wasn't affected by having to say goodbye, and it wasn't true, but there was nothing he could say to disguise the fact that he was leaving. All he wanted, right now, was to get away by himself and go home.

He might have known it would not be that simple.

Arabel had called Sophie's, one afternoon when he was with Sarah, to say she was arriving at the airport in Winston the following evening, on the eight-o'clock flight from Los Angeles— whatever was she doing *there*?

The town didn't look like the one Bob Jones had protected so staunchly in his memory. Something wasn't right. Its physical appearance was the same, but its aspect was foreign and flat, like a Hollywood set pretending to be a real place.

Bob stood with his company—Bernie Wilson, Mick Savely,

Howie Thurston, Dave Chubb, and the others—at the crest of the slope where the road dipped down to introduce the countryside through ranks of white houses, shuttered in red and green. Lilacs bloomed in every yard, and it was a balmy day, but no one was in sight.

"It looks so different," Bob mused. "Do you feel it, Howie? Maybe we've come to the wrong place."

"We're home, Bob—take it easy." Behind Bob's back Howie raised his eyebrows at the others, but they were all listening to Bob nevertheless. Since the episode at the major's house, he had been preoccupied and odd, yet whenever he spoke it was with a new authority, some passionate motive that impressed them and held their attention.

"What do you mean, Bob?"

"I don't know exactly. But I keep thinking of all those days sitting in the trench. Nothing to do but deal out another round of cards, smoke another cigarette, write another letter home, although you had nothing to say." Bob spoke easily, as if he had called them around a campfire for a story.

One would have thought the men wouldn't want to hear over what they knew by heart but their attention was rapt. Some inserted hands under the tight straps of their knapsacks to make themselves more comfortable; some leaned on their empty guns. They felt disappointed when Bob said, "Well, I don't have to tell you. You know all about it. The thing is, all that time I thought I was doing it for what I loved. For Peggy and the kids, the town, the whole country. I believed in that. I believed we were keeping the enemy from our homes."

"And so we were, Bob," Mick Savely said.

"You're pulling my leg."

"What do you mean?"

Bob stared at him. "What was the mutiny all about?"

"Mutiny!" Bernie Wilson exclaimed. "We got our marching orders. We're coming home!"

"Cut it out, Bernie. It's not a joke."

"I'm not joking, Bob." Bernie gave Bob a concerned look.

Bob winced. "You're putting me on, aren't you, you guys? Otherwise . . . The ambassador arriving, informing us it was all a put-up job, taking power from the colonel, the major's suicide . . . all that meant nothing to you?"

"Bob," Bernie said quietly, "the ambassador brought the orders to decamp. I was always in charge of our company. The major was strung up by enemy saboteurs he interrupted in the process of looting his home. You know that."

"You're lying, Bernie." Bob appealed to the others. "You're not going along with him, are you?"

"If it weren't for the fact that you're suffering from an extreme case of shell shock, Bob, I'd be tempted to have you court-martialed for that. Furthermore, you may continue to address me as 'Lieutenant' until you receive your final discharge."

"Knock it off, will you, Bernie? I knew you when you were just a punk. You can't pull rank on me." Bob looked down the main street. "Can't any of you *see*? Look at the place! It's the end of May and the doors are shut. Not one person has come out to say hello."

"Try to calm down," Howie suggested. "The sooner you get home and see Peg and the kids the better you'll feel."

"I *want* to see them, Howie. That's all I want. But let me ask you this. What am I supposed to tell them I was doing all this time? What are you going to tell Nan?"

"Tell her?"

"March on in and take up where you left off? Nine to five, Monday through Friday, golfing on Saturday, church and a barbecue on Sunday? Maybe you think everything's going to be the same. Maybe for you it will be, but I know I've changed for good.

"We weren't fighting. We went out there like sheep and we've come back like sheep. We're not heroes. We weren't in any war. I'm not saying there may not have been a war, I'm just saying we missed it. And I don't know about the rest of you, but I'm not going to pretend I didn't."

Flying Home

A river below reflected the moon above as the airplane, with its motionless wings, flew in such a straight line through the darkness it seemed not a machine under its own power but an object thrown, trapped somehow along the high point of its arc. In the river, the reflected moon kept pace. Arabel saw a brilliant serpent slithering at immense speed along the ground, and she imagined it hastening to the sea; there the moon's reflection would spread and cover the entire watery surface.

Not long ago, darkness had filtered into the emptiness around the plane as if a giant squid had squirted ink to put the aircraft off the chase, and the other passengers had stopped peering out the windows in search of whatever revelation they had expected to be vouchsafed now that they were off the ground. They watched the aisle for the approach of the stewardess. They longed for her to ask if they would like drinks before dinner; if they would like roast beef or fillet of sole; if they were finished with their trays . . . And by then the tall city's lights would be visible and in the plane's evil-looking nose the pilot would request permission to return to earth from the men in the tower, and in terse, codelike phrases these men would answer. In their economy was compressed a kind of love.

Passengers had to trust these men; when the sound of static announced the pilot's presence and then the smooth voice—smooth as the sleek plane—caressed their ears: "Ladies and Gentlemen, this is your captain speaking . . ." they knew their lives were in his hands. They were flying over Death Valley, where the dry wind preserved the voices of men who had died in the search for gold, singing, "Green grow the lilacs, all covered with dew . . . We'll change the green lilacs to the red, white, and blue . . ." but they knew this only because he told them—their pilot, up in front where they couldn't see him.

The passengers grinned as, from the end of the aisle, came the sound of ice cubes clinking into glasses. They began to chat with their neighbors, though continuing to ascertain from the increasing volume of fizzes and plinks how many rows back the stewardess was with her cart.

And all along the moon was in pursuit, as if to warn the plane of some impending danger, some fatal mistake about to be made, and Arabel kept her face pressed against the cold window and looked down at the swift, bright light.

It seemed to her Polly Farquhar was sending the moon, trying to persuade her not to count on Cyrus. But Polly was dead, and she had to trust someone.

Polly had left everything to Gabriel and Arabel. Nobody in Magnolia had believed she had a penny (and strictly speaking they were right), but what she did have was a sprawling house on a hillside overlooking Los Angeles, built for her by the husband she left to go back to Magnolia Junction. Arabel and Gabriel sold Aphrodite's remaining furniture, shut the door but didn't bother with locking it, and went west to survey their property. Frederick Chandler was the name of Polly's late and former spouse; "dead Freddy," Gabriel dubbed him. He had made of his house a testimonial to years of lovesickness. Life-size portraits of him hung in every room, his expression lovelorn yet accusing; his aftershave cologne cascaded from a miniature fountain in the master bedroom; his voice whispering, "I'll always love you, Polly," oozed from mysterious microphones whenever a light switch was flipped on.

The house spooked Gabriel and Arabel, and they spent their days by the swimming pool, dangling their feet in the water, eating the exotic canned goods dead Freddy had stockpiled: giraffe and whale and octopus meat; unheard-of fruits and vegetables from unheard-of countries. . . . Polly had left them the house but no income. Not only that but it turned out she had not paid the taxes since she inherited the place. "When we finish up all Mr. Dead Freddy's frog legs," Gabriel said with satisfaction, "we going to starve." It was at this point Arabel decided to use their last funds to purchase a plane ticket back East. She felt certain Cyrus would know how to help them out of their difficulty.

Dinner was brought now; row by row, the passengers were fed. They felt at ease, the food before them; that was why the airlines offered meals: to keep the passengers satisfied. They didn't want people to be tempted back to trains, which, though wonderful enough in their day (that soothing chug-chugging along the rails punctuated by an occasional exuberant whistle), belonged to the past. Life was too short now to spend time getting where you were going; flying, as the brochures had it, was the only way to go: up in the air, separate from the ground—that was the only smart place to be when the earth waged war.

"Ladies and gentlemen," the voice interrupted, "this is your captain again. Just wanted to let you know it won't be long now. We've begun our descent and in no time will be touching down in Winston City, and there will even be some Saturday night left for you folks to enjoy," as if there had been some question there might not be! It had been Saturday night all along, had it not? Not only in Winston but all over the country, in Los Angeles, Kansas City, New York—everywhere in this vast diversified terrain, land of pilgrims' pride, land where fathers died . . . It was a Saturday night and America was relaxing, taking time out—it needed to sometimes.

The plane had long ago left the river behind. Since the moon had disappeared Arabel had fallen asleep but now woke with a start.

"Ladies and gentlemen, the captain has turned on the seat-belt sign and we ask that you comply with his request at this time. Also, please extinguish all smoking materials until safely within the terminal building. We hope you've had a pleasant trip and thank you for flying with us."

Cyrus was standing by the gate when Arabel appeared. He gave her a hug and asked how she was; then he inquired where Billy was hiding himself these days. She said she didn't know; he was not at the Cottage. (She didn't add that she had called not for Billy but for Cyrus.)

Then they went to Sophie's. Sophie was so sweet to Arabel that Cyrus began to feel like a heel for resenting her. He remembered how dazed he had been after Lark's death. In his repentance he became very solicitous. He could tell from Sophie's occasional glances of amusement that she didn't believe Arabel wasn't his girlfriend—when he made Arabel take the guestroom and slept on the couch, he knew Sophie thought he was doing this for her benefit. He wanted to set her straight, but you didn't exactly say to your grandmother, Grandmother, I've never even gone to bed with her! She's *Billy*'s girlfriend. . . .

When Sophie and Arabel were both upstairs, Cyrus sat down at the dining-room table and wrote a letter. It took him innumerable drafts and several hours to finish it. The rejected pages he stashed in his suitcase. The approved version he folded, sealed in an envelope, and—just as he and Arabel were about to climb into the car the next morning to head off to Arborville—he feigned forgetfulness, ran back into the house, fetched the atlas he had purposefully left behind, and propped the envelope beside the stack of breakfast dishes Sophie had insisted they leave for her to wash.

"Goodbye, Grandmother," Cyrus said, giving her an affectionate embrace. "You have the telephone number in Arborville. Do you promise you'll call if you need anything? I'll be talking to you often, but if it's an emergency . . . you can get an operator to dial the call if you feel uncomfortable."

"Yes, yes," Sophie said impatiently. He was being provident

again, and she didn't trust him. "Now run along—you have a long drive before you."

Then she went back into the house. In the kitchen, she saw the envelope at once; she returned with it to the living room, where she sat down to read Cyrus's letter.

Dear Grandmother,

I apologize for writing in a letter what I have to tell you, but I don't have the courage to tell you in person. I am sorry for being such a coward.

Granddad lives in Winston City. He's at the Old Generals' Home on Elm Street. (The exact address and phone number are listed in the telephone book.) He came out here from Arborville right before I went to Fifield. He and Dad had a bad fight, somewhat over me (although it's a long story and not what I have to tell you about here), and that's why Granddad left. (That's why I left.) I haven't seen him since. You'll soon understand why not.

Do you remember the book you gave me? The night I had the nightmare, after I first came to see you? You said it was the only possession of Granddad's you ever found that you thought might be a clue to his past.

Well, I took a quick look at it the next morning, but then I forgot about it, until one day at Chive for some reason it caught my eye. Anyway, I decided to check it out further, and one weekend I drove up to New Jersey and went to one house after another whose picture was in the guidebook. That's how I found Granddad's family.

He has two sisters and a brother. Their names are Xy, Sammy, and George (Xilipheupia, Constantina, and Sigismund). Xy is the eldest, then George, then Sam. Xy is only a year younger than Granddad. Their last name isn't Street, it's Ludwicker, and before he left home (I think he was twenty-six), Granddad's name was Dagobert Ludwicker. (They called him Tad.)

First of all, I can't possibly describe everything about the Ludwickers to you in a letter (and you would have a hard time believing it even if I did), but I have to tell you a little background so that maybe you will be able to understand, somehow, how what happened could have happened.

The Ludwickers were (are) very rich, and they have never needed to work. There's been a kind of insane tradition handed down from generation to generation that their family is really exiled royalty (although they don't necessarily know from where or even why they got exiled). In my opinion, it originally started out as a kind of joke, but then the next generation forgot it was only a joke. I can't prove it, of course, but the thing is (and it is what I used to tell them in the beginning, until I realized it was hopeless to try to convince them), it doesn't matter if they are or not. It's not as if there's some throne they could get back. All that would happen would be that curious people would start hanging around the Cottage (that's the name Granddad gave their mansion. It's just his sense of humor—there are eighty-five rooms in it), or they would have to go on talk shows, and they would hate it. They're actually very nice people, although incredibly naïve about the world. (There is no way I can make you believe how naïve. You would have to see for yourself.)

Anyway, the point of telling you all this is to give you an idea of the kind of isolation they grew up in. None of them went to school; they never had any friends apart from each other. Their parents died when they were young. Granddad was only sixteen when his father died.

This is the hard part, Grandmother (or the beginning of the hard part).

Granddad and Xy were more than just brother and sister. They were lovers. I don't know how to tell you the rest. I guess the best way is just to tell it.

Granddad left home at twenty-six, but he came back once later (not when he was married to you—that is, living with you—but after that). He returned only for one night, which he spent with Xy. She had a baby, on November 8, 1951. Her name is Fritz Quadrata. (What I am about to tell you next will so to speak put the icing on the cake.) For almost five years now, Fritz has been my girlfriend.

That's the story.

I never told Fritz. In the beginning, when we first got involved, I didn't know she was Granddad's daughter. She was ashamed of what Granddad and Xy had done and she had made Xy and Sammy and George pretend she was adopted whenever strangers came to the house. Why I didn't tell them right away that I was their lost brother's grandson is another question. I still, to this day, don't know for sure why I didn't. At the time, it just seemed like the best thing to do (to keep it secret). It was such a shock to me I wanted to figure out what it all meant before I told anyone else about it. Thinking back on it, I have often asked myself if I really knew all along who Fritz was but refused to believe it. But I honestly don't know. It's like so many things, when you look back on them it seems as if you should have known what was really going on, yet you didn't. (I have found that, once you realize that this is the stupid way life is organized, it's almost impossible to do anything, because you can never see ahead of time the significance your action will have, and how can you take any action when you can't even know if what you're doing is right or wrong?) I'm not trying to say I'm not to blame for what happened. I'm mainly trying to explain why, among other reasons, I couldn't visit Granddad, or tell you, or tell Fritz. It seemed so much simpler to pretend that none of it was really happening. As a result, I let Fritz find out the truth on her own in a horrible accidental way, and she has left me, and I can't, frankly, even be sure she is ever going to want to see me again. How can I blame her?

I suppose I might not even be telling you this now, Grandmother, except for one thing. Fritz will try to see Granddad. That is something I never imagined happening, but I now know she will. Someone has to tell him before she does, and I can't do it.

So I'm telling you. As I said in the beginning, I am sorry for not doing so in person. I know this must be a horrible shock to you (although maybe you're glad at least to know, finally, what Granddad was hiding).

Please go to see him, Grandmother. He's totally blind now, I guess I should tell you. Also, I know it may seem irrelevant to

*say now, but I sometimes think that the only thing I've ever really
wanted in my life was for you two to be friends.*

Love,

Cyrus

After driving Arabel to the airport, Billy continued on to Amber with the intention of visiting his mother. He made it as far as the driveway to her trailer before deciding he could not bear to see her. He continued on past the trailer to where an old logging road led into the woods, turned around, and headed back south—to Magnolia Junction. Arabel had already left. After a week at the Calypso, during which he attempted to return to his "former" way of life, he drove back to the Cottage. He might as well have stayed there in the first place, he thought.

The Ludwickers, deserted by everyone, were overjoyed to see him. Perhaps their pleasure provoked increased somnambulistic activity. The morning after his arrival, waking at dawn, Billy thought he was in Amber, hearing what sounded like the whack of an ax—the same hollow echo of struck wood. Rising, he looked out the window. There, on the lawn, in his bare feet, dressed in red pajamas printed with blue baseball bats, stood Sigismund Ludwicker, playing croquet.

Billy threw on his clothes and went outside. Sigismund did not look up as he approached. The legs of Sigismund's pajamas were wet from the damp lawn and clung to his ankles; he shook first one leg, then the other, to loosen them.

"What are you doing up at this hour, George?"

No answer.

"George, are you all right?" Billy, alarmed, drew closer. Sigismund's eyes were open but he didn't seem to see. "What's the matter with you?" Billy reached out and grabbed his arm and shook him.

Suddenly Sigismund blinked. When he noticed Billy, he let out a wail. "I was winning!" he cried. "I was really winning! You've ruined the game. You've ruined everything!"

"What game? You were playing by yourself!"

"I was not. I . . ." Sigismund looked around him, bewildered.

Then Billy understood. "I think you were asleep, George. You were walking in your sleep. I mean," he said, laughing, "you were playing croquet in your sleep."

"In my sleep!"

"That can be dangerous. It's a good thing I woke up and saw you."

"What can be dangerous?" Sigismund shouted. "Just what?"

"Oh, never mind."

"Don't tell me never mind. I don't like never mind."

"Look, George, forget it. You're fine. I tell you what, why don't we go somewhere for a change—you and me, before Xy and Sammy wake up?"

"Go where? Why should we go somewhere?"

"To get out of here! We could go for a drive, see a bit of the country. Or wouldn't you like to see a real live baseball game?"

"No."

"Come on, don't you think it's about time you got out of this place?"

"About time?" Sigismund repeated, a strange light dawning in his eye.

"I think it's high time," Billy said.

"High time." Billy couldn't fathom Sigismund's sly expression. He didn't know that this phrase, like many another, bore a particular significance to the Ludwicker mind.

"Who told you?" Sigismund asked. "How do you know?"

"How do I know what? I just think you've been here long enough, that's all."

"Long enough," Sigismund repeated, pleased. "Long enough. Not too short and not too long." He suddenly sprang into the air. "Wait until I tell Xy! She'll be furious. She always said she would be the one to hear the summons but she was wrong. I heard it! I heard it first!"

Sigismund rushed into the Cottage, Billy in pursuit. He rushed upstairs, then back down, at last finding Xy in the sitting room, seated at a table, writing in her diary.

"Tad!" she cried, when Sigismund finally succeeded in waking her. She threw her arms around his neck. When she realized who he was, she slapped him. Billy listened, incredulous, as Sigismund announced to Xilipheupia that the moment had arrived for her to claim the throne. When at last she understood, she hugged him again and apologized for slapping him. Like children on Christmas morning, they raced off in search of Sammy.

"I'll knight you!" Xy shouted to Billy over her shoulder. "Don't let me forget!"

By noon they were dressed in their robes of state and heading for the Turnpike.

Charles could see flashes of light. When a breeze swayed the branches of the maple and the mottled pattern of sunlight on the grass shifted, he noticed. When someone intervened between him and a light source, he perceived the shadow. That was one way he had of telling when someone approached. He relied also on his senses of hearing and smell. Yet there were still other, subtler sensations informing him of another's presence: a kind of additional density in the atmosphere, a modification in the quality of silence— signs only the blind knew about.

He had already known that someone had crossed onto the lawn because he could hear the pause in the conversation accompanying the other generals' eternal card game. Sarah? he wondered. Or . . . could it be Cyrus, after all? His heart leapt. But, as the footsteps came closer, he knew they were those of a woman. Not those of any of the nurses—they would not approach from that direction. Not Rose's; she always warned him of her visits. Then he knew.

She stood a moment before speaking. "Charles?" she asked finally. Her voice was old, yet firm.

"Hello, Sophie," he calmly replied.

"So you expected me," she said. She sounded irritated.

"I've expected you for years."

"For years . . ."

"Besides," he added, with the hint of a smile, "no woman in the world calls me Charles anymore."

He imagined that she shrugged. "No one calls me Sophie either."

"Not Cyrus?"

"Cyrus calls me Grandmother."

"I always wanted him to know you."

"He first visited me after his brother died."

"So Rose told me."

"Is it true then?" she asked. "Cyrus has not been to see you in five years?"

"Yes, that's true."

"I didn't know that until recently, Charles." Could they be *true*, then, Cyrus's wild allegations? They could explain so much, and yet . . .

"I don't blame you for it," he said.

"You don't . . . You mean you think I persuaded Cyrus to avoid you?"

"Knowing you would be persuasion enough, Sophie." His self-satisfied expression disconcerted her. "I knew he would love you. He would ask himself what cause I could have given you to leave me. Finding you so lovely, he would conclude that it must have been something too dreadful even to speak of."

"But, Charles," Sophie said, abashed, "I did not turn him against you!" No, she could not believe Cyrus's story. She would not believe it.

"My Sophie . . ." Charles murmured.

"What did you say?" she exclaimed.

"If it comforts you, know that Cyrus did not visit me or correspond with me for nearly a year before he sought you out. You can only have confirmed a judgment he had already made."

"Why would he have made any judgment against you?" Sophie inquired warily.

"Evidently I did not live up to his expectations," Charles replied, adding, "He loved me once."

"Knowing Cyrus," retorted Sophie, "I imagine it more likely that if he has avoided you it is because he felt he did not live up to yours." The longer she sat there the more fantastical Cyrus's charge loomed—yet why would he have made it?

"What an absurd notion," Charles scoffed. "It was largely for Cyrus's sake I stayed on in Arborville. Harold resented me. Perhaps I ought not to have stayed, but I had had no one to . . ." He stopped, then went on staunchly, ". . . no one to care for, not since Rose had run away."

"Run away!"

"At fifteen. It was five years before I heard from her again. Perhaps Cyrus acquired the notion from her, although I don't believe she ever spoke to him about it. She never spoke even to Harold about it! She informed me I was not to contradict her story—that she had been in boarding school because I was too busy with my military duties. I agreed, despite the fact that this further prejudiced her husband against me—a neglectful parent, instead of a neglectful child.

"Cyrus was a happy child, Sophie. Then he changed—it was when Lark went to the Institute. Cyrus could not accept it. And because for once I was on Harold's side—Harold had had to make a difficult decision, but I believe he did what was best for Lark—Cyrus may have felt betrayed. In any event, that was when he began to turn against me. He began hiding himself."

"Like his grandfather," Sophie remarked.

Charles ignored this. "I urged Harold to send Cyrus away to school. I mentioned a place I thought might suit. Chap in my unit during the war ran it. Didn't tell Harold, though; it would have prejudiced him against it. He wouldn't hear of it, anyway. We argued about it, he and I and Rose—what was best for Cyrus."

"What right had you in the matter? He was their son, was he not?"

"Nominally," Charles replied, unperturbed. "A child belongs to one to the extent to which one loves him."

They were silent, then Sophie faltered, "You are cruel to me, Charles. I have paid enough."

He seemed puzzled by her response. Yet how else could that have been meant if not to taunt her?

"Too much is made of the ties of blood," he continued, as if in explanation. "Who is related to whom by the accident of birth. One is as much a father or a son—or a husband or wife—as one cares to be."

"But, Charles . . ." Could he be speaking of his—other—daughter? Might he actually *know* of her existence?

"I am not without hope," he continued. "I have reason to believe Cyrus may seek me out before long. And I do not intend to hold it against him that he has taken five years to decide in what relation he stands to me."

"Decide!" Sophie exclaimed. "But, Charles . . ." Now would be the moment to reveal the contents of Cyrus's letter. Yet she waited. Something compelled her to wait.

He looked amused. "Isn't that what you did with me? Not that I mean you to think I ever blamed you for it . . ."

"Never blamed . . . ! Please do stop feigning nobility, Charles. It has always been one of the characteristics of yours I could the least abide—the sense of martyrdom you conveyed."

"You imagine things, my dear Sophie."

"Do not dare to accuse me of that! It was the atmosphere you created of holding some obligation to a higher cause—greater devotion than yours to me—as if the reason you could not tell me about your past was because you were protecting someone else."

"Maybe I was," Charles remarked quietly.

"But what could give you the right?" Sophie demanded, too irritated to be startled at what he was suggesting. "Even if it were true! Was not your first responsibility to me, your wife?" She waited, but Charles made no reply. "Evidently you thought not. Your first responsibility was to your private world of suffering. You would not allow me entrance to it. You feared that I might be able to absolve you of your guilt—and you could not have borne that!"

"Sophie," Charles said calmly, "it is true I believed I deserved to suffer. I did not wish to. It was you who could not abide that necessity. Yet it is also true that I have never blamed you for leaving me, even though I have missed you my entire life."

Sophie now *was* startled. Nevertheless she answered readily, "That cannot be true. Why then did you refuse to see me?"

"Refuse to see you!"

She was gratified to see that, finally, something had unsettled him, though she was mystified as to the reason.

"Have you forgotten so easily, then?" she asked bitterly. "In nineteen fifty-one?"

"Nineteen fifty-one?"

"The letter I wrote you in February of that year . . ."

"I never received such a letter."

"You never received it? But it was not returned!"

"Sophie, the last communication I ever had from you was the note you left on the table in our apartment in Paris informing me that you were leaving. For a while, from time to time, I received news of your welfare and your whereabouts from mutual friends. That's all."

She gazed at him incredulously. He was staring blankly ahead.

"Charles, in the late autumn of nineteen fifty my great-uncle died and I returned to France and sold the château. It was the first time I had been to France since I left you to come to America. Inevitably, I missed you. When in Paris, where I stayed for four months, I visited all of the places we had frequented. I regretted what I had done. I stood before our apartment building. . . ."

"I have done so many times."

"You!"

"Why are you amazed?"

"Because I . . . Charles, are you telling me the truth? Because I am not crazed. My memory is intact. That February I wrote to ask if I might see you. I wished at least for us to be friends, if only for Rose's sake. I wrote to her as well, and neither of you answered. You are telling me now that you never received my letter?"

"I did not."

"But, Charles . . ." She was near tears, tears of frustration. "How is that possible?"

He had narrowed his eyes to think (a habit left from the days when he could see).

"When was this, you said?"

"February, nineteen fifty-one."

Then he sighed deeply. "My Sophie . . ."

"What is it?"

"Rose took the letters."

"Rose!"

"In February of that year, on a Tuesday evening, which I shall never forget as long as I live, I returned home to find that she had run away." He paused. "It broke me, Sophie. I left the service. I abandoned important work. My life had lost all meaning."

February of 1951. Sophie was calculating. November 8th, Cyrus had said. Yes, that could be. It was true, then. Cyrus had not known of his mother's running away from home. Had he known, it would still be possible to think he had fabricated the story; now it was not.

"What became of Rose?"

"The police could find no trace of her. For five years I did not know if she was alive or dead. Then at last she wrote to me from Arborville. Cyrus had just been born, and she asked me to visit. I went to her at once. Although she spoke painfully to me of her sorrow in having hurt me, she would never explain what had prompted her to run away. It distressed her so greatly when I questioned her that I refrained. A mistake, I perhaps knew even then, yet I felt I had no right to insist. It came to be an unspoken bond between us—our pain, each of us feeling we had wounded the other. At least, for the first time, I understand hers. But for what? Now when it is too late."

"Too late for what?" Sophie queried. But what was she saying? Her aim in visiting Charles had not been reconciliation! Not revenge either, certainly. (What would that serve?) Curiosity? Perhaps, if curiosity were not assigned its usual trivial aspect. To be justified? Justified for having left him?

The information contained in Cyrus's letter would certainly be justification enough, yet, even though she had not known the facts, had she not, she now said to herself, suspected his secret? She had perceived its outlines, its quality, its significance, the way one might, encountering a figure in a dark room, know before seeing its face or identifying it if its business was fair or foul.

But now his secret was hers. What could it profit her to give it back to him?

"Too late for what?" she asked again.

"To mend things," he said. "We are too old, you and I, and it is perhaps too late already for Rose as well."

"But, Charles, that is too stupid."

"It's not stupid, Sophie. It is simply our fate."

"Charles!" she cried. "For pity's sake, let us not compound our tragedy! We have all suffered enough. A sin can be paid for—I believe that—and we have paid for ours, even if I am not certain all the time of what it is. We are still alive. Let us stop, while time remains. Oh, Charles . . ."

"I cannot stop, Sophie. I haven't paid."

"But why not?" she beseeched him. "Tell me why, Charles. At least you owe it to me to tell me why."

"No. That is the punishment, not to tell you."

But now she knew. Yet suddenly Sophie was furious. He sat still as a statue, facing straight ahead. How very convenient to be blind!

"You never loved me," she accused him in a low, angry voice. "How could I ever have believed you did? Because when you love someone, Charles, you give that person all of yourself."

"I don't agree, Sophie. I loved you. In a way, I have never stopped. What you cannot accept is that we have loved each other for half a lifetime, unacknowledged, apart. The truth is that you do not wish to recognize that life itself may be unjust. As for my silence, as you call it, rendering false my love for you—I can only tell you, my dearest Sophie, that if I had ever relinquished what you are pleased to call my guilt, you would have despised me. You loved me for the same reason you think you hate me now. You would have left me, had I 'confessed.'"

"But you would not take the risk! *That's* why I left, Charles. I could not live with you any longer because you would not take it."

Could she now? She watched his face. He seemed to recede

from her, his face now expressing a great sadness. He might be spared looking into her eyes, acknowledging her anger, yet his blindness had made his own emotion more transparent.

"Charles . . ." she said again softly, then stopped herself. She could not afford to be moved by pity now! "Oh, what does it matter what you did, what I did?" she cried. "It is so long ago. For thirty years I have dreamed about you, argued with you in dreams . . ."

"What did you expect?" he asked, puzzled.

She stopped, speechless.

"Let us not be feeble-minded, Sophie, simply because we are old. It is not surprising that people whose lives were once joined and who are separated abruptly, whether by circumstance or intention, will dream about one another, even incessantly, the remainder of their lives."

"It is ordinary, then. It means nothing to you."

"I did not say that. Why do you persist in thinking I have not suffered from your loss, that you alone have suffered?"

She stared at him. How dare he not look at her? "Why do you not fight? Why do you not rage?"

"What would you have me do? Life is over, Sophie. Accept it."

"I will not accept it."

They sat then in silence, Sophie waiting for Charles to speak. But he did not. He would not, she saw. At last she said, "I must go, Charles. I am sorry. I am sorry if by visiting I have wounded you anew. But I haven't the strength to fight you anymore. I thought at first that I might, but I haven't. Forgive me, Charles, but I am not yet ready to die."

She stood. She waited a moment for him to speak, but when he did not she departed.

She did not cry on the way home, although she felt the tears behind her eyes, in her throat, in her heart. And there they would stay. Mourning would be an insult to the loss she had suffered; it would insult her love for Charles, which had never been allowed to live. Only something greater than herself—an earthquake, a volcano erupting, a tidal wave—or a war breaking out . . . yes, a war, why not a war? the subject of so much disagreement between herself and Charles—seemed sufficient to express her sorrow, though not for herself alone, but for all those who had never lived their lives with the person they loved, with the person they should have loved.

Sophie stood inside her front door for an eternity, motionless, aware of nothing except the expression in Charles's blind eyes. It was hopelessness, yet, even now, he still refused to ask help of anyone! Then she turned and ran from the house.

"Well, she's finally flipped!" her neighbors thought, as they watched Sophie scurry past, her hat awry; this time she carried no pocketbook. Discovering this herself after she had already boarded the trolley, Sophie announced defiantly to the driver that she had left her money at home.

"That's all right, dearie," said the driver, who knew her. "You ride as long as you want." When she disembarked, he gave her a transfer and another token.

"But I'm never coming back," she told him.

"I know that," he said. "But take it for a souvenir. Just say it's a little present from me to you."

When the trolley started up again, he shook his head and remarked to a passenger standing nearby, "See it all the time. Little old ladies like that running away from home."

"Running away? Where do they go?"

"Here she is again!" called the generals. "Here she comes, Charlie! Your vision has returned."

Generals! Sophie thought. It was nearly noon and they were still dressed in their pajamas. Not that it surprised her to see generals come to such an end.

"I'm back, Charles," she announced.

"Entertaining the troops, I see."

She sat down beside him on the swing.

"I'm not leaving you again either. You will come home with me."

"Did I ever say I wouldn't?" he asked her gently.

She ignored this. "A whole life wasted, out of pride. Two lives wasted. What prevented me from writing you again? Or you writing to me?"

"Sophie . . ."

"Never would I have thought such stupidity imaginable, had I not been so stupid myself. We have loved each other in secret for thirty years!"

"Sophie," Charles said, laughing, "far stupider things have happened in this universe."

"I can't think of any." Tentatively she placed her hand in his blind hand. She would never tell him. She did not care what he had done, and she would guard his secret as closely as if it were her own. She would hide him from his past—he had returned to it only when the future had deserted him.

"I was wrong, Charles. Love requires no conditions. It requires only the presence of the person loved."

"But, Sophie . . ."

"Don't confuse me, Charles. I'm an old woman and am easily confused."

"Sophie," he said, "my old Sophie . . ." He tightened his hand around hers. He was staring emptily ahead, but then she saw that he was crying. Transparent teardrops welled from his blind eyes and spilled onto his worn face.

"Don't cry," she whispered, beginning to cry herself.

He let go her hand and lifted his hand to her cheek.

"I forgot you would be old also," he said. Then, to her astonishment, he laughed.

"Yes, I am old," she said; then she too laughed, as if this were the silliest thing in the world. She sat without moving as Charles traced the line of her nose, up across the skull over her eyebrows, felt the hollows of her eyes while she closed the lids. When his fingers reached her hair she raised her hands and touched his temples, as if that would enable him to see again. She watched as surprise, then sadness, then tenderness succeeded one another on Charles's face.

"Is your hair white?"

"All white."

He let his hand fall to her shoulder and fingered the material of her dress. "Cotton. Flowers?"

"Yes."

"What color?"

"Blue and lavender, with darker purple flowers."

"You're still beautiful," he stated. "I always knew you would be a beautiful old woman." He took her hand again and held it.

"I doubt that very much. Don't try to deceive me. I know you're still imagining me as I looked when young."

"Try to stop me," he suggested.

They were silent. Then Sophie asked, "What shall we argue about now? We may have a long time left in which to argue before we die."

But he answered, "Let's not argue—not yet, anyway. Let's just sit here a little."

He reached for his cane and began to rock the swing slowly back and forth. He faced ahead. Sophie studied his face for a while. At last she laid her head on his shoulder and closed her eyes.

The Battle Joins on the
New Jersey Turnpike

They came from everywhere. They came east on Interstate 80 from Dover, Two Bridges, and Paterson, from Hope and Tranquility and Mount Freedom, from Panther Valley and the Jenny Jump State Forest. They came south on 87 and 91 from Troy and Schenectady and White River Junction. They came west on 287 from White Plains, Scarsdale, and beyond. They came north from Georgia and Wilmington, Delaware. They came from everywhere, as if it had been planned. Bib Block watched them come.

Before that, they had come from England and France and the Netherlands, from all over Europe, from Africa and India and China. And before that they came from somewhere else too: from Babylon or Carthage, from Atlantis or the Garden of Eden. Once they had all been homesick, but now they were at home—and traveling on the greatest highway system the world had ever seen. Bib himself still shivered whenever he saw the name spanning the highway on the huge green sign: NEW JERSEY TURNPIKE, ALL TRAFFIC RIGHT. Nothing ambiguous about that! The motion of swinging his cruiser over in obedience to that command still shot more amperes of power buzzing through his arteries than did any other single event in life. The road was destiny, but man had built the road.

From outer space, the network of highways covering the country would have seemed the ley-system of some modern religion, and Going Somewhere the form of worship its gods demanded—a celestial significance to every curve, intersection, merge, and metamorphosis of road surface. Yet even though no one on the ground could take in the network in its entirety, its existence was sensed, just as, approaching an altar, one knew one climbed the stem of the Cross, and God in his Turnpike Heaven looked down as the Memorial Weekend drivers received their communion tickets from the toll-booth priests and he sanctified them. Bib Block was sure that in any part of the country at all, whenever the name of this road was mentioned, people's hearts pivoted like Moslems to the east and flopped over. Sooner or later, he believed, at one stage of the journey or another, all roads led to the New Jersey Turnpike. Sooner or later, anyone who wanted to go anywhere ended up on this long gray path in search of his exit.

The New Jersey Turnpike was the greatest road in the country—so said its publicity brochure, though publicity, Bib thought, was hardly needed for such a famous stretch of highway. It was like a foreign country for which no passport was required. It had its own laws, customs, food, and history. It was a great asphalt river with its own inlets and docks, named after the distinguished men and women of the land: William F. Halsey, Molly Pitcher, Richard Stockton, John Fenwick. . . .

The New Jersey Turnpike was America's busiest toll highway; it was one hundred and eighteen miles long and had twenty-three exits and entrances. It stretched like a long gray snake with a green stripe halfway up its back from the George Washington Bridge to the Delaware Memorial Bridge; it was the country's most important north-south artery. Furthermore, the New Jersey Turnpike's safety record was the envy of highway officials throughout the land; its low accident rate consistently led that of all other roads. To enhance this incredible record, a fog-detection system had been installed, using the very latest engineering techniques.

Bib Block, standing in the parking lot of the James Fenimore Cooper Service Area, sipping his first cup of coffee of the day out of a white Styrofoam cup, watched the traffic getting heavier, everybody on their way north and south for Memorial Day, on the road that he had helped to build. This was what life was about, he thought; by Godfrey, it had made him see red recently when some young smart-alecky friend of one of his grandsons had asked him if he really thought it coincidence that the Feds had only gotten into the roadbuilding act after World War One, implying that the highways weren't there to benefit individual citizens at all. It was not the first time Bib had heard this insidious rumor, spread by unbelievers, that the Turnpike (like all the country's major roads) had been built for the use of the military in case of war. It outraged Bib to hear his government maligned like that, to have it suggested that it had ulterior motives at heart. Moreover, for that young cynic's information, not one single cent of taxpayers' money was used to build, operate, or maintain the Turnpike! No, the New Jersey Turnpike was self-sufficient; its high officials themselves refused financial reward for administering its affairs. They knew they would get their reward in the Turnpike Hereafter.

The lack of respect among young folk these days! It shocked and saddened Bib. *His* youth hadn't been like that—and he recalled his youth more and more vividly—in particular, how thrilling it had been, growing up with the country's roads. He would never forget when, in 1923, the first limited-access road opened or when, in 1928, the first cloverleaf interchange went into operation.

Once scarcely anyone had traveled. There had been no roads! No roads and no road maps! Until after the First World War roads hadn't even been numbered; tourists had constantly gotten lost. But now half the country relocated every five years—that meant the whole country moved once a decade! And how could they accomplish that without roads? Without roads, how would people visit their distant loved ones? The truth was the country would be lost. Its citizens would be unable to go home. In a way—it awed Bib to think of it—the road *was* home!

Bib was sixty-five now, officially retired, but on occasional holiday weekends the Authority asked him to help out. These were Bib's happiest times. Dressed in his crisp coffee-colored uniform and Smokey-the-Bear hat, he cruised the Turnpike, keeping the peace, though his mind was wandering far from the task at hand. He was back in the early days, before he joined the Authority, when he was working on the construction crew building the highway that was one day to become the Turnpike. And even though he was a father and a grandfather several times over, he had never forgotten that strange young woman who had driven out of the dawn one morning in 1931 in her Hispano-Suiza cabriolet, like a Good Fairy of the Turnpike, and he now discovered that, buried deep in his heart, the hope that she would come back still lived.

"For Pete's sake!" Bob Jones exclaimed. "Will you kids keep it down? I can't think! What *is* that smell?"

"Sulphur, dear," Peg replied calmly. "From the oil refineries. It's not the car, if that's what you're worried about. I just had it inspected."

"When are we going to be there?" Bobby demanded.

"I hope it doesn't smell like *this*," Emmy added.

"It won't, and I don't know. It depends on whether the traffic stays this heavy all the way."

"Where is it, though?" Emmy asked. "Where we're going . . . What's the name of it?"

"I told you, Emmy—I don't know the name. I don't remember seeing any signs."

"Then how do you know where to go?"

"Yes, how do you, dear?" Peg remarked. "Both the kids and I, I think, would enjoy looking at a map to see where we're headed."

Bob sighed in exasperation. "I've tried to explain to you—it's not *on* the map. I'm trusting my sense of direction to take me back."

The children looked at him suspiciously.

"It would have been nice if you had at least taken a picture," Peg said. "The mystery is being drawn out a little too long."

"I did take a picture," Bob replied, a little unwillingly.

"Where is it, then?"

"It didn't come out. Something must have been wrong with the camera. The entire roll of film was shot. Look," he appealed to

her, "trust me, okay? If worst comes to worst and we *don't* find the
house, we'll have had a nice drive trying to get there, won't we?"

"Can you believe this traffic?" Cyrus asked Arabel, as he wedged
his way into a line of cars commencing the ascent onto the bridge.
"What's the story? Is everyone migrating?"

Having accepted the ticket from the machine at the toll gate
on the other side of the bridge, he picked up speed again. When
the traffic spaced itself out a little, he began to whistle. He stopped
when he noticed what the tune was: "People Will Say We're in
Love" from the hit musical *Oklahoma*. God. His father had always
sung it to his mother when they went on trips. That and "Waltzing
Matilda." His father had always been in his best moods then. He
and Betsy squabbled in the back seat.

He glanced at Arabel—she looked so sad he wished he could
cheer her up. But what would he tell her? That you "got over it"?
And you did—that was the crime. When he had first begun driving
up from Chive to visit Fritz it had hurt every time he had driven
past the sign indicating the exit they had always taken (although
on the southbound side) when they went to see Lark, until once
he was turning off for Demetria before he realized he had passed
Lark's exit without remembering. Just by going on living you
betrayed the dead.

"Arabel?"

She turned.

"Are you all right?"

"I shouldn't have come back here," she said simply.

"Don't worry about that now," he said. "You had to go somewhere. We'll figure out something to do about Gabriel and that
house."

Meanwhile, in the cities, knowing that many city dwellers would
have abandoned their homes in order to honor the dead in a more
bucolic setting, burglars were scouting out the neighborhoods. By

the next morning, many valuable articles would have changed hands. In the pounds, boarded pets cowered and whimpered in their cages, believing their exile to be permanent. Here and there, someone who had not gone anywhere entered the house of someone who had and watered that person's plants. In Winston City, at the Old Generals' Home, all of the generals but three were eating lunch. Two had been missing since breakfast, though the staff did not yet feel alarmed. A strange mood descended upon the place toward Memorial Day; the management always made certain to provide the old soldiers with carnations and special meals and extra recreational activities to keep them contented on this day. It was to be hoped that this was all that was responsible for Generals Eastlake's and Martinson's disappearance. The third absent general, General Charles Street, was not present for lunch either, having departed in the company of an old lady. "I'm lunching with my wife," he had announced to the Home's attendants and what could they do about it? If General Street wanted to eat lunch with an old lady and cared to pretend she was his wife, they had no power to prevent him.

Just before noon, Sarah Simms, on her way to visit General Street, seeking as much to be comforted as to comfort (for that morning she had told Jason she wanted a divorce), had walked past the Old Generals' Home without stopping, for she saw that General Street already had company.

And meanwhile, all over the country, those awaiting the arrival of those traveling marched up and down supermarket aisles, stocking up on supplies. In honor of the coming Memorial Day, flags hung over the aisles, the union facing north, since the aisles ran east and west (if they had run north and south, the union would have had to face east; this was decreed in the rules and regulations concerning the hanging of the flag, which it was the custom to display on all significant holidays, including Mother's, although not Father's, Day). In addition to the flags, the store was decorated with red, white, and blue crepe-paper streamers.

In preparation for the holiday, shoppers were out in force, and carts jammed the lanes; it was impossible to exit from some where lines to the registers blockaded the turns. Gathering at the meat counter, outraged citizens demanded of one another,

"Will you take a look at these prices?"

"When is it going to stop?"

Glancing at the contents of each other's carts, they began to worry about supplies of certain vital foods running out—though they need not have worried; the supermarket management had the needs of its people at heart. With fond benevolence the supermarket personnel, watching through their closed-circuit screens for bottlenecks in the traffic pattern, observed the shoppers' relief at each point in their series of U-turns when they found the next item on their list still in supply: row upon row of dark red ketchup bottles, ranks a reassuring six deep; stockpiles of bouncy hot-dog and hamburger rolls; lockers of neatly stacked frozen-lemonade cans. . . . Nor did the shoppers need to worry if they hadn't been able to decide what to buy beforehand; the supermarket d.j. could help them out there. At intervals the easy-listening music was interrupted by a cheerful, exhortative voice over the public-address system announcing that red, white, and blue paper napkins were to be found in Aisle Nine, that there was a special on relish in Aisle Four. . . . After the interruptions, the supermarket anthem would come back on and the shoppers would feel embarrassed that, no matter how distasteful they found the music, they couldn't seem to help walking in time to it.

And at the same time somewhere else, though the sky was clouding up, threatening rain, it was a moment of truce, an occasion for the cessation of hostilities, for the coming and going of ambassadors, for deciding at the last minute to hurry out to the garden to pick the last lilies-of-the-valley and arrange them in a vase for the ambassador's room as if this were a custom.

Soon after, a knock came on the front door, and the major's widow opened it and greeted her guest. As she showed him in she said, "I'm afraid it's not the place it once was. I have been away so long."

"I'm so terribly sorry."

"Yes."

"The war . . ."

"It was kind of you to come."

(The ambassador had set out immediately upon receipt of Bob Jones's letter. The major's wife was being notified of her husband's death—that is, was being given the official version—but someone ought to tell her the truth. Bob intended to return to the major's house himself, but in case he should be prevented . . .)

"It wasn't the war that killed him, you know," she remarked.

"I did."

"You!"

"I left home without telling him. The soldiers carved 'Killed in Action' on his grave marker but I don't believe that. I never have believed in the war."

"I . . ." the ambassador said, then stopped. I never believed in the war either, he had been about to say. That is, not the war the men were given to understand they were fighting. But, if he said that, then she would be convinced she was to blame for her husband's death. The ambassador began to see how lies were born.

She was waiting for him to speak.

"Many people doubted the sense of the war," he said. "I did myself." Who was speaking? he wondered. Who was speaking and using his voice? "The men in the field suffered most of all. The lies of those in power are to blame for your husband's death, not anything you did."

"Do you really think so?" she asked.

"Yes, I am certain of it."

At the sad, gentle smile she then gave him, it seemed to the ambassador that all the ice he had ever had in his heart melted. He knew he would lie to her until the end of the world, if only she would smile at him like that.

Now he was in an upstairs bedroom, standing at the foot of the counterpaned bed, staring at the tiny white bell-like flowers on the dresser. Their fragrance filled the room.

She had put them there, he thought; she had picked them with her own hands and arranged them in the vase, even though her husband was dead and she believed it to be her fault—she had done this, and for him!

The ambassador turned to look out the window at the great lawn that stretched out before the mansion as far as the eye could see. The window had been raised, and a screen inserted in the opening, but there was no breeze. All was still, the birds hushed, awaiting rain.

The ambassador had always believed himself unsuited to the tasks set for him. When he had begun his diplomatic career, he had imagined himself as a bearer of goodwill from his homeland to the rest of the world. He had not wished to become an arbiter of disputes. He further resented the role that the diplomatic corps was asked to play in providing cover for clandestine activities, and the false position in regard to other people into which this deceit had forced him.

The ambassador knew it was believed that he had had women "all over the globe," dotting continents like the pins on strategy maps. The women he had met at diplomatic gatherings had never believed him to be a sincere man. They had thought him charming but untrustworthy; attractive but spoiled. Being no different from all human beings in wanting to be liked by those among whom he most frequently found himself, the ambassador had learned that it was easiest to adhere to others' impressions of him. He had practiced at being suave, witty, blasé; the sophisticated set had clamored for his company. Having abandoned hope that the war could be stopped (it had been considered gauche even to suggest such a thing anymore) they had been particularly pleased by the ambassador's ironic detachment, the discrimination that had allowed him to so entertainingly deliberate upon all points of conflict, knowing perfectly well all the while that no settlement could ever be reached. The ambassador had grown in popularity and loneliness.

But always until now he had blamed his solitude on the failure of others to recognize his true nature. He was a kind, solicitous man, who loved children and unpretentious people and had always preferred solitude to the company of people he did not know well. He had wanted to marry, to have children of his own, but he had not even come close, and it was the enduring sorrow of his life. But it was the price paid, he had consoled himself, for a life spent in diplomatic service. Only in light of recent events had he perceived his past differently. It now seemed to him that, even in the beginning, his pursuit of a diplomatic career had been motivated not by altruistic aspirations but by his private wish to escape the effort of having to make himself known.

Gazing out at the darkening sky, the ambassador felt as if he were all alone on top of a mountain in a vast, soundless space, surrounded only by air and more air. No illusions remained to him. But how could one continue to live without illusions?

He turned now from the window. I could have loved her, he thought, sitting down on the edge of the double bed he later would occupy alone, buffing his dinner shoes.

"Why?" he said aloud. "Why when it is too late?"

In his accumulated anguish, in a fit of self-loathing, he ripped the decoration he had been awarded for valor from his evening coat. However, it did not completely detach but dangled from his breast. He reached to tear it free, then thought better of it. He stretched out a hand and smoothed the bedspread of the old four-poster bed—the scene, he imagined, of conception, birth, death—smoothed the white bedspread with its protruding knots of thread as if it were a person he loved.

"Need any help?" Jake called out to Agnes, who was unloading groceries into the rundown farmhouse, a few hours' drive from Winston, on which they recently had made a down payment. For the time being it would remain a summer place, but someday, if Jake could build up his dog-training business and if Agnes could land a teaching job in the area, they intended to move up full-time.

Over the winter, Agnes had inherited a small sum of money and at the end of April they had taken a sentimental drive up to Swanbury, spent the afternoon exploring back roads, and come upon the ramshackle place, a hundred years old or thereabouts, with a FOR SALE sign attached to it, and it was love at first sight. We can't afford a house! they avowed to one another. We're out of our minds! Nonetheless, two hours later, having inquired at a neighboring farm and located the owner, they had signed a promise to purchase. What the hell, they agreed. It was worth the financial strain to have a place to call their own at last.

Now it was nearly June. Agnes, having handed in her dissertation, had moved up for the entire summer with Lilith; Jake had joined them for a month's leave of absence from his job. At the moment, he was in the garden planting lettuce.

"No thanks, love," Agnes called back, helping Lilith out of the car. She gave her lunch and put her to bed for her nap. Jake came in, his face ruddy with exertion. He washed his hands, then the two of them sat down to lunch on the porch.

"Any mail?" Jake asked.

"Mail!" Agnes exclaimed. "I knew I was forgetting something. Yes, as a matter of fact. You'll never guess in a million years who's written to us."

"Who? The pope?"

"Right. No—Fritz Quadrata. A postcard from Salt Lake City." Agnes went inside and returned with the card and handed it to Jake. "It's amazing—it's practically illiterate."

Jake read it, chuckling. "So she and old Pierre are fiddling their way around the country." He looked at Agnes. "Performing with the Mormon Tabernacle Choir? I think she's hoping we'll drop a word to Cyrus."

"You think she's not writing to him?"

"Anything's possible with those two. After that crazy comment she made about General Street . . ."

"Some kind of hysterical projection, clearly."

". . . although Cyrus has been scrupulously avoiding us. Among other things, I wanted to ask him if he has any interest in going into business with me. I have a little scheme up my sleeve. I'm disappointed in him, Agnes."

"So I've gathered," she said, laughing.

"Don't sound so indulgent," he said. "You remind me of Henrietta."

"Now wait a minute!"

"I *care* about that kid, Agnes."

"So do I."

". . . but he remains such a conundrum to me. He has so much going for him and yet he remains stuck somehow."

"You're too impatient, Jake. Have more faith in him."

"I've *had* faith in him. By now he ought to have done something to warrant it. He's not *moving*."

On the Turnpike the traffic was growing heavier. Once or twice, Cyrus had to bring the car to a complete stop.

"We'll never get out of here at this rate. Maybe we should stop and get something to eat. Are you hungry?"

"A little."

"Maybe in another half hour or so. There's a rest area it'll take us about that long to get to. Then it's not too far to the Pennsylvania Turnpike. Once we get onto that, the traffic should begin to thin out."

Ten miles ahead of them, Billy, sitting in the front seat beside Sammy, was thinking that he must have been out of his mind to come along on this expedition. What the hell was he going to do in Washington, D.C., with three insane old people who had never been away from home? Not only that, but who believed they were exiled royalty on their way to get crowned! He had finally understood—when it was too late to prevent them from leaving—that they were serious. What had he gotten himself into? Sammy didn't even have a driver's license, although that hardly mattered since

the car had no license plates. . . . He glanced nervously at each car
that passed; invariably people turned to stare at the elegant sedan.

Beside him, Sammy, dressed in a yellow seersucker pantsuit
and white ruffled blouse, looking quite contemporary except for
the fact that she was wearing a crown, kept her eyes on the road.
I, Princess Constantina Ludwicker, Sammy thought, am driving,
driving on the New Jersey Turnpike, on the way to Xy's coro-
nation. . . . Xy and George were in the back seat, dressed in red
ermine-trimmed cloaks and wearing their crowns. (Sammy had
put her cloak in the trunk.) George wore a football jersey under
his cloak. So Xy was finally going to ascend the throne; well, if
anybody wanted to know the whole truth and nothing but the
truth, Sammy couldn't have cared less. She just hoped there was
a modern fully equipped kitchen where they were going. She thought
of asking Billy Daphne but felt shy suddenly. Also confused. What
had she been doing, baking a cake in the kitchen at six in the
morning? She grew alarmed. It wasn't good to feel confused (or
alarmed); she knew this from an article she had read once upon a
time in *Zero-Stress Living*, one of her favorite magazines. Gradually,
though, Sammy forgot her confusion in the pleasure of driving.
She had driven past the Joyce Kilmer Service Area and now drove
past the Molly Pitcher Service Area; she thought she would stop
at the next one, the Richard Stockton Service Area, which was
right across from the Woodrow Wilson Service Area, which was
on the northbound side. She had often stopped there, during her
memorial drives in search of Bib Block—though she had not made
one for at least ten years. She didn't know who Richard Stockton
was, but once on the back of a cereal box she had read that Woodrow Wilson had taken America into World War One to make the
world safe for democracy, and that was a good, catchy quote, and
more than anything Sammy liked a good, catchy quote.

In the back seat, on the right-hand side, sat Xy, sitting up very
straight, looking at her hands. For long intervals she had been
keeping her eyes shut. It was horrible to see the landscape rushing
by. She had not been in a car since she was fifteen and then it had
been to drive at a slow pace along a country road, and Tad had

been at the wheel. Tad . . . She didn't want to rule without him. She didn't want to sit on the throne by herself. She had been perfectly happy in the Cottage, waiting for him to come back. She wished she were back there still.

At this moment, George, beside her, playing an electronic baseball game he was convinced was cheating—determining that his first act as Sports Chancellor would be to invent some way of punishing cheating electronic games—glanced out his window in time to see a car draw abreast in the outside lane. In it, Emmy and Bobby Jones turned to look. When they caught sight of Sigismund, their mouths dropped open.

"Mommy! Daddy!" they exclaimed. "There are kings and queens in that car!"

"Well, that's very nice, kids," replied Bob, without looking. (He had more important things on his mind.) "Kings and queens on the New Jersey Turnpike, what next?" He and Peg continued their conversation.

Bobby and Emmy shrugged. They turned and stared again into the huge antique car. Then, as if it had been agreed between them beforehand, they pulled down their lower eyelids with their index fingers, opened their mouths wide and thrust out their tongues at the man in the crown.

Sigismund gaped. Then, in a kind of exuberant fury, he not only made the same face right back at them but made it even more dreadful by spreading his nostrils with his two little fingers.

Bobby and Emmy could not believe it. In frantic haste, afraid that their father would pass the car, they contorted every single facial muscle into its most extreme and dreadful position, yet— they could not believe their eyes!—the man replied with a face just as revolting as theirs! If not worse! Desperately they rolled down their window and yelled at him,

"Prune face! Stupid idiot! Dumbbell! Ignoramus! Retard!"

Sigismund felt in his element. Here at last was a game he knew all about. Narrowing his eyes and grinning fiercely, he rolled down his window too.

"Toads!" he shouted back at them.

"Toads!" they screeched, laughing hysterically, pounding each other's arms. Gasping, they hurled back, "Elephant! Pig! Hippopotamus! Skunk!"

"Varlets! Commoners! Hemophiliacs!"

Bobby and Emmy did not understand these names; this made them furious.

"Fartface!" they yelled, and Peg turned in horror, realizing they weren't yelling at each other but at someone in another car. "You look like you got run over by a tractor! You look too stupid to be alive! You look like your mother dropped you on your head! We hope you die! We hope you fall in a hole full of snakes! We hope . . ."

"That is enough!" Peg shouted. "Shut the window this instant! What on earth has gotten into you two? As soon as we get out of this car you're both going to get such a spanking that you'll wish you'd never come on this trip! Now roll up that window at once, do you hear me? This is your mother speaking! Darling, the kids have gone wild! For God's sake, pass that car!"

But the joy of battle was too strong for Emmy and Bobby; they could not heed her.

"Goddamn son-of-a-bitch!" they yelled. "Goddamn son-of-a-bitch!"

"Don't let that car go by!" Sigismund shouted at Sammy. "Don't let it go by!"

"I can't pass, honey; the damn fool is racing me."

"Well, drop back then. Do you want us all to get killed?"

"You'll hang for this, you traitors!" Sigismund shouted. "You'll be hung, drawn, and quartered and fed to the hogs!"

"Idiot! Moron! Peabrain! Pervert! We'll kill you! We'll cut you up in little pieces! We'll eat you alive!"

"Traitors! Traitors to the crown! Vile knaves and traitors! Death is too good for you!"

"Stupid pig! Mongoloid idiot! Nincompoop! Get off the face of the earth!"

.   .   .

And all this while, General Eastlake and General Martinson were sitting in the back seat of the car driven by Fyodor Stoltzoff—his bride of twenty-four hours, Dora Stoltzoff, beside him. (She had a soft spot for old generals, and when they had discovered that she was traveling to the nation's capital—they didn't know it was on her honeymoon—and asked to be taken along, she hadn't had the heart to refuse. Fyodor, furious at first, then had begun to think how he might turn this inconvenience to his advantage. He still harbored the notion of taking revenge on Fritz Quadrata. Generals Eastlake and Martinson were not fond of General Street, and, perhaps, were he to denounce Street, they would support his accusations. What form, exactly, this denunciation would take, however, was not yet clear to Fyodor.) They sang songs to pass the time—songs from *their* war, "Oh, it's a long way to Tipperary . . ." and "Shrapnel and whizzbangs and pipsqueaks galore, we don't wanna go to the trenches no more . . ." and "Mademoiselle from Armentières," the song about the girl who had refused to kiss a general. . . . Refuse to kiss a general! And Dora laughed and said she couldn't imagine it.

> . . . *Oh, you might forget the gas and shell*
> *But you'll never forget the Mademoiselle!*
> *Hinky-dinky parlay-voo.*
>
> *Oh, Mademoiselle from Armentières, parlay-voo?*
> *Mademoiselle from Armentières, parlay-voo?*
> *'Twas a hell of a war as we recall*
> *But still 'twas better than none at all!*
> *Oh, hinky-dinky parlay-voo!!!*

When the ambassador went downstairs, he found the major's widow sitting in the kitchen, in a rocking chair, rocking, the whole world, as far as he could tell, in her lap. Her two children were nearby. The little girl was reading under a lamp at the table; she hunched over her book, her nose nearly touching the page. The little boy played beside his mother's chair. Soldiers were camped around her feet.

The ambassador said good evening, then knelt and spoke to the boy: "Who's winning?"

The boy didn't glance up. "I don't know. They're just fighting."

"I see." He smiled, trying to think of a pretext for continuing to kneel. He breathed the woman's perfume: a hundred kinds of flowers, names clamoring for choice: lilac, rose, daffodil, mock orange, jasmine, honeysuckle. . . . It was impossible for him not to feel hopeful in the presence of this woman and her alkahest.

Reluctantly he stood. "I wonder if I may trouble you with a minor matter. I caught my decoration on something and . . ."

"I'll bring you a needle and thread."

She rose—with one arm, he imagined, holding the globe like an infant against her hip. He had thought she would stand up close to him and keep one hand inside his jacket while she mended, but after threading the needle and knotting the thread she handed it to him. Nothing for it but to take off his jacket and deploy the dangerous slippery metal by himself.

He sat down on the nearest chair and began to sew. She laughed when he pricked himself and swore. He stared at her, then laughed himself. "To think that that was the last thing that princess felt before she went off to sleep for a hundred years," he said.

"Yes," she replied, "though I've never been sure what the moral of that story was. Whether it's that, no matter how careful you are, you can't protect your children from their fate. Or that, if you wait long enough, someone will come and wake you from whatever slumber your parents' carelessness allowed you to lapse into. But I've always preferred to take it as a suggestion that if you were to involve everyone, no matter how seemingly crotchety and embittered, in concern for a child's welfare, such calamities would never come to pass. What do you think?"

"I've never given it any thought."

"That's why men have always gone to war. They can never

know with certainty that their children are their own. They think if they can kill enough other men they can be sure of being fathers. They are angry because they have to take on faith what women know by heart."

"I never thought about that either, but perhaps you're right."

The ambassador gazed at her with admiration. Suddenly she looked away and began to rock harder. Then, to his secret delight, she began to cry.

The ambassador laid his jacket down and went over to her. He bent over the chair and smoothed her hair, pried her fingers loose from her eyes.

"The world will roll out of your lap if you don't hold on to it," he remarked.

She looked startled, then laughed.

"You leave her alone!" her son cried, jumping up and shoving the ambassador away.

"It's all right, darling. The ambassador was trying to comfort me."

"Don't comfort her! I don't want you to!"

She shrugged gently. The ambassador smiled at her and returned to his own chair.

"It's going to rain," she said. "Did you notice? Sometimes when it rains I feel there's nowhere else in the world. Especially if it's foggy as well. Sometimes in the mornings the fog comes right up to the house."

"Does it?"

"I'm glad you're here, Ambassador. The house seems less haunted now."

"The world seems less haunted now to me," he answered.

It was nearly three o'clock. Bib had migrated northward from the James Fenimore Cooper Service Area to the Grover Cleveland Service Area and thence back south again to the Richard Stockton Service Area. The traffic, he noted with satisfaction, was increasing steadily. He leaned against his cruiser, watching travelers going into and coming out of the cafeteria building. He had just seen a very strange sight.

Three elderly people wearing crowns (two of them wearing long red cloaks) had climbed out of a Model-K Lincoln and entered the service building, accompanied by a young man in ordinary clothing. Bib had been about to follow them in—with what intent he wasn't sure—when two other cruisers screeched to a stop beside his and two fellow members of Troop D, New Jersey State Police (the troop that patrolled the Turnpike), jumped out, and called to him.

"They're headed this way. Get ready for a showdown."

"Some people in crowns just went inside," Bib replied. "I've got to see what they're up to."

The two other troopers exchanged glances.

"Haven't you heard the all-points bulletin? And Mitch thinks he's spotted them just north of Molly Pitcher. He's going to shepherd them into our waiting arms."

Bib, not liking to admit his hearing wasn't as sharp as it once was (so that, standing outside his cruiser, he could hear only half of what was said on the radio), remarked, "Oh, that . . ."

"Oh, that!" a young trooper mocked. "Bib, have you been asleep? Two generals have been kidnaped!"

Cyrus and Arabel drove into the Richard Stockton Service Area.

"Look at those guys," Cyrus said, nodding at the cops. "What are they doing? Having a party?"

He parked and they went into the cafeteria building. When Arabel had disappeared into the restroom, Cyrus entered a telephone booth and dialed home. Harold answered.

"Hi, Dad. It's Cyrus."

"Cyrus!" Harold exclaimed. "Where . . ."

"Dad, I'm in kind of a hurry," Cyrus interrupted. "I've got to ask you something, but I'm in a phone booth on the New Jersey Turnpike. . . ."

"You're where?"

". . . and I've hardly got any change, so I can't explain right now what it's all about, okay?"

"Cyrus, are you all right? What's the . . ."

"I'm fine, Dad. Look—it's important. I need an answer to this question. Were you ever, even once in your life, in a place called Magnolia Junction? It's in the South."

"Cyrus . . ."

"Magnolia Junction, Dad. M A G N O L I A. There's an army base there. Also a bar called the Calypso . . ."

"Well, Cyrus," Harold said drily, "to the best of my knowledge, no, I've never been in Magnolia Junction. Nor have I been in Baton Rouge, Louisiana, or Boise, Idaho. Now, would you mind explaining what this is all about?"

"Oh, I just know someone from there, that's all. I was just curious."

"You were just curious? You stopped on the New Jersey Turnpike and used your last change to call me because you were *curious*?"

"It was just a spur-of-the-moment idea."

"This all sounds pretty fishy to me, buddy." Suddenly he lowered his voice. "Cyrus, are you sure you're all right? I mean—you're not being held by kidnapers or anything like that? I don't mean to be melodramatic, but these things do happen."

Cyrus burst out laughing.

"Cyrus, you sound hysterical. Now, listen. I understand that if someone's standing by with a gun pointed at your head you can't very well mention it. So just answer yes or no, ARE YOU IN DANGER?"

"Dad, I'm fine!" Cyrus shouted—so loudly that people waiting outside the phone booth turned to stare. He lowered his voice. "I'm not in danger! I'm not being held by kidnapers! I'm in perfect health, okay? Just answer one more question, will you? Have you ever had any periods of amnesia in your life, anything like that?"

"Cyrus . . ."

"Dad, please!"

"No, Cyrus," Harold replied, spacing the words out, "I have never had any periods of amnesia."

"You were in the Korean War. Sometimes, after wars, men still are shell-shocked."

"Cyrus, six months after I got home from Korea, I married your mother. She's not here at the moment, otherwise she could tell you herself what kind of shape I was in. I'll get it notarized if you want."

"I suppose even if you had amnesia you might have forgotten having had it," Cyrus said.

"Cyrus, in the name of all that's holy . . ."

"I mean, there's never any way of knowing anything for sure, is there?"

The operator's voice interrupted, announcing that only thirty seconds remained in the conversation. Simultaneously, Cyrus saw Arabel emerge from the ladies' room.

"Hey, I've got to go, Dad."

"Let me call you back, for God's sake!"

"Oh, no, no need to do that."

"Cyrus!"

"Look, Dad, I'll see you tomorrow, okay?"

"Tomorrow!"

"I'm on my way home. I was going to surprise you, but you seem so upset."

"Home? You mean to Arborville?"

"No, to the moon. Of course to Arborville, what do you think?"

"Don't ask me," Harold said. "It's obviously not a father's place to think. Just to answer absurd questions without any explanation."

He sounds like me, Cyrus thought. "I'll see you tomorrow, Dad."

"I'll believe it when I see you, Cyrus."

Cyrus hung up. When Arabel's back was to him, he slipped out of the booth.

"Looking for someone?"

She jumped. "Don't do that!"

He laughed. "Come on, let's get something to eat. I'm starving."

Entering the cafeteria, they walked into Billy, Sammy, George, and Xy, leaving with ice-cream cones. The six of them stood stunned. Then they all spoke at once.

"What on earth . . . ?" Cyrus said.

"Magnolia Junction too dull for you?" Billy asked Arabel.

"What are you guys *doing* here?"

"Cyrus, is there a good kitchen in Washington, D.C.? Because I didn't have time to pack anything. I have so many time-saving kitchen aids now, I would be distressed to return to the old ways of doing things."

"My first act as Sports Chancellor," George said, "will be to enact laws to govern electronic games. I may need your advice. I smashed my computer baseball game but I do not feel satisfied that the punishment made any impression on it. What do you suggest?"

"Cyrus," Xy said, moving close to him and speaking in a low voice, "you have arrived in the nick of time. I have changed my mind. I don't want to sit on the throne. I abdicate. I'm too old and I don't want to rule without Tad. Fritz can be queen—I must find her and tell her. I know she has never believed in the throne but now that Billy Daphne has told us where it is . . ."

Behind Xy's back, Billy was waving both hands at Cyrus.

"Will you marry Fritz then, Cyrus? You can reign together. Tad and I never did, but it would make me happy to see you and Fritz on our throne. I think I would even stop missing Tad if you were king and queen. Where is Fritz, Cyrus? I must find her."

Cyrus stared at Billy. Billy began to laugh uncontrollably.

"We're going to the capital," Sammy explained.

"There's a parade," George added. "We're going to be in it."

"That's terrific," Cyrus said. "Just terrific."

"You don't understand," Billy gasped. "Cyrus, come outside. I have to talk to you."

"It better be good, that's all I can say." Yet he felt strangely inclined to laugh himself. To the others he said, "Back in a flash, you guys. Go sit down with Arabel. Arabel, stay with them, will you? They may need help finding their way around."

"I can find my way around perfectly, Cyrus," Sammy said scornfully. "I came here for years."

"Sorry, Sam, I forgot. You should be the one showing me around."

Billy was waiting for him beside the Ludwickers' car.

"Are you crazy?" Cyrus began. "What are . . ."

"Look," Billy interrupted him. "I know what you're probably thinking, but it's not true! I didn't do anything!"

"They wouldn't have come on their own! You must have done *something*."

"I swear I didn't! All that happened was, I woke up very early this morning and couldn't sleep and then I looked out the window and saw George playing croquet—in his pajamas. And I went out . . ."

"Oh, no . . ." Cyrus closed his eyes for a moment.

"I said something to him and he didn't answer. I thought he was trying to get my goat so I went up to him and shook him. He was in some kind of a trance and I started to get worried."

"He was walking in his sleep, Billy. Jesus."

"I know. Because suddenly he woke up and started crying. He kept yelling, 'I was winning! I was winning!' "

"Billy, don't you know it's *dangerous* to wake up someone who's walking in his sleep? Didn't anyone ever tell you that?"

"I thought it would be dangerous not to wake him."

"Jesus," Cyrus said again. "So what happened next?"

"I don't know. I was just trying to cheer him up so I asked him if he wanted to go to a baseball game sometime. Suddenly he started jumping up and down yelling, 'The time has come! The time has come!' and then he ran in the house and woke up Xy.

"They were *all* asleep. Xy was asleep writing! Sammy was . . ."

"I know, I know. They did it a lot. But why are they going to *Washington*?"

"They think they're going to reclaim their throne."

"But why didn't you try to *stop* them?"

"Are you kidding? You should have seen them! A Mack truck

couldn't have stopped them. I figured all I could do was come along and maybe keep them from getting into too much trouble. Cyrus, you have to believe me. I didn't *know* they were really this crazy."

"I kept trying to *tell* you."

"Yeah."

"Where have you been, anyway? I tried to call you the day after I left."

"I drove down to Magnolia." He shrugged. "Arabel had already taken off for California. I hung around with the gang—just got back yesterday."

Cyrus was studying him. He was planning to explain that the only reason Arabel had called him was because she hadn't been able to get in touch with Billy, but to his surprise he said something quite different.

"You know what I think, Billy? I think you made Xy and George and Sam go on this ridiculous trip to get even with me for some reason."

"What? You're insane."

"I don't think so," Cyrus said deprecatingly.

"You think the whole world does things because of you."

"You're full of it."

"Oh, really? Who's the person who lies all the time? Who makes up insane stories to explain why he lies and then denies *them*?"

"What did I deny? I never denied anything."

"I don't go around getting in touch with old friends and making them think I want to see them and then treat them like dirt when I do see them."

"Now you really are full of it, Daphne. You're the one who had a chip on your shoulder. Why the hell did you visit if you hated my guts? All you had to do was write back and say, Sorry, buddy . . ."

"Don't tell me I hate *your* guts. You're the one who hates me."

"I *don't* hate you!" Cyrus shouted, utterly furious now. "I never did and I don't now!" Then he looked Billy in the eye. "Why

don't you believe me, that I like you? What do you want me to
do? Write it down and sign it in blood? You piss me off, Billy."

"Is that right? I'm so sorry to hear that . . ."

"Shut up!" Cyrus interrupted. "Will you shut up for once?"

"Why should I? I . . ."

Suddenly Cyrus hauled off and swung at him.

Next, two things happened simultaneously. Fyodor, pursued
by a cruiser, its light flashing, drove into the rest area, stopped,
jumped out of his car, and turned angrily on the trooper who had
chased him and who was now approaching, his pistol drawn. "This
is a free country!" he said. "Hands on the roof, sweetheart," replied
the trooper. And Bib Block drew his gun and shot Billy in the
leg. Billy, with a groan, slumped to the pavement.

Arabel and the Ludwickers, who had been anxiously observing
Cyrus and Billy through a window, raced outside. It took Cyrus
a minute to comprehend what had happened. It wasn't until he
saw Bib, gun still in hand, that he understood. For a moment he
couldn't think, but then Billy moaned again and Arabel, arriving,
burst into tears.

"What were you *doing*?" Cyrus shouted at Bib. "Are you out
of your mind?"

He knelt beside Billy, who was lying curled in on himself,
groaning.

"I feel sick, Cyrus, I think I'm going to be sick."

"Don't talk, Billy. You'll be all right. It's just your leg."

"I saw that!" Sigismund, near tears, shouted at Bib. "Why did
you shoot Billy Daphne? He never did anything to you! We're
going to throw you in prison. You'll rot there, with the rats and
the bats; they'll eat you alive. I knew I should have brought my
sword! I knew it!"

This invective finally woke Bib out of his trance, and he returned his gun to its holster. Ignoring Xy and George and Sammy
he said, "Out of the way, I'll handle this." To Cyrus he apologized,
"I was trying to hit you. I thought you were going to hurt him."

Cyrus looked at Bib incredulously. "All I did was punch him

once! You don't shoot at someone for that! It isn't even any of your business!"

"Everything on the Turnpike is my business, young man. I regret having wounded your friend, but I was trying to protect him."

"You're going to be sorry for this." Cyrus peered at Bib's name pin. "Bertram Block?" he read aloud in growing astonishment. "*You're* Bertram Block?"

"Most everyone calls me Bib."

"Bib Block," Cyrus repeated. "Sam!" he shouted. "I hate to tell you who this genius is."

But she had heard. She gaped at the balding, overweight elderly man. "Bib?" she whispered. But how could he be Bib? Bib had been so young, so slender, and . . . and so dirty! "You're Bib Block?" she queried, drawing nearer. "*My* Bib?"

He looked at her nervously. He was beginning to feel quite strange.

"Bib!" Sammy cried. "Don't you know me? It's Sammy, Sammy Ludwicker! Tell me you remember!" She flung her arms around his neck and began to sob.

"Sammy?" Bib repeated, patting her back awkwardly.

"Oh, Bib," she wept joyfully, "you *do* remember! It is you, even though you're fat and old and bald! I thought you had forgotten. I've never forgotten you! Ever! I did come back, honest I did, but by the time Tad left, you were gone."

"Tad?" Bib muttered. But now the road in his mind was stretching back, erasing as it went his years of employment, his grandchildren, his children, wife, house, lawn, his basement mock-up of the Turnpike with all its service areas and exits which would go to the Smithsonian Museum upon his death, until it had arrived at one dawn of his youth and he saw again a lovely young girl, exhausted but ardent. . . . "Who's Tad?" he asked.

"My brother," Sammy said, leaning back in his arms and looking at him. "Who did you think?"

"I had no idea. You never told me. How was I supposed to know?"

Sammy stared.

"You didn't tell me your name either. How could I find you? You said you would come back. You *said* you would, but then you never did. You were so beautiful," he mused. "Your hair was all sweaty on your forehead and you looked like you worked for a circus, but to me you were the most beautiful girl I had ever seen. You were like a princess to me."

"But I am a princess!" she declared.

"You said you loved me," he murmured.

"I still love you! I know you can't help it if you're fat and bald."

"You're no great shakes now yourself, Sam," he said, hurt.

She didn't understand this, but she could see that he was upset. "Don't be sad," she said encouragingly. "It's no use crying over spilt milk."

Bib stared at her.

"That's a quote," she explained. "I like quotes. Do you, Bib?"

"Depends. To tell you the truth, Sam, what I really like is the road. I don't like anything quite as much as I like the road."

"I like the road too. Very much."

"You do? Honest?"

"Especially the Turnpike. It always makes me think of you. To me you are the Turnpike, Bib."

She kissed him on the lips. Bib thought it was not unpleasant.

"Could you tell me your whole name again?" he asked.

"Sammy," Sammy said impatiently. "Princess Constantina Ludwicker. I'm on my way to Washington, D.C.—that's the capital—with my brother and sister. Xy is going to ascend the throne. She's next in line. Do you want to come?"

"The throne? What throne?"

"Ours. Whose did you think? Please say you'll come. We'll make you in charge of roads."

"In charge of roads?"

But Cyrus now interrupted with a shout. "What *is* this? Old home week? Here's Billy lying bleeding to death and you're chatting away and handing out royal favors! What the hell's wrong with all of you?"

Billy laughed, then grimaced. "I'm not bleeding to death, Cyrus. I only got shot in the leg. I don't think it's even very deep."

"You're still shot! It's not a mosquito bite, for Christ's sake!" Cyrus had taken off his shirt, ripped Billy's pants leg and was wrapping his shirt around the wound. "Hold still, will you? I'm trying to tie this. And be quiet. I can't concentrate. Okay. George," he called, "will you give me a hand getting Billy into the car?"

"Son, I think you better let me run you to the hospital," Bib said to Billy.

"You're not getting near him. Come on, George."

"I'm afraid you're going to require my assistance whether you like it or not," Bib answered. "Have you observed the traffic?" He gestured at the Turnpike. Cars had come to a standstill. "If you insist, you can drive the victim yourself, but I'll have to lead you. You'll never get out of here on your own."

Cyrus shrugged. He and Sigismund lifted Billy into the back of the limousine. He lay across a seat, his leg elevated. Sigismund got out, but Cyrus stayed inside.

"I'll never forgive myself for this," he said.

"*You* didn't shoot me."

"That's irrelevant. If I hadn't been acting like such a jerk it would never have happened."

"I pretty much forced you into it."

"Knock it off." They looked at each other. "Well, this is no time to argue about who's the biggest jerk. We've got to get you to the hospital. I guess that fool will have to lead us. Sammy can drive this and I'll follow. Don't worry, she's an excellent driver."

"I'm not worried. You don't need to come."

"Don't be ridiculous. Of course I'm coming."

"Why? All they have to do is bandage me up and give me a tetanus shot. It's not as if I'm in critical condition."

"Forget it, Billy."

"I'm fine, Cyrus! They'll take care of me."

"Xy and Sammy and George? And Arabel?"

"Arabel's not coming with me, Cyrus."

"Well, she's not coming with me!"

"Then she can stay here with Bib Block."

"Sammy's long-lost dreamboat. I can't believe it."

"It looks like true love."

"That's what scares me."

"Where were you headed?"

"Arborville."

"Then you should get going. You've got a long trip. I'm not an invalid."

"What about Arabel?"

"Why don't you ask her?"

Cyrus looked unhappy.

"It's no big deal about Arabel anymore, you know." Billy attempted to laugh nonchalantly. "I got her out of my system when I was in Magnolia."

"Well, that's good—I guess. But sort of beside the point. Now that we've run into you . . . I mean, she's not my responsibility. I'm sorry for what's happened to her, and since she hadn't been able to get in touch with you I asked her to come along. I had already made plans to go to Arborville and I didn't feel like changing my plans. Fritz skipped town, and . . ."

"What!"

"She left on a concert tour with Pierre."

Billy was looking at Cyrus strangely. "Why did she leave?"

"Why do you think?" Cyrus stared at him, unbelieving.

"You mean . . . it's true then?"

"Is what true?"

"About Fritz being . . . about your grandfather being her father?"

"Billy, do you really think I would make something like that up?" Cyrus asked angrily.

"No—I don't know. The night you got so drunk, remember? You told me it *wasn't* true."

"I don't remember anything about that night."

Billy regarded him steadily. "You must feel pretty lousy," he remarked at last.

They observed a moment's silence.

"Oh, well," Cyrus said brightly, "what's a little incest among relatives?"

Billy stared, then began to laugh. Soon they were both laughing hysterically.

"Damn!" Billy shouted. "My leg hurts!"

"Oh, God, your leg . . ."

Cyrus got up off the seat.

"Go on to Arborville, okay?"

"What are you going to do after you go to the hospital? You can't go down to Washington and limp around."

"Why not? I think it will be a blast. Show Xy and Sammy and George the sights . . ."

Cyrus, still in a crouch in the back of the spacious sedan, hesitated. "Do you still have my address in Arborville?"

"Eighty-four Summer Street."

"Will you write?"

Billy nodded.

"Swear?"

"If you'll write back."

Cyrus held out his hand; Billy took it. Then Cyrus exclaimed, "God, how ridiculous can you get! Shaking hands with someone who just got shot." He leaned over and hugged Billy quickly, then backed out of the car and slammed the door.

He went to Arabel. "What do you want to do?"

"What about?"

"Are you going to go with Billy?"

"Do you want me to?"

"Arabel, it's not what *I* want . . ."

"Then I'll go with you."

He squinted, assessing this; she held his eyes. Then his expression grew gentler. "I guess I'd like you to."

He walked back to the car. George and Xy and Sammy had now seated themselves inside.

"Don't do anything I wouldn't do," he said to Billy through the window. Billy grinned.

Bib returned to his cruiser. While he had been occupied with the Ludwickers, the scene with Fyodor and the generals had progressed. Dora had explained the situation to the suspicious state troopers, as Generals Eastlake and Martinson, enjoying themselves hugely, watched the drama being enacted for their benefit. The situation was on the verge of being settled amicably—a telephone call had been made to the Old Generals' Home—when Cyrus, Arabel at his side, walked past on the way to their car. Seeing them was the final straw for Fyodor, who was still outraged at having been stopped.

"That's General Street's grandson!" he exploded. "Dora—that's him! Arrest him!" he shouted at the state troopers. "He seduced his own aunt! His grandfather is a depraved general! Arrest him!"

Cyrus, horrified, stared at Fyodor.

"Who is that?" Arabel asked. "Do you *know* him?"

"Do you know this lunatic?" asked one of the troopers restraining Fyodor.

"Never seen him before in my life."

"Thought not."

"You liar! You're Fritz Quadrata's nephew! You lied to her! I am Fyodor Stoltzoff! I know the truth!"

"Do I need to listen to this?" Cyrus appealed to the trooper. The trooper waved him on.

"Are you following us?" Bib called.

"To the next exit," Cyrus called back.

"I have to take a man to the hospital," Bib explained to his fellows. "He's shot."

"Who's shot?" they exclaimed. "Who shot him?"

"Billy Daphne is his name," Bib answered. "And I did."

"You!"

"Only in the leg. He's going to be fine. I'll see you, fellas." He climbed into his cruiser.

"But how about you?" one of the troopers asked the others.

Soon the little caravan pulled out of the Richard Stockton Service Area, Bib in front, his light flashing, then Sammy, Xy, George, and Billy in the old Lincoln, Cyrus and Arabel bringing up the rear.

On the Turnpike, Bib had to drive down the shoulder; cars stuck in the immobilized line of traffic honked. An enterprising few pulled into line behind Cyrus.

At Exit 7, Bib pulled off to head back into Trenton; Cyrus, then Sammy, honked farewell. Cyrus inched on to the next exit: the Pennsylvania Turnpike.

"Are you sure you didn't know that man?" Arabel asked.

"Fyodor?"

"So you do know him!"

"He's an old boyfriend of Fritz's. But it's true I've never *seen* him before."

"What was he talking about, saying Fritz is your aunt?"

"It's a long story."

"That's what you say about everything. What were you and Billy fighting about?"

He grinned. "That's a long story too."

She looked disgusted.

"I'll tell you, okay? Just not right now. Right now I need a rest."

She shrugged.

He laid a hand on her arm. "Don't be mad at me. I really *will* tell you."

"I bet."

They didn't talk for a while. Arabel rested her head against the window and closed her eyes.

"Sleepy?"

"A little."

"Why don't you go to sleep?"

"I am."

"Lie down, I mean. You can put your head in my lap." She did so. "Want me to sing you a lullaby?"

"What lullaby?"

"I only know one. My grandfather used to sing it to me."

"If you want."

"Okay, but you have to keep your eyes closed. Arabel, I said close your eyes."

She closed them, and Cyrus sang softly, "Good night, go to sleep, go to sleep, go to sleep, go to sleeeeep, go to sleep, good night."

Parade

It had rained, but now the sun was out and the light infantry of trees guarding the streets of Arborville looked almost casual as Cyrus—with Arabel, asleep again—drove into town. The trees' trunks were rigid, as sentinels should be, but their branches spilled over, reminding Cyrus of mothers chatting while their hands restrained unruly children.

He slowed down, turning into Summer Street, letting his hand touch Arabel's soft hair. He wished she would wake up so that he could ask her where all the Arborvilleans were, why there weren't any cars parked on the street, and this a holiday morning in May. Why weren't people out working in their yards? Where was everyone?

He made a wide arc, crossed into the driveway of 84, and turned off the engine. Arabel woke with a start and sat up.

"Where are we?"

"We're home."

"Home?"

"We're in Arborville."

"This is Arborville?"

"Wake up, sleepyhead."

"Oh, no, I don't want to wake up yet, Cyrus."

"It's Arborville but no one is home."

"They're still sleeping. It's too early for anyone to be awake."

"No, it's not. It's after ten."

"Really? Why don't you honk, then?" She reached to press the horn, but he caught her arm.

"Let's exercise a little caution please here, miss. . . . Come along now."

They climbed from the car.

"It's so quiet!" she exclaimed.

"I know, I can't understand it."

While he sprinted up the walk like an eager son, Arabel thrust her arms into the unresisting air, then paced slowly back and forth across the lawn.

Cyrus came back out. "Nope," he called cheerfully, letting the screen door slam as he leapt from the porch over the steps onto the lawn. "Do you know how many years it took me to be able to do that?"

"Do what?"

"Oh, never mind, dimwit."

"Dimwit!"

"Yes, dimwit, I said!" he cried, and tackled Arabel and brought her down with him onto the lawn.

"Cyrus!"

"What, Arabel?"

He sprang up and jogged around back. She stood, brushing grass from her clothes, and strolled toward the house. Cyrus reappeared, looking worried.

"I just can't figure it out. No one anywhere, and I didn't see a note inside."

"Maybe they went on a trip."

"But the car's in the garage."

"They can't have gone far, then."

"Except they never park the car in the garage. They always park it on the street."

"They do?"

She looked up and down the empty street. Cyrus bit his lip. She caught this.

"If you're pulling my leg . . ."

"You'll what?"

"Oh, you make me sick," she said, climbing the steps to the front porch.

"Stay inside until I tell you it's safe," he shouted after her. "I'll go scout the place out."

Without replying, she entered the house. Cyrus started off down the street.

At the edge of town, in a field, the people of Arborville were mustering for their annual Memorial Day parade. Everybody in town was in it. It was an old Arborville tradition. Every Memorial Day at home, Cyrus had walked to the edge of town along with all the other inhabitants of Arborville, and at ten-thirty the Arborville High School band had struck up the Arborville town song and everybody had begun to march. Those who couldn't march— the very old and the very young, the sick and the crippled—rode in cars or horse-and-buggies, were pushed in wheelchairs or baby carriages, were carried. One of Cyrus's earliest memories was of sitting high on his father's shoulders shouting as they paraded through town, "Look, there's our house!" while his mother had shouted at him to be careful and hold on. Even some animals had marched in the parade, although Jonzo had been the only cat in Arborville history to do so. He had hissed at all the dogs.

Ever since a special day had been set aside in memory of those who had given their lives in the country's wars, most towns in America had had a Memorial Day parade. But, unlike in most towns, from the first no one in Arborville had been willing to serve as audience for the rest, so the entire population had gotten into formation and paraded past their empty houses, singing and laughing. When they got to the other end of town, they had a picnic.

People were lining up now, chatting with those next to them. Some were dressed up; some weren't. No one was required to.

Some wore their grandparents' clothes; some wore animal costumes; Mr. Swensen, the owner of the hardware store, was dressed in overalls hung with a hammer, a screwdriver, a tape measure, and even a small saw. He was pushing a wheelbarrow loaded with gardening implements, bags of peat moss and fertilizer. The town's doctor wore his white coat. A stethoscope dangled from his neck, but his pockets were full of lollipops. Children kept running up to him, pleading with him to listen to their hearts. June Greenmantle was wearing her grandmother's wedding dress; she was proud that she could fit into it. Her husband Hugh and a number of the other men wore their old army uniforms. Harold was wearing his. He had just finished complaining to Rose that it still felt too tight across the shoulders; he thought she had said she'd let it out for him.

Harold stood watching Rose laughing with Carrie Johnson and Susie Silton; Rose was tying Carrie's sash into a huge ridiculous-looking bow. Had he ever been in Magnolia Junction? What kind of a question was that, for God's sake? He must have run through that outlandish conversation of the previous day a hundred times and still could make no sense of it.

Harold hadn't told Rose that Cyrus had called. He hadn't told her he had been given a month's notice at his job either. What the hell was he going to do now? He certainly couldn't retire on what he had in the bank. He ought to be worried, he supposed, yet instead he merely felt gleeful. Cyrus was coming home.

Arabel had finished with the first floor and now climbed upstairs, trailing her hand along the banister. The house was so spick-and-span; it didn't even look as if anyone lived in it.

On one side of the upstairs hallway were the bedrooms of the children: Cyrus's, his sister Betsy's, and the one that probably had belonged to Cyrus's little brother who had died. The rooms were tidy; they had been kept as the children had left them. Arabel glanced at them, then crossed the landing and entered Cyrus's parents' bedroom. She was drawn by the dressing table; the objects upon it reminded her of Polly.

Sitting down upon the bench before the table, she examined

them: the lace bureau scarf, the hairbrushes and bobby pins and bottles of perfume and jewelry boxes arranged upon it. She picked up a hairbrush and brushed her hair, one stroke, then laid the brush back on the dresser, bristles down, took a vial of perfume, unscrewed the cap and sniffed, replaced the cap. She opened a drawer—it held gloves, belts, scarves, more jewelry boxes; she examined them all. Then, in the back of the drawer, beneath a pile of handkerchiefs, she discovered two letters: they were sealed with sealing wax and their seals were unbroken. She saw that they had been postmarked in Paris nearly thirty years ago. The letters were addressed to Rose Street and to Charles Street in Washington, D.C.; Arabel recognized the return address—53 Thornapple Lane, Newbridge—as the address of Cyrus's grandmother.

At the edge òf town, the parade had begun. The high-school band played the first bars of music, and people began to sing. Hearing the drums and horns and trumpets, Arabel looked up in astonishment, then went to the window, the letters in her hand. She couldn't see anything, but the music was growing louder. While she waited for the parade to come into sight, she held the letters up to the light, trying to read the words through the envelopes.

Cyrus heard the music begin too and broke into a run, catching up with the parade as it marched along the first street of its route. A couple of kids he didn't recognize turned to look at him; he said hello, but they didn't answer. Then he spotted his parents up ahead.

Sometimes, in coastal cities, when it was about to storm, seagulls flew low along the streets. Out at sea, waves gathered. Every so often, what at first appeared to be large, individual waves broke away from the general pattern, yet they did not crest into foam before diving back into the ocean. These were the whales—leviathans of the deep, orphans of the universe. Far beneath the ocean's surface, they called to each other, and their calls were overheard by men. They were strange, muffled, haunting cries; all is lost, they said, lost, lost. They were the most eloquent, mournful sounds in the world, though what the whales mourned for no one would say. As if despairing of any other means of making themselves

understood, sometimes the whales swam to shore, stranded themselves, and died.

In Arborville, the parade turned into Summer Street and as it
passed his house Cyrus looked up and saw Arabel at the window
and waved.

A NOTE ABOUT THE AUTHOR

Kathryn Kramer was born in Annapolis, Maryland. She received her B.A. from Marlboro College in Vermont, where she currently teaches, and her M.A. from Johns Hopkins University.